He lowered her to the ground, gently easing the chemise to her waist. He quickly tugged down her pantalettes to see all of her. Dearie made no move to stop him; instead, she helped him lower his trousers as if she was experienced at lovemaking.

Her actions both surprised and pleased him. He wondered if she'd had other lovers. Dearie stared at him with unbashed admiration. "I've never seen a man unclothed before," she told him honestly.

He laughed. "And I've never seen anyone as pretty as you."

Divested of his clothes, Tavish stood over her, his erect manhood fully visible. Although the size of him astonished Dearie, her passion was too great for her to feel any fear. When he lowered himself beside her, she pulled him to her.

With unaccustomed reverence, Tavish caressed every inch of her satin skin, kissing and suckling the taut nipples while Dearie arched, pressing her body against his. His fingers massaged the velvet softness of her stomach, ranging lower to the downy triangle between her legs. There he found her moist and open to his touch. Tenderly he teased her with his fingers until he was certain she wanted him as much as he wanted her.

For a brief moment he paused. "Are you sure you know where this will lead?"

She nodded her head. "Marriage," she said solemnly.

GRAYSON'S DAUGHTER

DIANA LEVITT

PaperJacks LTD.

TORONTO   NEW YORK

AN ORIGINAL

PaperJacks

GRAYSON'S DAUGHTER

PaperJacks LTD.

330 STEELCASE RD. E., MARKHAM, ONT. L3R 2M1
210 FIFTH AVE., NEW YORK, N.Y. 10010

First edition published September 1988

ISBN 0-7701-0899-7
Copyright ©1988 by Diane Levitt
All rights reserved
Printed in the USA

Dedication

To my darling Bernie without whose love and support I would never have found the words. And with special thanks to Rita Gallagher who always believed.

Chapter One

"Well, Tavish! What brings you to Philadelphia?"

"Murder, Cousin Alistair. Murder!" Tavish McLeod's handsome features were grim, his biting tone a reminder that scarcely a month ago he'd buried his father in Fayetteville, North Carolina.

"Uncle was murdered! God help us!"

"No. God help Matthew Grayson. It was he who drove Father to his death."

Alistair's aristocratic eyebrows shot upward. "Grayson? Not the infamous Philadelphia lawyer?"

Tavish nodded grimly. "That is why I came to you, Alistair. I need your help. I must have revenge against this wily fox who stole our home and business and forced the McLeods into bankruptcy."

"Grayson took over the McLeod factoring business?" Alistair was shocked. "Uncle Murdock was a successful factor for forty years, Tavish! He'd weathered bad times before! How could such a thing come about so quickly?"

Tavish raked his fingers through his sun-streaked brown hair. "Since the war, North Carolina factors have bartered with other states to supply their planters with seed and manufactured goods. The economy grew worse and the state bank notes were discounted when local banks could not pay in specie. The factors simply increased the amount of crops to make up the difference." Tavish paused to accept a brandy.

"Then last year, state banks refused to honor bank notes at all."

Alistair nodded. "The journals called it the Panic of 1819, but it was of little consequence here."

"Since the banks were not honoring notes, Murdock came to Philadelphia to see his longtime business associate, Sloan. He anticipated no problems since he had held Sloan's notes past maturity when circumstances were reversed several years back. But Sloan had died and Sloan's lawyer, Matthew Grayson, had taken over the business. Since the banks would not tender specie, Grayson demanded payment of the note Father had with Sloan. Father pleaded for an extension. Grayson agreed to wait for harvest, but demanded our home and business as collateral." Tavish's voice was choked with anger.

"Harvest was late and the crops were poor. Grayson, true to his kind, demanded payment in full on the due date. In a matter of months, we were bankrupt. He took over the business and we were put out of our home. We had to move to a rooming house near the outskirts of town. It was there that Murdock drank himself to death."

There was a long silence while Alistair absorbed the story, obviously stunned.

"What do you plan to do?" he asked quietly.

"I don't know, Alistair. Surely Grayson moves in your fashionable circle — I thought perhaps you might introduce me. He is wealthy . . . "

Alistair held up his hand. "Wealth alone does not guarantee entry to Philadelphia society. As you say the man is devious and despicable. An excellent attorney, Grayson has saved many a thief and murderer from the gallows — at a profit to himself, of course. He is a widower and he has a beautiful daughter. It must be for her sake that he attempts vainly to force himself upon us. Invitations to teas and soirees at the Grayson mansion are sent out regularly, but I have never attended his affairs. Although I know him by sight, my friends and I have nothing to do with him."

"I had hoped you might be able to help me," Tavish said, sighing heavily.

Alistair's face lit up. "Wait, Tavish! I believe another invitation arrived just yesterday." He walked over to a polished mahogany desk and flipped through a pile of letters on a silver tray.

"Success!" he cried, gleefully holding up an engraved invitation. "The Graysons are having a ball on Saturday next. I will send a servant for permission to bring a visiting relative."

Tavish frowned, his hazel eyes dark and questioning.

"Never fear, Cousin! Grayson will be so happy to have me as a guest that he will refuse me nothing!" With a broad grin, Alistair refreshed their brandies and sat down again. "What do you intend to do once you meet Grayson?"

Tavish grew thoughtful. "I don't know. But I swore on Murdock's grave that when I return again to Fayetteville, I will have the money he stole from us, and Matthew Grayson will be left a broken and bitter man. Murder is too good for him."

The sharp sound of breaking glass echoed in the parlor as Dearie Meade Grayson sent six china teacups crashing to the floor with one furious swipe of her slender hand. Shards of china were scattered across the plush Turkish carpeting and crunched under the young woman's feet as she paced back and forth across the large, empty room.

"I don't want to marry! Why should I? I'm happy here!" she said vehemently, reaching a long window and pausing to stare out at the manicured grounds.

A maid scurried in with a broom and a dustpan to sweep up the broken teacups. With an exasperated sigh Dearie flounced over to a high-backed settee. Another maid appeared with a tray holding more teacups and a steaming pot of tea. She glanced warily at her mistress before setting the tray down in front of her, then hurried off, shaking her head.

"Maybe someday I'll marry," Dearie told herself as she poured tea into one of the cups, "but not until *I'm* ready."

She sifted idly through the stack of invitations and calling cards on the gilded salver near the tea tray. The names of Philadelphia's three most eligible bachelors were on the cards she laid aside with an impatient sigh. William Warren was related to the Penns, and owned more property than anyone else in the city. However, at twenty-six, Jonathan Ridgeway was already one of Philadelphia's leading merchants. Malcolm Vandever, while not as wealthy, was certainly the most handsome of the three.

Dearie pursed her small mouth, pouting. The three men were the latest in a never-ending stream of suitors. They would have been destined to rejection like all the others had not Matthew Grayson ordered his daughter to choose once and for all.

"You've received a proposal from almost every unmarried man in the city," her father reasoned. "Soon they'll stop asking."

"Good," Dearie replied, her blue eyes flashing.

"Well, miss, you have three suitors of whom I approve. You will choose one of them before the month's out," her father had told her.

Dearie had been too astounded to respond. Her father had never before even raised his voice to her. Indeed she had only to shake her golden curls, stamp her foot, or begin to cry to have her way. But this time was different.

Dearie swirled the tea in her cup restlessly. She was momentarily distracted by the configuration of leaves at the bottom of her cup. The cook, Jessamine, had read Dearie's fortune several times and it was always the same.

"You going to marry someone strong an' handsome with a head on his shoulders like yo' daddy, chile," the old woman affirmed, a gap-toothed smile lighting up her dark face.

"That could be anyone, Jessamine." Dearie shook her head impatiently.

"No'm, he ain't jes' anyone and this one ain't like all the rest. He don't come from around here. I see a lot of tall skinny trees, taller than ten men — that be where he come from. You ain't seen him yet, but when you do . . . land, that all it take, Miss Dearie. Jes' you wait."

Dearie scoffed at Jessamine's prediction, but she sometimes wondered if it might be true. As time passed, however, the strangers she met were no different. And now . . .

Perhaps her father was right, Dearie mused, a frown marring her smooth brow. But which one should she choose? All three men professed to love her. Malcolm had even written a poem for her. Such rubbish! She was at a loss to understand how they could possibly be in love when they hardly knew her. She guessed men were just that way — at least the men she knew.

If Dearie was mystified by the men who constantly surrounded her, they were even more perplexed. She seemed not to care whether she was courted or not. Yet they were drawn to her like moths to the golden glow of a candle, and her nonchalance only increased their fascination.

"How can I choose? They're all so boring!" Dearie fumed. "Well, it's obvious that I can't. Surely Father will understand. I'll tell him I have to consult Aunt Sophie, and she's in Europe. If I can just delay things for a while, perhaps he'll give me more time."

Matthew Grayson paused in the parlor doorway, admiring the picture Dearie made taking her tea. Shafts of the afternoon sun played upon her hair, highlighting the curls that fell to her shoulders from ivory combs. He shook his head. It was no wonder her suitors lauded her beauty in poems. Her eyes *were* the color of the azure sky, her cheeks soft as rose petals, and her hair like brightest sunlight. Today, Dearie wore a rose-colored satin gown trimmed with tiny ruffles that made her look small and fragile. Grayson was gratified that others saw her as he did, although how could they not?

His own eyes were the same shade of sky-blue as Dearie's, but years of squinting had trained the skin around them into deep crevices. His gaze was constantly speculative, as if he sought to see deeper into the situation at hand. In fact, he was short-sighted. However he was too vain for spectacles, or perhaps was aware of the unnerving effect of his probing stare.

When his wife died ten years ago, Grayson vowed to become the wealthy by whatever means he could find. Thereafter, opportunities arose almost daily. He seemed to know intuitively about a new business scheme before it happened, and he quickly made himself an indispensable partner. He was merciless in the pursuit of his fortune. That his dealings left families homeless and hungry was no concern of his. Business was often unpleasant.

Rumors abounded that Matthew Grayson was unscrupulous, but nothing was ever proved and no one stepped forth to confront him. Grayson smiled at the talk, for in all his business transactions, he stayed just inside the law — but only just. . . . He worked tirelessly day and night, telling himself he did it all for Dearie.

"She shall have the finest dowry in Philadelphia," he had declared.

Matthew Grayson doted on his daughter shamelessly. When she look up at him with those vivid blue eyes, her face framed by a cloud of blond curls, he thought she was an angel come to life. How could he deny her anything? To do so would somehow invoke the wrath of God.

As a result of his indulgence Dearie was accustomed to having her own way. If a toy was broken or cast aside, it was immediately replaced with a new one. If Dearie expressed displeasure with a servant, the unfortunate person was discharged. Dearie grew from a beautiful child into a lovely young woman. It was like the fulfillment of a dream, and Grayson was continually awed by her. If she was indeed willful and headstrong, as her tutors hinted, it was simply a family trait. But now he saw he had to take a stand, rather than see her ruin her chances for marriage and future happiness.

"My little doll," he could not help but exclaim as he entered the room. He hastily gave his hat and cane to the butler trailing behind him.

Dearie looked up with a smile, but inwardly she winced at the endearment. All her life she had been referred to as a doll or a dear. Her mother had called her "dear baby," and her father had dubbed her his "little doll." Governesses and teachers had called her "little dearie," as if no name were good enough for their precious charge. From these expressions, Dearie had evolved. Her doting parents had formally adopted the endearment, thinking it original — and perfect for their beautiful child. To make matters worse, she had no other name to fall back on when she was old enough to realize what they had done.

To Dearie the name conjured up a simpleton, or a pretty face on a wooden head. Certainly a young woman who had been educated at the finest schools in Europe should have a proper name. But in spite of her protests, Dearie she remained.

"Just in time for tea, Father." Dearie rose to kiss her father's cheek and motioned for him to sit beside her.

"I planned it that way," he said, beaming down at her. He took the cup of tea she poured for him and stirred it methodically. "Well, my dear, have you decided?"

Dearie avoided his gaze. "Father, I need more time . . ." She felt her father's eyes boring into her.

"Surely there is one you favor?" he prodded.

"No." Dearie fixed him with a mesmerizing sky-blue stare. "I've never found anyone like you, Father."

A smile played at the corner of Grayson's mouth. He was flattered in spite of his determination to remain firm. "Dearie, you must have a life of your own . . . a husband . . . children. I've worked hard to provide you with a large dowry."

"One would think," Dearie pointed out impertinently, "that my marriage was more important to you than to me."

Grayson frowned, partly because there was some truth to his daughter's statement. He had already engaged an artist to paint her wedding portrait, and employed a seamstress to work on Dearie's trousseau. Moreover, he had to control his daughter's future. "Dearie . . ."

"Please allow me just a little more time. I should consult Aunt Sophie. After all, this is an important decision."

Grayson shook his head. "Tonight at the ball I'll announce your engagement to William Warren and set the wedding date."

Dearie stared at her father, aghast. "Father, what do you mean?"

"I mean if you won't choose, I'll choose for you! I'm getting no younger, my dear. And I intend to see my grandson before I die!" He affectionately patted Dearie's cold hand as he rose to leave. Inwardly he winced at the stricken expression on his daughter's face.

"It's for your own good, child," he said, his voice hoarse with emotion. He forced himself to leave the room as Dearie stared after him, too stunned to speak.

Already it was half-past seven and Dearie sat her dressing table, her hands clasped in her lap. The affair was to begin at eight o'clock, and soon the guests would start arriving.

Was it true? She imagined she'd awake any minute and find it was a bad dream. A tear caught and hung on her lashes, blurring her vision. Her father had never forced her to do anything before. And now, all of a sudden, he had decided whom she would marry!

The tear wobbled then fell onto her cheek, quickly followed by another. Nothing she said had moved him even slightly. She clenched her small hands into fists. This was a new century! Women were no longer told what they must do!

Aunt Sophie's pale, pinched face intruded into her thoughts. She, too, had refused several men and now she was alone. Matthew Grayson had often held up his sister as an example of a headstrong woman who sacrificed her happiness for independence.

"No one was good enough for Sophie," he had said, "and now there is no one."

Dearie knew it was true. She had no desire to be like Sophie, traveling the globe with no proper home. But she wasn't ready to marry . . . not yet.

Dearie sighed. Tonight she must tell William Warren she would be his bride. She shuddered involuntarily. How could she endure his caresses? Although he was older and his hairline was receding, many women found him attractive. Dearie considered him distinguished, but she couldn't imagine wanting his kiss or his touch. Oh, no! This was not the way she had dreamed it would be.

A chilling fear sent icy fingers up her spine and her body felt suddenly numb. Perhaps she was dying...

A soft knock on her bedroom door startled Dearie. "Who is it?" she called out.

The door opened to admit a maid Dearie had never seen before. She was dark-haired, and so small that Dearie thought she might be a child until she spoke out with a woman's voice.

"Colleen Mary-Katherine McCurdie, miss. Colleen, if you please. Mary and Katherine were me mum's two sisters. Colleen was me grandmum. She died before I was born, but they say I favor her." Colleen's eyes sparkled and her face had turned pink as she recited her speech in one long breath.

Dearie frowned. "I don't understand. We have plenty of maids." At Colleen's fallen expression, Dearie quickly amended, "Not that we couldn't use one more. But I usually hire the help myself." Dearie studied the girl. She appeared to be about her own age or younger.

"I was to be a surprise," Colleen blurted out. "I'm to go with you when you marry."

"Oh, no!" Dearie wailed, shaking her head.

Again, Colleen was perplexed. She busied herself about the room, picking up articles of clothing and folding them over her arm. "Your father is a nice man," she said as Dearie began to sob. "He...he picked me over five others, Miss Dearie. I have my references..."

Dearie waved her hand. "No, no. You don't understand. I don't want to marry!"

Colleen flew to Dearie's side and fell to her knees. "Oh, miss. That's natural," she said with a concerned look. "Do any of us want to marry? Not at first, I'll wager."

"But, I'm too . . . too young."

"Young?" Colleen scoffed. A dark curl, escaping her white cap, dangled over one eye. "Why, me own cousin married at fifteen. She has two bairn by now!" A dimple in each cheek indented with every new expression. "And me aunt, Mary not Katherine, ran away with a travelin' man when she was thirteen. No one ever thought a thing about it, except he was a juggler. And, you know, they say jugglers are never faithful."

The little maid's expression was serious now, her pert mouth set in a straight line. Through the fringe of her wet lashes, Dearie watched Colleen. She was suddenly struck by the humor in the situation the maid had described. "They toss up women as well as pins?" Dearie asked, a mischievous expression on her face.

"Who, miss?"

"The jugglers!"

The two women collapsed against each other in laughter.

When they'd recovered, Colleen quickly poured water into the basin and added a few drops of rose attar. She moistened a towel and padded Dearie's flushed face. "There," she soothed, "a little blush is becomin', but this much 'twould never do. They'll think you've been into the paint."

Colleen's words sobered Dearie and she sighed. "I don't know what to wear."

Colleen was already at the armoire. She pulled out a violet silk evening dress, shimmering with blue highlights. "Just the thing for a ball, miss. Why, this is the latest fashion abroad. And the flounces at the bottom are the perfect touch."

Surprised, Dearie was curious. Colleen seemed to have a wealth of information on every subject. "Have you seen many fashion plates?"

"Oh, yes, miss." Colleen nodded. "Me mum was a dressmaker and she taught me all she knew." She cast her eyes down for a moment. "She was set on opening a shop, but took sick on the way over. All our money went to buy medicines once we arrived. But in the end, she died anyway."

The poignancy of the maid's situation touched Dearie and she placed her hand on the girl's arm. "Colleen . . . I'm sorry. I hope you'll be happy here."

"That I will, Miss Dearie. Here, let me do up your hair."

In another fifteen minutes, the two women were chattering like old friends. Colleen had coaxed Dearie's hair into a waterfall of golden curls, interwoven with pearls and lilac ribbons. The last of a long row of buttons were secured and Colleen was adjusting the fichu of Mechlin lace around Dearie's low-cut bodice when another maid knocked at the door.

"It's time, miss," Colleen prodded. While Dearie pulled on long white gloves, Colleen hastily tied a sash of Scotch plaid around her mistress's slender waist. Then Dearie turned to Colleen for a last-minute inspection.

"You look like a princess in a fairy tale about to meet your Prince Charming, Miss Dearie."

Dearie's heart sank to her stomach. Like a fairy tale princess, her marriage had been arranged. But she was not marrying her Prince Charming. She blinked her eyes to stay the tears threatening to fall again as she left the room. Trembling with each step, she descended the stairs as though condemned to execution.

"At last, my dear. How lovely you are," Grayson said, extending his hand to Dearie. "Come, we must join our guests."

Dearie took his arm, smiling weakly as he escorted her into the parlor filled with guests.

The doors to the large room had been thrown open to an adjoining sitting room. Carpets had been removed, floors dusted with chalk, and chairs pushed back against the wall. Musicians on a raised dais had already begun the first waltz of the evening. Along one wall stood an enormous table laden with assorted delicacies. Terrapin, oysters, baked turkey, and thick slices of ham were arranged on a huge platter at the center, surrounded by breads and biscuits as well as cakes, pies, ices, and ice cream. Punch bowl and goblets stood on a smaller table nearby.

Dearie quickly scanned the guests, relieved to find that William Warren had not arrived. Her father propelled her to a tall, flamboyantly dressed gentleman dominating a small group. She knew at once that the man was Alistair Monroe.

Rumor had it that Alistair Monroe was a dandy. Dearie had heard he'd inherited money from his father and lived comfortably without working. He entertained elegantly and was seen in all the right places. His father, Dr. Archibald Monroe, had earned a reputation for being an intellectual leader of Philadelphia society. The elder Monroe had had a thriving medical practice and a chair at the university. His home naturally became a gathering place for the city's intellectuals.

After his father's death, Alistair continued the soirees. As time passed, however, they became more social than intellectual, more lavish than the simple fetes given by his father. The younger Monroe managed to lure visiting royalty and statesmen to his parties, and was always invited to every social affair in the city.

The Graysons had never been invited to a Monroe soiree, and, from the satisfied look on her father's face, Dearie supposed he was pleased that Alistair had condescended to attend their affair.

"Ah, Master Grayson. I cannot imagine how it is that we have not met. Of course, I know you by reputation, sir." Alistair affected a low bow. Only the barest metallic flicker in his eyes belied his sincerity.

Matthew Grayson inclined his head in an acknowledging nod. "It was good of you to come, Master Monroe. May I present my daughter, Dearie."

Although her lashes were demurely lowered, Dearie felt Alistair's eyes upon her. When she looked up, he was staring at her with unabashed interest. A pink flush spread downward to her breast. Alistair's eyes devoured her like a confection.

He licked his lips. "An unexpected pleasure." He grasped Dearie's hand and pressed her wrist to his mouth.

Dearie felt the heat of his kiss through her glove. She withdrew quickly her hand. "I understand you've brought your cousin."

"Yes. You must meet him." Alistair's eyes never left her face. "I hope I may ask for a dance later, Miss Dearie?"

"Her card is filled," Grayson answered, moving Dearie away from Alistair. "Please enjoy yourself, sir."

He escorted her to small group of merchants and their wives, then excused himself to speak with a client across the room. Rather than join in conversation with the merchants' wives, Dearie chose to look around at the other guests. William Warren would arrive any moment, and her life would be over.

"Miss Grayson, my husband tells me you were educated abroad," the woman next to her inquired politely.

"Yes, I — " Dearie started to reply when her attention was caught by a young man who had just stepped into the parlor. Tall and broad-shouldered, the man moved with the grace of an aristocrat. Aside from his handsome features, he had a rugged masculinity that set him apart in the crowd. Dearie wondered for a moment if he was visiting nobleman, but his face was tanned and he wore his sandy hair long, almost to his collar. He was American, she decided.

As Dearie watched him, his gaze suddenly locked with hers. She held her breath, lost in the golden brown warmth of his eyes. He smiled. She smiled boldly back at him, as if they were the only two people in the room. He walked in her direction and she took a step toward him, drawn to him in some inexplicable way. A deep, primordial instinct told her that she knew this man. . . . had waited for him all her life, exactly as Jessamine had predicted.

He reached her side and the nearness of him was overwhelming. She felt a warm flush on her face, and a wave of lightheadedness swept over her. No man had ever affected her this way. Shaking, she took out her ivory fan to hide the vivid color in her face.

"Madam? Or is it Miss?" Even his voice, deep with a slight scratch, was a sensual caress.

She nodded at "Miss," but she could say nothing else. Her body suddenly had a will of its own.

"Allow me to introduce myself. I am Tavish McLeod, Alistair's cousin."

What a beautiful name, Dearie thought to herself. Tavish McLeod.

Tavish gazed at her, awestruck. From across the room, he had been irresistibly drawn to the fair-haired beauty who stood like a bright angel. The noise had suddenly died out, the guests receded into the background, and they were alone. As he approached her, he could see the beautiful features of her face. Her eyes were so blue, it seemed he could see through them to the sky. His gaze took in the small but perfect nose above lush pink lips and the dewy rose of her skin. If only he could touch her, know somehow that she was real. When he finally found his voice and spoke to her, he saw the recognition in her eyes, as if the words, his name, were what she had expected him to say . . .

For a moment, they were suspended in time, neither speaking. Then the people around them began to dance and the strains of a waltz intruded upon their shared reverie.

"Will you dance with me?" he asked.

She glided into his arms without a word, her eyes never leaving his.

The room was a kaleidoscope of colors as they turned. Encircled in Tavish's warm embrace, Dearie was completely entranced. She looked up at him and his amber eyes blazed down into hers. He danced as he spoke, with an air of perfect self-assurance as he led her through the steps. She willed the dance to go on forever, but at last the music faded and they were forced to part.

"I hope I am not too forward in asking your name, " Tavish ventured, escorting her from the floor. He could not resist taking her hand in his and imprinting a kiss upon her glove.

Dearie only stared at the hand as if it had been kissed by a pontiff, blessed by a divine spirit. "Master McLeod . . . I— I — "

"Well, well. Master Tavish McLeod." The loud, booming voice of her father interrupted them and the couple looked up in surprise. "I understand from your cousin that you wanted to make my acquaintance. I am honored, sir. Allow me to put my humble services at your disposal during your stay here in Philadelphia. Matthew Grayson at your service. But I see you have already met my daughter."

Tavish's shocked glance moved from father to daughter, and his heart constricted so he feared he might collapse. "Daughter?" he choked out hoarsely.

"Happily so, good sir. Miss Dearie Grayson."

For a fraction of a second, Tavish's face darkened almost dangerously, and Dearie drew back startled. Perhaps it was her name, she thought. Once again she railed at her parents' foolish whim. Then, just as quickly, his smile reappeared. Everything was all right after all.

Tavish talked to Matthew Grayson for almost an hour, and it was obvious to Dearie that her father was impressed by the young man. In fact, when William Warren made his appearance, neither Dearie nor her father moved to join him.

"My family has lived in Virginia since it was a colony," Tavish told them. Alistair, passing by at that moment, raised one eyebrow inquisitively.

"We have quite extensive holdings in Virginia . . . over a thousand acres in one tract, I believe it is."

Grayson rubbed his large hands together. "I don't know how it is that we have not heard of your family before now. What was your name again?"

"McLeod," Tavish said, his voice low.

"I believe I have heard the name," Grayson said pursing his lips. "And, of course, we know Alistair well."

"Of course." Tavish's smile was thin, He would have liked to wring the old bird's neck. But there was a better way. He turned his attention to Dearie, who immediately blushed.

"H-how long will you be staying in Philadelphia?" Dearie asked timidly. Never before had she been so tongue-tied, felt so awkward around a man. Tavish was different. She looked into the smoky depths of his eyes and saw the mystery she had always longed for.

"I have some business and I shall be here until I conclude it," Tavish said, glancing sideways at Grayson. "It may take a while, Miss Grayson."

"Then you must have dinner with us some evening," Dearie heard her father say. "You and your cousin Alistair. Say, Thursday next. I'll send my man round to fetch you at seven, if that suits your pleasure?"

"Perfectly," Tavish excused himself. Sighing, Dearie watched him walk across the room. He made his way through the guests like a prince, smiling graciously at the women and nodding at the men.

"Now then, my dear. We must find William," her father said as he ushered her through the crowd.

"Father, I must speak to you immediately." Dearie broke away, forcing him to follow her across the hall into the library.

"Now, Dearie. Do not strain my patience. You will tell William and I will announce the engagement."

"No, Father. I will never tell him," Dearie said flatly. "I have just met the man I shall marry! It is Tavish McLeod."

"Child, what are you saying?"

"I've never been more sure of anything in my life," Dearie told him, her blue eyes wide. "Jessamine read it several times in the tea leaves."

"Tea leaves, what rot! Dearie, I'll have no more of your romantic notions. You've only just met the man — "

"And isn't that the same way you met my mother? She told me she fell in love with you at first sight."

Grayson rubbed his whiskers thoughtfully, trying hard to suppress a smile. "Oh, she did, did she? She told you that?"

"That she did, Father."

"Hmmm. But look here, you don't even know if the lad has a bent toward marriage. Better to hitch your dreams to a wagon than a star. And we know nothing about this Tavish McLeod. No, my dear. I'm afraid I have decided upon William."

Dearie's eyes blazed with a blue fire. "No, I will not marry him! You will be scandalized if you announce my engagement to William Warren! For then I will elope with Tavish! Heed me, Father!"

Chapter Two

Stunned by his daughter's declaration, Matthew Grayson had given in to Dearie's wishes . . . for the moment. The guests had all gone home and no announcement had been made. However the confidence Dearie felt earlier had now dissipated. With a candle in hand she returned to her room, her resolve wavering like the flame. What if Tavish did not wish to marry, or even worse was already betrothed to someone else? The thought of Tavish with another woman brought a swift pang of jealousy. Still, something wonderful had passed between them in that first meeting, as if God himself had arranged the tryst.

Yet, like Alistair, some men showed no desire to marry. Could Tavish feel the same? Then she remembered with a renewed surge of excitement how his eyes had lingered on her breasts, then moved down to scrutinize the rest of her figure. The amber flame igniting his gaze had belied his outward composure. He was a man, after all. She simply had to convince him that he could not live without her. And this, she would surely do, no matter what it took. Dearie smiled to herself, and rushed up the stairs to her room.

"Ah, Colleen," Dearie said, twirling around her bedroom while the little maid scurried behind her trying to unfasten the buttons on her dress. "Tonight I met the man I am going to marry!"

"But of course you did, Miss Dearie. There's a good lass. You've set the date. And you told him you would marry just like your father wanted. See, 'twas not nearly so bad as you thought."

Dearie stopped long enough for Colleen to grasp the first row of buttons, which she hurriedly undid.

"No, no, Colleen. Not that one." Dearie collapsed onto the chair at her dressing table in happy exhaustion. "This man was like Jessamine said. He was tall and handsome and smart, like Father. He's a planter from Virginia. Just like she said, he'd not be from here . . ."

Colleen frowned. "Stand up a minute, Miss Dearie."

Dearie stood obediently and Colleen pulled the dress over her head.

"He is so handsome, so unlike the other men I've met. His eyes went right through me . . . as if he looked into my very soul." She shivered with delight.

"But . . . your father was to announce your engagement . . ." Colleen said, trying to understand.

"I told him I was in love with Tavish and we would elope if he announced my engagement to William Warren."

Colleen gasped, her dark eyes wide with disbelief. "No, miss! You didn't!"

Dearie nodded smugly.

"And you've set your cap for this one after meetin' him only once?"

Dearie smiled, a faraway look in her eyes.

Colleen took out a satin night dress and helped Dearie slip into it. "Oh, Miss Dearie. I've seen that look before," she sighed softly. "It's so much better when the man catches it first."

"Catches what, Colleen? What on earth are you talking about?"

"Lovesickness. If the man catches it first, everything is bound to work out fine. But if the woman catches it first . . . well, anything can happen."

"Oh, Colleen," Dearie laughed and hugged the maid impulsively. "Everything is going to work out fine. Tavish will ask for my hand and Father will agree. I know it." She walked over and flopped down on the bed.

"How can you know it? Have you the sight, then, that you may predict the future?"

Dearie smiled, hugging her knees to her chest. "I can't say, Colleen. But I know that I will marry Tavish McLeod as surely as I sit here."

Colleen shook her head. "I've never seen it work when the woman gets it first." She grasped Dearie's hand. "Take your mind from him, Miss Dearie. Forget you even met him and turn your attention to your other suitors. If this one comes around, well-a-day. Then you kin favor him with a bit of your time."

Dearie sighed in exasperation. "Colleen, you're asking me to do something I don't want to do. It's dishonest."

"Dishonest!" The little maid was shocked. "Me cousin was trysting with another right up to her wedding night, she was. You don't burn your bridges until you're sure the new one will hold."

Dearie smiled indulgently. Colleen was the most opinionated person she had ever met. "I'll keep that in mind, Colleen. Please turn down the lamps."

"They say there's no cure for lovesickness," Colleen whispered, blowing out the lamps. "The lass that thinks with her heart instead of her head ends with her heart broken." Colleen closed the door behind her with a soft click.

Dearie tossed and turned, unable to get comfortable. Finally she fell into a troubled sleep. She dreamed that a bridge was burning and while she was running frantically to put water on the blaze, Colleen sat placidly on the opposite riverbank. Then Tavish drove up in a splendid carriage annoyed that the bridge was out. Without a word to Dearie he got back in the carriage and drove away. Meanwhile, the fire raged out of control. It nipped at her long skirts as she ran back and forth to the river carrying buckets of water.

Dearie awoke drenched in perspiration. For a long while she stared at the ceiling before she finally drifted off to sleep again.

Tavish was coming to dinner. It had been a week since they'd met and Dearie had thought of nothing else since. She had spent the entire day supervising preparations for the evening's entertainment. In the morning, she had consulted with the cook to make sure everything was in order — that they had enough pheasants, turkeys, roasted meats and potatoes, corn, and seafood salad. Then she had personally inspected every room to make sure that all were spotless. The rest of the day was spent deciding what gown to wear.

Colleen went back and forth between the wardrobes and, in the end, had to fetch her sewing basket to combine two dresses for a new look. Dearie insisted that she look her best, and her black velvet was too severe. Colleen added a pink satin petticoat and an overskirt of white crepe decorated with gray fox fur. More of the fur was fitted around Dearie's low-cut bodice and lined the pink satin sleeves. The final effect was breathtaking, as the dress was grand enough for a queen. Indeed, it was a copy of a similar one worn by Queen Charlotte.

Dearie's pastel beauty was further enhanced by the gray and pink, but the black made her look truly aristocratic. Colleen arranged her mistress's hair in a braided coil at her neck. From the pink satin she fashioned roses and wove them into the coil.

When at last they were finished, Colleen shook her head, her dark eyes glistening. "Miss Dearie, sure an' you're the most beautiful lass I ever did see. The young master could not help but fall in love with you tonight."

Dearie's cheeks flushed almost the exact shade of pink in her dress. "Oh, I hope so, Colleen."

Outside a carriage pulled up to the door. Dearie drew Colleen to the window. "Look, there, the taller one," she urged the maid, just as Tavish removed his hat.

"He looks fair like Bobby Shaftoe," Colleen said.

"Bobby Shaftoe?"

"Y'know, mum, the rhyme. 'Bobby Shaftoe's gone to sea, silver buckles on his knee. He'll come back and marry me, pretty Bobby Shaftoe. Bobby Shaftoe's back and fair, combing out his yellow hair . . .' Now I've forgot the rest . . ."

Dearie hugged Colleen to her. "Oh, Colleen, you're wonderful."

A moment later, Dearie hurried down the stairs to the parlor. Taking a deep breath, she settled herself on the settee. She was joined shortly by her father.

"You look ravishing, my child," Grayson said. "What an extraordinary dress."

"Colleen made it from bits and pieces of other dresses." Dearie smiled up at him.

He returned her smile. "You like the little maid, then, I gather."

"Oh, yes, Father. Thank you. I am . . . so happy."

A splendid coach and four had arrived for Tavish and Alistair. The doors of the coach were painted a cerulean blue over which an elaborately scrolled "G" was embossed in white. The driver and footman wore blue frock coats that matched the color of the coach.

Tavish was impressed by the showy display. He followed his cousin into the coach and sat rigidly while Alistair chatted about the soirees he had recently attended.

The Grayson mansion was on Third Street above Spruce and occupied a huge allotment of land. The house was three-storied and set back from the line of the street some fifty feet. The main entrance was approached by a circular gravel carriageway, and huge wrought-iron gates with open tracery were unlocked by gatemen in blue livery. A stone baluster, lined with shrubs, ran from the gates to a low wall fronting the house. Looking around him, Tavish was awed. It had been too dark to clearly see the outside of the mansion on the night of the ball. Even Alistair was impressed by the artful landscaping of the grounds. The lawns were filled with statuary, crisscrossed with stone walks, shade trees, and parterres, and covered more than three acres.

Tavish's chest tightened and he felt his confidence waning. Matthew Grayson was a rich and powerful man. How did he, Tavish, who had little in comparison, expect to outwit him? And Dearie . . . wouldn't she have hundreds of suitors to choose from?

Alistair broke into his thoughts. "Good heavens. It was hard to tell last week with so many carriages. This is lovely . . ." he gestured with his lace handkerchief. "I had no idea he was so . . . uh . . . prominent. Perhaps I shall attend his soirees from now on." He glanced sideways at Tavish. "He certainly seems to be taken with you, as does his daughter."

"Hmm," Tavish grunted in response.

"I had no idea she was a delectable little — "

Tavish turned toward his cousin, hazel eyes blazing copper.

Alistair cleared his throat nervously. "I meant to say, she is a lovely creature."

Tavish pulled a square of linen from his pocket and wiped tiny beads of perspiration off his forehead.

"Alistair, I shall need to borrow some money from you temporarily."

Alistair's eyebrows shot up. "Oh? Have you thought of a scheme to beat Grayson?"

"Yes. And I imagine I should be able to repay you within a month, six weeks at most."

Alistair looked skeptical. "That soon? but how could you possibly hope . . . " He looked from Tavish's face to the enormous house as the carriage pulled to a stop in front of the magnificent red brick structure. "Oh, I see . . . " he said.

They were helped out to marble steps, leading up to the door. It was as if they were ascending up to heaven. And Tavish, slowly climbing the stairs, let out his breath in a prayer.

"God give me strength," he said aloud . . .

The butler knocked lightly on the parlor doors, then opened them. "Master Alistair Monroe and Master Tavish McLeod," he announced.

Dearie's heart fluttered and she took out her sandalwood fan to hide her confusion. If possible, Tavish was more handsome than the week before. She'd been afraid that she might be disappointed. Instead she was further awed by his bearing and presence.

He strode into the room as if he owned it, attired in a deep blue broadcloth coat that hugged his broad shoulders. His waistcoat and trousers were of white kerseymere, and Wellington boots gleamed beneath. Both the trousers and the boots clung tightly to his legs, outlining his strongly developed muscles. Alistair was also elegantly arrayed, but Dearie couldn't take her eyes off Tavish.

Tavish came to her immediately and put her hand to his lips. Briefly their eyes locked, blue on hazel. His eyes were somewhere between brown and gray, the color of a pond in summer, Dearie thought dazedly.

"Miss Grayson," he said, his breath warm on her hand. He lowered his eyes to her creamy cleavage outlined in gray fur. How soft and pink she was. He wanted to bury himself in her sweet softness. Slowly, seductively, he raised his eyes again to meet hers.

In a fraction of an instant he had set her senses reeling. A completely new sensation surged through Dearie's body. She desperately wanted to speak, but again her voice had deserted her. She could only nod.

"Welcome, Master McLeod, Master Monore." Grayson's eyes narrowed as his gaze rested on Tavish.

Tavish remembered himself and released Dearie's hand. He walked over to shake hands with Grayson and accepted a snifter of brandy.

"Please, gentlemen, make yourselves at home," Grayson gestured expansively.

The house, Tavish mused, was even more beautiful than he'd remembered. The parlor walls were papered in a small floral print, and fine oil paintings hung in gilded frames. The settee and chairs were covered with deep red damask and the highly polished walnut tables held brass candelabras with dipped tapers. Oriental rugs covered gleaming oak floors.

In the midst of all this splendor Dearie sat on the high-backed settee, a rare jewel in a perfect setting. She seemed to be a natural part of such elegance, yet her unusual beauty, her striking coloring would draw the eye immediately in any background, Tavish thought.

It was with great effort that Tavish tore his gaze away from Dearie and turned to talk to her father. Alistair, however, was openly appreciative in his scrutiny.

While the men talked, it was difficult for Dearie to sit still. There were a thousand questions she wanted to ask Tavish. She wanted to know everything about him, every detail of his life before they had met. So intense were her feelings, she found herself feeling jealous of his past, of any girl he had previously thought pretty.

Tavish sat in a wingback chair close to the fire. From across the room, Dearie studied his profile — the strong, square jaw, the thick sandy-blond hair curling slightly at his collar. Why, she wondered was he so much more appealing than other suitors? Perhaps it was the golden bronze of his skin that gave him such healthy glow. Or, could it be the way his trousers clung to his muscled legs, or the thick bulge at his crotch?

Dearie blushed at her own response to him. Never had she felt so attracted to a man. She had lost control of her senses. Why did he affect her so? She listened to the easy drawl of his deep voice and compared it to Alistair's high-pitched prattle. Then she knew. He was a real genuinely vital man, and masculine. That was why she was drawn to him.

The maid came to announce dinner and Tavish rose gracefully.

"Allow me, Miss Dearie," he said, offering his arm.

It was the first time he had called her by name. She met his gaze directly. "Thank you, Master McLeod." His nearness caused her very skin to prickle with tingling goosebumps that she hoped went unnoticed.

The meal was a sumptuous repast, fit for royalty. Turkey, venison stew, pheasant, and roast were served, along with a seafood salad, various breads, butter, and relishes, topped off with Madeira wine. The men fell to with great gusto, but Dearie only picked at her food. She wished desperately to be alone with Tavish instead of at dinner with her father.

Dessert was followed by brandy. After another round of brandy the gentlemen rose to leave. Dearie watched the butler bring them their hats and cloaks with a heavy heart. Tavish would leave and she might never see him again.

"I ask your permission, Master Grayson, to take Miss Dearie for a carriage ride on Sunday afternoon," she heard him say.

"Well," Grayson reflected, frowning, "the weather — "

"Father," Dearie interjected.

"Perhaps the air would do her good," her father amended reluctantly. His frown remained. Grayson silently resolved to send a man to Virginia to investigate the elegant Master McLeod.

Tavish smiled down at Dearie. "Until Sunday, then."

"Until Sunday," she echoed softly, surprised that the look in Tavish's eyes did not reflect the warmth of his smile.

She watched him shake her father's hand stiffly before taking his hat and cloak from the servant. Then, without another glance in her direction, he left the house with Alistair.

Dearie felt strangely deflated by his odd behavior. Surely he was everything she had ever dreamed of in a man, but his manner was so distant.

She shook her head to dispel the notion that something was wrong. After all, she had known him but a short time, and she was delighted at his request to see her Sunday next.

Sunday was bright and warm. Tavish called for Dearie in Alistair's open rig. Although he brought rugs to keep them warm, Dearie was immediately glad she had worn her brown woolen pelisse over her pink taffeta gown. Just as they were leaving, Colleen came running after her to give her an enormous bearskin muff.

As they rode through the city, Dearie pointed out Independence Hall, the Masonic hall, and various theaters along the way. After a time, they stopped at the Phoenix Tavern at the intersection of Germantown Road and Sixth Street. Alighting there, they walked through the spacious grounds to several benches set close to a rippling stream.

Few couples were abroad. Most remained inside by the fire, for the wind had picked up. Tavish led Dearie to a bench partially obscured by a stand of elms. They stood silently for a while, watching the steady course of the stream. Then without a word Tavish pulled her close to him. The action seemed as natural to Dearie as when they had danced. She slid willingly into his embrace.

His kiss held a deep, urgent hunger. He kissed her roughly, bruising her lips, yet Dearie had no will to resist. She pressed closer to him, returning his kiss with equal ardor.

Tavish deepened the kiss with his tongue and Dearie was only surprised at the pleasant rush of sensations coursing through her veins. He cradled her in one arm while his other hand touched her cheek. His fingers traced the outline of her jaw and moved down her slim white neck. He kissed her golden lashes as they fluttered against her cheek.

She felt his hand beneath her pelisse, caressing her back, then reaching within her dress to touch her breasts. Dearie pulled away. But it was only the fear of detection that made her place her hand upon his shoulder.

"You don't know how I've wanted to hold you, to touch you like this," he whispered between soft kisses.

They were the words Dearie had so wanted to hear. She had dreamed he would hold her like this.

He kissed her again even more ardently.

"Tavish, someone might see," she protested breathlessly.

He tightened his arms around her, plunging his hand into her bodice to cup one firm breast. His lips on hers were heated as he found the nipple he was seeking and pressed it like flower between his thumb and forefinger.

Dearie moaned, arching toward him. Never had she felt such a delicious sensation. "Please," she managed.

"Perhaps 'tis too soon to tell you this, Dearie" — he massaged the nipple between his fingers — "but we are meant to be together." In fact it seemed that God had provided the circumstances to suit Tavish's purpose. He bent down to kiss the rosebud nipple before covering it, like a priceless jewel, with her bodice.

He suddenly pulled away and Dearie shivered as the cool air whipped through her open pelisse. She desperately wanted him to hold her again, but he turned to stare at the rushing stream. A frown creased his brow, and it was obvious that his thoughts were elsewhere. In a moment he retrieved her fallen muff from where it lay on the ground beside them.

"What do you mean, Tavish?" she asked, searching his face. "Do you love me?"

"How could I *not* love you? You are beautiful, educated . . . everything a man could want in a woman." His words did not match the expression on his face, as cold as the wind whipping around them. More than anything in the world, Dearie wanted to believe him.

"And I love you, Tavish," she said.

He adjusted her pelisse and smoothed the golden tendrils of her hair, then pulled her arm through his. "I suppose the next step is to speak to your father." He smiled stiffly.

Dearie knew that her father was formidable, and she imagined that any young man would be intimidated by him. Still, Tavish's strange manner was puzzling.

As he walked her back to the carriage, Dearie again searched his face for some clue to his thoughts. After all that had just happened, surely there should be some warmth in his expression. His face was an impassive mask.

Was this what Colleen meant? Dearie asked herself. Was it possible that her love was not returned? Had she been too forward? She had just told him that she loved him; words she had never said to a man before. Dearie ignored the sinking feeling in her stomach. Tavish must love her. It simply had to be.

He handed her into the carriage, settled the wrap around her, and climbed up beside her. His actions were methodical rather than tender, and Dearie was even more bewildered.

"Tavish? You do love me, don't you?"

He flicked the reins without looking at her, but she could discern a muscle working in his jaw. "I said so, didn't I? Why do you ask?"

"Well, if we are to be married . . . I . . . just thought . . . we should be sure."

He laughed. "Shall I kiss you again to show you I mean what I say?"

Dearie smiled with embarrassment, her cheeks flaming crimson. "No, I think I have had enough for one day. And I do believe you."

Despite his laugh, his answer left her wondering. He was darkly preoccupied during the ride back. Was this the way lovers behaved? If so, it was not as she had imagined it. Doubt edged its way into the back of her mind. Did he really love her? But of course he did, she chided herself roundly. Whyever else would he want to marry her?

In the weeks that followed, Dearie had scant opportunity to reflect upon Tavish's strange behavior. The usual round of spring parties had begun. This year there were even more, and, as a result of Alistair's social standing, Tavish was always in attendance.

Tavish proved to be a model suitor. His manners were impeccable, his gifts were well timed and tasteful. He never failed to ask permission to escort Dearie to a soiree. Once there, he made sure to compliment the hostess and spend a certain amount of time speaking with Matthew Grayson. Philadelphia society was charmed by the young Virginian. If Matthew Grayson was looking for a flaw in the young man's character, he found none.

After the interlude at the Phoenix Tavern, Dearie thought of Tavish constantly. He had awakened desires she'd never dreamed she had, but although she longed to be alone with him, they seldom had the opportunity. The few stolen kisses on moonlit verandas only fired her imagination.

"Colleen," Dearie asked the little maid when they were out shopping one day. "What happens between a man and a woman on their wedding night?"

They were in a milliner's shop and the proprietor had gone into the back room for more bonnets. Colleen's face turned bright red. "Miss, 'tisn't proper to speak of such things."

"Oh, pooh. I've done things properly all my life and it's boring."

Shocked, Colleen shook her head so vigorously that her cap fell off. "Why, miss, what are you sayin'? You've your reputation to think of." Colleen had no idea what Dearie had in mind, but she saw an alarming look in the girl's azure eyes.

Dearie tapped a finger on her chin. "Colleen, I want to know what it's like to be a woman. Have you been with a man?"

The color in Colleen's face now reached the very roots of her dark hair. "Well, I . . . no, miss. But I did come close once with Jimmy McGregor in his uncle's loft. Her voice was a husky whisper. " 'Tis by God's own grace that his younger brother come to fetch him and not a minute too soon."

"What was it like?" Dearie clutched Colleen's sleeve.

Colleen rolled her dark eyes expressively. "From what I could tell, there's naught else like it. I wish . . . " She paused, her eyes misty. "Ah, well, that's past. But you know, once the lovin's started, there's no turning back. And if there's no ring on your finger, may heaven help you! That much happened to my second cousin, Rosie."

"Why? What do you mean?"

"Well, you know, miss. She got in the family way." Colleen raised a dark eyebrow.

"Oh." Dearie let out her breath quickly.

"Aye, and to make matters worse, it was twins. If that's not the Lord's way of telling — "

The milliner's return with an armload of boxes abruptly ended the conversation. But Dearie spent the rest of the day contemplating Colleen's words. Did Tavish really intend to marry her or had he been swept away by the moment?

The more she thought about it, the more convinced she was that she needed to be alone with Tavish. Perhaps if he lost control again he would speak to her father and they would be married right away. She told herself that was what she wanted. Colleen's admonitions only made her realize that she had to have Tavish. And there was no reason why she shouldn't have him. She'd always received everything else she had ever wanted.

Chapter Three

Dearie was thrilled when Tavish asked to take her rowing on a Sunday afternoon in late March. At last they would be alone.

The Schuylkill River wound down snakelike from the mountains. Smooth and dark green, it cut a zigzag path through a dense forest. The water was peaceful as it flowed along its primeval course. Only a boathouse in the distance served to remind the observer that man had been there at all.

The weather was unseasonably warm and Jessamine packed them a picnic lunch. As usual, Dearie hardly spoke. Tavish wore a plum-colored coat, accentuating his ruddy, suntanned complexion. *How well we match*, Dearie thought, for own dress was flowered plum-colored silk. Seated next to him on a carpet of pine needles, she was entranced by him. She toyed with her food while he ate heartily.

His nearness filled her with an inner excitement she could hardly contain. Her face was flushed, her skin warmed by his very presence. Just when she thought she would die for a kiss, he leaned over and nuzzled her cheek, then traced the line of her jaw with kisses.

Her senses reeling, Dearie leaned back on her elbows, fully aware that he was afforded an ample view of her breasts in her low-cut bodice. Lips parted, her eyes closed, she waited for his kiss. When it didn't come, she opened her eyes to find him staring at her, a strange expression on his face.

"Perhaps we should take a boat ride," he said clearing his throat.

Puzzled, Dearie jerked her shawl back around her shoulders and nodded. "That would be nice, Tavish."

Once in the boat, she could not keep her eyes off his strong shoulders. He'd taken off his frock coat and cravat and rolled up the sleeves of his white cambric shirt. As he rowed, she could see muscles rippling in his corded arms. He paused, wiping perspiration from his head and neck, then opened his shirt. The vee at his collar revealed a thatch of dark brown hair.

Dearie too, felt the heat. But she knew it was the reaction of her own body to the man across from her. Her shawl fell loosely from her shoulders, then the wind caught it and threatened to whip it away. As she lurched forward to catch it, Dearie fell onto Tavish. The boat tipped dangerously, and before they knew what was happening they had fallen into the icy water.

"Oh, my goodness," Dearie gasped, reaching the surface, "I . . . I didn't mean . . . " Quickly righting the boat, Tavish retrieved the oars and took a firm hold on Dearie with his free hand. "Hang on to me," he told her, pulling both Dearie and the boat onto the bank in a remote part of the park.

Once he'd tied up the boat, Tavish peeled off his shirt. Although she was shaking with the cold, Dearie watched with an amused smile on her lips. He acted as if he were alone. At the sight of his chest bared to the waist, Dearie took in her breath sharply. He was every bit as handsome as she had imagined. Beneath the wet silk, her nipples hardened in response.

He strode over and handed her a blanket that had been miraculously saved. "You must take off your clothes. We can lay them out here to dry." He made as if to walk away and leave her to undress in privacy, but his eyes locked with hers.

Boldly Dearie began to unbutton the front of her bodice. Her breathing was staccato, every button loosening the hold she had on her reserve. She wanted him so badly. She peeled the sodden gown from her shoulders and let it fall into a heap at her ankles. Still looking at Tavish, she began to unlace the ribbons of her chemise. Finally it, too, hung around her white shoulders, revealing firm, uptilted breasts glistening with crystal drops of water.

Now, Tavish could not have left if he had wanted to go. She was like some fine statue, perfectly formed by a master sculptor. He gazed hungrily upon her lovely torso. How he longed to trace those gentle curves and make them his own.

"Tavish," she called him to her.

He took her in his arms with a moan and she melted into him instantly becoming a part of his body. She waited, her lips moistened and parted. He claimed them urgently, molding her mouth to his. The touch of her erect nipples against his chest drove him to thrust his tongue through her white teeth. Instead of resisting, Dearie urged him on, moving her rosebud nipples back and forth seductively. Did she know how she drove him mad?

He lowered her to the ground, gently easing the chemise to her waist. He quickly tugged down her pantalettes to see all of her. Dearie made no move to stop him; instead, she helped him lower his trousers as if she was experienced at lovemaking.

Her actions both surprised and pleased him. He wondered if she'd had other lovers. Dearie stared at him with unabashed admiration. "I've never seen a man unclothed before," she told him honestly.

He laughed. "And I've never seen anyone as pretty as you."

Divested of his clothes, Tavish stood over her, his erect manhood fully visible. Although the size of him astonished Dearie, her passion was too great for her to feel any fear. When he lowered himself beside her, she pulled him to her.

With unaccustomed reverence, Tavish caressed every inch of her satin skin, kissing and suckling the taut nipples while Dearie arched, pressing her body against his. His fingers massaged the velvet softness of her stomach, ranging lower to the downy triangle between her legs. There he found her moist and open to his touch. Tenderly he teased her with his fingers until he was certain she wanted him as much as he wanted her.

For a brief moment he paused. "Are you sure you know where this will lead?"

She nodded her head. "Marriage," she said solemnly.

He took in his breath sharply and he seemed about to speak, but twining her fingers through his sandy hair, Dearie pulled him back to her.

His hands were strong, yet amazingly tender, and Dearie's body sprang alive everywhere he touched her. A master magician, Tavish instantly called forth her most ardent responses. When at last he positioned himself over her, she was delirious with longing.

His breathing matched her own and, murmuring low, he buried his face in her hair. She felt him enter, thrusting against her maidenhead. There was a sharp pain, but she urged him further, coaxing him deep within her. The pain subsided and a growing sense of euphoria spread throughout her body. Something wonderful was happening. They moved in thrilling unison to a symphony only they could hear, whose music touched their very souls. The intensity of their need for each other was frightening. When at last Tavish released all the passion within him, Drarie's corresponding response was almost perfectly timed. They were left breathless and spent, in awe at the wonder of their love.

They lay quietly intertwined, neither one speaking. For the first time in her life, Dearie was totally happy. This was surely love. She imagined that they would go and speak to her father as soon as they got back. Her dream faded when Tavish roused himself and dressed hastily without a word.

Dearie watched him in silence, not wanting to break the spell.

"You must dress," he said curtly, avoiding her eyes. He knew that if he looked into her eyes again, he would stay and wrap himself in her warmth once more. He was irritated for giving in to his feelings. "We cannot be gone all day." His voice was gruff, almost harsh.

Dearie was visibly shocked. "I don't want to dress." She stretched provocatively, lifting her hand in invitation. "I want to stay here. Come back to me, Tavish."

He closed his eyes to the vision of her lying upon the green carpet of the woods. He felt her come to him, winding her soft arms around his neck and he sighed, unable to resist kissing her face and hair. He rested his head in the curve of her neck. "We must go," he said in a muffled whisper. "Else we'll stay here forever."

Dearie was about to propose that they do just that when he wrapped a blanket around her and scooped her up in his arms. "Shall I take you home like this?" he grinned mischievously.

She shook her head in mock alarm, then scrambled out of his arms to dress hurriedly.

Tavish's mood sobered as they approached the Grayson mansion. Dearie wondered if she had said or done anything to displease him. Perhaps she had been too free with her love and he thought her loose. Yet he knew he was the first . . .

At Dearie's behest, Tavish drove the carriage to the servants' entrance. Avoiding her gaze, he jumped out to help her down. He saw her through the door, but when she turned to say good-bye he had gone.

How strange! she thought, mystified. She was completely unable to interpret his actions. Tavish was the most wonderful and mysterious man she had ever met.

Having made love to Tavish, Dearie could think of nothing else. Over and over again, she dreamed of having him near her, whispering softly in her hair. She remembered with a warm rush the gentleness of his hands as he caressed her body. His touch had made her body respond exactly as he'd wanted.

Tavish courted Dearie extravagantly. Almost every day Colleen brought in flowers or some small trinket from him. But when Dearie tried to speak to him, he was remote. She expected some secret lover's signal, a squeeze of her hand, a stolen kiss. There was nothing. Not even the barest flicker of longing appeared in his amber eyes.

Weeks passed and still he had not spoken to her father. Dearie was consumed by doubt. Colleen was right. She had given herself entirely to him and there was no ring on her finger. What if she shared the same fate as Cousin Rosie?

Dearie had never worried about a man before, but Tavish dominated her every thought. She realized that she was hopelessly in love. Gazing at her image in the glass over her dressing table, she knew her blond beauty was arresting. Why wasn't Tavish affected? A pout formed on her small mouth. She must do something to force his hand. Fate responded to Dearie's predicament in a fortuitous catastrophe which occurred on Easter Sunday.

Over her father's objections, Dearie had invited Tavish to accompany them to the popular Chestnut Street Theater where a troupe of English actors were putting on a production of *As You Like It*.

"You worry me, my dear. You are spending too much time with this young man."

"Father, I've told you. I'm going to marry him!"

"Dearie, I've made inquiries. No one knows anything about him. I've yet to hear back from Virginia but — "

"Father! Don't you believe him? Hasn't he been the perfect gentleman? He's answered all your questions about his past! I'm surprised at you, Father. Jessamine said he was just like you, and I believe her."

Grayson pursed his lips. "Just like me, eh? That's not at all the sort of marriage I had in mind for you, miss."

"But I don't understand. I should think you'd be pleased."

"I am not. The lad is a stranger to us. For all we know he could be penniless and looking to fatten his purse by marrying you."

Dearie's eyes filled with tears. "How could you even suggest such a thing?"

Grayson's heart constricted at the sight of her distress. He took her trembling hand in his. "I'm sorry, my little doll. You say that you love the young man and I'm willing to give him the benefit of doubt. I just want to make certain."

Later, nettled by her father's words, Dearie sat quietly while Colleen worked on her hair. Surely her father was overcautious and perhaps a bit jealous. After all he stood to lose his only daughter very soon. Any father would react so, she told herself. Dearie shook her head, as if to dispel any doubts, and Colleen's carefully constructed curls tumbled down around her shoulders. "Aye, now you've done it, Miss Dearie. We'll have to begin all over again."

Dearie smiled. "We have time, Colleen. Besides, I want to look especially good tonight."

When Tavish arrived, Dearie's eyes sparkled. In her hair she wore the flowers he had sent. They matched her dress perfectly. He pressed her hand to his lips. Nodding at Grayson, he handed the older man a packet of his favorite pipe tobacco. Grayson smiled grimly. "You think of everything," he said, following the young couple out to the coach.

The theater was filled to capacity, and the performance proved a lively one. During intermission Tavish was attempting to work his way through the crowd in the lobby when a cry of alarm was heard. There was a fire in the theater! Having started backstage, the fire spread through the building with lightning speed. The wooden props and velvet curtains were ready tinder to the fire, and within minutes, the theater became a smoldering inferno.

An alarm bell clanged. Panic and confusion followed, for the building had been plunged into total darkness. The only light came from the flickering flames. The exit was soon blocked by several women who had fainted from lack of oxygen.

Reacting instinctively, Tavish threaded his way through the crowd, returning to Dearie and her father. Dearie was clinging to Grayson as he attempted to break through a boarded-up window.

"Come with me quickly," Tavish directed tersely.

Taking Dearie's arm, he led them upstairs to the balcony. Once there he tore down a heavy velvet curtain and, anchoring one end to a sturdy wooden table, lowered the length out through an open window.

"What do you intend us to do?" Grayson asked, shaken by the panic around him. "Jump?"

"Lower yourself down. Hurry, sir! We must get Dearie out. The smoke's about to overcome her."

Goaded into action, the older man climbed gingerly out the window, holding on to Tavish's strong hand. As Tavish looked down into those cold blue eyes, now filled with fear, he had a sudden impulse to let go of Grayson's hand and watch him drop to his death below. But he pushed the thought from his mind. Instead he helped Grayson get a firm hold on the heavy drape and talked him down

"Easy now. That's it, sir. Not too fast."

Holding a handkerchief over her nose, Dearie swayed at Tavish's side.

"Now, sir," Tavish prompted him. "Now you can drop down

Grayson fell to the ground below. Although the drop was not too far, he did not immediately stand up. Tavish wondered if he had been hurt. In a moment, however, the older man had revived and positioned himself under the end of the drape, ready to receive Dearie.

In a half-swoon, Dearie could no longer hear what was going on around her. She only vaguely remembered that her father had been lowered out the window. It was not until she felt the sting of Tavish's slap on her cheek that she came back to full consciousness.

"Oh," she cried, touching her cheek. "Did you hit me?"

"Yes. You must get hold of yourself!" Tavish commanded her harshly. "Your father is waiting to catch you. You'll have to climb out."

"No . . . no . . . I can't. I . . . don't know how . . . !" With a muttered oath, Tavish tested the drape. Then without warning he threw her roughly over his shoulder and began to climb down. They had gone about halfway, when the velvet ripped apart and they fell to the ground, Dearie on top of Tavish. Stunned by the fall, Tavish lay on the ground, hardly able to move. He was fairly certain that something was broken. But the cries of those still trapped within the burning building forced him to his feet. With a herculean effort, he dragged himself back over to the twisted drape, now torn in half. Painfully he began to heave himself back up the drape.

"Where are you going, Tavish?" Grayson asked in disbelief. We're all safe now. Surely, you're not going back . . . ?"

The clamorous confusion swirling around them drowned out Grayson protests as Tavish climbed tediously upward. Once inside the theater, he came upon several people struggling to find an exit.

"Come with me," Tavish urged them.

They followed Tavish blindly up the stairs, where he tore down another curtain and fashioned a more secure rope. Working quickly he helped person after person out the window. Soon, however, the smoke became too intense and Tavish was forced to follow them down the rope.

By now, a group had gathered beneath the window. A few men congratulated Tavish for his brave action, but he was too spent to do more than nod. Dearie, now revived by the fresh air, rushed to his side.

"Oh, Tavish, you saved our lives!"

Matthew Grayson pursed his lips and nodded. "We're beholden to you, Tavish. Is there anything at all I can do to repay you . . . ?"

Tavish gave a vague smile and collapsed in front of them.

Upon Dearie's orders, Tavish was taken to the Grayson mansion where Matthew Grayson's personal physician was immediately summoned. After a thorough examination, the doctor announced that Tavish had nothing more serious than a broken collarbone.

"The young man should be confined to bed for at least a week," the doctor advised.

"Then he shall certainly stay here," Dearie informed her father, giving him no choice but to comply.

The morning papers hailed Tavish as the hero of the day: "None could have acted more courageously than did young McLeod when he helped many trapped theater-goers gain freedom from the burning edifice."

Dearie and her father learned later that the theater had burned completely to the ground. Fortunately, due largely to Tavish's efforts, there were no fatalities.

Tavish was the talk of the city, and the handsome stranger had dozens of visitors every day. Dearie took great pleasure in surpervising Tavish's convalescence and catering to his every need. There were fresh flowers in his room each day, and she insisted upon checking his bandage regularly. In the evenings she brought a book and read aloud.

"I'm not sure I ever want to get well," he teased her, touching her soft cheek.

"Tavish, why haven't you spoken to my father?" Dearie blurted out, her cheeks coloring.

Looking into her blue eyes, Tavish felt a sudden stab of guilt. His expression darkened. He wasn't at all sure that he could go through with his plan.

"Tavish?"

"Soon," he told her, his mouth tightening into a straight line.

Several times during that week, Matthew Grayson stopped by to pay Tavish a visit.

Dearie smiled at her father's concern. *He is finally coming around*, she thought. However, when passing close to the open door one morning, she was saddened at the conversation she overheard.

"Well, Master Tavish. How are you feeling today?"

"Much better. Thank you, sir."

"Have you informed your family of your injury? Perhaps we should write them since you are convalescing. Where is your home?"

"In Virginia."

"Ah, yes. Where in Virginia?"

Tavish lowered his eyes. "It's a small town some distance from Richmond. I doubt that you have heard of it, Master Grayson."

Grayson waited expectantly, but when Tavish gave no more information, he cleared his throat noisily. "I have been thinking ... I knew a McLeod at one time some months ago ... "

"It's a very common name," Tavish informed him curtly.

"I daresay," Grayson said. "And your family originally settled in Virginia?

Tavish nodded.

"I have a friend living in Richmond. I wrote to him recently inquiring as to whether he might know your family. I have his letter here. He knows of no McLeods in the vicinity." Grayson narrowed his bright blue eyes shrewdly. "I wonder how that can be?"

Tavish's heart had leaped to his throat, but his eyes held Grayson's steadily. "I can't imagine. What is your friend's name?"

"Marcus Welhouse. He's said to be a prominent attorney there."

Tavish raised a brow skeptically. "He can't be that prominent. I have never heard of him."

Obviously irritated, Grayson rose, stuffing the letter into his pocket. Again he fixed Tavish with his ice-blue gaze. "One of you is not telling the truth. And I intend to find out, sir." He turned to go. "For your sake, I hope it is not you, Master McLeod."

Matthew Grayson marched down the hallway, so preoccupied that he failed to notice Dearie standing outside the door. When she entered the room, Tavish's dark expression reflected the same angry distrust.

Dearie's spirits fell. How could they be so at odds? She was further disheartened when later encounters proved equally awkward. At the point of despair, she remembered what Jessamine had said. Tavish was just like her father. She relaxed then, realizing that they were both strong men. It was inevitable that they would come into conflict at first. In time they would surely become reconciled to the situation.

The doctor returned the following week and pronounced Tavish well enough to move back to his cousin's house. Dearie was sad to see him leave. And still he had not spoken to her father. On the morning of his departure, Grayson and Dearie saw Tavish out to the carriage. Dearie noted gratefully that her father appeared to be in much better spirits.

"Tavish, we can't thank you enough for all you've done," Dearie told him. Her eyes locked with his. She longed to kiss him, but she knew that it was impossible.

Tenderly, Tavish placed her hand to his lips. "No, Miss Grayson. I am in your debt for the hospitality you have given me since the fire." He raised his eyes briefly to glance at Grayson.

Grayson cleared his throat. "We do appreciate your assistance, Master Tavish. You'll be sure to honor us with another visit as soon as you are able. I only wish there was some way to repay you . . . " Tavish's eyes darkened and he quickly released Dearie's hand.

You'll pay, he thought, smiling cordially at Grayson. *With your daughter and a huge dowry.*

He turned to the footman standing ready to help him into the carriage. "I'll think of something," he said solemnly before the door closed between them.

Chapter Four

Tavish contemplated his situation during the coach ride to Alistair's house. Soon his funds would be completely exhausted, and he would be forced to leave Philadelphia.

I must act quickly, he told himself, *or the opportunity will be lost. But what if Grayson refuses my suit?*

Matthew Grayson was a wily old man. Already he was beginning to doubt the story Tavish had concocted. If he learned the truth, all would be lost. His mouth curved into a sardonic smile. The lawyer would not be so quick to refuse if he knew that his daughter had already been compromised. What sweet pleasure it would be to see the look on Matthew Grayson's face when he heard that news. Just then the image of Dearie's beautiful, trusting face appeared before his eyes.

Tavish reasoned with himself. Dearie's large dowry would restore the business, and the McLeod name would mean something once again. He struck his fist against his hand. *I cannot fail! I am too close!*

Like some exquisite phantom, Dearie continued to haunt him, tugging at the strings of his heart, eroding his determination to seek revenge. What of her? Her eyes told him she was in love with him. He'd seen that look before . . .

Tavish had a way with women. Since the servant girl who had introduced him at an early age to the pleasures of the flesh, Tavish had never lacked for female companionship. His rakish, cavalier attitude left women tantalized and uncertain.

Having no desire to settle down, Tavish held a tight rein on his emotions, carelessly wounding many hearts. Generally, he confined his liaisons to lower-class women, always making sure they understood that he had no intention of marrying. One girl, however, nearly succeeded in changing his mind.

Georganna Arms, the voluptuous young daughter of Gregory Arms, Fayetteville's blacksmith, was a woman of the world at sixteen. Although she had her pick of the local swains, she'd decided that Tavish was the one she wanted.

At first she flirted openly when Tavish dropped by her father's shop. She found various reasons to be out front — sweeping the floors, pouring water for the horses or serving cider to the waiting gentlemen. She performed menial tasks with a seductive grace, teasing with the soft swaying of her full hips as she swept, the glimpse of rounded breasts she showed when bending over, and the attractive pout of her red lips when she sighed. Tavish was intrigued in spite of himself.

Knowing Georganna's reputation, Tavish dropped by one afternoon when Gregory Arms was not in the shop. Georganna was caught unawares in the stable, her bodice unbuttoned to reveal a thin chemise beneath. Without a word, Tavish sauntered over to the girl and took her roughly in his arms. Highly outraged, Georganna slapped his face. " 'Tis only by the grace of God that you aren't dead," she cried out. "If me father were about, you most surely would be." She then flounced into the shop, slamming the door behind her.

Tavish was left standing in the stable, an abashed look on his face.

The humiliating incident plagued Tavish until he found some excuse to return. He strolled into the blacksmithy two weeks later, leading a lame horse he had borrowed.

Georganna was not immediately in sight, but she appeared presently. From her expression, it was obvious that she was shocked to see him again.

"Master McLeod." She inclined her head with a solemn, chastising look. At that moment, her dark brown hair tumbled from the knot atop her head to spill over her full, white breasts.

Tavish watched her bend over to twist her curls up again. From his vantage point, he could see the dark tip of one breast in her loosened bodice.

From that day, Tavish courted Georganna judiciously, quickly learning the little things that please a woman. His ultimate goal was to bed her, and, when he finally had his way, he was not disappointed.

"Yes, Tavish. You may touch them," Georganna told him as he lowered her bodice to her waist. "But just this once . . . "

As a result of Georganna's wiles, Tavish felt privileged to receive what others had obtained with much less effort. And Georganna, determined to win him, artfully used her soft, rounded body to bring Tavish pleasures he'd only dreamed of before.

The affair raged for several months, until Tavish realized that Georganna was out to trap him. He suddenly began to see far less of her. Desperate and hurt, Georganna schemed to force a marriage by becoming pregnant. But Tavish left for Philadelphia before she could put her plan into action.

After leaving Fayetteville, Tavish continued to think about Georganna. He even fancied that he might love her until he met Dearie Grayson. Then all memory of the blacksmith's dark-eyed daughter vanished completely from his mind . . .

Thinking of Dearie, Tavish's expression softened. He gazed distractedly out the coach window. She was everything he had always wanted in a woman — beautiful, intelligent, and soft . . . so soft. If only she was not Matthew Grayson's daughter! Because she was, he could not, must not, care for her. He reminded himself that she was only a tool to achieve his goal.

The marriage would be a temporary arrangement, merely a means of regaining what was rightfully his. He had no doubt the spoiled girl would soon tire of rustic country life in North Carolina. Then he would send her back to her father and the affair would be settled, to his satisfaction.

Tavish underestimated Dearie's appeal, however. Just when he was certain that her charms had no effect on him, she would find an excuse to be alone with him. Then she would press her softly curved body against his and he'd forget everything else. Afterwards, he was consumed with guilt. She was an innocent girl, completely unaware of the game she played.

Dearie was unable to sleep or eat. What little she did eat made her immediately sick to her stomach. Her porcelain skin took on a pale translucence, then became suffused with color at the mere mention of Tavish's name. When she knew that Tavish was coming to call she spent hours picking out what dress to wear, and fussed over her hair until she cried.

Colleen watched her mistress with sinking heart. "Aye, miss. You've got it bad, y'do. I've never seen such a case."

"Now don't start on the love sickness again, Colleen," Dearie told her crossly. "This time I really am sick. I can't imagine what I must have eaten. . . . We must send to the doctor for some medicines. Tavish is coming to dinner tonight."

Colleen shook her dark curls solemnly. "There are no medicines for what ails you, Miss Dearie."

Dearie sat at her dressing table, combing through the shimmering gold waves of her hair. "Please, Colleen. I'm not of a mood to argue."

Colleen stood silently behind her.

"Colleen? I can't imagine what's got into you."

"You've got yourself with child, Miss Dearie," Colleen blurted out. "I've seen it too many times not to know." The little maid lowered her dark eyes.

Dearie peered closer at her image in the glass, as if seeing it for the first time. Then she pushed back the chair to survey her entire figure. Her expression betrayed no emotion. Then she smiled. "If that's true," her voice trailed off, "then it's wonderful news. Tavish will be so happy!"

Dearie's reaction was not at all what Colleen had expected. "But, miss, you aren't yet wed . . . "

"Tavish will ask for my hand tonight, I'm sure of it," Dearie assured her. But Colleen's doubtful look was unnerving.

What if Tavish didn't speak to her father? What if it was months before they married?

Dearie grasped Colleen's hand. "He said he would talk to Father. But why hasn't he? Do you think he loves me? How does he seem?"

Colleen was at a loss. For all his good looks, she thought him remote and sometimes moody. But she smoothed Dearie's golden curls. "Ah, Miss Dearie, of course Master Tavish loves you. How could he not?"

"Then surely he will speak to Father."

"He will, miss. Don't you fret."

With great effort Colleen forced herself to smile and tell a humorous story as she brushed Dearie's hair into gleaming curls. But she inwardly offered up a silent prayer. She had no idea what the future would bring. She did know it wasn't the best way to begin a marriage . . . if there was to be a marriage.

Dearie badgered her father until finally three weeks after the fire, he extended another dinner invitation to Tavish.

"After all, Father," she reminded him. "Tavish saved our lives."

"Yes, yes," Grayson grumbled, "but how far must our gratitude extend? My own physician nursed him back to health. He dined on our food for a week. Where does it end?"

Dearie shook her golden curls. "Why, Father! You act as if it were all a part of some elaborate scheme Tavish has planned."

Grayson rubbed his chin, speculatively. "I wonder . . . "

"Oh, tush! And I suppose he set the fire in the theater, too!"

Shortly before he was to arrive, Tavish sent a message requesting a private audience with Matthew Grayson. Dearie was elated. At last Tavish would ask for her hand! Everything was going to be all right after all.

When Tavish arrived the servants ushered him into the parlor with great ceremony. He was still regarded as a hero for his bravery during the fire.

Grayson was seated in one of the wingback chairs in front of the fire. He motioned for Tavish to seat himself opposite. Dressed in a gray velvet coat with a high stock at his neck, Grayson looked every inch the aristocrat he aspired to be. He settled his sharp gaze on Tavish. A servant brought two glasses of brandy.

"Well, Tavish," Grayson said, holding up his glass. "It seems you've really made a name for yourself in the city."

Tavish bowed his head modestly. "That wasn't my intent."

"No?" Grayson inquired lightly. "What was your purpose in coming to Philadelphia, if I may ask?"

Caught off guard, Tavish took refuge in his brandy. He paused to take a healthy sip. "I . . . had some business to conduct with my cousin."

"Ah. I wasn't aware that your cousin was a businessman. He certainly hides his occupation well." Grayson smiled evenly. "In any case, we are all grateful to you for your gallant show of courage."

"Thank you, sir."

The men sipped their brandies in silence, each studying the other over the rim of his glass. Finally Tavish cleared his throat.

"Sir, I've come to say that I'll be leaving soon."

"Oh?"

Tavish hated Grayson's unflappable composure. It was almost as if the older man knew what he going to say. "I believe I told you that I have an older brother who is running the plantation in Virginia . . . "

Grayson continued to sip his brandy, although his eyes narrowed.

"The family also has a plantation in North Carolina, a smaller one, not far from Fayetteville. I'm to take over the management of it, and I hope to make it produce as much as the other one."

"Indeed. Well, Tavish, you are full of surprises."

Tavish took another sip of brandy. The liquid burned his throat and made him cough. "Yes, I'll be leaving within the next few weeks."

Grayson nodded.

"I'd like to take Dearie with me," Tavish continued. Grayson slammed his glass down on the table beside him.

"As my wife, of course," Tavish finished quickly.

"What made you think I'd give my consent to such a proposal?" Grayson's eyes were ice-blue. He saw now that things had moved too fast.

"I assumed you approved of my suit, since you did not discourage me from courting your daughter."

Grayson waved his hand. "Dearie has any number of suitors."

Tavish leveled his gaze at Grayson. "But none that she wants to marry."

Grayson cocked a silver eyebrow. "You are quite confident, Tavish. Have you spoken to Dearie?"

"I have, sir."

Grayson's expression was an inscrutable mask. "Dearie is my only child," he said at last. "I confess I've allowed her . . . em . . . to have her say on things in the past. But I must intercede for her best interests. Dearie will marry one of our own Philadelphians. Had you been able to establish yourself here . . . in some business . . . perhaps then . . ." His voice trailed off and he sipped his brandy. He then smiled genially. "I'm afraid, Master McLeod, that a marriage between you and my daughter is quite impossible."

That must have been the way he smiled at my father the day he took his home and business, Tavish thought. The blood rushed to his face and he felt the rage his father must have felt. He stood abruptly. "Perhaps you should speak with your daughter, Master Grayson."

Grayson rose to face the younger man. "Dare you question my decision? What say has Dearie in this? She is but an innocent girl."

Tavish's mouth was a tight line as he nodded, turning on his heel. "We shall see. Good even, sir."

Something had happened! From the sitting-room window, Dearie watched Tavish march stiffly out the door. He was leaving and dinner was waiting to be served!

She rushed into the parlor to find her father pacing back and forth in front of the fire.

"Father, what has happened?"

Grayson continued to gaze at the fire, a solemn expression on his face. "Tavish has asked for your hand," he said without looking up.

Dearie clasped her hands expectantly. *Tavish does love me!* she thought with a rush of joy.

"I have turned him down. There is much we don't know about him and it bothers me." He raised his eyes to see the stricken expression on her face. "Tavish is unsuitable, Dearie! I will hear no more about it!"

"You cannot do this, Father!" Tears of anguish sprang to her eyes, and she shook with anger and disbelief.

"I have already made my decision." Grayson shook his head, looking at the fire again.

"I am to have his child!" Dearie cried out, her face taut and white.

Grayson's head snapped back around, his face purple with shocked rage. "What! He has taken your innocence! You let him . . . I knew he was a scoundrel! I should never have let him near you!"

Blue eyes blazing, Dearie challenged him. "Scoundrel or not, I *will* marry him! Else I'll have your grandson in a convent!"

Less than a week later, a servant admitted Colleen to Alistair's parlor, where Tavish was taking tea alone.

"I've come with a note from my mistress, Master Tavish." Her face flushed, Colleen shakily retrieved the note from her reticule. Aware of the girl's discomfort, Tavish offered her a cup of tea.

"Thank you, sir. I'd be most beholden," she said as he rang for a servant. Then he opened the note.

Dearest Tavish,

My father has reconsidered his decision of Thursday last. We both request your company tomorrow night when we may discuss plans for the wedding. Dinner will be served at 7:00.

With warmest regards,
Dearie Meade Grayson

Colleen's cup clattered against the saucer and she smiled nervously.

"I'm to take your reply, sir," she said, wondering if his dark expression meant that he would refuse the invitation.

"You may tell them that I shall be happy to come." His tone was pensive and his expression grim.

"Yes, sir. And thank you, sir."

Colleen hurried out the door, anxious for a breath of fresh air. The tension in the Grayson mansion was unbearable and she'd welcomed the chance to escape for a while. But Master Tavish's mood was worse still.

"I've seen happier folk on the third day of a wake," she muttered to herself, shaking her head.

When Tavish arrived on Thursday, Dearie was waiting for him in the parlor. He was again rendered speechless by her beauty. She was an ethereal vision in ivory satin. Her golden hair was twisted into a coil atop her head and a soft cloud of ringlets framed her face. She smiled, and it seemed she drew all the light in the room to her.

"Oh, Tavish," Dearie said, motioning for him to sit near her. "I'm so glad you've come. I was afraid that Father . . . had discouraged you."

Tavish moved mechanically, unable to tear away his gaze. For a moment he forgot where they were. The vivid blue of her eyes and the blush of her pale cheeks made her seem like a Dresden figurine come to life. Yet the warm surge in his loins reminded him that she was real and passionate. His eyes followed the folds of smooth satin clinging to her hips, molding her full breasts. His heart hammered wildly, and suddenly he felt a rush of joy that she would soon be his.

"I am not so easily discouraged," he assured her, smiling. Matthew Grayson entered the room, and the light seemed to dim. The older man's expression was grim, and his face was ashen. Tavish's muscles tensed in response.

"It was good of you to come, Master McLeod." Grayson slowly lowered himself into his chair. "Our last meeting was . . . uh . . . unfortunate. Under the circumstances," he paused to look at Dearie, who flashed him a radiant smile, "I have changed my mind regarding your proposal. We will arrange to have the wedding as soon as possible, if you are in agreement."

Tavish smiled. "I am, sir." Grayson's look of resignation bothered Tavish. Dearie must have badgered him into submission, but Matthew Grayson was not easily subdued. He was curious to know how Dearie had won him over.

The formal dinner was lengthy. Matthew Grayson said nothing, but Tavish could feel the older man's sharp gaze boring through him. Dearie prattled blithely about the wedding preparations and where they would live.

"It's all so wonderful," she exclaimed, clasping her small hands together. "We shall go to live on a plantation. How romantic it will be! Are there hundreds of trees lining the drive, and will there be dozens of servants? What do the wives of planters wear? I'll warrant 'tisn't nearly so cold." She put a finger to her chin. "I shall need ever so many parasols for the summertime . . ."

Tavish smiled wanly. Plantation life wasn't nearly so glamorous. In fact, he thought as he gazed around the room, it would seem like the frontier compared to the luxury of Philadelphia. "It is hard work," he commented.

"Of course it is, Tavish. But I'm sure you have many people to help you."

Matthew Grayson's blue eyes narrowed and Tavish took it as a warning.

"Yes. But it will take time to build up the place."

Matthew Grayson wiped his thin lips with a linen napkin and cleared his throat. "I have not had much time to think of a fitting wedding present," he said with a pained look, "but I lately recalled that I have a factoring business in the area." Grayson had taken over countless businesses in the past few years. He made it a practice to dispose of the original documents and rename the old business to avoid any legal entanglements. When Tavish mentioned North Carolina, he had been reminded of his account there although he had long since forgotten the circumstances under which he'd acquired it. "You say your plantation is not far from Fayetteville?"

Tavish, his eyes fixed on Grayson's, nodded like one in a trance.

"I have paid very little attention to it, but perhaps you could build it into something for you and Dearie. The income might see you through until the plantation is profitable."

Tavish sat immobile, as if he'd been cast into stone.

"Unless you don't want it, or think you might not have time for it," Grayson continued, unable to interpret Tavish's strange expression.

"No, I'm obliged, sir," Tavish finally replied, his voice husky with emotion. "I believe I can handle both responsibilities well. I'd like to try my hand at factoring."

"Well, I shall expect a monthly report."

Dearie smiled happily and thrust her arm through Tavish's. "You see how well everything has turned out," she whispered.

Tavish only nodded, a queer grin turning down one side of his mouth. Grayson had just given him his father's business, and a healthy settlement as well.

But as Dearie smiled trustingly up at him, his triumph dwindled into sadness. It was she who would pay the price of his success.

Calvin Buie, Planter.
Robeson County, North Carolina.

April 10, 1820

Dear Calvin,

I aim to make good my promise. I'll be back before harvest. I am to be married first, though. Please don't mention this to anyone, as I would like to break the news myself. I will explain everything when I return.

Put down some money on the old Suggs place in my name. I'll make good on the loan as soon as I arrive. Be sure to tell Duncan and anyone else you see, I'll be back factoring when the wheat is in.

My best to everyone and tell my mother not to worry.

　　　　　With regard,
　　　　　Tavish.

Tavish McLeod, Esq.
In Care of Alistair Monroe
Sixth and Chestnut Streets
Philadelphia in the State of Pennsylvania

April 28, 1820

Dear Tavish,

We had despaired of hearing from you after so long a time. Now to hear that you will be married within a month was a surprise. I am bound to tell you your mother has not been well.

As you requested, I put money down on the Suggs place, although I'll warrant I could give the banker no good reason as to why you might want it. Had we more time, I might have persuaded him to pay us for it instead. In all honesty, I cannot, for the life of me, figure what you are about in this matter. I have been told there are only four good rooms with a roof still overhead. If I can get away I'll have a look for myself.

I must confess that I didn't guess you would be back on your feet so quickly as to meet the June harvest, but I can't think of anyone I would rather have as my factor. Duncan and I are full of questions the length of this paper will not permit. I can only assume you have done well with your venture there. I eagerly await your reply.

Your Friend,
Calvin.

Tavish McLeod, Esq.
In care of Alistair Monroe
Sixth and Chestnut Streets
Philadelphia in the State of Pennsylvania

May 2, 1820

Dear Tavish,

Although I have not as yet received your reply to my last letter, I felt duty bound to write you as to the condition of your recent purchase. The place is a shambles, certainly not fit to live in at the present time. I have hired some free blacks to clean up the exterior, but they have no carpentry skills. I remain at a loss to know what you have in mind here. Please write and inform me.

With best regards to your future bride,

Calvin.

Tavish began a hurried note back to Calvin in an effort to explain his decision. But in the end, he crumpled the paper in his hand. It was impossible to explain what he intended to do.

With the wedding barely a week away, Tavish wondered if he could go through with it. Dearie's face haunted his dreams, and her sky-blue eyes, so filled with love, held no inkling of his dark motives.

To make matters worse, Tavish's feelings for Dearie constantly fluctuated. One moment she held him spellbound with her witty chatter of places she'd been and people she'd met. However, he had only to see her with her father to become convinced that she was as shallow and greedy as Grayson, with her talk of parties and finery.

Two days before the wedding, Tavish could endure his indecision no longer. He packed his bags and ordered his servant, Clarence, to saddle two horses. Alistair appeared at the stable door.

"What's happened, Tavish? Surely you aren't leaving?"

"I can't go through with it, Alistair." Tavish shook his head sadly. "It will break her heart when she learns the truth."

Alistair dropped his hand on Tavish's shoulder. "This would be even worse. Your leaving would create a scandal, and Dearie's reputation would be ruined. This way she can return to her father after a while, and still be able to hold her head up. Grayson will be furious, of course. But you will have bested him, especially if you keep the dowry."

Tavish watched him brush an imaginary speck of lint off his velvet morning coat. "Believe me, Tavish. You've gone too far to turn back now."

Chapter Five

The wedding was the most splendid affair Philadelphia had ever seen. Matthew Grayson sent invitations to everyone of importance. Most came largely out of curiosity, knowing that he would spare no expense to see his only daughter married in style.

The mansion had been completely transformed. Pastel ribbons formed a colorful rainbow against the whitewashed brick and streamed across the carriageway like a heavenly canopy. In evidence everywhere was Grayson's flair for extravagance. Brass lanterns swung from chains decorated with fresh flowers. Hundreds of other flowers had been placed in the ground alongside jonquils and tulips.

As the wedding was to be held outside, servants in pastel satin scurried through the throng of guests, serving chilled cider or punch in crystal glasses. The bridal path to the white latticed summerhouse was strewn with more flowers and white satin streamers were woven in among the bushes and trees. It was a fairyland, awaiting only the arrival of the beautiful princess and her dashing prince.

Dearie spent hours at her toilette. Colleen, equally nervous, employed several other maids to see that all the skirts and petticoats were ironed and hung in the separate wardrobes reserved for the wedding accessories. Dearie's extensive trousseau was stored in six other wardrobes in the upstairs rooms and would be packed away later into several enormous traveling trunks.

At last, Colleen helped Dearie into her wedding gown. The dress was elaborately fashioned of white satin. It was trimmed with white gauze and ornamented with tiny satin bows. A rouleau of white satin edged the low-cut bodice and lined the edge of Dearie's full skirt. Once the gown was snapped in back, Colleen adjusted the full puff sleeves on Dearie's arms and tied the silken tassels. Next she endeavored to secure the veil of embroidered silk on Dearie's head.

"Oh, Miss Dearie," Colleen fussed, adjusting the veil, which was attached to a coronet of flowers. "I hope I can get it like the drawing."

"Colleen, you're more nervous than I am!" Dearie smiled at her in the glass.

"Thunder!" the little maid fumed as one side of Dearie's coiffure collapsed and a golden braid fell down.

Carefully, as if she held a queen's crown, Colleen settled the veil on the bed and returned to Dearie's side. She deftly rebraided the loose tresses and secured the braid across the other bandeau atop Dearie's head. Golden curls framing her face, Dearie looked like a Saxon princess from a Nordic legend. Colleen retrieved the veil, securing it properly in place. The final effect was dazzling. Colleen stepped back to admire her work.

"I declare, miss. Ye'll put them all to shame." Tears glistened in the maid's eyes. "How wonderful it is to be marrying the man you love."

Dearie caught Colleen's hand and squeezed it affectionately. "Oh, Colleen. It *is* wonderful! But we'll soon be off to North Carolina, and with all the young men there, I'm certain you'll find your true love, too."

"Aye, miss," Colleen nodded, forcing a brave smile. "Mayhap 'twill be. But today is yours alone. And young Master Tavish must surely know what a prize he has won."

For a brief moment, Dearie's eyes lost their sparkle and she frowned. Did he? she wondered. Did Tavish really know how very much she loved him?

"What is it, miss? Are the fastenings too tight?"

Dearie waved at her and smiled again. "No, Colleen. Where are my gloves and reticule?"

Colleen quickly handed Dearie a pair of linen gloves that she had personally designed and sewn.

Dearie inspected them appreciatively, her eyes twinkling. "Oh, Colleen. They're beautiful. I never dreamed you were so gifted."

Colleen cast down her eyes shyly. " 'Tis the only gift I have to give you," she said, voice breaking. Pulling a handkerchief from her sleeve, she turned away.

"There, there," Dearie chided. "You'll set us both to crying."

The opening strains of the wedding music sounded suddenly from below. Dearie hastily pulled on her gloves and snatched up her reticule.

"Your flowers and book, Miss Dearie." Colleen thrust a nosegay and Bible into Dearie's hand before she hurried out the door.

Grayson met his daughter at the bottom of the staircase. Resplendent in a deep blue coat richly embroidered with gold, and a starched ruffled shirt, white knee breeches, and white silk stockings, he embodied elegance.

"You are as lovely as your mother was," he said, his craggy features lighting with a smile.

Dearie beamed. It was the highest compliment he could have paid her, for in his eyes, his dead wife had no rival among mortal women.

"Oh, Father," Dearie whispered, reaching on tiptoe to kiss his cheek. "I am so happy."

Grayson proudly led his daughter through the open double doors and into the gardens where the guests waited expectantly. Slowly, in time to the melodious strains of the music, they proceeded down the flower-strewn pathway.

Looking neither right nor left, Dearie heard exclamations of awe as she passed.

"How lovely!"

"A vision, surely."

"The most beautiful bride I have ever seen."

As they approached the gazebo, Dearie's heart suddenly stopped. Where was Tavish? Her eyes strained to find him in the crowd. Moments later, Tavish stepped to the center of the gazebo in front of the minister and Dearie breathed a sigh of relief. Compared to Grayson, Tavish was somberly dressed. His plain black broadcloth suit fit snugly over his broad shoulders and clung to his long, muscular legs. The simplicity of his attire emphasized his warm coppery complexion and his fair, sunstreaked hair. He waited there with his legs apart, his hands clasped behind his back. When he saw his bride, he heart began to thump loudly in his chest.

Tavish involuntarily sucked in his breath as Dearie approached him. She moved as if she floated on air, lace and gauze like a halo of light surrounded her flushed face. He drank in every detail of her beautiful face and hair, feeling a heady warmth spread to his loins. Then he saw Grayson.

The rapid beating of his heart stilled, as if a cold hand had gripped it. Suddenly sober, Tavish turned back toward the pastor.

The service was over quickly. Only once, when the reverend asked "Who gives this woman to be married" was there a pause as Grayson's eyes locked with Tavish's in a look of challenge.

A strange feeling suddenly clawed at Grayson's insides. Something was not right. He'd had doubts all along, but now he felt there lurked a malevolence in the young man's eyes that he'd never seen before. Grayson's momentary hesitation caused an awkward silence to fall over the wedding party. The next instant the cold look was erased from Tavish's eyes, and Grayson was left feeling puzzled. His instincts had never failed him before. Dearie sighed with exasperation.

"Who gives this woman to be married," the pastor repeated.

"I do, sir. I give this woman to be married," Grayson boomed out loudly, never taking his eyes from Tavish.

"Very well then. May I have the ring?" the pastor continued.

At the end of the ceremony, Tavish gave Dearie a passionate kiss for all to see. He held her so closely that her head was tilted back and her veil would have tumbled to the ground had not her father held it in place.

Dearie's heart beat wildly, and her face flushed a bright red when the pastor gently nudged them apart. She was both thrilled and a touch embarrassed.

Grayson, clearly affronted, ground his teeth in silent fury. The young man was clearly a scoundrel. Perhaps he should have sent Dearie abroad for a year or two.

Tavish shot Grayson a defiant look before taking his bride's arm and leading her back down the aisle.

Now I have him, Tavish thought to himself. But again, his triumph was short-lived. Affectionately squeezing his arm, Dearie looked up at him with eyes as blue and depthless as the sea.

"I've never been so happy in all my life," she whispered.

The full impact of what he'd done momentarily stunned Tavish. He had chosen a wife who would be a constant reminder of Grayson. What he had seen as a solution to his problem had merely caused another that was some-how even worse.

The wedding celebration lasted late into the evening. There was dancing, a lavish dinner buffet, and glass after glass of imported champagne. Dearie felt lightheaded with excitement, but Tavish wore the same serious frown throughout the evening.

"Is it so difficult to give up your freedom, my love?" she whispered timidly when they had a moment alone.

A strange expression flitted across his features, as he was reminded of yet another complication in this tempo-rary arrangement. " 'Tis an odd thing to say," he retorted. "I hadn't given it a thought. But now that you mention it, I don't intend to give up my freedom." His grin was only half joking.

Bewildered, Dearie fiddled with the bows on her gown. "Ah, well. I didn't mean 'give up' your freedom. Cer-tainly, I do not intend to be your jailer, Tavish. 'Tis but an expression . . . " She sighed deeply.

He caressed the soft skin of her chin and tilted it up. "Why such soulful sigh, my Dearie?"

She searched his eyes, emboldened by his genuine con-cern. "It is just that I seem never to say the right thing. I only wonder when I will learn your . . . ways. So that I might . . . please you." As she listened to her own words, they seemed cloying and subservient. Never had she humbled herself so before a man. Men had always fallen at her feet happy to do her bidding regardless of what she asked. Tavish was different. The tables had suddenly been turned and Dearie didn't know how to behave. She constantly searched for ways to win his favor. Although she did this willingly in the name of love, she longed to know that he felt the same.

Tavish looked away, wondering what to say to her. His silence only added to Dearie's consternation. "You do please me, Dearie," he said finally, pulling loose a golden curl and watching it spring back into place. How lovely she was! He bent low and she felt his warm breath in her hair. "I will show you just how much you please me tonight." He brushed a light kiss across her cheek and left her, weaving his way back into the crowd.

Dearie nodded, a wan smile on her lips. She had just married the man of her dreams, but she felt suddenly empty. Watching him move away, she sensed that something important was missing — a piece of the elusive puzzle that was Tavish.

"Men have a funny way of showing what they feel," Colleen had said. "I knew a man who never once told his wife he loved her until just before he died. And the two of them lived together for nigh onto thirty years."

At the time, Dearie had wrinkled her brow in doubt. "Tavish does seem to enjoy kissing me," she had offered.

"Well, there you go, miss. They have no way to say it — to put into words how they are feeling. So they just show it."

Perhaps Colleen was right, Dearie thought now. Tavish was not unlike other men she knew who felt awkward expressing tender emotions. He had said he'd show her how she pleased him, and she guessed she'd know by then. What more could any woman want?

Taking a glass of champagne from a passing servant, Dearie turned back into the room, a determined smile on her face.

Matthew Grayson had offered a guest cottage for the newlyweds to live in until their departure for North Carolina. A miniature of the main house, the cottage was a perfect hideaway, almost hidden by the foliage at the back of the garden. It was there that Tavish was to bring his bride after the wedding festivities ended.

Dearie envisioned her groom sweeping her up at the end of the evening after the guests departed, and carrying her across the threshold. But the hour grew later and later and still Tavish and Alistair continued to play cards.

Finally Dearie excused herself to go upstairs and supervise the packing. Another hour passed before her father knocked on the door. His expression was dark and foreboding.

"You'll want to say good night to your guests."

Dearie looked up brightly. She and Colleen had been laughing like schoolgirls, and she had no idea of the time. "So soon? Where is Tavish?"

Grayson's expression darkened even more. "He will not be of help to you. He is indisposed."

"Indisposed?"

"In his cups," Grayson almost shouted. His disapproving scowl brought Dearie quickly to her feet "I . . . guess it must be getting late . . . "

She followed her father downstairs and graciously bid their guests good-night. There was no need to inquire as to Tavish's whereabouts. Peals of raucous laughter issued steadily from the sitting room. Her face suffused with color, Dearie felt her father's embarrassment, but she took consolation when the guests treated the groom's behavior with good-natured indulgence. After all, it was a night to celebrate.

Matthew Grayson, however, felt no such tolerance. When the last guest had departed, he turned on his heel and strode into the sitting room. The next moment she heard Alistair's high, nasal voice uttering an indignant protest.

"Upon my word, Master Grayson," Alistair exclaimed. Tavish walked stiffly into the hallway, his gait unsteady. Seeing her standing there, he smiled and moved toward her.

"Come, Dearie," he said, taking possession of her hand. " 'Tis late and we've much to do on the morrow."

At his touch, a searing warmth spread rapidly through her limbs. Thinking of what was yet to come, she briefly closed her eyes, anxious to be held and loved by him once again. "Yes, Tavish," she breathed, smiling up at him.

A servant carrying a lantern preceded them into the ribbon-strewn garden. He led them along the curved walkway through trees until finally they arrived at the little cottage. Then the servant bowed politely and handed the lantern to Tavish.

Tavish opened the door and led Dearie inside. He deposited the lantern on a table, then turned to gather up all the candles, lighting them from the lantern. Soon the cottage was ablaze with light. Streamers hung from the ceiling, and huge bouquets of flowers filled the air with a heady scent. The table was laden with fruits, breads, and cheeses, along with several bottles of imported wine.

Dearie clapped her hands in delight. "Oh, look! Father thought of everything!"

Tavish's face darkened. "As always..."

"What do you mean, Tavish?" she asked, touching his shoulder.

He moved away without an answer. Instead he busied himself by opening a bottle of wine. Taking the bottle with him, he sat down heavily in one of the chairs.

"Tavish?"

He stared at her as if he was looking through her, his expression inscrutable. "You'd best go to bed, Dearie. I'll be along in a while." Dearie took this to mean that he wished her to retire first so that she might have her privacy. *How thoughtful of him*, she thought. She would undress and be ready to receive him with open arms. Smiling, she took a lighted taper, and turned toward the bedroom. She looked back at Tavish, but he was staring intently at the candle on the table next to him. A gentle wind from the open window caused the flame to flicker and nearly die.

Were all men as moody as her husband? she wondered, closing the door behind her. From his somber mood, he might have just arrived from a funeral. She shook her head.

It was just his way she told herself, but her lips trembled. Doubt was taking root in her heart.

She selected a gown of lace and pink silk and laid a satin peignoir on the chair beside her. Then she lifted off her wedding veil, letting her heavy braids fall to her shoulders. She attempted to unsnap her dress, but try as she might, she could not reach the fastenings. She stared at her image in the glass, her mouth pursed in thought. Whether he wanted to or not, Tavish would have to help her, she decided with a helpless sigh.

Tavish didn't look up when she opened the door. As she neared the table, Dearie noticed the half-empty wine bottle. Her groom's eyes were closed. He was asleep!

"Tavish!"

His head jerked up quickly, and for a moment, he seemed not to recognize her. "What is it? What is wrong?"

Dumbfounded, Dearie stared at him. Then she quickly recovered herself. "Can you help me with my dress?"

She turned around slowly. She felt his hand fumble at her back, then one by one, the fastenings came open, leaving her back bare except for her pantalettes. He gently lowered the dress off her shoulders and over her slender hips. His hands lingered at her back, tentatively caressing the soft flesh.

His touch sent ripples of liquid fire throughout Dearie's body. She desperately wanted him to continue. His fingers traced the curve of her spine and outlined the slope of her shoulders. She trembled with delight when, the next moment, she felt his mouth moving over the same course his fingers had just traveled. Now his tongue was drawing a smoldering circle along her back and shoulders. A wave of heat followed his kisses, starting a familiar ache in the lower part of her abdomen.

She felt him rise up to stand behind her. His breath was upon her hair, and still she did not move. His fingers slid down her arms to rest in the bend of her elbows before trailing back up again to her shoulders. The feeling was deliciously sensual, unlike anything Dearie had ever felt before. He touched her neck, gathering a stray curl before pulling the heavy braids over her shoulders. With slow deliberation, he loosened each plait. Then he raked his fingers through the shimmering mass until it streamed down her back in a glowing golden curtain, halfway to her waist.

"So beautiful. Your hair is so beautiful . . . like spun gold," he said softly.

Dearie was silent, unable to break the hypnotic spell that held them.

Tavish's kisses on her neck and shoulders left her weak and trembling. It was as if he had melted her very bones with the heat of his touch. When she could tolerate no more, she turned to face him, shamelessly bared to the waist. The hardening tips of her nipples betrayed her passionate need as she raised her eyes to his. He had but to touch her and she was his. Surely, he knew that, she thought desperately. By now her body was so alive and tingling, and hungry for him that she could hardly breathe.

Tavish stared down at her through eyes of smoldering amber. His eyes caressed every inch of her body, telling her without words how much he wanted her.

Dearie's heart beat painfully and she ached to press herself against him. When he knelt down to take a swollen nipple in his mouth, she sighed with relief. Plunging her fingers into his tawny hair, she urged him closer. He moved from one breast to the other, suckling the rosy tips to painful tautness. Dearie felt the insistent throbbing between her legs increase when Tavish loosened her pantalettes with one swift motion and letting them fall limply to the floor. His fingers explored the damp curls below her abdomen and the velvet recesses beyond, causing her to sway into him helplessly.

He broke away for a moment to quickly pull off his clothes. Dearie watched in awe as he lifted his white linen shirt, revealing his muscled shoulders and the thick whorls of dark hair that matted his chest. She never tired of looking at him. Her eyes remained fixed on him as he pulled his breeches down over his lean hips.

Tavish smiled at her obvious fascination, and pulled her to him roughly. Dearie could feel his fully erect manhood straining against her.

"You look at me so strangely. What do I see in your eyes?"

She shook her head, moving her hands across his firm buttocks. "A reflection of the man I love."

His lips claimed hers with a ferocity that startled Dearie at first. But soon she found herself responding in kind. She arched her body toward him, drawing him nearer. Her doubts dissolved in the wave of passion that threatened to sweep her away. Instinctively she knew that he felt the same way.

Suddenly impatient, Tavish lowered her gently down to the Turkish carpet, pillowing her head on his clothes. His mouth left hers and his lips moved slowly down the scented column of her neck to the swell of her breasts.

Dearie moaned with unrestrained desire, raking her nails across his shoulders as he alternately teased and suckled first one rigid nipple then the other. Never had she experienced such exquisite pleasure.

Suddenly Tavish pulled away from her. "Touch me," he urged her, placing her hands on his chest. Free to caress him as she had in her dreams, Dearie shyly explored his body. She felt the sculpted planes of his chest, traced the curling mat of his hair down to where it ended in a mound of dark curls surrounding his manhood. She touched him tentatively at first, then, emboldened by his response, she continued her gentle, teasing exploration until he ceased her ministrations by lowering himself over her.

She was ready when he entered her. She drew him in further and they began to move slowly together. They rocked as one, deepening each other's pleasure, and Dearie knew how right it was, how integral a part of her Tavish was. Soon, their rhythm increasing, they were lifted beyond time and place. As he plunged deeper, Dearie's legs wound about him more tightly, fusing them together. They climaxed as one, the fiery explosion igniting them both — shattering hundreds of stars into pinpricks of light. It seemed that the heavens had opened up for a moment in a brief flash of penetrating light. Surely Tavish had felt it too. Dearie longed to ask him. But her new husband had collapsed, exhausted, beside her, his face hidden against her shoulder.

Dearie lay quite still for a long time, her eyes wide open, her body sated but exhilarated. When she finally drifted off to sleep she knew with certainty that she was truly in love — for the first time in her life.

Barely an hour later, she awoke to find herself in bed and Tavish sitting in a chair opposite. He was staring at her with an indefinable look in his eyes.

"Tavish? Why are you over there? Come back to me, my love."

He shut his eyes tightly, as if the endearment pained him. He shook his head.

"Tavish, what's wrong?"

He avoided her eyes. "I have been thinking. Dearie, you should stay here in Philadelphia. When I've established the business in a few months, I'll send for you."

She sat up straight in bed. "No, Tavish! My place is with you. Don't you want me with you?" He came and sat beside her on the bed. "Yes, of course I do. I only thought . . . "

"I'll hear no more about it," she said, smoothing the bed sheets invitingly. "Besides, I won't be able to travel later."

"Why not?" Tavish asked her, frowning. She took his hand, pressing it against her cheek. Her blue eyes glistened in the dim light. "I am to have a child," she said softly, searching his face.

She'd imagined that he would cry out with joy, or pull her to him in a passionate embrace. Instead she saw pain, and an infinite sadness turn his hazel eyes dark.

"Why?" he asked, shaking his head as if he didn't even know she was there. "Why?"

He began to pace back and forth as if in a trance, his eyes unseeing. Then without another word, he walked out of the cottage and left her alone.

Feeling unutterably lost and afraid, Dearie turned her face into her pillow and cried, until she fell into an exhausted sleep.

Chapter Six

Tavish did not return that night. When Dearie awakened, she was still in the cozy cottage alone. There was no sign of Tavish. Trying to calm her rising sense of panic, she told herself that he could not have left her so soon after their marriage.

She splashed water on her face, chiding herself for choosing such an inopportune moment to tell her husband she was with child. Of course he would be shocked. In the short span of a few hours he had taken on the responsibility not only of a wife, but of a child as well. Although having children is second nature to women, men are not so easily reconciled to the idea, she reasoned.

Dearie dressed carefully. She must look her best for Tavish. With a warm rush of emotion, she remembered their lovemaking last night and was reassured. Tavish had certainly demonstrated his feelings for her in just as he'd promised. Then, realizing that the trip to North Carolina might be arduous, he'd thoughtfully suggested that she stay behind for a time. What a wonderful husband he was! He deserved a wife equally so! She smiled at her reflection. Although patience wasn't one of Dearie's virtues, she vowed to wait until Tavish came around. And surely he would. It was just a matter of time.

When Dearie arrived at the main house, she found Tavish sitting on the veranda with her father. The two were so deep in conversation that neither noticed her approach.

"I shall expect to receive reports on a regular basis," Grayson was saying, his mouth set in a straight line. "To my mind the business could be made profitable. The former owner was not much of a businessman, I'll warrant."

Tavish merely nodded, his face expressionless. But Dearie saw that he gripped the arms of his chair so tightly his knuckles were white.

"Then there's the matter of my daughter's dowry. Since you will be in charge of the money, I'd suggest that you put it in a bank straightaway."

"Tavish?" Dearie came to stand at her husband's side, her hand resting lightly on his shoulder.

Tavish's eyes brightened at the sight of her, then he quickly looked away. "I quite agree, Master Grayson. Dearie's money will be quite safe with me."

"I daresay." A muscle worked in Grayson's jaw.

Perhaps I'm getting old, he thought. *The young man seems the same as always. And, judging from the smile on Dearie's face, she is happy with her new husband. There is the grandson to think of now. Best leave well enough alone*, he told himself.

"Have you been here long, Tavish?" Dearie asked. "I'm sorry I was such a sleepyhead."

"Not long."

Tavish's answer was cold, and Dearie hesitated. "Should I leave you two alone, then?"

"No, no, my little doll." Grayson rose. "We're finished now. I'm sure you have much to do before you leave."

Dearie watched her father walk stiffly back into the house. He suddenly looked older. She felt a stab of guilt for defying his wishes. *But after all*, she reminded herself, *I have done exactly as he asked. But I simply chose my own husband.*

Now gazing at Tavish's brooding expression, she wondered at her choice. Then, as had become her habit of late, she shook her head to dispel all doubts. "Well, my husband. Shall I serve tea or have you already eaten?"

Tavish rose abruptly. "No, thank you. I must be off to my cousin Alistair's. To bid him good-bye." Without meeting her gaze, he moved quickly past her.

Dearie's bottom lip trembled. "But I want to go with you."

He paused, and a slight frown creased his brow. "I'm sure you have much to do with all the packing . . . and," he added, turning to look at her at last, "you shouldn't tire yourself."

"But, Tavish," she protested, catching his arm. "The packing is almost finished, and I have nothing to do. I feel . . . marvelous."

Tavish said nothing as she walked along beside him.

"Please. I'd like to say good-bye to Alistair, too." Her soft lips grazed his jaw.

Tavish acquiesced, but his displeasure was obvious. He wanted to forget about Dearie . . . forget that he had lost his head the night before, probably because of the champagne. Had he known she was with child, he would surely have left her regardless of the scandal. A child definitely was not in his plans. In fact, Dearie was only temporarily in his plans. Guilt consumed him ever time he looked at her, especially now that he had given in to his passion for her. He felt like a thief, for he had sold her a false bill of goods and taken pleasure in the doing.

Was he such a weakling, to be influenced so by a mere girl? But thoughts of Dearie haunted him, even when she was not there. She had permeated his entire being. With a heavy sigh, Tavish drew her arm through his and guided her toward the waiting carriage.

Staunchly determined to lighten her husband's mood, Dearie prattled on. "Is all in readiness for the journey tomorrow?"

"Alistair has taken care of it."

"Such a nice man. I wish I had thought to get him a gift."

"He will be recompensed, I assure you," Tavish replied with a thin smile.

His manner is so cold, Dearie thought, fighting back tears of frustration. *Surely*, she prayed, *I will begin to understand this man I married.*

But even as she prayed, she saw that Tavish had forgotten the wonder of their wedding night. It was as if last night never happened. He was like a stranger sitting beside her.

The carriage rolled through lush gardens to the mansion gates. Tavish gazed out the window, a set expression on his face.

Alistair had been expecting them. He ushered them into his spacious parlor and a servant immediately brought chilled cider and buttered buns. Dearie ate with relish while the two men spoke in monosyllables.

"Shall we take a turn on the veranda, Cousin?" Alistair suggested.

Tavish nodded. "If you'll excuse us a moment, Dearie. We have some business to conclude."

Dearie's appetite had increased over these last few weeks and she was grateful to be left alone to continue eating. However, when the men had failed to return after ten minutes, she grew restless. The door of the veranda was slightly ajar, and she pushed it open. They were standing with their backs to her, facing the garden.

"I must congratulate you, Tavish. I must say that I had my doubts that you could accomplish it all in so short a time. I understand that the dowry was considerable. And to think that I played a small but significant part in it all." Alistair sighed.

"I will repay your money as soon as I can."

Alistair waved it away as if it were unimportant. "As you will, Cousin. You see now that it is better that you stayed."

"No. It is far worse."

"What do you mean?"

"She is with child," Tavish said. From the corner of his eye, he glimpsed a flash of satin. He turned to see the veranda door close quickly.

Visibly shaken, Alistair pressed his handkerchief to his lips. "You don't suppose she heard?"

"It would serve her right if she did," Tavish growled. He turned and angrily retraced his steps to the house.

Dearie was quietly drinking her cider when the men entered. She forced a bright smile, her expression as open and guileless as always.

"If you are ready," Tavish urged her, "we must go. I think we have successfully concluded our transaction, am I not right, Cousin?"

"Quite so," Alistair agreed readily. Then he gallantly lifted Dearie's hand to his lips. "Philadelphia will miss its fairest flower," he said gushingly.

"Thank you, Alistair. You must be sure to pay us a visit in North Carolina."

The men exchanged glances, and Tavish's eyes narrowed.

"Ah, well. I seldom leave the city except occasionally to travel to the coast," Alistair replied. "But . . . who knows?"

An awkward silence fell over the newlyweds as they returned to Grayson Mansion. Finally Tavish broke the heavy silence.

"I'm sorry if you overheard anything that may have distressed you, Dearie," Tavish volunteered. "Perhaps that is the price one pays for eavesdropping," he added trying to assuage the guilt he was feeling.

"Eavesdropping? I hardly think — "

"Alistair and I had . . . an agreement."

"A loan, you mean?"

"All right then . . . a loan." Irritation showed in Tavish's eyes. "And we were discussing the circumstances under which it is to be repaid. That is all."

Dearie knew that was not all. Her fears had returned in a rush. Tavish had thought of leaving her, and Alistair had persuaded him to stay! Then they had spoken of her dowry. But surely, she told herself, Tavish did not intend to use that money to repay Alistair. It was unthinkable! But why had Tavish, who came from wealthy planters, incurred such a debt in the first place? Her stomach began to churn and she thought she might lose her breakfast. Pressing a scented kerchief to her nose, Dearie closed her eyes. She tried desperately to block out the doubts assailing her. Then Tavish's hand covered hers.

"Don't think of it, my Dearie. 'Tis of no importance, and I don't want a misunderstanding to spoil our last day in Philadelphia." Tavish was suddenly himself again. He leaned to kiss her tenderly, and Dearie's misgivings vanished.

How could I have doubted him? she chided herself. *Tavish is my husband now. Have I not vowed to support him in whatever he did?*

She was suddenly ashamed. "I am sorry, my love. 'Twas truly none of my concern," she said, her long golden lashes brushing her cheek. "Of course, it will not spoil our day."

Dearie spent the rest of the afternoon with Colleen, making certain that all was in readiness for their departure the following day. Five enormous trunks were filled to overflowing with dresses of every color, shoes, reticules, and gloves all to match. Stacked next to the trunk were twenty hat boxes.

Colleen shook her head. Due to the heat, she had discarded her lace cap, and her dark curls cascaded in tight ringlets over her shoulders. "I don't know, miss. Looks as if we'll need another trunk."

"I'll send for one," Dearie assured her. "I couldn't leave my hats and parasols. Why, the people in North Carolina would think me uncivilized."

Colleen agreed, dimples indenting her cheeks. "People are wont to judge by appearances."

"They are, aren't they?" The image of Tavish conversing with Alistair suddenly arose in Dearie's mind. "One really has to look deeper to get the true picture, don't you think?"

"I would say so, Miss Dearie." Colleen studied her mistress. "If I may say so, miss, you've been stewing all afternoon. Is there aught I can help you with?"

Dearie sighed and settled on the bed. Hesitating for a moment, she then told Colleen of the conversation she had overheard between Alistair and Tavish.

"I . . . I don't mean to doubt my own husband, Colleen. But I cannot help wondering . . . "

Colleen shook her head. "Master Tavish is a good man, Miss Dearie. Oh, he has more than his share of moodiness, and he keeps his own counsel, but that's the worst you can say of him. Of course he may have thought of leaving. 'Tis a big responsibility for a man, especially with a child coming. Did you not hue and cry about being too young to marry?"

Dearie nodded contritely.

"If he did take a loan from his cousin, then I wager he had a good reason for doing it. After all, 'tis the planting season, did he not say? Surely, his funds would be low until after harvest."

Dearie clasped her hands together in relief. "Why, of course, Colleen! Why did I not think of that? He must have run short until money from the harvest comes in. Naturally, he would borrow money from Alistair, and since we are to leave, he would want to have his debt cleared." She embraced the little maid warmly. "Thank you, Colleen, you've set my mind at ease."

Later, when Dearie left again for the cottage, Colleen sat for a long time in Dearie's room. She gazed vacantly about the room, now stripped almost bare of its lavish furnishings. She wondered if she had done the right thing giving Dearie such sage advice. What did she know? Could she really say with certainty that Tavish was a good man? In her heart she felt that he was, but his actions certainly contradicted that feeling.

She looked out the window at the sun setting behind the houses of the city. It was the last time she would see Philadelphia, and no one knew what lay ahead of them. She shut her eyes tightly and took a deep breath.

"Dear Lord, I'll watch after Miss Dearie and do all I can to help her, but I would be beholden if you would keep an eye out for me as well. I reckon I would feel a sight better knowing you were not far away . . . "

Matthew Grayson sat in the sitting room of his enormous mansion, a house he would now occupy alone. On a table beside him, a glass of brandy remained untouched. In his lap was another letter from Marcus Welhouse of Richmond, Virginia. With an exhausted sigh, he picked up the letter and read it again.

Master Matthew Grayson, Attorney-at-Law
Third and Spruce Streets
Philadelphia, Pennsylvania

My Dear Master Grayson,

In accordance with your wishes, I have searched the countryside round to locate your McLeod family, but to no avail. There was one family by that name, but they moved west, mayhap to the frontier. I have been unable to locate any other family by that name in Richmond or the surrounding areas.

I am sorry to be of so little help in this matter. If I may be of further assistance, I am at your service.

Your humble servant,
Marcus Welhouse, Attorney-at-Law

Even before receiving the letter, Matthew Grayson had decided that there was no truth to Tavish's claims. The young man was an impostor. He drummed his fingers on the table. For the first time in his life, Grayson was at loss. There was the child to think of, and Dearie was obviously in love with the scoundrel. After such an extravagant wedding, it would certainly look better if she stayed with him for a little while. At least until the child was born.

Grayson pursed his lips and nodded. "When the child is born, I'll fetch them both home and say that young Tavish had a hunting accident. Perhaps a hunting accident could even be arranged."

Having made his decision, he settled back in his chair and sipped his brandy. He drew a deep breath and relaxed for the first time in weeks. He would miss Dearie, but she would not be gone for long.

He would make sure of that.

Dearie had returned to the cottage with renewed hope. Now she was eager for the morrow, confident that she had made the right decision. Upon entering the cottage, she was surprised to find Tavish sound asleep on the bed. She studied his features in repose — the straight nose, the determined jaw framed by sandy hair. He seemed so young, so innocent . . . like a boy. She was strangely moved. Then her eyes dropped to his broad chest, half covered by the blanket. Her emotions heightened and suddenly she had to be near him, even though he was asleep.

Quickly, she took off her clothing, leaving it exactly as it fell on the floor. Then, completely naked, she slipped beneath the coverlet, next to Tavish.

He stirred as she nestled close to him, and his arm went around her. Still asleep, he drew her close until she felt his heart beating against hers. There, in the circle of his arms, she was secure, protected.

Suddenly, Tavish turned over, pulling away from her. As always, she was chilled by his absence. Cold doubts edged into her mind. She was leaving the only home she had ever known to go to a strange place with a man she hardly knew. If only Tavish had been from Philadelphia!

Dearie chided herself for her fears. Women married and left their families every day. They survived . . . and so would she. She burrowed close to Tavish again and was comforted by his warmth. He was her husband, her life mate, the man for whom she had waited so long. Tomorrow they would be on their way to a new home and a new life. A renewed surge of anticipation welled up inside her. Everything would be exactly as she had dreamed.

She was sure of it.

Chapter Seven

The day was bright and clear. *A good omen*, Dearie thought happily, watching the servants load her trunks on the coach. When they had finished there was just room enough inside for Tavish, Dearie, and Colleen. Clarence, Tavish's black servant, had to ride with the driver.

All was in readiness for their departure. Matthew Grayson came out to bid his daughter good-bye. He hugged her to him as if he couldn't bear to let her go. The sight of his affection was so tender that Tavish was forced to look away suddenly wracked by guilt.

"You must come for a visit very soon, Father," Dearie told the older man.

Grayson nodded, kissing her tear-streaked face and handing her into the coach. His eyes then locked with Tavish's. "I wish you a safe journey. And I shall expect to hear from you soon."

"You will, sir."

As the coach pulled away from the luxurious gardens of Grayson Mansion, Dearie chatted animatedly with

Colleen. She failed to notice when they passed well-manicured lawns fronting the elegant houses on tree-lined streets, or the theaters and clubs where the Philadelphia elite entertained.

She takes it all for granted, Tavish mused, gazing out the window. *There will be none of this in North Carolina.* A wave of sadness washed over him, for he knew that she would be shocked. Very shocked, indeed.

The first two days of the journey passed quickly without incident. On the third day, a light spring rain impeded the coach's progress and they arrived at the inn very late in the evening.

The innkeeper was very hospitable for having been awakened, and hastily set about warming up a pot of stew. After dinner, everyone retired. Exhausted, Dearie immediately fell asleep. When she awakened the next morning, she realized that it was quite late.

"I thought it best to let you sleep, Miss Dearie," Colleen told her. "The driver has gone ahead to check the roads."

"But where is Tavish?" Dearie demanded.

"Mayhap he went with the driver. Now come along, Miss Dearie, and have something to eat. We must be ready to go when they return."

Colleen brought her oatmeal, cream, and a steaming cup of hot coffee. By the time she had finished eating, Tavish had returned. He walked through the door, but instead of speaking to Dearie, he sought out the innkeeper. They talked for a few minutes, then Tavish counted out a sum of money and dropped it into the innkeeper's hand.

Puzzled, the women watched the transaction. In a moment, Tavish joined them. His face was devoid of color and his manner was preoccupied. "I have just received word that my mother was visiting relations in Fayetteville and became ill. I must ride on ahead immediately."

Dearie clutched Colleen's arm. "Tavish, no! I must go with you."

He shook his head. "You can't. The ride on horseback would be too arduous for you, Dearie. And the coach would delay me several days. By then, it may be too late."

"But I — "

" 'Tis only a few days longer, and the coachman knows the roads well. Clarence will be here with you. I am sorry to leave you, but I have no choice in the matter."

Dearie saw the anguish in her husband's face. It was true that he had no choice. But she couldn't bear the thought of parting with him. Not now . . . so soon. A tear trickled down her cheek.

Tavish caught it with his thumb and brushed it away. "We will not be parted for long." It tore at his heart to see her blue eyes fill with tears. She was so fragile. He wondered for a moment if she would be able to continue the journey without him.

Then just as suddenly her eyes brightened. She placed her hand firmly on his arm. "I will be fine, Tavish. Colleen will keep me company, and time will pass quickly. Please send my prayers to your mother. I wish . . . "

Leaving the sentence unfinished, she turned and walked with Tavish to his horse. Once mounted, he leaned down to kiss her. His lips clung to hers, sending a fiery current racing through her body. He felt it too, for he took off his hat and kissed her again, hugging her tightly to him.

Gently, she pulled away, laying her hand on the saddle. "Godspeed, my love."

Tavish jammed his hat on his head and tore his eyes away from her with an effort. He spurred his horse into a gallop, half afraid to look back.

It was hard to leave her. Too damn hard.

The driver returned before noon to report that the roads were clear. Shortly after lunch, they set out once again. Though Colleen tried to engage her mistress in conversation, Dearie stared morosely out the window.

"Now, miss, don't fret. 'Tis the lot of women to be left behind. Me own sister Margaret saw her first husband but two times in five years. Just long enough to plant three bairn in the oven."

"Three?"

"Twins, mum." Colleen smiled and dimples indented her cheeks.

"What happened to him?"

"He died at war, never did come back the last time. But 'twas good for Margaret. For then she married a tailor with a clubfoot. I guess she thought he never would leave home. Now, after ten years, she wishes he would. But Margaret never would be satisfied. Some aren't, y'know."

Dearie smiled despite herself. Colleen was certainly entertaining. She had such an endless supply of family anecdotes, Dearie wondered if they were really true. But she didn't dare ask. Colleen seemed so sincere.

Obviously trying to make up for lost time, the driver continued after dark. Colleen and Dearie could hear Clarence's loud complaints above them. "Don't want to go on much after dark. We seen a number of wild boar and no end of deer last time."

The driver muttered something indistinguishable.

"Well, I'm agin it even if there ain't no place to stop. We — " His words were cut off suddenly. "Great Lord in heaven!"

The coach swerved suddenly, then lurched forward at breakneck speed. Dearie and Colleen were thrown violently to the side of the coach. "What's the matter with the man! Can't he slow these horses down? We'll lose the trunks," Dearie shouted to Colleen. As she spoke, one of the trunks tumbled over the side.

Furious, Dearie pulled open the window and stuck her head out. "Driver! Hold up, Mr. Strake!"

He couldn't hear her over the noise.

"Cut 'em loose," they heard Clarence yell.

Dearie wedged herself further out the window. "Driver! Stop, I say!"

"No, Miss Dearie, don't! You'll fall," Colleen cried grabbing onto her skirts wildly.

Suddenly the coach wheel hit a rock and tilted crazily on one set of wheels. Dearie was thrown from the careening vehicle before it jounced down into a ditch, coming to a rest on its side.

An ominous silence fell. The horses, cut loose at the last minute, trotted blithely off down the road. There was no sound other than the soft call of night birds.

Thrown against the side of the coach, Colleen scrambled to the other side. The door latch was jammed, but she was able to push back the window covering. Clinging to the side of the coach, she crawled out of the ditch. "Miss Dearie! Where are you?" She stumbled over a soft body lying across the road.

"Have we died and gone to heaven? Then Lord, why do I feel so bad? Uh oh. Maybe we didn't all make it. Please, Lord . . . I been good . . . except for that time . . . " It was Clarence.

Clarence slowly turned over and pushed himself up on his elbows. "Oh, my head. Now I know I ain't dead. You don't feel a thing when you're dead. And there ain't nothing I don't feel."

"Hello, anybody hurt?" Mr. Strake emerged from the ditch. He set a lantern on the ground and it cast a dim glow on Clarence's dark face.

"Should of cut them horses loose sooner."

Strake shook his head. "Tried to, but I was afraid to let go."

"We have to find Miss Dearie," Colleen said, jerking the lantern away from Strake. "She was thrown from the coach."

The driver followed Colleen down the deserted road. Colleen held the lantern high to cast as much light as possible around her. "Miss Dearie? Where are you?"

She heard a low moan coming from the side of the road, and she rushed over to find Dearie lying face down in the grass. Setting the lamp next to her, she knelt beside her mistress. "Oh, Miss Dearie. Thank the Lord we've found you."

Dearie moaned again.

Gently, Colleen tried to turn her over. "No," Dearie screamed. "Don't . . . don't touch me!"

"But miss, we've got to help you." Colleen's fingers touched something sticky as she eased Dearie to her side. Raising the lamp, she saw that Dearie was lying in a pool of blood. "Oh, no. Miss Dearie."

Strake approached the women and knelt beside Colleen. "Is she hurt bad?"

"I . . . don't know. There's blood all over. I'm afraid for the baby."

"Merciful heavens," the man said, dropping his head to his chest. "If only I'd cut the traces."

"We've got to get help, Mr. Strake! Or she won't make it."

Colleen's words spurred the driver into action. "Yes, ma'am. I'll get help if I have to walk all night. I'll take the other lamp and leave you this one."

After Strake left, Clarence hobbled over. Colleen immediately ordered him to make a fire.

When the fire was burning strong, he retrieved the water bag from the coach. Colleen tore off some of her petticoat and dipped it in cool water. She pressed the cloth against Dearie's lips, then placed another strip of moistened cloth on her forehead. The night was cool, but Dearie's skin was burning.

"Tavish . . ." Dearie murmured. "Tavish. Where is Tavish?"

Right where they always are when you need them — gone! Colleen thought to herself. She smoothed back Dearie's hair. "He'll be along soon, Miss Dearie. Don't you worry." It wasn't the truth, but the slight smile on Dearie's lips justified the falsehood.

The night wore on and Dearie's breathing became shallow and labored. Colleen grew frightened. What should she do? Dearie's temperature had dropped drastically in the last hour. Her hands were now like ice.

"Oh, Miss Dearie! Please don't die! You've your whole life before you." Tears welled up in the little maid's eyes. She felt as close to Dearie as to her own sister.

Dearie shivered. Colleen hugged her close as if she was small child, trying to will her own warmth into her mistress's limp form. The rocking motion prompted her to sing. It was all she could think to do. She sang the "Ballad of Barbara Allen" in a high clear voice.

" 'Tis so beautiful, Colleen. I ... . I've never heard it sung so sweetly," Dearie whispered.

Colleen was relieved to know that Dearie was conscious. "Me mum used to sing it to me when I was a wee bairn. It always made me sleep and dream ... such pretty dreams. You know they say 'tis the story of the Sweet William rose," she said, looking down at her mistress, but Dearie had fallen asleep.

Colleen judged it to be about midnight when Strake returned with a farmer named Kiley who lived nearby.

The men peered down at Dearie's inert form. "Is ... she ... ?" Strake asked.

"Sleeping," Colleen reassured him.

Wrapped in blankets from the coach, Dearie was gently moved to the farmer's wagon. Within the hour they had arrived at the small farmhouse. A plump, rosy-cheeked woman stood in the doorway as the wagon pulled to a stop. Colleen saw that her gray hair was tucked into a neat bun atop her head and she wore a clean apron.

"Well, you took your time, Amos," Mrs. Kiley scolded her husband. "Poor thing's probably half froze by now."

Dearie scarcely stirred under the blankets when she was moved again. "There, that's it. Put her yonder in our room."

The men had hardly settled Dearie on the bed when Mrs. Kiley shooed them out. She and Colleen removed the blankets, and were visibly shocked at the amount of blood they saw.

"Oh, my soul," Mrs. Kiley exclaimed, covering her mouth.

"I . . . I think she may have lost the baby," Colleen ventured when she could speak.

"Mercy me," Mrs. Kiley clucked. "Hardly more'n a baby herself. Well, we've got to remove these clothes and bathe her before we can tell much of anything. Never did see so much blood. It's a wonder she has any left."

Woodenly, Colleen helped the farmer's wife undress Dearie, all the while praying that her mistress would live. But Dearie's small hands were even colder and her face was so pale that it was almost translucent.

Mrs. Kiley brought pots of hot water into the room. Together the two women bathed the unconscious girl, taking care to dry her carefully and cover her well to ward off chill.

"Well," Mrs. Kiley pronounced, rolling down her sleeves. "'Tis a mighty shame she lost the baby, but it looks like she'll pull through. 'Course we can't tell for sure, but the bruises are mainly on her arms and legs."

Her breathing barely moving the coverlet, Dearie looked like a beautiful princess under a spell. Colleen gripped Mrs. Kiley's arm. "She's lost so much blood. Will she really live?"

"If we can get some food down her, I reckon she will. She's young."

Colleen nodded, stifling a sob. What if she didn't live? What would she do? Where was Tavish when they needed him?

Voicing her own thoughts, Mrs. Kiley asked, "Is that big man her husband?"

Colleen shook her head. "Master Tavish rode on ahead to attend to his mother who is dying."

Mrs. Kiley's lips tightened into a straight line and she shook her head as if to say, Isn't that the way of it. The three of them were bound by the suffering of all women who wait for their men. For a time Colleen and Mrs. Kiley sat in a pensive silence.

At last Dearie stirred. Colleen jumped up and flew to her side. Mrs. Kiley hurried to fetch a bowl of broth and a bit of bread. With some difficulty, Colleen roused Dearie enough so that Mrs. Kiley could spoon down some of the soup. Dearie's eyes remained closed and in a moment she fell back asleep.

It was almost three o'clock in the morning and Colleen was nodding in spite of herself.

"You'd best get some sleep. I'll keep watch for a while," Mrs. Kiley told her.

Since the men were already asleep in another room, Colleen sank gratefully to a pallet in front of the fire. Hours later, she was awakened by the loud clatter of pots and the smell of bacon frying.

Mrs. Kiley was cooking breakfast. Half-awake, Colleen studied the woman. She had not slept all night, but she was as energetic as ever. She reminded Colleen of her own mother. She sat up, rubbing her eyes.

"There's water on the grate. You can fix yourself some tea if you've a mind to," Mrs. Kiley said.

After warming herself at the fire, Colleen fixed a mug of tea. She started to check on Dearie, but Mrs. Kiley stopped her. "She's still sleeping. Wait a spell." Then, as an afterthought, she asked, "Did you tell me her name?"

"Mrs. McLeod. Dearie McLeod," Colleen answered. The name sounded strange as it rolled off Colleen's tongue. It was the first time she'd said it aloud.

Mrs. Kiley nodded. "Well, she appears to have more color this morning."

Colleen was heartened by the news.

The Kileys insisted that they stay for three more days. Mr. Strake agreed, even though the delay would put him behind schedule. He had rounded up the runaway horses and mended the traces in readiness for the journey. But he felt to blame for the accident and he was anxious to see Dearie up and about.

She began eating on the second day, and by degrees, she began to gain strength. Colleen and Mrs. Kiley ministered to her tirelessly, but still she asked for Tavish.

When she was strong enough, Colleen felt duty-bound to tell Dearie about the baby. "I'm sorry, Miss Dearie. Mr. Strake keeps saying he wished he could have cut the traces sooner, but the team ran away. He did what he could."

"He shouldn't blame himself. It was I who leaned out the window." She shook her head sadly. "Oh, what will Tavish say?"

Colleen hung her head. She couldn't imagine what his reaction would be.

Dearie brooded on her misfortune and nothing Colleen said seemed to help. Mrs. Kiley took Colleen aside when Dearie was sleeping. "They always act that way over the first one. I would have ten children if they'd all lived. But the Lord saw fit to leave me five. I love those He kept just as much, especially the first."

Nothing the women said could lift Dearie from her sorrow. Silently she wondered if she had deserved to lose her child.

Am I being punished for selfishly scheming to entrap Tavish and marry him to spite my father? Dearie repeatedly asked herself. Perhaps Tavish would never have married her if she had not seduced him. And she had willfully defied her father, after all he'd done for her. Shame and remorse overwhelmed her and she cried constantly.

" 'Twill do no good to cry, Miss Dearie. And what would your new husband think to see you this way?" Colleen tried to shake Dearie back to her old self.

But Colleen's words planted new doubts in Dearie's mind.

"Oh, Colleen," she wailed. "What if Tavish does not come back at all?"

"That's nonsense, miss. Of course he'll come back. But you can be sure he won't come back here. He's expecting to meet us at the plantation."

"That's right, Colleen! Then we must be on our way immediately," Dearie commanded suddenly, showing more animation than before the accident.

"Are you sure, miss?" Colleen saw the determination in her mistress's eyes, and she was relieved Dearie was on her way to recovery.

"Tavish will be worried, Colleen. We must hurry."

After a lengthy farewell to the Kileys, during which Mrs. Kiley hugged and kissed them both in tears, the group departed. They set out early so as to make up as much time as possible. Dearie's spirits were high in anticipation of seeing Tavish again.

"Surely he will send word to one of the inns," Dearie said.

"I hope so, miss," Colleen replied. She was reluctant to build up Dearie's hopes. "Of course we don't know what weather he may have encountered. The driver said there had been storms reported up ahead."

There was no message waiting at the inn that night, but the landlord confirmed the fact that thunderstorms had made the roads impassable for a few days. Dearie took the news calmly, but after three more days with no word from Tavish, she became distraught.

"What if he was injured somehow? He is alone, with no one to aid him!"

"Aye, but Master Tavish is familiar with the roads. Don't fret, miss."

Dearie was temporarily comforted by the maid. But the farther they traveled into North Carolina, the more puzzled she became. "Where are the towns, Mr. Strake? And the plantations? I see nothing but plank roads and pine trees."

Strake rubbed the stubble of his beard. "That's all there is, ma'am. The only towns to speak of are Raleigh and Fayetteville. If you'll pardon me for saying it, they don't hold a candle to Philadelphia. I don't know about the plantations. Clarence, you would know more about that."

Clarence shifted his eyes away for a moment. "Yes'm, there's Greenhill. That belong to Duncan McNeill. And Mr. Calvin Buie live over to Rosalee."

"Is that all?" Dearie was astounded.

Clarence wagged his head. "No, I reckon there's some more down on the Cape Fear River. But I don't know 'bout them."

"Such pretty names," Colleen remarked. "Greenhill and Rosalee."

Dearie pursed her lips. "Looks like a bunch of pine trees to me."

The rest of the journey passed quickly. The only delay was a wheel change.

On the last day of the trip, Dearie donned a lemon-colored cambric gown, ornamented around the border with strips of muslin. Colleen had parted her hair in the latest fashion, down the middle in two bands that were tucked beneath a straw carriage hat with bright feathers. Tan kid shoes and gloves, and blue wool cape completed the ensemble.

"Perhaps the neighboring planters will throw us a welcoming party," Dearie suggested to Colleen. "That happens in Philadelphia, you know, whenever newcomers arrive. We call it a housewarming. Of course this is a plantation and the custom may be different."

"Yes, miss," Colleen agreed. However she felt vaguely apprehensive.

"I am sure I shall have to inspect the servants, in any case."

Colleen nodded. "Well, Master Tavish will be there — and a welcome sight he'll be."

As the day wore on, there was no change in the monotonous landscape of trees and gently rolling hills. Indeed, the land hardly looked settled. At the worried look on Dearie's face, Colleen's misgivings grew. Her heart began a slow descent to her stomach.

It was almost dusk when the coach lumbered off the main road onto a narrow lane, more a bridle path than a highway. Here the vines were overgrown, and caught at the coach as it passed.

"Not much further, Miss Dearie," Clarence leaned down to announce.

Dearie sat like a Dresden statue, her small pink mouth set in tight line. In her lap was a white silk parasol, a wedding gift from her Aunt Sophie in Paris.

After an hour on the bumpy road, the coach arrived in a desolate clearing. The men jumped down.

"Can this be it?" Strake asked Clarence.

"Well, I reckon so . . . "

"We're here, Miss Dearie!" Colleen announced brightly, in an effort to hide her misgivings.

"Please run ahead and tell Master Tavish to come get me, Colleen."

"Yes, miss."

Colleen scrambled out of the coach. In a few minutes she returned, out of breath.

"You must come quickly, Miss Dearie!" she cried out.

"What is it, Colleen? Where is Tavish?"

"Miss, I've seen nothing of Master Tavish. But the house . . . the plantation . . . It's burned down!"

Chapter Eight

They were in the middle of a pine barren, and dusk was falling rapidly around them. Picking her way with difficulty through the overgrown shrubs and weeds, Dearie reached the two men. They stood staring at the charred remains of the plantation. The front porch was still intact, but the roof and one entire wing lay in blackened ruins.

"Oh, Tavish! Could Tavish have been killed?" Dearie suddenly weaved unsteadily, and for moment Colleen thought she would faint.

"Oh, no, ma'am," Clarence said, shaking his dark head. "This here been this way for a long time. See them weeds? Master Tavish, he ain't here."

The news brought Dearie up short. "Well, where is he?"

"Don't know. I expect he still in town. But he done sent out a wagonload of supplies. They out in the shed."

"Did Tavish know the house had burned?" Dearie demanded to know.

Clarence shrugged. "I don't know. I only been here once a long time ago. It weren't burned then."

Dearie let out her breath in an exasperated sigh. "Then what are we to do? Surely he didn't intend for us to stay here?"

The driver had gone through the charred door to inspect the house. He emerged shortly and motioned the group forward. "This part of the house is still standing. It will have to serve for the time being."

Clarence and the women stepped gingerly through refuse and rotting wood to the front door of the house. To the right of the foyer only blackened timbers remained, but to the left were three whole rooms.

"Look, Miss Dearie. There is a sofa, chairs, and a table!" Colleen exclaimed.

Dearie was unable to share her maid's optimism. Everything seemed utterly hopeless to her.

They explored the other rooms and found beds, lamps, and a serviceable fireplace. Someone had obviously lived in the rooms after the fire.

"You see, miss? It's not so bad in here. Why, if you don't look out the window, it's almost cheery — like a little cottage. And we have all we need. We'll do just fine, Miss Dearie." Colleen hoped that she sounded more confident than she felt.

Dearie looked unconvinced, but she allowed Colleen to help her out of her elegant traveling costume and into a blue merino dress. "And . . . and there are no servants," Dearie said. She felt like a small child, lost and abandoned.

"No, ma'am. Just us. But we'll do it ourselves."

Dearie had never cleaned a room in her life. However, she followed Colleen's lead, and was surprised to find the work rewarding. At least she was doing something constructive. The women cleaned and rearranged the furniture as best they could in the cramped quarters. Soon a fire was blazing, and an evening meal simmered in a pot provided by the Kileys.

"We'd best make enough for Tavish, in case he arrives late," Dearie said.

Nodding, Colleen said nothing. To her mind, Master Tavish had some explaining to do.

But Tavish did not arrive that day or the next. The driver, reluctant to leave the women alone, delayed his departure. He helped clear away some of the debris and gathered firewood. "I'm sure that Master McLeod plans to move you elsewhere, considering the condition of the place, but I'll lay up a supply of firewood in any case," he said.

Dearie wore a brave smile as she and Colleen busied themselves about the house. But all the while she wondered desperately where Tavish was. She often grew despondent, imagining that he was lying wounded and alone somewhere along the road. The she consoled herself with the knowledge that Tavish knew the area better than they. Surely, he would know where to get help in an emergency.

After several days, the driver reluctantly prepared to leave.

"I'll ask after Master McLeod when I'm in Fayetteville. I'm sure he'll be along directly." But as he drove away, Strake shook his head. "A man should see after his womenfolk. Pity. She's such a young thing, too," he said to himself.

Watching the coach pull out of sight, Dearie felt desolate. It was as if they had lost their only link with civilization. "Well, Colleen, we'll just have to make do until Tavish returns." With bits of soap and torn-up curtains, they washed the windows and floors until they sparkled. Then they surveyed the damage done by the fire.

"This here was a beautiful place until the fire," Clarence said.

Dearie squinted her eyes, looking at the wide porch that wrapped around the exterior of the building. She tried to imagine what the house must have been like. "It was beautiful, I can see that now." She paced back and forth, her hands on her hips. "And it will be again. We'll call it Beauvais," she said with a determined look on her face. "With some repairs, paint, and cleaning, it will be the most beautiful plantation in the state!"

Colleen smiled weakly at Dearie's declaration. What she saw was a facade that hid a mass of burnt timbers and charred brick. The fields were completely overgrown with weeds. The task of restoring the mansion to its former grandeur seemed monumental.

While the servants stared vacantly at the plantation house, Dearie's head buzzed with ideas. Together, she and Tavish would rebuild the house and cultivate the land. They would make Beauvais as profitable as his other plantation in Virginia. Then wouldn't his family be proud?

Dearie paused suddenly in mid-thought. Where was Tavish's father? And his brother? Had they not come to Fayetteville to be by his mother's side?

"Clarence," she asked, "wouldn't Tavish's father have come to be with his wife if she were so ill?"

"No, ma'am. Master McLeod been dead for a while now."

Dearie was shocked. Tavish had never mentioned his father's death. "But what about his brother? Wouldn't he come?"

Clarence looked at her strangely. "Master Tavish ain't got no brother. He the only boy in the family. And his sisters all moved away."

"What about the plantation in Virginia? Who's running that?"

Clarence shrugged. "I don't know nothing about no plantation in Virginia. But Master Tavish, he don't tell me everything."

Dearie suddenly felt weak and dizzy. Her father's words echoed in her ears, *The young man is a scoundrel. For all we know he's a pauper, looking to fatten his purse by marrying well.* Dearie shut her eyes, valiantly trying to hold back her tears. "There must be a plantation. Tavish wouldn't lie to me!"

For the next two days, Dearie was tormented by her doubts. What if he had lied? Or worse, taken her money, never to return again!

Dearie was sweeping the porch when she heard a rider on horseback coming up the narrow path. Shading her eyes to see who was approaching, she recognized the sandy hair, burnished by the sun. It was Tavish! Her hand flew to her throat and she took in a sharp breath.

"Tavish!" she called out to him.

Sweeping up her skirts, Dearie ran down the steps and up the path to greet him. He leapt off his horse and stood there, waiting for her. When she reached him he swung her up into his arms and held her so tightly that she could feel his heart beat.

"I've missed you so," he whispered into her hair. His fingers touched her golden ringlets and brushed the tears from her soft pink cheeks. It seemed like years since they had parted. Holding her tightly against him, he kissed her hungrily, over and over again. Then suddenly he frowned. Over her shoulder, he saw the ruined house. It was far worse than he had remembered. He was suddenly ashamed. He set her down, away from him. "I hope you have not been too uncomfortable here."

"Well, no . . . I . . . we have made it . . . livable," Dearie said. She searched his face for some explanation, but he said nothing refusing to meet her eyes.

Tavish took her hand and kissed it. "You must not work so hard, Dearie," he said in a low voice." There is the child to think of."

Dearie looked away, tears filling her eyes once again. "I . . . no, Tavish, I lost the baby. There was an accident. The horses ran away and I was thrown from the coach."

Tavish felt as if the air had been knocked out of his lungs. Seeing the anguish in her eyes, was almost too much for him to bear. He had left her, and she'd had to suffer the pain and heartache alone. Then she'd come to be mistress of an elegant plantation . . . and found this — an ash heap! He could find no words of explanation or comfort. There were no words to say to her. He'd wanted revenge against Matthew Grayson, and he'd wreaked it upon his daughter — an innocent — instead.

He ground his teeth, feeling utterly ashamed. Dearie tried to interpret his expression. He seemed more angry than sad. Was he displeased with her for losing the child? Suddenly seized with remorse, she remembered that she had taken a chance by leaning out the window. "Tavish, I'm so sorry."

Her words stung his conscience even further and he couldn't look at her.

"Please tell me of your mother," she pleaded. She would do anything to dispel his anger.

His voice was a hoarse whisper. "We buried her yesterday. She lingered some time before . . . I guess she was waiting until I got there, but when I did, she didn't know it." He shook his head, his eyes dark and unfathomable.

"But what of your family, Tavish? Where were they?"

"My father has been dead for some time, now." Dearie clutched his arm desperately. "You never told me, Tavish."

He shrugged. "It never came up." It didn't seem to matter now that she knew. The entire episode would be over soon enough.

Tavish walked toward the house with long strides. Dearie followed him, running to keep up. He gasped audibly when he saw the inside of the house from the front door. "Oh, no!" he said harshly.

"This way, darling," Dearie urged him, pulling him away from the ruins. "These rooms aren't so bad. Look, we've cleaned them up. Tavish what happened? When did it burn?"

He shrugged off her question, glancing quickly at the rooms. He noted that everything in the small rooms had indeed been washed and scrubbed. It reminded him of the boarding house his family had lived in after the bankruptcy. His mother had bravely cleaned and re-arranged the shabby furnishings as if nothing at all had happened.

It depressed Tavish even more to see Dearie's fine clothes crammed into a crude wardrobe in the corner of one room. He felt suddenly drained. Surely he had sunk to the lowest point in all his life. He was worse than a thief, since a thief took only material goods. He had taken a young girl, seduced her, lured her away from her home to . . . this hellish monstrosity of a plantation. And he had done all this to get even with Matthew Grayson.

Dearie waited near him expectantly. She was sure that Tavish would comment on the work they had done. But he only shook his head. "It was a mistake to bring you here," he said. "I shall make arrangements to send you back to Philadelphia immediately."

"No, Tavish! Really, I'm just fine," she said, forcing a bright smile. After all, he *had* suggested that she stay behind until he had arranged things, and she had re-fused. She could not go back now!

"Look, my love," she said with a genuine smile. "We have cooked you a delicious meal. Mrs. Kiley, the woman who nursed me back to health after . . . the accident. . . . sent us several pots. Colleen found greens down by the stream. Tomorrow Clarence said he'll bring home some fish to fry. Tavish, I have so many plans. I cannot wait to tell you."

Tavish sat down stiffly, but he ate very little. He could not stop berating himself for allowing all of this to happen.

Dearie watched her beloved husband sadly. He had so much on his mind. It would be selfish to bother him now. There would be time enough for talking later.

After dinner, Tavish took a long walk alone. Dearie reasoned that he must want to evaluate the fire damage. When after several hours he had not returned, she took a lamp outside to look for him. She found him sleeping on the porch, his head on his saddle.

She smiled at the sight. What a thoughtful husband he was, to consider her physical condition over his needs. She set down the lamp and bent to kiss him.

Tavish stirred ever so slightly, and a smile curved his lips. Dearie picked up the lamp and tiptoed back into the house, to sleep alone one more night.

Dearie awoke the next morning filled with new hope. Now that Tavish was here everything would be taken care of. They would move into town until renovations were completed. Of course they would rebuild. She had already decided that whitewashed columns would line the porch. And the kitchen would be attached to the house in back. She had seen this done in Europe, and it was much more convenient. Each bedroom would have its own sitting room so that their guests would be comfortable, and the parlor would be large enough to hold a ball! Dearie couldn't wait to tell Tavish all her ideas. She wondered what he would say.

Dearie entered the main room wearing a new muslin dress. She had expected to see Tavish eating his breakfast, but the room was empty. Colleen was outside washing clothes and she had seen no one except Clarence.

The barn, some distance away from the house, had not been touched by the fire. Dearie found Clarence there sweeping the floor.

"Where is Tavish?" She asked him.

"Oh, Master Tavish left early this morning. Said to tell you he got to get back right away. The wheat's in, and he say he got no time to lose. But he say he's going to send some men along to clean up this place. And I told him we needed some horses and a wagon." He beamed as if proud of his request.

"But . . . but when will he back?" Dearie asked, stunned.

"I don't know, ma'am. He didn't say."

It was useless to question Clarence further. Fighting back tears of fury and disappointment, Dearie retraced her steps to the house. She was at a loss to interpret her husband's actions. They had been apart for so long! Why couldn't he have stayed? Tears rolled unchecked down her cheeks.

"Who is this man I married?" she wondered aloud. "I love him, but does he love me?" She reviewed mentally everything she could remember of the day before to try to discover what could have driven Tavish away.

Perhaps he was disappointed in her. The rigors of the journey had proved too much for her, just as he had feared. Why hadn't she listened? Wistfully, she thought of her father's comfortable mansion, of servants catering to her every need.

"It was a mistake to bring you here," Tavish had said. Did he really mean to send her back? Fresh tears welled up at the thought.

"No, I won't go! I will prove to him that 'twas no mistake to bring me here," Dearie vowed, clenching her her small fists. "I must find a way to make him love me. Then everything will be all right."

Another week passed and still Tavish did not return. However, a group of free Negroes arrived in a horse and buggy. By law, the freemen were required to register with the town clerk. Cloth badges bearing the word "free" were sewn on their left shoulders. Clarence immediately set them to work cleaning up the debris littering the gounds.

Swallowing her disappointment with a supreme effort. Dearie busied herself about the house. But soon she and Colleen had done all they could without help.

"Tavish is busy with the harvest," Dearie told Colleen. "I'll find workmen who can rebuild the plantation house. When Tavish returns, the work will already be underway."

"But, miss. We know of no carpenters, and we have no money to pay them."

"I have some money, Colleen. And I have my jewels." Dearie asked the workers where she might find good carpenters.

"Mr. McFarland might know," one man volunteered. "His farm is about five mile down the road."

That afternoon, Dearie set out with Clarence to talk to Mr. McFarland. They rode through several swamps and through pinewoods covered with bright evergreens. The road wound endlessly, until the pinewoods gave way abruptly to neatly plowed fields planted in wheat. They followed the road through the fields to where it ended a short distance from a small frame house. Four or five hunting dogs lay at the edge of a weed-choked path leading up to the whitewashed house.

The howling dogs brought a woman to the door. She was wearing a poke bonnet and a faded blue dress. Dearie, by contrast, wore a blue velvet riding habit and black kid gloves. She had wanted to look her best to meet her new neighbors. The woman drew back into the dark recesses of the house as Dearie approached.

Dearie knocked on the door while Clarence quieted the dogs. After several more knocks the woman reappeared.

"Go away," the woman cried harshly. "I'll have naught to do with ye." With that she shut the door in Dearie's face.

Dearie looked questioningly at Clarence.

"They don't like strangers around here," he explained. "Y'know, ma'am. There be witches and demons about."

"What? That's nonsense, Clarence. This is the nineteenth century." Again she rapped on the door, this time more impatiently.

"Mrs. McFarland! I am your neighbor, Dearie McLeod."

After a moment, the door opened a crack. "There are no McLeods around here." Mrs. McFarland started to close the door again, but Dearie caught it with her foot.

"But we *are* your neighbors. We live just over there five miles."

The woman followed the direction of Dearie's black-gloved finger. "There ain't nothing there but a pine barren. The old Suggs place burned five year ago."

Dearie frowned. She had no idea when the McLeods had purchased the plantation. She'd assumed it had been in the family for years. She sighed in exasperation. "I'm looking for your husband. I was told that he might know of some carpenters."

"Ain't home. Down at the punch house at four corners. But he ain't done nothin' wrong. He's a good man," she said, slamming the door shut.

"What a strange thing to say," Dearie remarked to herself. "I can only hope that Mr. McFarland is more hospitable than his wife."

With some difficulty, they were able to locate the tavern at the intersection of four roads. The building was a log cabin, with no sign other than a jug hanging from the branch of a tree. But there were horses and a wagon tethered to a log in front.

Dearie marched bravely through the door. The tavernkeeper had been sweeping the floor, and he dropped his broom when he saw her.

"Excuse me, sir," Dearie said, smiling. "I'm looking for Mr. McFarland."

The tavernkeeper only stared at Dearie as if she were an apparition.

"I was told that Mr. McFarland was here," she repeated.

"Angus McFarland?" the tavernkeeper whispered.

"I suppose so."

"Out back," the man pointed, without taking his eyes off of Dearie.

Irritated and perplexed by the man's reaction, Dearie walked through the tavern and out the back door. Outside, four men sat at a wooden table, playing a game called All Fours. At one end of the table were several bottles of rum. The men looked up in surprise at Dearie.

"I'm looking for Mr. McFarland," she said.

The men looked at one another without speaking. The silence grew uncomfortable. Finally one of the men laid down his cards. "I am Angus McFarland. There's no betting here. Just an honest game."

Dearie's shoulders sagged. Did the man think she would turn him in to the constable? "I am just looking for a carpenter, Mr. McFarland. I was told that you might know of someone. I am your neighbor, Dearie McLeod." She walked closer, but Mr. McFarland's face was like granite.

"Neighbor? These here are my neighbors. There's naught else around."

"No, our place is five miles from you. I believe it must have burned some time ago."

"The Suggs Place," all the men said in unison.

Dearie smiled weakly. This was turning out to be more difficult than she ever imagined. "My husband and I are planning to rebuild the house. I am trying to locate some carpenters."

The men conferred among themselves and decided upon someone. "Billy Spears could do it," McFarland told her. "I'll send word over to his wife tomorrow."

"Thank you, Mr. McFarland," Dearie said, extending her hand.

The farmer only stared at her gloved hand before sitting down again at the table.

Dearie hurried back to the wagon. The experience had shaken her. When they arrived at the plantation, it was almost dark. Colleen ran to greet them, a worried look on her face.

"Oh, Miss Dearie. you were gone so long! I was afraid that you had come to harm on the road." She embraced her mistress warmly.

"As a matter of fact, Colleen, I believe that we were perfectly safe. But our neighbors appeared to be afraid of me. It was so strange! Both the McFarlands acted as if they had seen a ghost."

Clarence shook his head and snorted. "Oh, no, ma'am. It worse than that. They see ghosts around here all the time. But it ain't every day they see a witch."

"A witch!" both women echoed in disbelief.

"Well, yes, ma'am. That's what they think. Else what would a woman that looks like you be doing out here in the middle of nowhere? These country folks believes in all that. Yes, ma'am, they do."

"But, Clarence, a long time ago they accused women of being witches. Of course people were uneducated and fearful then . . . "

"Yes, ma'am, I heard tell of it. They burned the women at the stake."

Colleen's dark eyes widened in alarm. "Oh, how terrible!"

"But . . . but that practice is unlawful now. Thank goodness our society has advanced a great deal since then. Nothing like that could happen in this day and age."

"No, I reckon not." Clarence's dark eyes shifted to the charred remains of the plantation house.

Dearie shivered involuntarily. The temperature had dropped suddenly, and a rising night wind whistled through the pine trees. She picked up her skirts and hurried into the house.

Chapter Nine

Billy Spears arrived at the plantation the next day. With him were his young son, his father, and a wagonload of supplies. A tall, thin man with a gaunt face, Billy looked as though he hadn't eaten for days. In fact, the family gazed longingly at the biscuits on the table when they entered, and Dearie immediately urged them to sit down.

"Please have some breakfast with us, Mr. Spears," she said.

Colleen quickly brought mugs and poured hot coffee for the men.

Dearie soon learned that Mrs. Spears had died a year ago, and the young boy, Jake, did all the cooking now. It was obvious that the men appreciated Colleen's cooking, for they ate with relish. While they ate, Dearie talked to Billy about the renovations. She had sketched several ideas out on paper, which she now handed him. Billy studied the drawings with a critical eye.

"This one here looks more like the place did before it burned," he said.

"Oh," Dearie exclaimed, surprised. "Did you know the people who lived here?"

Billy exchanged a look with his father, then shook his head. "Knew of 'em. Name's Suggs. Ole Mr. Suggs come here before the Revolutionary War. They say he brought a bundle of money with him. He cleared the land and built a beautiful place. Then he went back to England, married him a fine-lookin' gal and brought her back. Things went along well enough for a while. The plantation turned a profit and the Suggs, well, they were a fine couple. But for a long time they never had children. Finally, they had a child, little girl named Louisa. When the little girl was about five, the old man just up and died, all of a sudden. Everyone tried to help the widow and the little girl, but they didn't want no part of it. They just stayed to theirselves."

Billy helped himself to another plateful of biscuits. He seemed completely unaware that both Dearie and Colleen had been raptly listening to his story. In fact, he concentrated so on his food that Dearie had to prod him to continue.

"What happened to them, Mr. Spears?"

Again Billy exchanged a glance with his father. "Well, they acted pretty strange — the two of 'em. Never left the house at all. Sent an old negro woman to town to do the shopping. Long about two year ago they said Mrs. Suggs died. But there never was a funeral or nothing. Then there was just the girl, Louisa, who must of been about nine or ten. Some of the ladies in town rode out to see if she wouldn't come live with one of them. But she plumb scared 'em off." He shook his head.

Billy Spears's father had remained silent while his son recounted the story, encouraging the boy by a nod now and then. Dearie had the feeling he knew more than anyone else.

"One of the ladies took to her bed for a week after," Billy told them. 'Louisa was wild as a March hare,' she said. After that nobody wanted to go near the place. Even the Negro woman stopped coming into town. 'Course everybody was wondering how Louisa got her food. And, you know, the McFarlands would be missing a chicken or two every once in a while. But they never said a thing about it."

"Then she took to riding around at night," Jake added, "scaring folks to death."

"Now, Jake," Billy protested.

"But 'tis true, Papa. Ole man McLaughlan fell over dead one night after seeing her."

"Well, it got so nobody knew what was what anymore," Billy continued. "If something happened out of the way, y'know, they said it was her — Louisa. Somebody said they saw her riding through the pinewoods, wearing black cloak with that long white hair streamin' out behind her."

"White hair!" Dearie exclaimed. "I thought you said she was only ten years old!"

"There was another strange thing," Billy agreed. "Some said it was kinda light yellow, but others said it was white as a sheet. There was rumors . . . "

"They said she had a fever one time and her hair all fell out," Jake supplied, his ruddy face animated. "And when it come back in it was all white."

Billy shrugged. "I never seen her myself. But once when I was out huntin' late, I heard someone go atearin' down the road wailin' or cryin'. I was too far away to see."

"But what happened to her?" Colleen wanted to know.

"Nobody rightly knows what happened. But one night the house burned to the ground, and Louisa went with it."

Dearie shivered. She felt cold again, as she had the night before. She drew her shawl around her shoulders and cleared her throat. "Well, Mr. Spears. We're going to make Beauvais beautiful once again. In fact, I intend to make it a showplace!"

"Yes, ma'am," Billy Spears said, jamming his hat on his head. "Well, we'll be back on Monday morning, early."

Dearie frowned, puzzled. "But why can't you begin today?" she asked.

For the third time Billy Spears and his father exchanged a meaningful look. "It's Friday, ma'am. Can't begin a piece of work on Friday. It's ill luck. I'm thinkin' there's been enough of that already." He touched his hat and nodded, then sauntered through the door. His father and son followed.

"Well, I declare! Never in all my life have I heard such nonsense. Oh, how I wish Tavish were here. I cannot believe the people here are so . . . backward." Her hands on hips, Dearie watched the men climb into the wagon and drive away.

After the men left, Dearie and Colleen tried to busy themselves about the house. But the story of the ill-fated Louisa had left them edgy.

"You don't suppose, miss, that we . . . should poke through the ruins a bit . . . ?"

"Certainly not, Colleen! If the men were to find . . . anything . . . they would take care of it."

"Yes, miss. I'm sure y're right. I only thought . . . why, the poor thing deserved a proper burial."

Dearie sighed heavily. "Honestly Colleen! Sometimes I think you deliberately imagine things for us to do, as if we didn't have our hands full enough now! But I don't suppose that you will rest easy until we have checked to see . . . " Dearie's reprimand was fueled by her anxiety, for she, too, wanted to know if the mansion was haunted. They felt safe, for it was high noon and certainly no spirits would be about with the sun blazing overhead.

Cautiously, the two women picked their way through charred timbers. The house had been built in the popular Georgian style, with wide halls and high ceilings. Here and there a piece of a baluster remained, and Dearie could see they had been beautifully carved. From the look of it, there had been four large rooms on each floor, each room with a fireplace. Upon closer inspection, Dearie and Colleen found pieces of velvet curtain and snatches of silk and lace fluttering from a broken armoire. Old frames held bits of blackened canvas. Searching the ruins was a gruesome task, for after so long a time, very little remained. After hours of fearful looking, they were relieved to find no trace of Louisa.

"Perhaps she got away, miss," Colleen suggested hopefully.

"Yes, perhaps she did," Dearie agreed.

Then the same thought hit them both at once. The women stared at each other.

"Then where do you suppose she got to?"

They gazed into dark, silent woods. Not even a birdcall disturbed the silence.

Dearie had trouble sleeping that night, wondering about Tavish and the dead girl, Louisa. In her dreams she saw Louisa riding through the woods on a white horse. Suddenly, she saw Tavish on horseback, riding after the girl. Dearie ran after them, but she was on foot and couldn't keep up. Finally, she was left alone, staring into the blackness.

Billy Spears came early Monday morning with his father, Jake, and four free Negroes. Immediately, they set to work clearing away what was left of the timbers. Then they began to rebuild. The men worked quickly, resting only an hour at noon, and continuing until sundown each day.

At the end of the week, Dearie surveyed the work and was pleased. Her blue eyes sparkled with delight — her dream was coming true! But when she gave Billy Spears his first payment, she realized that the money Tavish had left her would not last long.

"Colleen, you'll have to go into town soon and ask Tavish for more money." She paused, deep in thought.

" 'Twould be a shame to bother him during harvest time," she said finally. "Mayhap my jewels would bring a nice sum . . ."

"Oh, no, Miss Dearie! You can't sell your jewels. Y'know your father paid me a year's wages in advance. I had it put by as a start for me own shop one day. I'll gladly loan it to you if need be."

Dearie hugged Colleen. "Oh, Colleen, I wouldn't dream of using your money. We'll manage somehow. Tavish will return soon, I know it." But Dearie was not so sure. When would Tavish return? Surely, he did not intend to leave them alone indefinitely. Now that her health was completely restored, Dearie's desire for Tavish had returned and was doubly strong. She thought of his warm kisses, and longed to sleep next to him at night.

By the end of another week, the exterior of the house was almost completed. Soon, the bricks would be laid and mortared with lime made of crushed oyster shells. Dearie clapped her hands in excitement. If only Tavish could see what she had done . . .

Tavish sat in the same office that his father had occupied two years before. He sensed his father's presence in the room with him. He could almost see the ruddy face, the piercing blue eyes, could feel the firm hand on his shoulder.

"Well, laddie," Murdock would have said. "What do you aim to do now?"

The business was flourishing, and after only three weeks, all their old customers had returned. Barrels of flour stood in the warehouse behind the office, ready to ship downriver. Soon there would be corn and tobacco.

Tavish could imagine Murdock rubbing his chin thoughtfully. "I can see that the business is booming, me lad. That's not what I meant. What are ye going to do about *her*?"

What *was* he going to do about her? Dearie was in his thoughts constantly since he had returned to Fayetteville. Her sky-blue eyes followed him wherever he went, questioning, pleading, deepening his guilt. He had been unable to stay with her for even a day, although the thought of lying next to her nearly drove him mad. Now the very image of her brought a warm rush of sensation to his loins.

It was time to make a decision. He had left her alone long enough now. No doubt she would beg him to allow her return to her father. After living a month in that burnt-out, haunted plantation, she would be only too ready to leave, her dreams dashed, her schoolgirl notions of marriage destroyed. What else could she do? Perhaps she had left already. The thought pained him more than he cared to admit. That he might never see Dearie again was unthinkable. He must see her just one more time . . . kiss her one more time . . . before he sent her back where she belonged.

At dusk the following Friday, Tavish arrived at the plantation. As he approached the house, he noticed that the path had been widened, and grass along the roadside had been cut. It almost looked like a real road. When he saw the house, Tavish reined his horse up short.

He rubbed his eyes, for the mansion rose like a mirage before him. Gone was the blackened shell, the fallen timbers, the brick rubble. In its place a new house had been raised. Tavish drew in his breath sharply. How in heaven's name . . . ?

Upon closer inspection, he saw that the renovation was not yet complete. The brickwork had only been finished on the front of the house, and the interior still needed much work.

"Tavish!" Dearie ran to him with open arms.

At sight of her, Tavish was filled to bursting with an emotion he couldn't understand. Instead of the anger and resentment he had expected, here she was — loving him as though nothing had happened. He was amazed, but relieved at the same time. He gathered her into his arms, folding into his embrace all her softness and warmth.

He carried Dearie into the house, past Colleen, and into the tiny bedroom. Without a word, he placed her on the bed. He undressed her slowly. She was more beautiful than he'd ever seen her. The simple blue merino dress showed off her pastel beauty better than any of her fine clothes. Her golden hair was twisted into a loose knot atop her head, and curling tendrils framed her flushed face. Her cheeks were rosy pink and her steady, azure gaze warmed him dangerously.

"I missed you, Dearie," he whispered into her hair.

"And I you, Tavish." She buried her head in his shoulder. She could hardly believe that she was really in his arms. Everything in her world was righted by his touch. It no longer mattered that he'd been gone for weeks, that she had been left alone in unbearable circumstances. It was enough that he was simply here . . . now.

Tavish's fingers were drawn like a magnet to her liquid-soft skin. Lower and lower her dress fell, over her arms, then down to her waist, seemingly of its own volition. Dearie's taut nipples pressed against the thin material of her chemise, and Tavish circled them gently with his finger. Dearie arched toward him.

Tavish paused to divest himself of his doeskin breeches and white cambric shirt. Then, his manhood clearly aroused, he knelt beside her on the bed.

Her eyes locked with his, Dearie untied the laces of her chemise and hastily pulled it down, freeing her porcelain breasts. Hungrily, his mouth found a rosebud nipple and suckled it to a marble hardness.

Dearie emitted soft, kittenlike moans and her hands clutched his sandy hair. His mouth moved from one swollen nipple to the other as his fingers slid down the length of her silky abdomen to the curve of her thigh. Ever so slightly he shifted his body, pulling her hand to him. Lovingly, she grasped his manhood and bent her head to place light kisses along his straining shaft.

Tavish was touched by her gentle ministrations. He could not remember ever having been caressed so tenderly. Taking her face in his hands, he drank in the deep, wondrous blue of her eyes. He kissed her softly on the lips, then more and more passionately. They seemed to mesh skin to skin, soft flesh to hard muscle, their arms and legs intertwined as one.

Although her body ached for release, Dearie's joy was all-encompassing. She could have remained interlocked with Tavish forever. His shaft throbbed against her leg, and her own body's response told her that it was time. Gently he rolled on top of her, and entered her warm moist passage. Dearie's soft undulations welcomed him, pulling him deeper into her.

His rhythmic thrusting drove her passion to the very heights of ecstasy. Every pore, every nerve, tingled with anticipation, cried out for more. Like a fine crystal goblet, she felt she would shatter from the exquisite vibration. But when at last it came, their shuddering release sent them both soaring far above anything they had known or felt before.

They lay against each other limply, like two who had ridden a huge wave into shore after a raging storm. They were spent, but somehow changed. They looked at each other questioningly, wonder in their eyes. Neither one could explain it. They knew now that what they'd experienced before had just happened again. And because it had happened again, they could believe what they'd felt. But what was it . . . love?

Dearie called it love. In her mind there was no other word for what she experienced with Tavish. And yet, the confines of the word seemed too small to encompass the power and depth of her emotion.

Tavish was perplexed. This was more than what he called coupling. It was more . . . much more. In fact, the experience was so powerful, it was frightening. He felt vulnerable that he could be so moved. It was as if all his secrets were revealed, that his soul was laid bare to her.

He looked at Dearie. Did she now know his innermost thoughts? Tavish looked away. He wanted to hide his nakedness from her, to shut himself away so that she couldn't see all that he was thinking. He drew away abruptly. His best and only defense was to somehow ignore the emotions that threatened to overcome him.

"We must dress, Dearie," he told her, unable to meet her gaze any longer.

"But why, Tavish? I want to stay here with you. There is naught to do."

Dearie touched his shoulder with her fingertips, sending a shiver of delight through him. He felt a resurgence of desire seize him. Moving quickly out of her reach, he covered himself with a blanket. Had he no control over his own body? His reaction made him furious with himself. In a fit of impatience, he stalked over to gather up his clothes.

"There is much to be done. And I must go back to town. Do you not realize that the harvest is in? I must work for a living, Dearie. Surely, you know that."

She was stunned. The pink flush from their lovemaking was still upon her face and breasts. But now she, too, pulled up her dress to cover herself. She lowered her golden lashes, ashamed. "I . . . I'm sorry, Tavish. Of course I know how hard you must be working. I only thought . . . "

But Tavish had already pulled on his shirt. He was fastening his breeches as he walked to the door. Without a backward look at her, he left the room.

Scrambling off the bed, Dearie dressed hastily. *Surely, he won't leave again*, she prayed. *He can't. I won't let him!*

Tavish stalked through the front room and out onto the porch, fully intending to ride back to town. Things had not turned out as he had planned. He had not made sure that she would return to to Philadelphia. He looked at the house and shook his head. He couldn't believe all the work she had done.

As he mounted his horse, Dearie caught up with him, breathless. "Tavish! You aren't leaving? But you can't! Colleen has cooked a wonderful dinner, and I . . . have so much talk to you about. Tavish, please!"

Her stricken expression melted his resolve. Taking his hand in hers, she tugged at him gently. "Come along, Tavish. Dinner is waiting."

He allowed her to lead him back inside, where an oaken table was set for the evening meal. The enticing smell of bacon and potato cakes reminded Tavish that he hadn't eaten since breakfast. Why shouldn't he stay and sample the pleasures of his home? he told himself. After all it was his to enjoy . . . *she* was his.

As if nothing at all had happened, Dearie sat calmly in the chair next to her husband. She smiled sweetly into his dark eyes, searching her memory for something she might have done to displease him. She finally decided that he must be preoccupied with business worries. She recalled her own father acting the same way upon occasion.

Dearie heaped Tavish's plate with bacon, potato cakes, and greens. Smiling at his appetite, she stole furtive glances at him while he ate. She thought she would never tire of looking at him. He was so handsome! Her eyes traced the line of his square jaw to his chin. There was a determined set to it, but that was good, she decided. His expression, ever brooding and thoughtful, puzzled Dearie. Was he never happy? Still, she was strangely intrigued by his distant manner.

Tavish stayed for two days. During the day he kept busy cutting wood or working with Clarence in the barn. After the evening meal he walked around the plantation with Dearie. But never once did he comment on the changes she had made.

Finally, she could bear his stubborn silence no longer. "Tavish, you have said nothing about the house! Does it not look wonderful?" she finally asked, her blue eyes begging for some sort of praise.

Tavish's eyes darkened and a muscle worked in his jaw. He was sorry he had ever purchased the place, sorry he had brought her here. "There's still a lot to be done," he said gruffly, ignoring her fallen expression.

"You must see the plans. Mr. Spears says it will be a showplace indeed," she informed him curtly. Her eyes flashed as she fought back her anger.

"Showplace!" Tavish laughed. "I doubt it Dearie. Your head is full of romantic notions. Fairy tales have no place here, I'm afraid."

"How can you say that, Tavish? Is it not your family plantation? Do you not wish to build it up . . . like the one in Virginia?"

He realized the extent of her misperceptions at his hand, and decided that it was time that she knew at least some of the truth.

"There is no plantation in Virginia. I have no family. This" — he gestured at the parched fields and the half-finished house — "is all there is."

Dearie's anger was uncontrollable now and her eyes blazed blue fire. "But you said . . . you told us you were from Virginia! That you were a planter! That is not true?"

"No."

"Why did you deceive me?" She was crying now. Her fury was mingled with shock and heartbreak, and she could contain her misery no longer.

"Would your father have considered me as a suitor if he knew that I had . . . very little?"

His words gave her pause. Matthew Grayson would never have permitted her to entertain a suitor who was not of their social standing.

"Believe me when I say I love you, Dearie," Tavish said, moving toward her.

"No," she said. "I don't believe you. How can I now? Do you think me some kind of fool? Leave me, Tavish," she cried, picking up her skirts as she ran up the steps to the house. "I don't care if you never return!"

The front door slammed, jarring loose a shingle from the porch roof. It dangled for a moment, then fell into the dirt at Tavish's feet.

Chapter Ten

The moment she'd uttered the words, Dearie regretted them. She had told Tavish to leave, that she didn't care if he never returned. But that was not true. Tears trickled down her cheeks unheeded. Wearily, she sought refuge in the tiny bedroom.

Tavish was right. Matthew Grayson would never have accepted him as a suitor had he not had a sound financial standing.

She smiled through her tears. Tavish *must* love her to be willing to risk so much on her account. Had he been exposed as a fraud, his reputation and Alistair's would have been ruined. It was no wonder that Tavish had been so preoccupied. He had borne this burden alone, not knowing how she would react to the truth.

Dearie chewed her lip thoughtfully. *I behaved abominably. When he needed assurance of my love, I sent him away. Tavish is my husband now, and my place is by his side, no matter what.* Her wedding vows echoed in her mind. "For better, for worse, richer or poorer . . . " She had accepted him fully, regardless of future hardship.

There was a soft knock, and Colleen opened the door. "The workmen are here, miss."

"Tell Mr. Spears I'll be along in a minute. And, Colleen . . . "

"Yes, Miss Dearie?"

"We have a lot of work to do before Master Tavish returns again."

Colleen nodded, a tight smile on her lips.

They *would* build a life together, Dearie vowed, silently. Tavish would never regret marrying her or bringing her to North Carolina. Momentarily she thought of the other men she could have married. She shook her head. No one captured her imagination as Tavish did.

Dearie ran short of funds soon after Tavish departed. In desperation, she sent Colleen into town to ask her husband for more money. "If you don't happen to find Master Tavish, here are my jewels. Perhaps you could trade them for supplies until we receive an allowance."

Clarence drove Colleen into town. The maid was not looking forward to meeting with Tavish. She knew he'd had words with her mistress, and she feared reprisal. Never had she seen two people more often at odds than her employers. If Dearie smiled, Tavish frowned. She was the sun trying always to peek through the dark cloud of his mood. Colleen imagined that it was because they were from two different worlds. He was from the country, while she was used to the culture of the big city. Dearie's solution to the problem of her new life was to civilize her surroundings. But while she might rebuild the house and cultivate the fields, it would never be Philadelphia. Colleen, however, was immediately at home in the rough, unsettled country. It reminded her of Scotland.

As the wagon pulled into Fayetteville, they crossed a granite ledge and bumped over a desolate track of sandy pinewoods and swamp. Colleen was relieved when this gave way to parklike shrubbery lining the road. Fayetteville was a busy metropolis. They passed houses of painted weatherboard, a lawyer's office, a bank, a doctor's clinic, and a general store. She noticed the slave block in the center of Fayetteville Street, and the town market. The wagon pulled to a stop in front of an office next to the store. The newly painted sign over the door said, "McLeod and Son."

Colleen alighted and rang the bell, but there was no answer.

"He could be out on business or down at the mill," Clarence suggested.

Colleen decided to set aside the things she needed at the store, then come back to the office later. Duffy's General Store was a completely new experience for her. She walked up and down the crowded aisles, amazed. There were barrels of salted meat, bags of fresh flour, strings of dried fruit, tubs of homemade preserves, and imported spices. Displayed along the shelves were felt hats, metal needles, bone buttons, suspenders, and bolts of colorful material. She had only to look to find everything she needed, from cleaning supplies to farm implements. In addition, there were various luxury items such as Brazilian coffee, Cuban sugar, nails, and osnaburg cloth. Colleen was enthralled.

Mr. Duffy was measuring out the supplies when Colleen glanced out the window. Her attention was caught by the sight of a handsome man walking arm and arm with a dark-haired woman. It was Tavish! Colleen stared at them aghast.

Mr. Duffy followed her gaze. "Looks as if Georganna has her cap set for Tavish McLeod. She said that she would marry him, and I'll warrant she'll have her way afore long."

Colleen was too stunned to speak.

"Now then, the total comes to thirty-six dollars, ma'am."

Shaking, Colleen fished in her reticule and withdrew the pouch containing Dearie's jewelry. She hadn't the heart to face Tavish now. She took out a garnet necklace and matching earrings.

"I . . . I'm sorry," she stammered. "But my mistress . . . we are short on funds. We were hoping you might take these in trade."

Mr. Duffy frowned, fingering the delicate necklace. "Well, now. I've traded nearly everything except jewels." He rubbed the stubble of his beard. "I wouldn't know what these are worth, but I'll allow my wife would look right smart in 'em."

"The garnets are set in gold," Colleen told him. "I'm sure they would be worth thirty-six dollars."

"Or much more than that." A tall man came to stand by Colleen. His sharp features were offset by lively blue eyes. With long fingers he picked up the necklace and held it to the light. "This is worth well over a hundred dollars," he declared, handing it back to Colleen.

"Well, ma'am, I'm afraid it wouldn't be worth that much to me," Mr. Duffy said, shaking his head.

The stranger swiftly counted out the exact sum and pushed it toward the storekeeper. "I'll settle up with this young lady, Mr. Duffy. See that the goods are loaded into her wagon." He took Colleen by the arm and led her out of the store.

Colleen, dazed by what had just happened, responded mechanically. "Please, Mr. . . . I . . . you shouldn't have . . ."

"It's Buie, Calvin Buie." He took off his hat and made a low bow. Colleen didn't know what to do. Never before had such a fine gentleman bowed to her. Her face flushed bright red and she stood staring at him, tongue-tied.

"May I ask your name, lovely lady?"

Was he talking to her? Colleen almost looked around her, then she recovered herself. "I . . . me name's Colleen McCurdie, sir, and I'm much beholden for your help. Me mistress, Dearie McLeod, sent me to town for supplies, but Master Tavish was not in his office so I thought to purchase supplies with her jewelry." She paused to take in a breath.

Calvin had been watching twin dimples indent her cheeks as she spoke. She was lovely, like a breath of sweet spring air. Then he thought about what she'd just said. "Your mistress is Dearie McLeod? Tavish McLeod's wife?"

Colleen nodded vigorously, loosening a dark curl from her cap.

Calvin frowned. "But I was under the impression that your mistress was unhappy here, and would be returning to Philadelphia soon."

"No, sir!" Colleen said firmly. "I mean, things are hard, but me mistress has no intention of returning. And you may tell Master Tavish that when you see him."

Clarence and the storekeeper came out of the store loaded with supplies. Calvin helped the men load the goods onto the wagon. When they were finished, he untied his horse from the hitching post and tossed the reins to Clarence. "Since we are neighbors, I'll ride out with Miss Colleen, Clarence. You ride my horse for me."

Colleen smiled, thrilled to hear him say her name. But when he returned her smile, she looked shyly away. Suddenly Calvin lifted her onto the wagon seat, then he climbed in beside her. He was twice her size, and his long legs made two of hers. When their bodies touched from the movement of the wagon, an electrical current seemed to pass between them.

As they pulled out of town, Calvin rested his arms on his knees and turned to Colleen. "I've been meaning to pay my respects to Mrs. McLeod. And I'd have come sooner if I'd known that you were there." His easy grin revealed straight white teeth.

Colleen blushed again. He certainly wasn't handsome. His hawklike nose and high cheekbones were too sharply defined. But there was definitely something about him.

Perhaps it was his twinkling blue eyes or his gentle smile. *He is a man who doesn't care about his looks*, Colleen thought. *He's as unaffected and simple as the countryside around him.*

Calvin drew her into conversation easily. Colleen found herself telling him everything about her childhood in Scotland, and about her mother's death after the long trip over. When she told of Dearie's marriage to Tavish, he frowned.

"The marriage was very sudden, then?"

Colleen dropped her eyes. "There was an accident on the road. Miss Dearie lost the babe."

Calvin shook his head sadly. "I didn't know."

When they arrived at the plantation, the workmen were busily applying finishing touches to the outside brickwork. Calvin gave a low whistle. "I was here just two months ago! I cannot believe what I see. It is beautiful!"

Colleen beamed proudly. "Miss Dearie got the workmen herself and drew up the plans."

When Calvin lifted Colleen down from the wagon, his hands lingered at her waist. His eyes locked with hers. "I have a feeling that I may be a frequent visitor."

Flustered, Colleen pulled away from him and led the way into the house.

Dearie was stirring a pot of peaches. It was the first thing she'd ever cooked. When they were done, the peaches would be put in jars with brandy, or put by for peach preserves. She looked up, startled, when Colleen entered.

When Calvin saw Dearie, he was awestruck by her beauty. He simply stared. With a sinking heart, Colleen watched his blue eyes absorb every detail of Dearie's lovely face, from her rosebud lips to the pale cloud of golden curls framing her face. Obviously, he thought she was beautiful.

When no one spoke, Dearie smiled cordially. "I'm Dearie McLeod," she said.

Calvin found his voice and managed to snatch his hat from his head. "Calvin Buie, ma'am. My place is no more than a half day's ride."

"But, of course! I know I've heard Tavish speak of you. How wonderful it is to meet another neighbor! Some of our other neighbors have not been too friendly."

Calvin grinned, still staring in fascination at Dearie.

Well-a-day, Colleen sighed, *he's in love with my mistress. No use to waste a thought on him now.* Her heart breaking, she busied herself about the room. In few minutes, she had prepared a meal. Calvin tore his eyes away from Dearie long enough to nod when Colleen invited him to stay for dinner.

Throughout the meal, Dearie chatted animatedly with Calvin. They had been to many of the same places in Europe, and they had friends in common in Philadelphia.

Colleen contributed nothing to the conversation. Eyes cast down, she ate her food in silence, thinking how foolish she had been to imagine that Calvin was interested in her.

When the meal was finished, Calvin lingered, apparently reluctant to leave. He talked about the plantations near Fayetteville and the economy since the war. Colleen had long since cleared away the dishes, and now stood at the washtub while they talked. Finally, her pride sorely wounded, she slipped out the door unnoticed.

When Calvin rose to leave, he promised to return within a week. "Tavish is very busy now," he reassured Dearie. "It is difficult for him to get away, but I'll be glad to stop by."

"Please do, Mr. Buie," Dearie exclaimed, delighted.

"Calvin," he corrected her with a smile, wondering how Tavish could leave this woman here all alone. He turned to speak to Colleen, but she had vanished. He jammed his hat back on his head and thanking Dearie for a fine meal, left.

Dearie watched him with amusement, for his head barely cleared the door frame.

"Colleen, isn't it wonderful?" Dearie commented later. "We have Mr. Calvin Buie as a neighbor. He seems such a nice man, too."

Colleen smiled weakly. "I'm not feeling myself, miss. Perhaps if I rest ... "

Dearie caught her arm. "But, Colleen, you haven't told me. Was Tavish well? What did he say?"

Colleen frowned. "I didn't speak with him, miss."

"You didn't see him? Then ... then how did you pay for the supplies?"

"Mr. Buie paid for them, miss."

"But where was Tavish?"

Colleen looked away. "I don't know, Miss Dearie. I didn't see him." She hated to tell a lie, but the truth would break Dearie's heart.

Dearie sat down with a heavy sigh. "Then we are indebted to Calvin. What a generous man."

"Yes, miss. Good night, Miss Dearie."

As he had predicted, Calvin became a frequent visitor. Each time he arrived with a gift. Sometimes it was a sack of flour or bushel of cornmeal. Once he brought a basket full of plums which he set down before Colleen.

"I've had a hankering for plum jelly," he said, a twinkle in his eyes. But Colleen nodded without a smile, and took the basket from him.

Another day he appeared with planks for a fence. In the back of the wagon was a young black boy holding a small pig.

Dearie was astounded. She had never seen a pig before.

"In a few months, he'll make bacon, sausage, and chitlins."

Dearie's blue eyes grew wide. "You mean I ... I have to kill it?"

Calvin chuckled. "No. Clarence will take care of that when the times comes."

Colleen was convinced that Calvin had fallen in love with her mistress. He found a reason to drop by almost every week, and he spent hours talking to Dearie.

Weeks passed and there was no word from Tavish. Dearie began to look forward to Calvin's visits, hoping to hear something about her husband. Calvin always reassured Dearie that Tavish was working hard and simply could not get away. But Dearie resolved to go into town herself.

She was preparing to leave when a note came from Calvin. He offered to escort the ladies to the Independence Day celebration in town where Tavish would join them. Dearie was filled with excitement. She would see Tavish again!

"Oh, Colleen, what shall I wear?"

Colleen rummaged through the trunks and wardrobe to retrieve a violet sarsnet with narrow flounces caught up in scallops. Another search produced a matching bonnet of violet silk trimmed with bows of pink ribbon. Dearie clapped her hands. "It's perfect, Colleen."

After much primping and preparation Dearie was ready. But she realized that Colleen still wore her faded house dress. "Colleen, we must hurry. Why don't you wear one of my dresses?"

Colleen shook her head. "No, miss. You go on without me. I've not been myself lately."

Studying the little maid, Dearie grew concerned. The color had gone from Colleen's cheeks, and lately she hardly ever smiled. "Nonsense, Colleen. The fresh air will do you good. Why, there'll be political speeches, and horse races, and games. And I'll wager there might be a handsome young man or two . . . "

Colleen frowned and shook her head stubbornly.

Dearie fixed her with a steady gaze. "I'll not have you staying here alone, Colleen. You must come."

Colleen gave in to Dearie's urging and allowed her mistress to select for her a dark blue merino dress bordered with blue velvet. After she had combed and arranged her dark hair in long curls, she had to admit she was pleased with the effect.

"You need a hat, Colleen," Dearie decided, searching through the boxes. "At last," she cried, holding up a straw hat with pink and blue ribbons.

"But that's your new hat, miss." Colleen cried.

Dearie ignored her protests and placed the hat on Colleen's dark head. "Just right," she pronounced, beaming.

Calvin was splendidly dressed in a dark blue broadcloth coat, drab trousers, and a white waistcoat. Colleen thought him the most elegant man she had ever seen. His eyes twinkled when he saw her, and she was momentarily heartened. However when he shifted his gaze to Dearie she abruptly looked away, fighting back tears.

"I'll be the envy of all the gentry today, for I am escorting the loveliest ladies in the county," he said, beaming.

Dearie laughed gaily, wondering if Tavish would be included in the ranks of the envious. It had been almost a month since they had parted.

During the trip, Calvin entertained them with stories of his ancestor, Archibald Buie, who had sailed from Scotland with Black Neil McNeill. Calvin was a natural storyteller, and the women couldn't help but smile at his genial humor.

Fayetteville was alive with activity. In addition to the thirty-five hundred residents, people from the surrounding areas now wandered the streets of the city. Strung from building to building were flags and banners advocating candidates for public office. The Fayetteville Light Infantry marched in tune to a brass band in front of the town hall.

How will we ever find Tavish? Dearie wondered.

Calvin ushered the ladies through a crowd of merry-makers who were freely passing jugs of whiskey and brandy. They arrived at the front of the group just as Judge Robert Strange ascended the dias.

After a recitation of the Declaration of Independence and a lengthy speech, the judge directed the crowd to the open field outside of town where a picnic and horse race were soon to commence. The three were carried willy-nilly along with the crowd to a dirt track near a shady grove of sycamores. Beneath the trees, the town women had set up long picnic tables filled with fried chicken, smoked hams, biscuits and thick gravy, roasted yams, hominy, and garden vegetables swimming in butter. On other tables stood pumpkin pies and cakes in abundance.

Calvin led them over to the tables. One of the women was Mrs. McFarland. Dearie started to say hello, but Mrs. McFarland turned to whisper in her neighbor's ear. The neighbor looked at Dearie and nodded solemnly. Dearie quickly followed Calvin and Colleen.

Their plates full, they found a spot beneath the trees with a good view of the racetrack. Dearie scanned the faces in the crowd, but could not find Tavish among them.

"Calvin, where is Tavish?" she asked finally.

"He'll be along directly. He must — he's in the race," Calvin told her with a wide smile.

One by one, horse and rider appeared at the starting line which was designated by a white line of flour poured across the road. The men all wore white shirts, with different colored scarves tied around their necks. They were to race in pairs to a large rock where another white line had been drawn.

Just as the referee held up the gun for the first two riders, Tavish appeared on a prancing black stallion. The crowd cheered as if he was a celebrity. He waved and took his place beside another rider, making the group six in all.

Like the other men, Tavish wore a white shirt, but his neck was bare until suddenly a dark-haired woman ran up and tied a red scarf around it. Dearie bristled as Tavish smiled down at the woman.

I should have been the one who tied the scarf around his neck, she thought angrily, chewing her lip in frustration.

Then she remembered. She had told Tavish not to return! Apparently, he'd taken her at her word, and found female companionship elsewhere. But how could he? She watched him, mesmerized.

The gun went off and the first two horses charged over the white line. The spectators were left in a cloud of red dust as the horses pounded down the dirt road. In minutes, the race was over, the victor a bay stallion.

Tavish and his opponent readied themselves for the second race. Pushing her uneaten plate of food aside, Dearie stood to gain a better view.

The gun went off a second time. The black stallion leaped to the fore. Dearie cheered along with the rest of the crowd, and hugged Calvin with delight when Tavish crossed the finish line first. Without thinking, she lifted her skirts and ran toward him. Pushing her way through the men crowding around him, she stood gazing up at him.

"Dearie!" He slid off his horse and gathered her into his arms, "I wasn't sure you'd come!"

Her arms went around him and the tears ran unchecked down her cheeks. "I . . . I am sorry, Tavish. I didn't mean what I said. Please forgive me."

He brushed the tears from her cheeks and lifted her chin. "There is no need to dwell on it. I'm sorry for the pain I've caused you, Dearie. Mayhap some day you will understand — " He looked away, unable to continue.

"But I do understand, Tavish. And I have behaved like a spoiled child."

He shook his head. Her gaze went through him, catching at his heart. She did not understand, and she never would.

"The house is almost finished, Tavish," she was saying. "And I thought we would clear the fields for planting in the spring."

Tavish frowned suddenly. "Dearie, what are you thinking? You know nothing about planting, and I cannot help you now. I have an obligation . . . to your father . . . to get the factoring business going again. It is taking all of my time, so the plantation will have to wait. When I have the business turning a profit then I can think about planting."

"I only wanted to help." She looked away.

He patted her arm affectionately. "You can help by being patient."

"I know but — "

"Tavish!" At the sound of his name, Tavish looked around quickly. The dark-haired woman appeared at his side. She glanced haughtily at Dearie, an amused smile on her full lips. She wore a cream-colored muslin gown, cut low to reveal a wide, ample bosom. From her bodice she retrieved a lace handkerchief, and reaching up, she dabbed at the drops of perspiration on Tavish's forehead.

Irritated, Tavish pushed her hand away.

"Tavish, I must speak with you right away," the woman said. Her eyes were dark and mysterious, as if she had some secret to tell him.

Dearie watched her in awe, hardly believing what she saw. Then, to her surprise, Tavish nodded.

"I'll be with you shortly," he said to her.

She smiled broadly, almost victoriously, at Dearie and turned away.

Tavish took Dearie's arm and led her back to the trees, where Calvin was standing with Colleen.

"Who was that woman, Tavish?" Dearie asked.

He shrugged, as if he was surprised at her question. "Just an old friend. It will be a while longer before I can get away. I am readying the produce for market. Send Clarence in every week for supplies, and anything else you need."

"But, Tavish . . ."

"I must go now," he said. With a quick kiss on her forehead, he disappeared into the crowd.

For a moment, Dearie thought of running after him, of throwing her arms about his neck and begging him not to leave her. But she did not want him to know how desperately she needed him. She would wait until he returned.

And he would return. He had to — she loved him.

Chapter Eleven

Colleen had been happily chatting with Calvin when she saw Tavish and Dearie in the distance. A dark-haired woman went up to Tavish and spoke with him, ignoring Dearie. It was the same woman she had seen walking with Tavish outside Mr. Duffy's store. Her mouth compressed into a tight line of disapproval, Colleen stopped in mid-sentence.

"Has the woman no shame, to parade herself so in front of a married man?" she muttered, half to herself.

The conversation between Tavish and Dearie was over quickly. Dearie rejoined them moments later, her face pale and her expression preoccupied.

"Miss Dearie? Will Master Tavish be joining us?" Colleen asked.

"No. He is very busy now. He . . . must ready the crops for market. It is very difficult for him now, you see. He must make the factoring business profitable, so he has no time for anything else." Dearie recited the words as if she were trying to convince herself.

Calvin nodded thoughtfully. He had forgotten how little money Tavish had. He knew that his friend was too proud to take a loan, and it saddened him to think that Tavish had struggled in silence these past few months. "Perhaps the expense has been too great," he suggested. "If the fields were planted, he could expect some return from the land."

"But he has no time to devote to planting now. His energies are all to the business in town." Dearie hung her head. All her plans seemed hopelessly optimistic and doomed to failure.

Calvin rubbed his chin. "Perhaps we could help Tavish," he said.

"But how? I know nothing about planting, and the fields have gone to broomsedge and pine seedlings."

He nodded. "True. But after the harvest, my men will be free to clear ground. Perhaps they can do your land as well as mine. Then come late October or November, we could sow winter wheat, and after the frost — maize and corn. I'll wager the fields will be fertile, having lain fallow for so many years."

Dearie clapped her hands together enthusiastically. "Oh, Calvin, that will be wonderful! Tavish will be so pleased."

Calvin smiled. He wondered if, indeed, Tavish would be pleased. He didn't understand Tavish of late, and his attitude toward Dearie was even more puzzling. It seemed as if he couldn't wait to see her, but then, having seen her, he couldn't wait to get away again. And what of Georganna Arms? Why hadn't she given up on Tavish now that he was married? Calvin had misgivings about offering help without Tavish's knowledge, but Dearie needed assistance, and there was no one else to give it.

A light summer rain began to fall, hurrying picnickers into their wagons and carriages. Dearie scanned the faces of the departing crowd, but Tavish was not among them.

Again she thought of the dark-haired woman. Who was she, and what did she want with Tavish?

The three were silent on the trip home, immersed in their own private thoughts. When they arrived at the plantation, the rain had turned into soft drizzle. Calvin accepted a mug of cider before departing for home.

"I'll be by on Friday," he promised before driving away.

Dearie looked wistfully after him. He was her only link to Tavish, but often he seemed as perplexed about Tavish's behavior as she was.

Calvin had been gone but a short while Colleen motioned Dearie to the window. Several wagons were driving up the narrow path.

"Perhaps our neighbors have come to welcome us at last," Dearie said, smoothing her hair.

The wagons stopped short as Dearie and Colleen stepped out onto the porch. Dearie recognized the McFarlands, and another man who had been at the Four Corners Tavern. However, their expressions seemed anything but friendly.

For a while no one spoke. Finally, urged by Mrs. McFarland, Angus McFarland climbed slowly down from his wagon. The man from the other wagon followed suit.

Angus cleared his throat. "Things have been happening . . . since you moved in here, that we ain't got an explanation for." He looked at his neighbor.

"A month ago two of my hogs just up and died one night. No reason," the neighbor said.

"'Bout the same time we found some of the chickens with their necks plumb wrung off," Angus said, looking at Dearie as if for an explanation.

Dearie shrugged her shoulders sympathetically. "Well, nothing like that has happened here. Of course, we haven't any livestock."

"No, ma'am. I wouldn't think anything would happen to you," the neighbor said. "Since then, the butter won't churn and half our cream done turned bad. All of a sudden like."

Dearie began to suspect that they held her responsible somehow. But she thought it best to listen to their grievances before replying.

"Several of us have found sacks of grain and flour strewn all over the yard or the storeroom.... Then today, this . . . "

Angus produced a small doll fashioned from mud and clay. Her hair was made of corn shucks, and she wore a crudely sewn calico dress. His neighbor produced a similar one.

"Why, they're little dolls!" Dearie exclaimed.

"We found them on our doorstep when we come from town," Angus said, taking the doll from his companion and shoving them both into Dearie's hands.

Dearie examined the dolls more closely. The faces were delicately carved, and one bore a resemblance to Mrs. McFarland.

She looked at the men, puzzled.

"Waxen images," Mrs. McFarland rasped out from her seat in the wagon. "That's what they air."

"These dolls are made of clay," Dearie pointed out.

"Don't matter. They're one and the same," Angus said.

"I . . . I don't understand," she stammered.

"We're sayin' that before you came nothing like this ever happened."

"C'mon, Angus," Mrs. McFarland called from the wagon.

Angus snatched the dolls back from Dearie and walked slowly back to the wagon. His neighbor followed him.

"I didn't leave the dolls." A frown indented the smooth skin of Dearie's brow. She was irritated at their ignorance. How could anyone be so superstitious in this day and age?

"Things is stirred up something terrible. It bodes ill for us all" were Angus McFarland's parting words.

The wagons pulled slowly away, then stopped halfway down the lane when the McFarlands' wagon became mired in the mud. Angus climbed down and gave Dearie a withering look as he searched for a rock to slide under the wheel.

Dearie turned to Colleen. Her face had gone white during the interchange. "Say a prayer, Miss Dearie. Say a prayer, quickly," she urged her mistress.

"But this is all ridiculous, Colleen. Look! He even thinks I made his wagon wheel stick in the mud!"

Finally the wagons departed, but an uneasy silence fell over the house. Shortly afterward, the sky darkened and the rain began again. At first it fell in heavy sheets, then the wind picked up and became a driving gale.

Soon the rain brought hailstones the size of small eggs, and the wind bent tall pine trees until it seemed they would snap in half.

Halfway through the storm, Clarence burst into the house. He was dripping wet. "Looks like the devil himself is pushing this storm," he said.

"Warm yourself a bit, Clarence," Dearie ordered him.

"It'll work havoc on the crops, I'll bet." Clarence moved toward the fire.

Dearie exchanged a glance with Colleen. "And they'll say I was to blame," she sighed.

Clarence produced a tiny black kitten from his jacket. "I ain't the only one got caught in the storm. I found this little fellow stuck in the fence wicket," Clarence said, placing the kitten in front of the fire. "Hope you don't mind, Miss Dearie."

"Oh, what a precious kitten!" Dearie rushed over to cuddle it.

Colleen shook her head, frowning. "It's a black cat, Miss Dearie. We can't keep it."

"Nonsense, Colleen. We aren't going to let superstition rule our lives. I know that Tavish would want me to keep it." The kitten looked up at her with large green eyes. "We'll call it Wicket."

The storm raged for two days, growing in intensity before finally abating on the morning of the second day. Clarence went out to check for damage, and reported that a tree had fallen against the barn, but the barn roof was still intact. Dearie was vastly relieved to hear that the house had sustained no damage.

When the roads were again passable Billy Spears and his son drove by to see how Dearie had fared through the storm.

"Haven't had a storm like that for as long as I can remember," Billy remarked. "You were lucky. The McFarlands lost pretty near everything. Their whole corn crop is ruined, and a tree fell on their house — dead center. Like someone took a big ax to it."

Dearie shuddered at the description. "I'm sorry to hear that," she said sincerely.

"And his neighbor, John Woolsey, fared poorly, too. He lost most of his crop." He raised his eyebrows in question. "Ever hear of storm-raisin'?"

"No, I haven't."

"They say a witch can cause a storm to come and destroy people she don't like," Jake supplied with mischievous grin.

"Surely you don't believe in all that, Mr. Spears."

"Oh, no, ma'am, I don't," Billy said, his attention momentarily distracted by the appearance of the black kitten.

Following his gaze, Dearie nervously explained. "That's Wicket. Clarence found her stuck in the gate during the storm."

Billy nodded. "Yes, ma'am. It's a wonder it warn't drowned. Well, I'm pleased to see you fared so well."

He clucked to his horse, and Dearie thought that he left rather hurriedly. She picked up the kitten and hugged him to her. Did they all really think she was a witch? How could they hold her responsible for natural occurrences? She shook her head and walked back into the house.

When Calvin came by after the storm, he laughed at Dearie's fears. "Everyone was hard hit," he said. "Several of my trees were uprooted, and there was damage to the poultry house roof. We lost several chickens before it was over."

"But, Calvin, they think I'm a witch because we had no losses."

Calvin shrugged. "You had nothing to lose — no livestock, no crops."

But in the weeks that followed, one incident after another increased Dearie's agitation. It was as if the storm had unleashed all the demons in the woods.

Clarence saw a bridge collapse and float down Cross Creek. People on the bank just stood and shook their heads, he reported. Livestock came through broken fences and wandered freely though the overgrown fields of the plantation. To make matters worse, they decided to stay, congregating around a small pond at the corner of one field.

"Oh, no," Dearie wailed, shaking her head. "Why do they stay? I suppose our neighbors will blame me for this, too!"

"Yes, miss," Colleen agreed. "People are wont to place blame elsewhere whenever they can. Their own poorly mended fences could never be at fault."

Disgruntled neighbors trekked over to round up their livestock, but none stopped to share a word with Dearie. Instead, their expressions were ominously dark and unfriendly.

Then Dearie, too, experienced unexplainable occurrences similar to those of her neighbors. At first, she thought that her neighbors were wreaking revenge, when the small pig Calvin had given them suddenly disappeared.

"Coulda been a weasel, I reckon," Clarence commented, "but then the fence warn't damaged. And he couldn't have gone under. It was packed too good with bricks and mortar. I seen to that myself. No, it had to be something big. But I'm switched if it don't look like something done reached down and scooped him up."

Dearie's blue eyes widened. "What sort of something, Clarence? A wolf?"

"No, ma'am. I think somebody stole the little fella."

Dearie's shoulders sagged. Were her neighbors trying to get even with her?

"It bodes ill, Miss Dearie," Colleen said. "Mayhap when Master Tavish returns, we should think about leaving. There's no accountin' for what people may do if they band together against you. Why, once in me own village they ran off a man just because they didn't like the way he looked. He had been burned in a fire, you see — "

"Yes, yes, Colleen," Dearie interrupted with an impatient wave of her hand."Well, we'll not be leaving. This is my home, and I won't be driven from it."

Three days after the pig disappeared, Wicket did not return for her evening meal. After a thorough search, they concluded that she had been lost. Thoroughly despondent, Dearie collapsed into the chair by the fire.

"If only Tavish were here! He could help us." Her eyes filled with tears.

Colleen placed her hand on Dearie's shoulder. "Master Tavish said he'd be here in a few weeks, Miss Dearie. That's not so long now."

Dearie nodded absently. "But when he learns what has been happening, he will surely send me back to Philadelphia."

A knock sounded at the door, startling the women. Clarence opened the door tentatively. It was Angus McFarland. Dearie followed Clarence to the door, but the scowl on her neighbor's face forced her to remain well behind her big servant.

Angus held a small cloth bag, which he thrust into Clarence's hand. "Me wife thinks ye've sent this to do the devil's work. I have no knowledge of witchcraft, but you best keep it to home. Too many things have happened that cannot be explained." He shook his head and left.

Clarence opened the sack and Wicked pranced out. She quickly took her place by the fire.

"For goodness' sake," Dearie exclaimed, exasperated. "When will all this end?"

A second storm came within three weeks of the first one. This time the wind was not so strong, although lightning streaked through the dark, moonless sky. Wicket disappeared again and Dearie, thinking that she might have gone to the neighbors, went out in the storm in search of the kitten.

She ran out of the house with only a thing shawl covering her head. Imagining that the kitten had taken refuge in the barn, she hurried there. But Wicket did not respond to her calls. As she came from the barn, a streak of lighting briefly illuminated the edge of the forest. Dearie stopped dead in her tracks.

Like a statue carved from stone, a young girl sat on a white horse. Her face, hair and dress were all a deathly white. Dearie's heart was in her throat. It was the ghost of Louisa!

No thoughts came to Dearie's mind, no words to her lips. She remained frozen, oblivious to the pouring rain.

Then Louisa laughed. Dearie realized vaguely that her laugh was like that of a small child's. "You are looking for her?" The wrapped figure asked.

Dearie saw that Louisa had a sheet wrapped around her shoulders. From within its folds, she produced Wicket.

Forgetting that she stood facing a ghost, Dearie advanced to take the kitten from the girl. The hand she touched briefly was warm to the touch, hardly that of a spirit. "Thank you," she whispered, as if in a trance.

Upon closer inspection, Dearie saw that the girl wore faded muslin. Both she and her horse appeared to be alive, and as if to prove her suspicion right, the horse snickered at being reined in so tightly. Louisa smiled and again laughed lightly. "Thank you for making my house pretty again. Good-bye."

She gently kicked her horse with a bare heel. The animal reared at her touch and galloped quickly away. Childish laughter rose above the pounding hooves, growing faint and fainter.

Colleen had come from the house in search of her mistress. "Miss Dearie," she cried, grasping her arm. "You'll catch the augue, sure."

Dearie allowed herself to be led back inside. She said nothing as Colleen peeled off her sodden clothing and threw a warm wrapper around her. "You look like you've seen spirit from beyond the grave."

"I have, Colleen," Dearie told her calmly. "I just saw Louisa."

Colleen gasped. "Oh, miss. Ye saw Lousia? Say a prayer, quickly, Miss Dearie. Merciful heavens! It's these storms that stirred things up."

"Colleen, she isn't dead! She's alive, and riding around on a white horse like Billy Spears said!"

"Saints preserve us, Miss Dearie. This isn't a safe place. I must pack our things . . . "

Dearie caught the maid's arm. "She found Wicket, Colleen! And she thanked me for restoring her house."

Colleen's dark eyes widened. "Did she now! Well, what next!" The women looked at each other in amazement. What more could happen?

After the second storm, Dearie saw Louisa several more times. Once she had been gathering blackberries in the woods nearby and had stopped at the pond to water her horse. Lost in her thoughts, she hadn't seen the girl until Louisa turned and smiled. By daylight her face was pinched and childlike, and most definitely human.

"You are Louisa, aren't you?" Dearie heard herself asking the girl.

"Yes," she said, tossing her white-blond hair.

"But where do you live?"

"There," Louisa nodded toward the woods.

"In the woods?"

Louisa laughed gaily. She turned to her horse, and from the saddlebag she retrieved a doll. "Here. I made this for you."

The doll was exactly like the ones her neighbors had received, only this one was much prettier. Dearie was touched. "Thank you," she said.

"Your name is Dearie. I've heard them say. . . . Such a funny name."

This time Dearie laughed with her. "Yes, it is."

"Well, good-bye, Dearie." In a flash, Louisa was upon her horse. A moment later she had disappeared into the woods.

It was like a strange dream. Colleen feared that the events of the preceding weeks had been too hard on her mistress until she, too, encountered Louisa down by the well. Bending over to bring up the bucket, Colleen suddenly saw a strange, childish face in the water next to hers. The little maid was so surprised she almost fell in. Luckily she only lost her cap in the water below.

"Oh, tarnation," she muttered, more irritated now than afraid."

Louisa laughed. "I'll help you."

Together they managed to spear the cap with a sharp stick. But when Colleen turned to thank her. Louisa had gone.

"Do y'suppose she wants her house back, Miss Dearie?" Colleen asked later.

"No, I don't think so, Colleen. Do you know, I just think she wants to be friends."

Clarence continued to bring home reports of strange incidents he heard from Mr. Duffy, the storekeeper. Soon Dearie began to associate these happenings with Louisa. Whenever a chicken disappeared, or a cow wandered off, she imagined that Louisa had needed something to eat. She discussed this with Colleen, who immediately agreed.

"That's probably right, miss. The child needs food. All this witchcraft is nothing more than a lonely child needing company and a good meal."

But Dearie's efforts to help Louisa went for naught. The girl had grown used to foraging for herself in the forest. When Colleen offered her a basket full of breads and preserves, she only laughed and shook her fair head.

"I have my own food," she sang out, and gaily rode away.

After that, Louisa began bringing chickens, pigs, and even a baby calf as presents to her new friend, Dearie. The chickens had been plucked, but she led the calf on a rag rope behind her horse.

"Louisa, where did you get these chickens?" Dearie asked her.

"I found them," Louisa said, smiling. "I have more than I need. So I brought you some."

That was all she said before disappearing again.

"I am sure she is stealing these animals from our neighbors," Dearie told Colleen. But there was nothing she could do.

The neighbors, however, did not take kindly to the depletion of their stock. One or two chickens were not missed, but now the thefts had become a nightly occurrence. The men began to hold meetings at the tavern at Four Corners.

When Dearie learned of the meetings, she ordered Clarence to drive her over. No longer would they accuse her of witchcraft, Dearie vowed.

Clarence complied, but a worried frown creased his dark face. "Don't want to mess with these folk, Miss Dearie. They liable to string you up."

"No they won't," Dearie assured him. But she quailed inwardly at the thought.

Dearie marched into the tavern dressed in a rose-colored taffeta dress with muslin ruffles. She looked as though she was going to a dinner dance instead of a confrontation with hostile neighbors.

Once again, the tavernkeeper was shocked to see her. Women seldom frequented his establishment, and certainly no women like Dearie. Finding none of the men inside, she made her way to the back door.

Seated at the tables were some twenty men drinking either cider or rum. An ominous silence fell when Dearie stepped boldly into their midst. Angus McFarland stood up abruptly, an angry frown on his face.

"Mrs. McLeod — " he began.

"I am a householder and a neighbor, Mr. McFarland. As my husband is away at the moment, I have the right to be here. I have a few things to say, and then I shall leave. We, too, have been prey to strange happenings since the storm. And I think there is a simple answer to it all."

She paused and the men whispered among themselves.

"Louisa Suggs has been living in the woods, not far from our property. It is she who has depleted your stock, I'm afraid."

"What!" Angus sputtered. "She's been dead for two years!"

"No, Mr. McFarland. She's not dead. But she is a very sick child. She spends her time making dolls, and when she is hungry, she takes your pigs and chickens. I hope that this explains these mysterious incidents to your satisfaction. Good evening, gentlemen." Dearie nodded curtly and left them talking among themselves.

Dearie felt confident that her announcement would end the talk of witchcraft, and the silly behavior of her ignorant neighbors. Secretly, she felt that Tavish would be proud of her.

"Now we can get back to the business of running the plantation," she told Colleen.

Days passed and neither Dearie nor Colleen saw Louisa again. They missed the girl's visits, and wondered if she might be sick. Then one evening she appeared at their front door.

Her huge gray eyes were wild, and her cheeks held a faint flush. Dearie reached out to touch her, but Louisa drew back sharply as if she were frightened.

"You . . . you told them I was a witch," she told them in her childish voice.

"No, Louisa, I didn't tell them you were a witch. I would never do such a thing. You . . . you must believe me," Dearie protested, moving toward the girl.

Staring at them accusingly, Louisa backed away, and scrambled onto her horse. "I thought you were my friend. Now they will hunt for me and kill me! And it will be your fault!"

"No, Louisa! Stop!" Dearie ran after her, but the girl had been swallowed by the woods.

"Don't fret yourself, Miss Dearie. The child's not well. Surely she's imagining things."

"But what if they do think she's a witch? What can we do?"

"She's just a child, miss. No harm will come to her. Besides, that horse can outrun anything, I'll warrant."

As always, Dearie was comforted by Colleen's words. Still, Louisa had seemed so distraught. By now she felt almost responsible for the girl.

The next day Dearie sent Clarence into town for supplies, and to inquire after Tavish.

Tavish had promised to return in a few weeks. It had been almost two months. Dearie's eyes filled with tears at the thought. Did he not care for her? she wondered again. For what seemed the umpteenth time.

"Clarence, tell Master Tavish that I miss him," she said, her voice choked with emotion.

Dearie and Colleen went about their household tasks. They were surprised when two hours later Clarence had returned. He jumped quickly down from the wagon before it stopped at the front door.

"Miss Dearie, you must come quick! They've got that chile, Miss Louisa, down at the tavern! I don't know what they're aimin' to do. I b'lieve they going to string her up!"

Chapter Twelve

Dearie, paying no heed to her appearance, grabbed her sunbonnet and climbed into the wagon beside Clarence.

"I done told you, Miss Dearie. You don't want to mess with these folk. No tellin' what they can do," Clarence grumbled, angrily slapping the reins against the horses. "They done switched their fury from you to that pore girl."

Dearie said nothing. Louisa's words echoed in her mind. *"They'll hunt for me and kill me. And it will be your fault!"*

As they drove she said a silent prayer. When they arrived at the tavern, no one was there. The tavernkeeper only shrugged his shoulders.

"They left," he said. "And they took the girl with 'em. She was biting and clawing like some wild animal."

"Where did they go?" Dearie demanded.

The man rubbed his chin, obviously debating whether he should divulge the information. "They was going to get a preacher and then go to the river."

Dearie and Clarence drove away quickly, but they had no idea which direction to take. "It's a long river," Clarence said. "Can't tell where they'll be."

"Why would they get a preacher? To baptise her, I suppose," Dearie said.

Well, maybe. But there's all kind of ways to test out a witch, and some of 'em have to do with water."

Dearie frowned. Louisa had been right. They *had* hunted her down like an animal. But were they going to kill her, too?

They drove along the river for almost an hour. Finally they came upon a small gathering of horses and wagons partially obscured from the road by a thick outcropping of brush.

An old woman in a poke bonnet sat on a wagon seat, a snuff stick in her mouth. Dearie alighted and walked over to her wagon. The woman sat immobile, her eyes trained on the scene in front of her. She didn't acknowledge Dearie's presence, even when she cleared her throat.

"Excuse me, ma'am. Do you know the girl they have, there?" Dearie asked.

"It's a witch. She's been a'makin' havoc hereabouts," the old woman said, taking out her snuff stick. She spat out the juice just an inch away from Dearie's foot.

"What are they going to do to her?"

The woman turned slowly to Dearie, a solemn expression on her withered face. "They're going to swim her, I reckon." She pushed the snuff stick back into her mouth and turned away.

Dearie had no idea what the woman meant, but there was an ominous tone to her words. Ordering Clarence to stay with the wagon, she joined the women standing at the edge of the crowd. With her bright hair hidden by her bonnet, Dearie looked like the other women, for they all wore faded muslin dresses and poke bonnets.

On her tiptoes, Dearie could see Louisa. She'd been forced into a kneeling position at the feet of the preacher, who was uttering an unintelligible incantation over her. The girl had ceased struggling, and her chin had sunk down to her chest. Was she conscious? Dearie wondered. Her heart beat rapidly as she tried to think of what to do.

"Swim her! Swim her!" some of the women demanded.

Dearie quickly scanned the faces around her. Their utter hatred was almost tangible.

When the preacher had finished, two men lifted Louisa and untied the ropes binding her arms behind her back.

She is as limp as a rag doll, Dearie thought, biting her trembling lip.

When her bonds were cut, the men proceeded to tie her right thumb to her left big toe.

Dearie clutched the sleeve of a woman near her. "What are they doing?"

"They're going to swim her. They've tied her so she's crossbound." There was a satisfied look on the woman's face.

"They're going to put her in the water like that?"

The woman nodded, absorbed in the show going on in front of her. "Yes. And if she floats, she's a witch for certain. There's been some who just up and soared over the water like birds."

"And if she sinks?"

"She's innocent. But I don't reckon there's much chance of that."

"But she could drown, tied up like that!"

The woman shrugged and looked over at Dearie for the first time. "Either way we'll be rid of her."

They carried Louisa to the banks of the Cape Fear River. They were about to drop her in when Dearie rushed to the center of the group.

"No, no! You can't do this! She's just a child. A . . . a sick child. Give her to me. I'll . . . I'll take care of her. I promise she'll never bother your chickens again . . . "

Mrs. McFarland stepped forward and took Dearie's arm in a firm grip. "She's evil. She must be dealt with. It's God's will!"

Dearie tried to shake off the woman's grip, but she was held fast. The men carried Louisa to the bank of the river. There was a five-foot drop to the water from where they stood. Louisa's head bobbed limply on her chest, and Dearie saw that she had fainted. The men swung her back and forth.

"Noooo!" Dearie screamed as they threw her into the water.

She broke free of Mrs. McFarland, and ignoring the protesting crowd, she jumped off the bank behind Louisa. It was only when she hit the water that Dearie remembered that she couldn't swim. She beat frantically against the water, struggling with her long skirts. The skirts wound around her legs, weighting her down like lead. She fought uselessly, grasping for air, until the waters closed over her face. As she sank to the bottom, she vaguely felt the water moving around her. A man was swimming toward her. She thought that it was Tavish, but no, he wasn't here. She must be dreaming. Or had she already died?

Dearie's eyes fluttered open. The heat of the afternoon sun beat down on her. She felt very uncomfortable. Turning, she found herself in the bed of a wagon, covered with a quilt. Beside her lay Louisa. Dearie propped herself up on her elbows for a closer look. The child seemed to be dead. Her face was even whiter than before, and her silver hair lay in wet strands. She was so still that it was impossible to tell if she was breathing. They had killed her!

Dearie's attention was diverted by loud arguments nearby. One voice was familiar — it was Tavish!

"If either woman dies, you will hang for it, McFarland!"

McFarland hung his head. "I didn't want to do it. . . . My wife . . . she hasn't been the same since we lost our little girl a few years back. And so many things happened. Well, we didn't want no more of it . . . "

"It makes no difference, Angus. You can't take the law into your own hands. Surely you know that."

"I didn't know your wife would jump in after her like that."

"Tavish!" Dearie called out to him.

Instantly he was by her side, touching her soft cheek with eager fingers. He hugged her to him closely, rocking her like a small child. "I thought . . . I didn't know . . . if I got to you in time. You took in so much water. Thank God!"

Her arms wound around his neck automatically. It no longer mattered that she was chilled to the bone, or that her clothes were soaked. Tavish was here at last! His face was so full of love for her that Dearie was immediately suffused with warmth.

"What about the girl?" McFarland asked, peering into the wagon.

"That's up to you, Angus," Tavish said, his eyes dark.

"What do y'mean?"

"I mean that you did this to her, so it's up to you to nurse her back to health. If not . . . you can stand trial like any other criminal."

Angus scowled. It seemed that he might protest, but then thought better of it. "All right, Tavish. I'll allow that's fair, since she ain't got people. But only 'til she mends."

Dearie grabbed Tavish's sleeve. "No, Tavish, they'll harm her . . . "

Mrs. McFarland came to stand by her husband. Her face was exactly as Louisa had carved it on her doll — solemn, unflinching, and hard.

"No, ma'am. She'll come to no harm in our house. If we was wrong, we aim to do right by the girl. We're Christians, after all."

Tavish nodded and Dearie released her hold on his arm. But she still cringed when Angus picked up the girl's limp form and carried her to his wagon.

"Are you sure, Tavish?"

"I know these people, Dearie. I've dealt with them all my life. But you can feel free to visit often to ease your mind."

Dearie heard someone mutter aloud. "Well, she warn't a witch. That much was clear. I heared tell that a real witch will float just like a cork."

Her head on his lap, Tavish sat with Dearie in the back of the wagon as they rode back to the plantation. Dusk settled over the tall pines, and bathed the landscape with a soft, rosy glow.

"Tavish," she said. "I still don't understand how something like that can happen. How one minute people can think of murdering a young girl, then the next minute take her into their home to nurse her back to health again."

"They aren't bad people, Dearie. You don't understand them or their ways. They're superstitious and ignorant. They're afraid of anything strange, especially strange people."

Dearie frowned. "I'm not strange, Tavish. They are."

He shook his head. She was so naive. "You're from a different world. You stand out like a sore thumb."

"But they've gone against the law."

Tavish shrugged. "It happens all the time. There are duels, lynchings, and killings every day."

"Not in Philadelphia," she assured him.

He flinched, and she could see a muscle working in his jaw. "No, I suppose not in Philadelphia."

Dearie felt the warmth leave his touch and he moved away from her. Now what had she said? A sadness too deep for tears welled up within her. Would she ever understand her husband? She was beginning to doubt it.

Dearie's words had brought Tavish up short. It was obvious that she didn't belong here. Rural North Carolina was no place for a gentlewoman bred to a civilized life. Dearie didn't understand the ways of commonfolk. And she'd almost died trying to save a child she hardly knew. His mouth tightened in a grimace. He could not for the life of him understand why she stayed.

Tavish stayed only for week, long enough to make sure that Dearie had mended. During the day he chopped wood, butchered a hog he bought from Calvin, and laid in a supply of grain and dried fruit. Dearie was curious. It seemed that he was storing provisions for the winter.

At night, he slept beside Dearie without touching her, his long body cramped into a small space on one side of the bed. Dearie lay awake, longing to hold him. But she could not bring herself to make the first move. She studied his strong shoulders and the firm muscles of his back, memorizing every line of his torso.

One night she fell into a fitful sleep and dreamed that Tavish came to her. He wore the same tender look of love he had after he'd rescued her. Suffused with warmth, her desire was heightened by his touch. His hands touched her everywhere, until she burned with need for him. She felt him rise over her, then come deeply within her, fueling the blaze of her passion higher and higher, until she could bear it no longer . . .

The heat became too intense all of a sudden — it was suffocating her! She thrashed about frantically, trying desperately to escape the heat. Lurid colors of orange, red, and yellow danced around her, but now it was not Dearie, but the plantation that was burning! Tavish had wrapped her in a quilt and carried her outside. There he stood, stoically watching their beautiful home burn.

"Tavish," she screamed. "Get water!"

But Tavish only shook his head. "It's no use," he said dully. "It can't be saved."

"Yes, it can!" she sobbed hysterically. "Yes, it can! I know it can . . . "

Dearie awoke sobbing and drenched with perspiration. She sat up, confused. The dream had been so real that she was sure the plantation had burned again.

Tavish rolled over. "What's wrong?"

"I . . . dreamed the plantation was on fire and you . . . just let it burn. You said it was no use to save it," she hiccupped.

Tavish took her in his arms and dried her tears. "It was only a dream. Go to sleep now, Dearie."

Tavish ordered Clarence to pack his saddlebags, and Dearie watched him without speaking. She yearned to throw her arms around him and beg him to stay but she could not bring herself to plead with him.

"I must take the grain to market," he told her.

"But why must you go? Can't you ship it to market?" She knew that it was futile to argue, but she could not understand why he had to leave.

"I must trade with the merchants in the coastal cities to buy seed and goods for my planters. Else they will have nothing for the winter months ahead."

"You have certainly learned about factoring in these past months. One would think you had always been a factor, instead of a planter."

Tavish smiled ruefully. "I'll be gone for over a month."

Dearie looked away. She tried to remind herself that Tavish had to make a living, but she couldn't help thinking that they hardly had a marriage. It wasn't right for a husband to leave his wife alone so much.

"I'm sorry, Dearie. I'll be back before winter, but until then, I've left you well provided for. If you need anything else, Clarence can go into town."

She forced a thin smile. "Will it always be like this, Tavish?"

He didn't answer. He hadn't thought that she would stay this long. He looked out the window to the fields of broomsedge and pine seedlings. In the spring, he'd send her home to her father. For now, he needed the old man's cooperation one more time.

Dearie was morose for weeks after Tavish left. Over and over again she tried to reason things out. This was not what she'd expected from marriage.

She sat down to write her father. She had written him several letters, but she'd revealed nothing of her misgivings, nothing of the pain she had endured since leaving Philadelphia. Now, as she sat trying to compose the letter, she thought of telling him the truth. But try as she might, she could not bring herself to write the words. She knew that if she gave even one hint that all was not well, Matthew Grayson would be on the next stage to North Carolina. So she wrote him another glowing account of beautiful Beauvais, and more about her wonderful husband, Tavish. She closed by telling her father how well she was. She hadn't had the heart mention that she lost the child, for she worried about how he would react. He might hold Tavish responsible somehow.

The letter made Dearie feel better. She thought of Tavish and told herself that he was right. After the months she had spent in North Carolina, she had not adapted well to her new surroundings.

"I am still a stranger here," she said aloud.

Tavish would be much happier, she decided, if he saw that she had made the adjustment well. Any man would.

Just how she planned to adapt herself to rural life, Dearie didn't know, but her first project was to call on Louisa. As Clarence drove the wagon over narrow, weed-choked roads to the McFarland home, Dearie was filled with trepidation.

"They say the child's hung on, but they don't know if she'll make it." Clarence verbalized her own fears.

"I pray that she does."

Their approach set the dogs to barking, and Mrs. McFarland came to the door. She stood watching silently as Dearie and Clarence approached.

"I've come to visit Louisa, Mrs. McFarland," Dearie said, trying to ignore the woman's severe expression. "May I come in?"

Mrs. McFarland pushed open the door. "She's still ailin'. But she'd probably like company."

Dearie walked into a cabin as neat and clean as a Dutch cottage. The house had only a sod roof, but the mud and brick walls had been whitewashed a gleaming white. Pots and pans hung over the stove, and rag rugs crisscrossed the dirt floor. In the far corner was a small wooden bed. Dearie could see Louisa's frail form outlined beneath the covers. Mrs. McFarland gingerly lifted the girl to prop a pillow up behind her. Then the older woman uttered something low and soothing.

"She's up now," Mrs. McFarland said, motioning Dearie forward.

When Louisa saw Dearie, a faint smile curved her pale lips. "Your name is Dearie."

It was like their first meeting, and Dearie could hardly stay her tears. "Yes, Louisa. I'm Dearie. Are you feeling better?"

Louisa nodded.

"I brought you some biscuits and blackberry jam. Remember when I gathered the blackberries? Colleen made them into jam."

Louisa's gray eyes were blank, but her soft smile still played at her mouth.

Mrs. McFarland brought a plate for the biscuits. "She don't eat much. Don't have much interest in it."

Dearie noticed the clean bed linen, and next to the pillows, some of the dolls Louisa had made, including the one she had made of Mrs. McFarland.

Dearie stayed for almost an hour. Although the child seemed distracted, Dearie was convinced that she was slowly recovering. As she put on her bonnet to leave, she turned to Mrs. McFarland.

"Louisa seems much improved, Mrs. McFarland."

The woman nodded. "She's gettin' on."

"Won't be long until she's out and about again."

Mrs. McFarland frowned. "It'll be a while, yet."

Dearie nodded, reflectively. "It'll be a shame to see her go back to living in the woods."

Mrs. McFarland looked away. "I reckon she kin stay on here. If she's a mind to."

Dearie smiled. "That would be nice. Louisa needs a home."

Mrs. McFarland said nothing more, but Dearie thought that the older woman's expression had softened momentarily.

In the wagon on the way home, she thought about Louisa and the McFarlands. *Tavish is a wise man*, she thought proudly. *Louisa has a family to take care of her, and the McFarlands have a daughter to replace the one they lost. I wonder if he knew . . .*

Calvin came by again and brought two slaves, Temperance and Bess, to help with the chores. The older woman, called Tempie, soon took over the kitchen, while her daughter Bess, who was only ten, did odd jobs inside and out.

"Tempie can cook like an angel," Calvin remarked with a sigh of appreciation.

"Oh, Master Cal," Tempie pursed her lips, "you always did like my cookin' better than anybody."

"Surely you didn't bring her from Rosalie?" Dearie asked.

"Oh, no. Tavish asked me to buy her. She belonged to a neighbor who recently died. The widow is moving in with her sister who has no room for extra servants."

"How thoughtful of Tavish," Dearie smiled.

Calvin smiled, too. Tavish had not exactly asked him to buy the two servants. He had taken it upon himself to do it for his friend. Dearie and Colleen needed help, after all.

"If the weather holds, I'll send my men over to clear the fields. Tavish won't recognize the place when he returns."

Even as he said the words, Calvin hoped that he was doing the right thing. Tavish might very well resent his help.

Well, I'll deal with that later, he told himself.

He looked to Colleen for a reassuring smile, but the girl had disappeared again. Why was she never around when he came to visit? He had begun to believe that she didn't like him. *A girl as pretty as she probably has a beau*, he thought with a sigh of disappointment.

Tempie and Bess quickly settled into the routine at Beauvais, leaving Dearie and Colleen with much more time. While Colleen once again applied herself to her needlework, Dearie consulted Gales's North Carolina Almanac. She was fascinated by John Beasley's calculations. He predicted the weather, the cycles of the moon, and the eclipses.

"It's not hard to understand why people hereabouts are so superstitious, with only this to go by," Dearie remarked to Calvin.

"But it is sometimes very accurate," Calvin said. "I use it myself. I have seen too many cases where people ignored the lunar cycle and ended up with a poor crop."

"Not you, too, Calvin," Dearie sighed. "I would think that since you have been to the university, you would not be superstitious."

"Not superstitious, just careful," he laughed. "And," he raised his eyebrows emphatically, "my crops have always been good."

As Dearie read the almanac, she began to understand a little why her neighbors felt as they did. Their lives depended on the land. Were they to lose a crop, they could not easily afford to wait until another year when the weather was more favorable. In fact, she learned more about her neighbors by reading the almanac than she could have if she'd lived for years in North Carolina.

Dearie continued to visit Louisa every week. The girl steadily improved, and had begun to help Mrs. McFarland around the house. Dearie noticed that the young girl had changed. Her wild look had vanished, and she wore a peaceful expression of acceptance as she busied herself around the tiny kitchen. She wore a clean apron over a new calico dress, and her white-blond hair was twisted neatly into a braided coil at her neck.

Although Louisa's recovery was amazing, the really astounding change was in Mrs. McFarland. Whereas she had been suspicious and withdrawn, she now opened the door without hesitation when Dearie arrived. She didn't smile, but in her eyes was a warmth Dearie had never seen before. The day Mrs. McFarland made a social overture, Dearie was so delighted she had to bite her lip to keep from giggling.

They were sampling some jelly cakes Louisa had made when Mrs. McFarland turned to Dearie. "We'll be having a quilting bee here Thursday next. We'd be obliged if you'd come, Mrs. McLeod."

Dearie was glad the older woman looked away immediately, for she was sure she hadn't disguised the surprise she felt.

"We've been 'apromising Louisa since she's been feeling better that we'd have one. So it's set."

Dearie put her hand lightly on Mrs. McFarland's arm. "Thank you for inviting me. I'd be delighted to attend."

Louisa clapped her hands in happiness. "Oh, Dearie! It will be so lovely. We've invited all the ladies hereabouts."

Dearie left for home filled to overflowing with anticipation. *Tavish will be so proud of me*, she thought. *And when I show him the lovely quilt I've made with Mrs. McFarland's help, he'll see how well I've adjusted here!*

Then she caught her breath. *Oh, my goodness! Whatever will I do? I've never sewn a single thing in all my life, and I have certainly never quilted!*

But she assured herself that Colleen would teach her. After all, she had a whole week to learn.

Chapter Thirteen

The McFarlands' small cottage had been completely transformed. All the furniture had been moved to accommodate two long tables. Ten women were already situated around them working industriously when Dearie arrived.

Taking a seat next to an elderly lady, Dearie took out her thimble and needle. Her companion did not look up, but continued to sew diligently. Out of the corner of her eye, Dearie watched her, trying to learn the stitches. With painstaking slowness, Dearie threaded her needle and began.

This is not so difficult, Dearie thought. *Perhaps I can have a party of my own one day.*

Several other women sat down near Dearie. One put a snuff box in the middle of the table. Presently, the box was passed around. Dearie observed each of the quilters withdraw a snuff stick from her pocket and dip it in the box. Then, to her surprise, they plopped the snuff sticks in their mouths and continued to sew.

How strange, Dearie mused. *North Carolina is full of unusual customs.*

The box moved around the table and finally came to rest in front of Dearie. For a while, she ignored it. Then her elderly companion poked her in the ribs.

"I got an extry if y'want it," she said, retrieving a stick from her pocket.

Dearie started to protest, but feeling the eyes of the other women upon her, she flushed bright red.

"Thank you," she said, taking the stick.

Tentatively, she dipped the blackened stick into the snuff box. Smiling bravely, she put the stick in her mouth. Immediately, a wave of nausea swept over her, and she looked around her in panic. Still smiling, she rose and left the room.

Finding a secluded place away from the dogs, Dearie spat out the vile powder, coughing and retching at the same time. She turned to find Mrs. McFarland at her side.

"Dipping snuff ain't fer everybody," she said, handing Dearie a dipper of water. "Don't care for it myself."

Dearie accepted the water gratefully. She studied her hostess over the rim of the dipper. The look in the older woman's eyes was almost kindly.

"Thank you," Dearie said.

The rest of the quilting bee passed without incident. At the day's end, the quilt was finished, and the women gathered their utensils into baskets. Dearie noticed that many of their faces were smeared with snuff.

Lousia hugged Dearie as she prepared to leave. The child had completely recovered. Mrs. McFarland joined Louisa and put her arm around the girl.

"I'm obliged to you for coming, Mrs. McLeod."

Dearie smiled. "I've never been to a quilting bee. I enjoyed it."

Mrs. McFarland nodded, as did the other women when they passed. The unfriendly looks were gone and Dearie was glad. She would never be a seamstress, but she had contributed her share. More importantly, the women accepted her now. She had earned their respect.

Dearie thought of Tavish. he had said that she did not understand rural folk, but he was wrong. She did understand, and for the first time she felt at home in her new life. She knew he would be pleased.

Tavish thought of Dearie as he boarded the stage bound for Philadelphia. He was sure she must be unhappy here in North Carolina. It was so different from what she had known. She was meant for fine clothes, afternoon teas, and balls. Now all her finery was stowed away in trunks, and she wore muslins and poke bonnets instead. He grimaced and shook his head. She would have wanted to go with him to Philadelphia. And so she would, in the spring. But now he had to face Matthew Grayson again . . . alone.

Having sent the grain to market, Tavish now had to collect the balance of the bills. With this money he would buy manufactured goods for the winter, and more seed for the spring planting. In addition, he sought to establish new markets for the new clients he would have come spring. He planned to repair the dilapidated warehouse behind the office, and purchase several wagons to transport grain to the Cape Fear River. Since he had already used most of the money in Dearie's dowry, he hoped to convince Matthew Grayson to contribute more money toward the venture, as the factoring business was already realizing a profit. Tavish was loath to report the full extent of the business profits to Grayson, since he would then expect a much larger share each month. So he'd adjusted the figures to reflect a small but steady margin of growth.

The leaves were beginning to turn by the time Tavish reached Philadelphia. Inclement weather delayed him on the road for days at a time. Dirt-stained and with a week's growth of beard, Tavish arrived at Alistair Monroe's door.

"Is that you, Tavish?" Alistair surveyed his cousin disdainfully. "This will never do, Cousin. I am having a soiree this evening and you must attend." He cocked his eyebrow. "After all, your father-in-law will be in attendance."

Tavish frowned. He hadn't expected to face Grayson so soon. But he said, "Of course I will attend."

The Monroe house at Sixth and Chestnut was made of brick with a double front, two stories high, and a hipped roof. Although it was not large, it had the appearance of time-worn stability, as though it had been there since the founding of the city.

Once a month, the parlor doors were thrown open to a large sitting room, and the chairs were pushed back against the walls. A mouth-watering buffet was spread over a large walnut table, and guests passed freely through the rooms. On this evening, an accomplished violinist was accompanied by a pianist in one corner of the parlor.

Tavish was already sampling a plate of food when Matthew Grayson entered the room. The older man wore a brocade coat over a green silk waistcoat and white trousers. His dress was as gaudy as the plumage of a large parrot, Tavish observed. Matthew Grayson obviously enjoyed exhibiting his wealth.

After paying his respects to Alistair, Grayson strode over to Tavish.

"I heard you were back in the city." Grayson's expression held no trace of a smile. "I have received only three reports since your departure. Can you tell me why, sir?"

Tavish smiled evenly. "Business has been slow. There has been little to report. But I have brought you the returns for the last several months. I think that you will be pleased with the progress."

Grayson took a glass of punch from the table. His eyes never left Tavish's face. "I gather that Dearie is well. Her letters contain glowing accolades of the plantation and life in North Carolina. Frankly, I find it hard to believe that she is so happy. However, I suppose the prospect of having a baby has overshadowed all else."

Tavish felt a jolt of surprise. Dearie had not told her father about losing the baby. Why? he wondered.

"She is well, isn't she?" Grayson asked, trying to interpret his son-in-law's sudden change of expression.

"Yes," Tavish replied truthfully. "She is."

"I shall plan a visit come spring. When Dearie is up and about again." Tavish nodded. No doubt Matthew Grayson would see his daughter back home before he ever left for North Carolina.

"Tomorrow I shall expect to see you in my offices at nine o'clock. Good evening, Master Tavish." With a curt nod, Grayson moved back through the crowd.

Tavish was ushered into offices as plush as any he had ever seen. Grayson sat behind a carved wooden desk like a magistrate. He looked up with an irritated look when Tavish entered, as if a servant had disturbed him at his work. He motioned Tavish to a seat opposite him.

"I have brought reports from the factoring business." Tavish handed his father-in-law a sheaf of papers.

Grayson studied them for a moment without comment.

Tavish cleared his throat. "As you see, the figures indicate a steady margin of profit."

Grayson looked up, arching a silver eyebrow.

"As I am talking with clients weekly," Tavish went on, "I am confident that the business will continue to expand. With this in mind, I believe that we should repair the warehouse in back of the office — "

"We?"

"Well, I had supposed, after looking at the figures, that you would want to expand. At present, we have only limited space in which to house the grain before market.

And to cut our expenses further, it would be prudent to purchase wagons to transport the gain to the river."

Grayson gazed at Tavish stonily. "You have funds at your disposal, I believe."

Drops of perspiration were beginning to form on Tavish's forehead. "Much of the money has gone toward building up the business."

"Much of the money?"

"Almost all of it."

Grayson laid the papers down on his desk and folded his hands on top of it. "Then you have very little to show for it."

Tavish hated Grayson more than ever now. Of course there was money left. But he didn't want to use it. It was money Murdock had paid for with his life. Tavish swallowed his anger and faced Grayson with an expression equally as cold. "Of course, Master Grayson, the decision is entirely yours, as is the business. I have done my best to make it profitable again. I only thought that if these improvements were made, rapid growth would be possible. It is sound business practice to — "

"It is not sound business practice to pour money down a rathole." Grayson cut him off sharply. His blue eyes narrowed. "How do you account for the slow progress? Only recently I heard the crops have been good this year."

"The people there are slow to change. Many of the planters had factors in Wilmington, and small farmers traded their goods with the storekeeper. It's been a struggle to win them over."

"I see." Matthew Grayson made a steeple of his fingers. "Dearie writes me that the plantation is doing well. That should be your mainstay. I had thought that the factoring business might tide you over if you needed extra funds. Since you do not, 'tis of no consequence. But I'll not put another penny in it until I see real progress." He smiled genially. "Enjoy your stay in Philadelphia, and give Dearie my love. Good day, sir."

Tavish saw that he had been dismissed summarily, as Grayson returned his attention to the other papers on his desk. He rose abruptly, turned on his heel, and left.

After Tavish left, Grayson picked up the reports again. Something was wrong. Unless Tavish had no head at all for business, the figures could not be correct. With the bountiful harvest this year, he would have had to turn clients away. He shook his head. The young man was obviously skimming cream from the top. But why?

He would never begrudge his only daughter and her husband money if they were in need. They had only to ask. But according to Dearie, things were going well with the plantation. And now Tavish had come asking for more money.

Grayson frowned. More than ever, he was convinced that he had a scoundrel and a crook for a son-in-law. He would get to the bottom of this regardless of Dearie's feelings. It was a matter of principle.

On the first of October, Calvin arrived with twenty slaves to clear the fields of Beauvais. While the men worked, Calvin sat in the parlor with Dearie. They discussed crops and planting, fertilizers and irrigation.

As she sewed by the fire, Colleen watched them furtively. Every time she saw Calvin, her heart wrenched within her bosom. She couldn't explain her feelings even to herself. She hardly knew the man, after all. But there was something about the look in his eyes when he did notice her. It was a sparkle . . . a light that touched her very soul. Then, when he turned his attention back to Dearie, she was devastated, as if the sun had left the sky. She pricked her finger with the needle.

"Tarnation," she said out loud.

Calvin looked over at her and smiled briefly. Colleen swept up her sewing basket and left the room.

Calvin's smile faded as he watched Colleen leave. He forced his attention back to Dearie. "You'll need at least twenty-five men," he told her. "We can rotate the men from Rosalie, or else we can hire free blacks."

Dearie frowned. "What will Tavish say?"

"I'm sure he would agree," Calvin assured her. Someone had to see after these women while Tavish was gone. The Lord only knew when he would return, and winter was almost here. Tavish was working hard, Calvin knew. At least he could help his friend this much.

Dearie could not help thinking about Tavish. He had been gone for over a month now. She often wondered if he preferred to be away. Then she chided herself roundly. Of course he would want to be home if he could.

"I'll be happy to take care of the matter for you," Calvin was saying.

Dearie nodded absently. "Do what you think best, Calvin."

One afternoon, Calvin sent a note inviting the ladies to Rosalie for Sunday dinner. Dearie immediately accepted the invitation and set about deciding what she should wear. She decided upon a gown of sapphire-blue taffeta and a cashmere shawl.

"Now, Colleen. We must find something for you to wear."

Colleen shook her head. "No, miss. I'm not feeling well. Me head's pounding like a drum."

"But Calvin specifically requested that you attend!"

"He did?"

"Yes. Now I'm sure you'll feel better once you have on a lovely frock and your hair is done up."

Dearie looked like a queen, Colleen decided. Her heart sank even lower. She could not compete with her mistress, and she had no will to try. "No, miss. I'll not be going today. But give my regards to . . . Master Calvin."

Dearie was growing worried about Colleen. In the past few months, the little maid had lost weight, and her mood was always somber. Many times she had excused herself to go to bed, when it was not yet even dark.

Dearie concluded that Colleen was ailing, and should see a doctor. She resolved to take her to town the following week.

Rosalie was set back from the tree-lined road, across a large expanse of green grass. A great columned porch fronted the house of whitewashed brick. Behind the house stretched well-tended fields bordered by rail fences. Dearie was astounded at the pristine beauty of the house and grounds. Rosalie was exactly as she had envisioned a plantation would be.

A black butler greeted Dearie at the door and led her to a large parlor off the main hallway. Another couple was seated on a couch across from Calvin. The gentlemen rose immediately as Dearie entered.

Calvin rushed to greet her, taking her hand in his. Then his eyes looked beyond her, as if he were waiting for someone else. "Miss Colleen . . . ?"

"I'm sorry, Calvin. She wasn't feeling well."

Calvin quickly masked his feelings and escorted Dearie across the room. "It is time you met another of Tavish's friends. Dearie McLeod, allow me to introduce Duncan and India McNeill."

Dearie said hello to the handsome couple. Duncan was tall with auburn hair and flashing green eyes, and his wife, India, was a striking woman with black hair and deep blue, almost violet, eyes.

India smiled warmly. "I'm so sorry we haven't called on you before, Dearie. India looked at her husband guiltily. You see, we didn't know . . . "

"Tavish was keeping you a secret," Duncan grinned. "And I can certainly see why."

India raised an eyebrow in mock-jealousy, but he squeezed her arm affectionately. "Calvin told us that Tavish had married, and we demanded to meet you," India continued.

"I'm very glad to meet you both. I'm only sorry that Tavish cannot be here," Dearie said, dropping her eyes.

There was an awkward moment until Calvin clapped his hands together. "Well, now that we're all friends, let's see what the cook has in store for us tonight."

Dinner was a sumptuous repast of chicken and dumplings, with stewed apples and corn. While they ate, Duncan and Calvin joked about problems they'd had during planting season. Then Duncan entertained them all with several anecdotes about their Scottish ancestors.

"Remember the one Murdock used to tell about the farmer who gave his soul to the devil?"

"I don't remember. Tell it again, Duncan," Calvin urged him.

"Well, as Murdock told it, 'twas a hot and dusty day. And the devil, looking for another soul, happened upon a farmer who had a whole field to clear.

Says the devil, 'I'll clear your field for you if you give me your soul.'

The farmer saw he was dealing with the devil, but told him to go ahead anyway. The devil worked quickly, clearing the stumps and broomsedge from the field in half the time. When he was through, he came up and demanded the farmer's soul.

The farmer took out his knife and cut the sole off the bottom of his shoe, and handed it to the devil.

Well, the devil was hoppin' mad and went off acursin'. 'I might have known I'd get a Scotsman,' he cried as he disappeared."

Everybody laughed, including Dearie.

"I suppose you've heard all these stories from Tavish," Duncan said, smiling.

Dearie shook her head. "Actually, Tavish has told me very little about his family."

"That's like Tavish," Calvin commented.

"But surely," Duncan persisted, "he told you stories about Murdock . . . "

Dearie was puzzled. "Who is Murdock?"

They all exchanged glances. "Murdock was Tavish's father," Calvin told her.

Dearie sighed. "No, I'm afraid I haven't heard about him."

Although Dearie enjoyed the dinner, she came away from Rosalie with the growing fear that she really knew very little about her husband. She had been married for six months, but she had hardly seen Tavish, and she could not understand why. She was almost jealous of the relationship that Duncan and India shared. Obviously, they shared many common interests, including the management of their large plantation, Greenhill.

"Please come and visit Greenhill," they had said.

But the thought of visiting them and their children only made Dearie sad. She longed for a life such as theirs. If only Tavish would return!

Dearie returned to Beauvais later that evening with a heavy heart. She fell into a troubled sleep that left her tired and wan the next morning.

When she appeared for breakfast, she was surprised to find Colleen sitting by the fire, dressed in her best traveling suit. Next to her feet was a leather valise.

"Colleen! What's happened!"

Colleen looked up, wearing a look of discomfort. "Well, miss, I've been meaning to tell you. I'm aimin' to go back to Philadelphia. Now that you've got help, I don't feel so bad about leaving."

"Leaving! But, Colleen, why? I thought you liked it here in North Carolina. You said . . . it reminded you of Scotland." Tears sprang to Dearie's eyes.

Colleen looked away. "Yes, it does. But I've had a hankering to open a millinery shop. There's naught for me to do here, Miss Dearie."

Dearie rushed to the little maid and threw her arms around her. "Oh, Colleen, please don't leave! I can't bear it. What will I do?"

Now Colleen was sobbing too. "I . . . Miss Dearie. I haven't been meself lately, and I think the change would do me good." The little maid shook her head sadly.

Dearie could see that she was determined to go. "But why Philadelphia? Why not open a shop in Fayetteville? Then I could visit you."

"Oh, miss. I know nothing about Fayetteville."

"You know even less about Philadelphia, Colleen."

"Well, that's true."

Dearie saw that Colleen was wavering, and she pressed her advantage. "After all, we have met people here. There's no shop in town, and I for one would be happy to see one. I'm sure the other ladies would agree."

"Well, I don't know," Colleen said.

"Colleen, tomorrow we'll go into town and see if there is a suitable place for a shop. If not, I'll pay your passage back to Philadelphia. Do you agree?"

The little maid nodded tiredly. Perhaps Dearie was right, but she hoped she'd never see Calvin Buie again. He was in love with Dearie, and she had to forget him. However, the chances were slim that he would come to her shop. Men seldom frequented millinery establishments.

"Colleen? What do you say?"

Colleen managed a weak smile. She hated the thought of leaving Dearie. She'd become like a sister. Perhaps opening a shop in Fayetteville was the answer. "All right, Miss Dearie. It wouldn't hurt to have a look."

Dearie breathed a sigh of relief. She had promised to help Colleen establish herself in a shop when the time came. However, the time had come much sooner than she had expected. She only knew that she could not lose her one friend. Not now, when she needed her most.

Chapter Fourteen

Dearie accompanied Colleen to Fayetteville the following week. The storekeeper, Mr. Duffy, referred them to a small building which belonged to an attorney, Charles Atwood.

Mr. Atwood's office was on the second floor, and he was interested in renting the first floor. The building was small, but ideally located next to the bank, and the space available had several large windows and a back room for storage.

"It's absolutely perfect, Colleen," Dearie exclaimed.

Colleen agreed, but when Mr. Atwood quoted his price, she frowned. "I'll not get the shop. 'Twouldn't be right. Your father gave me a year's wage, and I've stayed but six months. I had intended to give half back, but I'd need it to buy merchandise and pay the rent."

"Nonsense, Colleen. I'll not hear of it. You've earned twice your wage. After all, you saved my life after the accident. Had it not been for you, I might have . . . might have . . . " Dearie's eyes filled with tears at the memory.

Colleen rushed to Dearie and hugged her warmly. "There, there, Miss Dearie. I won't have you crying."

"I just want you to be happy, Colleen."

Looking around the small space, Colleen's eyes brightened, and a flush touched her cheeks for the first time in weeks. "I am happy, miss. I never thought my dream would really come true."

Thank goodness, Dearie thought. *The change has already done her good.*

Colleen worked feverishly to ready things for her shop. While a sign was being painted, she cleaned the rooms until they sparkled. She ordered fashion plates from New York, and fabric, bonnets, millinery supplies, and boxes from Raleigh and Charleston. Then, with what supplies she could purchase in Fayetteville, she set about making gloves, reticules, and shawls.

Soon lace curtains were drawn back to display bonnets and hats of all styles in the store window. There were leghorn hats decorated with strips of plaid silk, carriage hats made of striped gauze or crepe, and straw bonnets trimmed with lilac ribbons. She had walking bonnets of silk decorated with chenille or velvet flowers, dress hats for the evening, and black velvet hats trimmed with feathers. In addition, she had racks of dresses, shawls, reticules, and gloves, many of which she had fashioned herself.

When the store was ready for business, Colleen was pleased with her inventory and anxious to open. There was nothing like it in Fayetteville. With Dearie's help, Colleen composed an announcement to be printed in the newspaper.

Miss McCurdie announces the opening of a millinery shop in Fayetteville. She has satin and silk bonnets of the latest fashion, Leghorn bonnets, plain and open-work straw bonnets, Ruffs and Turbans; shawls of muslin or silk; Ladies' kid gloves or lined gloves, hand-worked; band boxes by the dozen, or single ones. There will a good and general assortment of millinery and dresses of the newest fashion, the proprietress having weekly correspondence with New York.

Dearie was there on opening day. When at least ten ladies stood waiting outside for the store to open, she was as excited as Colleen. There were loud exclamations of appreciation as the women seized upon a bonnet or a pair of delicately worked gloves.

As the day wore on, and more women filed in, Colleen began to wonder if she had ordered enough merchandise. Already she had sold six bonnets, and orders had been placed for five more. In addition, she had been commissioned to sew a wedding dress for the following month.

"My dear," one matron took Colleen aside, "you don't know what you've done for the ladies of this town. We've had to order from catalogues, or go to Raleigh to buy fine things. I had thought of opening a shop myself, but my needlework does not begin to compare to yours."

Colleen beamed with the praise. Dearie had never seen her friend so happy.

"I see I shall have to come to town more often, Colleen." Dearie hugged her. "You won't be able to get away."

Dimples indented Colleen's cheeks. "Of course I will, Miss Dearie."

Dearie touched her arm. "It's just 'Dearie' now, Colleen."

The little shop flourished. The location proved to be a godsend. Many of the ladies made a habit of dropping by while their husbands were at the bank. Colleen was so busy that she had no time to reflect upon her feelings for Calvin Buie, until one afternoon three weeks after the shop opened.

Colleen was sewing in the back room when two women entered the shop. The women browsed for a while, and were deep in conversation when Colleen appeared. Colleen frowned, immediately recognizing the dark-haired Georganna Arms.

"Georganna, you are not getting younger. You can't wait forever," her companion was saying.

Georganna placed a bonnet on her head, and turned to survey her appearance in the glass. "I don't intend to. I plan to be married in the spring. Perhaps I'll be a June bride." She pursed her lips in the mirror. "Tavish has told me that the marriage was one of convenience only. He expects to have it annulled as soon as he returns. Of course you know what that means?" Georganna shot her friend a meaningful look.

"No, tell! Will you marry Tavish?"

"Certainly! Why else would he seek an annulment? He says she is young and naive. A man like Tavish could only be happy with a real woman. I know that for a fact." She pinched her cheeks to bring color to her pale skin.

"But what will the poor girl do?"

"Poor girl, indeed. I hear that she has money and a lot of it. She'll go home to her family, I expect."

"So Tavish has proposed, then?" her friend inquired.

Georganna whirled around quickly. "You know that it would be improper for him to propose while he is still married. But he will. I'll see to that."

Colleen cleared her throat and the ladies looked around. "May I help you?" She tried desperately to be civil. After all, the women were customers. But she had despised Georganna Arms since the day she had seen her walking with Tavish.

"I'm interested in a walking bonnet," Georganna said.

"Of course. These hats are really for the evening," Colleen told her. "I wouldn't imagine you'd want anything so dressy for the day."

"Oh, I don't know. I do love to dress up."

Georganna picked up a hat that Colleen had intended to redo. It was crimson velvet and garishly decorated with rose-colored feathers. Georganna set it jauntily on top of her head and fluffed out the curls along her forehead.

"It certainly is colorful, Georganna," her friend commented.

Colleen thought that it looked like a red rooster perched on the girl's dark head. "I can change the feathers. I have some dark green. They're all the rage — "

"No, I like the rose. I just know Tavish will like them, don't you, Charlotte?"

Colleen bristled at Georganna's audacity. For a moment, she considered telling the woman exactly what she thought of her. But then she thought better of it, she would do no good that way. "It's charming, miss," she said, certain that Tavish would hate the bonnet.

After Georganna left, Colleen was lost in thought. Certainly Dearie should know what Georganna had in mind. But the news would break her heart! What if it were true, and Tavish did plan to seek an annulment? What would Dearie do? Colleen felt sure that she would not go back to Philadelphia — not now.

Suddenly the face of Calvin Buie came into her thoughts. If Dearie were free, wouldn't Calvin ask for her hand? Then she would be mistress of Rosalie plantation, and have no worries at all. Colleen's heart sank. Until now, she had never considered that Dearie might one day be free to marry Calvin. The very idea left her shaken.

She spent the rest of the day trying to convince herself of why she should not tell Dearie about Georganna. Eventually she concluded that the information, all hearsay, would devastate her former mistress. She, Colleen, had no right to infer that Tavish really intended to annul their marriage. It might well be only the wishful thinking of a jealous rival. Having convinced herself that she was doing the right thing, Colleen had to admit her own selfish interest. She still cherished the small hope that Calvin would someday see he had chosen the wrong woman. She needed time — all the time she could manage.

Somewhat satisfied with her decision, Colleen returned her attention to business. She thought no more about the matter until Dearie rushed in one day, her face flushed with pleasure.

"Oh, Colleen. I must have a new dress! Calvin is giving a ball, and since Tavish is away, he has invited me to be his hostess."

Dearie was too excited to see Colleen's mouth drop open in amazement. Colleen turned quickly away so that Dearie couldn't see her expression. "I have just got some new materials in, miss, and some plates from New York. You can browse through the plates while I get the dress materials."

Dearie leafed happily through the plates, never suspecting that Colleen had gone into the back room to get control over her emotions. She was happier than she had been since she left Philadelphia. She was going to a ball!

Colleen, on the other hand was miserable. She splashed cold water on her face, but she still felt overheated. After a few minutes, she gathered up some bolts of material and retraced her steps.

"Calvin is such a nice man, Colleen. He would make a wonderful husband, I just know — "

The colorful bolts of material fell loudly to the floor. Bending down to recover them, Colleen could not stay her tears.

"Colleen! Here, let me help you." Dearie knelt down beside her. "But you are crying! Have I said something to upset you?"

Colleen shook her head, dark ringlets framing her small face. "No, miss. It's just me nerves again, what with all that's going on."

"And I thought those spells had passed since you left the plantation."

"Well, they have. But every once in a while . . . "

"Colleen, can I help in any way?" Dearie grasped her hand. "I can leave the plantation for a while and help you here. I want to see you get a good start."

Colleen regained her composure and began stacking the bolts on the table beside Dearie. "No, Dearie, I'm fine. Here, let's take a look at these plates. Fashioning a dress always cheers me."

Dearie thought about Colleen on the way back to Beauvais. She acted almost lovesick. That must be it! Colleen had a beau! Dearie clapped her hands together. For a moment Dearie wondered if it was Calvin, but then she shook her head. No, if that was true, Colleen would have told her, she was certain. Then who could it be? Perhaps the girl had met a gentleman since her move to town. Dearie knew that Mr. Atwood was a widower, but he was almost old enough to be Colleen's father.

On subsequent visits, Dearie watched Colleen closely. However, the girl was a model of perfect composure. *Perhaps I was wrong*, Dearie thought. But time would tell.

At Dearie's last fitting, however, Colleen was strangely withdrawn. Colleen had designed a magnificent ballgown for Dearie. The gown was tulle, over white satin, trimmed with full-blown red satin roses.

"It is a work of art, Colleen," Dearie cried twirling about the shop. "I shall outshine every woman at the ball."

"That you will, miss. I've made a few of the dresses meself. And this is my favorite." Her small mouth tightened into a straight line. "I wish . . . "

"What do you wish?" Dearie returned quickly to her side. Colleen shook her head.

"It's nothing, Miss Dearie. I was only daydreaming. Now turn around and let me finish the back." She put pins in her mouth as Dearie obeyed.

"Honestly, a body would think you were in love the way your mood changes, Colleen. One moment you're gay and happy, then the next you've tears in your eyes."

Colleen almost swallowed a mouthful of pins. "Why, no! I . . ."

Dearie studied her friend closely. Colleen's discomfort was obvious.

"I don't believe you. Look at your hands! They're shaking. Who is it? Mr. Atwood?"

"Heavens no!" was Colleen's outraged reply. "He's old enough to be me father!"

"You must tell," Dearie implored, grasping her arm. Colleen looked away quickly. "There was someone. But it's over now. He's in love with someone else."

"Ah, I'm sorry, Colleen," Dearie said, feeling for her friend.

The night of the ball was crisp and clear — like the night she had met Tavish, Dearie reflected on the way to Rosalie. She remembered having opened her casement window and seen the moon glancing off the cobblestone streets. But here, the moon shone down on a road cut through a thick pine forest, and the air was sweet and clean. How different things were now!

The festivities were to be held in the plantation dining room. When Dearie arrived, Duncan and India McNeill were busily attending to the musicians and refreshments. India embraced Dearie warmly.

"You look lovely, Dearie. We're so sorry Tavish couldn't come."

India wore a gown of violet satin that matched the blue violet of her eyes. *What a striking woman*, Dearie thought.

In a moment Duncan joined them. Gallantly, he kissed Dearie's hand, then placed a proprietary arm around his wife's waist.

"Tavish has been gone too long, I'm thinking. You know the saying about all work and no play," he grinned.

Dearie studied her ivory fan. "Yes, I agree with you. But I don't know if Tavish has heard that saying!"

"We'll remind him when he gets back," Calvin said, joining the group.

Dearie smiled up at him, marveling at his height. He looked every inch the successful planter, in his claret velvet coat and striped breeches.

"Everything is ready, Calvin," Duncan told him. "The musicians await your signal."

Calvin held out his arm to Dearie. "Then let's open the ball."

The dining room was already filled with guests. Dearie hadn't realized the room was so large. Without furniture, there was ample space for musicians and dancers. It was gaily decorated with huge floral wreaths, and yellow ribbons swung from the enormous chandelier to the four corners. When Calvin nodded, the musicians began playing a waltz.

For a moment, Dearie was transported back in time. She remembered when she had first seen Tavish. "Will you dance?" he had asked. She closed her eyes. How she wished he was here!

"May I have this dance?"

Calvin touched her arm and Dearie was jolted out of her reverie. "Certainly," she said.

She glided into Calvin's arms, but the tall, lanky man felt different from Tavish. They bobbed up and down in an awkward fashion, for Calvin was no dancer. Hating to dampen his enthusiasm, Dearie only smiled when he stepped down heavily on her white satin slipper. More than ever she longed to be in her husband's arms.

"I love dancing," Calvin told her, breathless with exertion.

"I can see that you do." Dearie laughed. She silently prayed that he would be too busy greeting guests to dance every dance.

Dearie joined Calvin at the doorway. Each time another couple entered, Calvin introduced her as Mrs. McLeod, causing several eyebrows to rise in question. "I didn't realize Tavish had married," one woman commented.

"I must chastise Tavish when I see him next," Dr. Prescott said. "He's been keeping you a secret, my dear." He patted her hand in a friendly fashion.

Dearie was puzzled. Why hadn't Tavish told anyone he was married? A cold feeling of dread crept over her. Perhaps he didn't wish to acknowledge her!

Halfway through the evening, Georganna Arms appeared with another planter, Owen McKay. He was a widower, and some years older than Georganna.

"Good evening, Georganna," Calvin said stiffly. "I'm delighted that you could come."

Georganna smiled sweetly. "Well, my invitation must have been lost, Calvin. In any case, Owen received one." She rested her hand on the older man's sleeve.

Georganna's full breasts were clearly visible in her low-cut bodice. Her gown of nile green silk had a broad sash of striped ribbon. Dearie recognized Colleen's handiwork in the expert design of the dress, and felt somehow betrayed.

"What a lovely dress." Dearie's smile was strained.

"Why, thank you. I had it made especially for the ball."

"Have you met Mrs. McLeod, Georganna?" Calvin asked.

Georganna nodded primly, as did her escort. "I'm glad to make your acquaintance at last, Mrs. McLeod," she said. Then the aging planter ushered her onto the dance floor.

Dearie watched the saucy brunette waltz away. Georganna smiled and waved to all the men as she danced. She was the same woman who had tied the scarf around Tavish's neck at the Fourth of July celebrations with such a proprietary air. Dearie decided that she disliked the girl immensely.

"I wish she hadn't come," Calvin said.

Dearie agreed wholeheartedly, but she said nothing.

Calvin had no talent for dancing, but he was a perfect host. It was clear that everyone liked him. Several older matrons fussed about him while their husbands drank brandy in the parlor.

"Why is it that some pretty thing has not caught you," one lady asked.

Calvin sighed. "I don't know. I've been available."

"For too long," another added.

"Yes, it's high time you married, Calvin. You'll get too set in your ways." The ladies nodded at each other sagely.

"The ladies are right," Dearie told him later. "You should marry, Calvin. Surely someone has taken your fancy."

Calvin looked away. "Well, I did take a liking to someone . . . but she was not of the same mind."

"Ah, I'm sorry, Calvin," Dearie said. Later she realized the she had recently said the same thing to Colleen. What a shame that both her friends should have loved and lost.

Dearie enjoyed the evening until Georganna Arms accosted her at the refreshment table.

"I understand that you'll be leaving us soon, Mrs. McLeod." Georganna had emphasized the "Mrs." in her name, and she wore a sly smile.

"Perhaps you misunderstood. I've only just arrived here in North Carolina."

Georganna gave her a knowing look. "Well, it can't be nearly so civilized as Philadelphia."

"How did you know I was from Philadelphia?" Dearie asked evenly, studying her adversary over the rim of her punch cup.

"Tavish told me."

"Oh?"

"Yes. And he said that you'll be returning to Philadelphia in the spring." Dearie's face flushed bright pink. "Well, I'm sorry to disappoint you, Miss . . . "

"Arms."

"Miss Arms. But I am not leaving North Carolina."

Georganna's full lips curved into cold smile. "Don't be sorry. It's not me you've disappointed, Mrs. McLeod." She tossed her dark curls and flounced away.

Dearie set down her cup, her hand shaking. The woman had the gall to insinuate that Tavish intended to. . . . Suddenly, she was very frightened. Had Tavish really told Georganna that his wife would leave in the spring? There was no doubt that he knew the woman possibly quite well. Did he really plan to send her back to Philadelphia? Is that why he had told no one of their marriage? Dearie's heart beat so loudly she thought that someone would surely hear. Her thoughts raced ahead wildly. And if Tavish sent her back, then what — an annulment?

No! No, I won't go! She balled her hands into small fists. *Our marriage has not even had a chance! If Tavish would stay with me for a while he would see.*

Georganna waltzed in front of Dearie and waved gaily as she passed. Joining Dearie, Calvin was alarmed at her expression.

"Dearie, is anything wrong?"

"Who *is* that woman, Calvin?" She nodded at Georganna.

"Well, she is the daughter of Gregory Arms, the blacksmith."

Dearie shook her head. "No, I mean how does she know Tavish?"

Calvin looked away, obviously flustered.

Dearie tugged at his sleeve. "Calvin, I must know. Please."

Calvin cleared his throat. "Well, Georganna and Tavish . . . uh, knew each other before . . . before Tavish met you, of course."

"How well?"

He laughed, embarrassed. "Dearie, it can't matter now, after all . . . "

"It does matter," she said, her mouth straightening into a determined line.

"It was no secret that Georganna planned to marry Tavish."

Dearie nodded grimly. "And she still does."

"What! But that's absurd!"

Dearie leveled a fiery blue gaze at Georganna. "Yes, it is absurd."

When Tavish returned she would speak to him of Georganna. Perhaps together they would pay a visit to the girl and set her thinking straight. Dearie breathed a sigh of relief at the thought.

Everything would be resolved . . . when Tavish returned.

Chapter Fifteen

"Tonight! Tonight is the night of all nights, Tavish! I will at long last see her. The lovely goddess haunts my dreams and colors my thoughts with her bright beauty. Sweet Helena! Have you ever seen a woman so fair?" Alistair was describing his latest lady love, the true queen of his heart. Sweet Helena, however, had many predecessors, all equally bright and beautiful. She was destined to join her sisters in the never-ending chronicle of love. For Alistair's affairs were doomed to failure since the objects of his affection were inevitably married. Alistair played a dangerous game, but by some miracle, he always managed to avoid detection.

He recounted his adventures to Tavish with a certain relish. He was like the highwayman who kept one step ahead of the king's guard. Tavish suspected that it was the risk involved that made the women so desirable to Alistair.

Since he was a dandy, the husbands generally did not take Alistair seriously. They thought nothing of leaving their wives in Alistair's keeping while they enjoyed a brandy with their friends. How surprised they would have been to find Alistair reciting a sonnet he had had composed, or even caressing one of their wives during a garden walk.

"Once I made love to Lady Braithmore in the parlor while her husband was conducting business in the library," Alistair confided to Tavish. "They were my houseguests for a fortnight last winter. Fortunately, her husband is quite long-winded. Ah, but she was a lovely creature ... almost as lovely as Sally Foxworth. I believe you met her at a soiree last spring. Now she was a real beauty, don't you think?"

Tavish endured Alistair's rambling by thinking of Dearie. Alistair's question brought him reluctantly back to the present. He smiled ruefully. "What?"

Alistair sighed impatiently. "Sally Foxworth? Do you not think her one of the most beautiful women you've ever seen?"

Tavish shrugged. He had no recollection of the woman, or for that matter of any other woman he had ever admired. Every face but Dearie's had been erased from his mind. Next to Dearie, all other women were pale and wan. Nothing could compare to the sky blue of her eyes, or the bright gold of her hair, the effervescence of her laughter. Dearie was undoubtedly the most beautiful woman he had ever seen.

"What a pity her husband took Sally away soon after we met."

"You have been very lucky, Alistair," Tavish told him.

Alistair shook his head. "But I am also irresistible. Sally moved away, and within a fortnight, Helena appeared to take her place."

Helena Merwin was the pampered wife of one of Philadelphia's leading merchants. Uriah Merwin was known to be hot-tempered and jealous. Rarely did he allow the lovely Helena out of his sight. On one of these rare occasions, Alistair was immediately on hand with a poem and a kiss. Bored with her older husband, Helena had encouraged Alistair. After several surreptitious meetings, he had fallen hopelessly in love.

"She has promised to steal away with me at the soiree tonight," Alistair sighed.

Tavish frowned. "Won't her husband be there with her?"

"Of course. We will be careful." Alistair arched his dark brows.

"Well, I wish you good luck. I must pack, for I will be leaving tomorrow."

"What! You are not coming with me? Tavish, this is the last soiree until the holidays. Surely, after all I've done for you . . . "

Tavish sighed with resignation. "All right, Cousin. I will come. But I think you play a dangerous game."

Alistair smiled smugly. "Yes, I do, don't I?"

The soiree was being held at the home of Horace Vandever, the father of Dearie's former suitor. They learned at the gathering that young Malcolm was away visiting friends.

Horace greeted them cordially at the double doors of his Georgian mansion. "Come in, Alistair and Master McLeod. Please make yourselves merry. We have much to eat and drink."

The parlor of the large house was already crowded with guests. Alistair had assured him that the elite of Philadelphia would be there. Tavish quickly scanned the faces for Matthew Grayson. After their last meeting, he had no wish to see his father-in-law again. But Grayson was not present. Tavish breathed a hearty sigh of relief.

Alistair waved gaily to Helena, who was standing close to her husband.

"Alistair," Tavish hissed under his breath. "What are you doing? She is with her husband."

Alistair pouted with exasperation. "Oh, don't be so stuffy. He isn't looking. See, his head is turned."

Frowning, Tavish followed his cousin into the room and took a brandy to steady his nerves. Tomorrow he would be on his way home, and this would all be a memory. He longed for the red clay of the North Carolina countryside and . . . Dearie.

The evening passed agreeably enough. Tavish managed to establish business contacts with another factor and several merchants. At half past ten many of the guests had begun to leave, but Alistair was nowhere to be found.

A quick look around the room told Tavish that Helena Merwin was also absent from the group. Her husband was deep in conversation with a banker in the corner of the room. Soon, Tavish realized, her absence would be noticed.

He took another brandy, sipping it as he observed the merchant from the corner of his eye. More guests left, women kissing and waving good-bye, men laughing loudly as they took their hats and coats. Tavish paced back and forth in front of the long buffet table. He had no idea what to do.

Horace Vandever strode up to Tavish. "Your cousin tells me you are a factor?"

Tavish smiled and thought of his father. At long last he could again claim the title. "Yes, he said. My office is at Fayetteville."

"In North Carolina?"

Tavish nodded. "I am here on business."

"And your lovely wife did not accompany you?"

"No, she . . . could not come."

Horace looked around him. "Where is your cousin, by the way? I've wanted to speak to him all evening."

Little beads of perspiration formed on Tavish's forehead. "I was just about to look for him. Perhaps he went for a walk in the garden."

Uriah Merwin had finished his conversation and was now looking around him, frowning.

"I'll see if I can find Alistair," he told Horace Vandever hastily." I'll tell him you'd like a word with him."

"Yes, do," Horace called after him, but Tavish was already striding through the French doors leading to the garden. He picked his way carefully over the uneven garden path. This time Alistair had gone too far.

"I must find my wife, Horace. Then we'll be off."

Tavish heard Merwin's voice behind him, and he quickened his pace. He must find Alistair first!

After a few minutes, Tavish spied a summerhouse in the distance. It was an obvious place for a tryst. He hastened to the house and opened the door, but all was dark and still. No one was there.

Angrily, Tavish shut the door and took another path. Halfway back to the house, he heard giggling. He stopped suddenly, trying to determine from where the laughter came.

"Oh, Alistair, I'm freezing! Listen, my teeth are chattering."

"Here, what luck to find these blankets. They must belong to the groom. Come closer, love. Ooh, that's more like it. Did I tell you your" — the words were muffled by giggles, "like rosebuds, so soft and tantalizing."

They were in a rose arbor some distance away, partially obscured by a row of evergreen bushes. Tavish hurried toward the sound and ran headlong into Uriah Merwin.

"Oh, Alistair! Kiss me again. I don't feel cold anymore," Helena giggled.

Shoving Tavish aside, Merwin bellowed like a charging bull and crashed through the bushes. He parted the foliage with one swipe of his beefy arm. Plunging into the arbor, he emerged minutes later, carrying his shocked wife. Alistair followed, an abashed look on his aristocratic face.

"Uriah ... I — " Helena started to protest.

."Silence!" he bellowed. Setting her down abruptly, he ordered her to the coach. Then he turned his face, purple with rage, to Alistair. "You, sir, I will meet at sunrise. Have your second ready." Taking a leather glove from his coat, he brought it down across Alistair's face with a loud slap. Then he threw the glove at Alistair's feet and stalked off.

For a moment, both Alistair and Tavish were too stunned to speak. Finally Alistair swallowed hard and grabbed Tavish by the sleeve. "What does he mean, do you think?"

"A duel, Cousin. He's challenged you to a duel tomorrow at sunrise. I am sorry, Alistair. I warned you. I will be leaving for North Carolina — "

"A duel!" Alistair twisted the material of Tavish's coat into a knot. "The man is an expert marksman! He will kill me! You can't leave, Tavish. I have no one else to help me. Please!"

There were tears in Alistair's eyes, and Tavish was ashamed for him. "Oh, Alistair, why?"

Alistair hung his head. "I just can't help myself. She had the softest — "

"Enough," Tavish shouted exasperated. "Hers may well be the last soft skin you ever touch."

"Then you will stay?"

Tavish nodded grimly. After all, he had come to Alistair for help. With difficulty, he pried Alistair's hand from his sleeve. "I will be your second. But beyond that, I can't help you. The man seeks vengeance, and he certainly has cause."

That night Alistair slept fitfully, moaning the name of his lady love each time he turned. In the room next to his cousin, Tavish did not sleep at all. How had this happened? Tavish asked himself over and over again. At one o'clock, Tavish was startled by a knock on the door. The servants were all in bed, forcing him to answer the summons.

A coachman stood outside, his hat pulled low and his collar turned up against the chill. Behind him a carriage waited. All was still, even the horses stood as motionless as carved statues.

"Master McLeod?"

Tavish nodded slowly.

"My master, Jonathon Burns, begs a word with you in his carriage."

Pulling his coat around him, Tavish followed the servant to the carriage. Once inside, he recognized the banker from Horace Vandever's soiree. The banker motioned for Tavish to sit beside him. He was an older man, graying at the temples, but distinguished-looking. His greatcoat was lined with fur, and a diamond stickpin sparkled in his cravat.

" 'Tis late, I know," Burns said. "But we must settle our business ere dawn."

Tavish shivered. A sick feeling of dread crept over him. More than ever he wished he was back in North Carolina.

"Master Merwin supposed you would serve your cousin as second. Is that correct?"

Tavish nodded.

"This is not a business I like. I have known Merwin for many years; he is a hot-blooded man. He is a southerner, and they always settle their differences this way. I understand that his father was a participant in some fifty duels." He sighed as if he were bored by the discussion. "I have told him the authorities frown on duels here in Philadelphia, but to no avail. In any case, he believes that his honor is at stake."

Tavish looked down at his hands. "My cousin truly regrets his actions . . . "

"I daresay. With any other man, a severe tongue-lashing might serve. But not Merwin, I'm afraid. The hour is set at five. There is a plot of land off the Germantown Road. You must take the right fork at a sign marked 'Clear

Point.' To mark the turn we will leave a red kerchief. Continue on the road until you see my carriage. Have I made myself clear, Master McLeod?"

"And there is nothing we can do to stop this from taking place?"

"No. Of course the choice of weapons will be up to Master Munroe."

Tavish thought quickly. Alistair had no interest in hunting or fencing, and had never been in a fight. Poor Alistair even hated to get his hands dirty. He did own pistols, however. Remembering that fact, Tavish assumed that his cousin had some prowess in shooting.

"Pistols," Tavish said.

"Very well. You know, of course, that Merwin is an excellent shot."

"I have heard as much."

"It is a shame," Burns said, clearing his throat. "I always liked Alistair." He spoke as if Alistair were already dead. "I have already arranged for a physician. Of course, you may bring your own as well."

The whole thing was like a bad dream. Tavish shut his eyes for a minute, and hoped that when he opened them the nightmare would be over. But there was no escape. As he moved to reenter the house, Burns caught his sleeve.

"I know well that Alistair Munroe is a gentleman and will therefore, honor such a challenge. But mark me, Master McLeod, and advise your cousin not to play the coward. Though he might escape with his life, his reputation will be ruined in Philadelphia. Uriah Merwin is a very powerful man."

Tavish stepped down and watched the carriage pull out of sight. The night was dark, for there was no moon. Suddenly, and for no apparent reason, Tavish thought of Dearie. He remembered when he had first met her, how she had glowed with an ethereal beauty. She had been like the brightest star on a night as black as this.

How he wished she was here! Sighing, he walked back into the house.

Another hour passed before Tavish awakened Alistair. His cousin staggered groggily to the basin and splashed water on his face.

"Have you been up all night, Tavish?"

"Merwin's second came by an hour ago."

"He's actually going through with it?"

Tavish nodded. "Have you any knowledge of pistols?"

"Some. More of pistols than swords."

"Have your pistols been cleaned recently?"

"Not recently."

"Then I will clean them. And I should like one for myself."

"Why? Surely you don't expect to duel!"

"I expect to be prepared for whatever happens, Cousin. As your second, I have that right."

Alistair delayed their departure another hour, spending an inordinate amount of time fretting over what he would wear. "What do you think, Tavish? The claret velvet with my patent pumps?"

Tavish lost his patience. "What does it matter, Alistair? You could be killed, you know!"

"All the more reason to look my best," he sniffed.

Alistair still did not grasp the gravity of the situation, Tavish thought, amazed. He was more concerned with his appearance than whether he lived or died. Finally, they set out on horseback instead of using the coach. Alistair preferred to keep the incident from his servants. "Servants talk, you know."

Tavish shook his head. In another hour, it would hardly matter.

After a lengthy ride, they arrived at the Clear Point marker and continued down the right fork as they had been instructed. Soon they saw several carriages parked near a stand of oak trees. Dismounting, they led their horses to the trees. Walking past the carriages, they saw a wagon containing a bed.

"What is that for?" Alistair asked.

"I expect it is to be used as an ambulance."

In the clearing, Merwin paced back and forth, his large arms folded across his broad chest. Behind him followed the physician, his shirt-sleeves rolled up in readiness. Burns hopped behind Merwin like a bird, talking and gesturing with his hands. But from the look on Merwin's face, his mood had not improved.

"Won't you reconsider? What if you are killed, Uriah?" Burns was saying. "What then?"

"I never miss. And I certainly won't miss this time."

Merwin stopped abruptly, scowling as Tavish and Alistair approached. Alistair's teeth chattered so loudly that Tavish could hear them. His body, when Tavish tried to steady him, was as frail as a girl's, and his very bones shook.

"Well, you're not a coward after all," Merwin boomed out.

Alistair's knees buckled. He would have fallen had not Tavish reached out to support him.

The first pink light of dawn crept through the trees. It was time. Burns hurried over and took Tavish aside.

"We must select the dueling ground and clear away the brush. There is a small clearing beyond those trees . . . "

Tavish followed Burns, and together they picked up twigs and branches. Then they each stepped off ten paces in opposite directions. There they placed long sticks as markers where the combatants would stand.

Tavish returned to Alistair, who was leaning weakly against a tree. Talking quietly to his cousin, he loaded the pistols.

"Surely he doesn't mean to go through with this," Alistair asked.

"Yes he does, Alistair."

Burns nodded at Tavish. "If you are ready, Master McLeod, we will toss a coin for position and word."

"I am ready."

Burns won the toss. "Now I'm obliged to tell you the rules. I will ask if you are ready. Silence will indicate that you are. Then I will call out, 'Fire-one-two-three-stop!' I will hesitate briefly between each word. But you will not fire before or afterwards."

Though the air was very cool, Burns wiped the perspiration from his forehead with a handkerchief.

Alistair removed his coat, absently handing it to Tavish. Merwin also removed his coat. He stalked over to Alistair, who cringed at his approach.

Tavish gave the loaded pistol to Alistair, placing it barrel-down in his left hand. When he was at the marker, he would switch it to his right hand.

"Are you ready then?" There was no sound except for Alistair swallowing.

"May the best man win," Merwin said with a cruel smile.

Burns positioned the men back to back. Tavish winced to see that Alistair was at least a head shorter than Merwin. In the last few hours he seemed to have shrunk. His bony shoulders stuck out from his white cambric shirt, and his silk hose bagged down over his patent pumps. Alistair's facade had completely fallen away, leaving a scarecrow draped in fine clothes.

Merwin held his pistol firmly, but the weapon in Alistair's hand wobbled noticeably. Burns exchanged a sympathetic glance with Tavish. There would be no contest, that much was painfully clear.

"All right, gentlemen. To your markers!"

Tavish's heartbeat kept time with each footfall. They measured out ten paces away from each other across the isolated stretch of grass.

The silence was suddenly shattered by a loud boom. Both Tavish and Burns whirled at the sound of the explosion. At first Tavish assumed that a pistol had accidentally misfired. Then the smoke cleared. Alistair fell to the ground, shot in the back. Merwin had turned before the count, and fired.

"Uriah, you've killed the man! You did not wait for the count!" Burns shouted.

"He got what he deserved!" Merwin yelled, unrepentant.

"And so shall you," Tavish said, pulling forth his own gun. He fired before he could think, and Merwin, a startled look on his face, crashed forward like a felled tree.

For what seemed like eons, Tavish and Burns stood frozen. Then Tavish sprang toward Alistair. He was still breathing, but blood stained his white shirt.

"What happened?" Alistair rasped. "Am I dying?"

The physician appeared at Tavish's side. He shook his head when he saw the blood oozing onto Alistair's shirt. "We'll put him in the ambulance. He needs immediate attention."

He helped Tavish carry Alistair to the wagon. Alistair was placed on the wagon bed, then the physician hurried over to Merwin. Burns was kneeling beside the merchant's inert body.

"How is he?" Tavish asked.

Burns shook his head. "He's beyond help. He's dead."

"Oh, no," Tavish groaned, passing a hand over his eyes. He hadn't meant to kill the man — he'd just reacted instinctively.

"McLeod," Burns said, "think no more on it. If you hadn't killed him, I would have. He disobeyed the rules. It was not a fair fight . . . but it ended fairly."

Tavish shook his head sadly. *I have taken revenge on an innocent young girl, and deceived her family. And now I have committed murder,* Tavish thought disconsolately. He was filled with self-loathing.

The ride back to town was interminable. Alistair's moans only echoed Tavish's inner turmoil. Alistair had lost more blood, and by the time they arrived home, he was barely breathing.

The doctor was a long time ministering to Alistair. He finally emerged from the room shaking his head.

"I have my doubts that he'll make it. If he makes it through the day, he'll have a chance. In any case, I'll be back tomorrow."

For the second night, Tavish sat by Alistair's bed. He spent hours trying to compose a letter to Dearie, but he wadded up each one and threw it on the floor.

The one he finally decided to send sounded oddly formal, as if it were written by a stranger.

My Dear Wife,

Cousin Alistair has had an unexpected accident. The doctor can give me no assurance that he will live.

I regret that my return had been delayed. Under the circumstances, I have no choice but to stay a while longer in Philadelphia. I am sure you understand. May this letter find you in good health.

Your loving husband,
Tavish

Tavish sighed and reflected upon how different his life would have been had he never come to Philadelphia in the first place.

The next morning, Alistair was still alive but just barely. The doctor returned, and after the examination, was more encouraging.

"Your cousin is stronger than he looks," he said. "But he will be a long time recovering."

Alistair hovered between life and death for ten days, then he began to mend. At the end of two weeks, he was strong enough to eat solid food. Gradually, the color returned to his cheeks, and he could sit up in bed. Tavish was encouraged, and again packed his bags.

"I will be leaving soon for North Carolina," Tavish told Alistair one morning. "I am glad you are on the road to recovery."

"What!" Alistair choked. "You can't leave, Tavish! The doctor says I mustn't leave bed for weeks yet. Who will manage my affairs? I'll starve if I'm left alone like this."

"Alistair, I have my own business to manage."

"A little more time won't make much difference. Just wait until I'm on my feet again."

Tavish looked out the window. It had begun to snow. It seemed that the elements were in league with Alistair. "All right, Alistair. I'll stay a while longer . . . until you improve."

Chapter Sixteen

It was almost two months before Dearie heard from Tavish. With Colleen in town and no one to talk to, she grew despondent. She took frequent trips into Fayetteville until the weather turned cold. Then she was forced to stay indoors.

The plantation fields were cleared and ready for planting. In November, the workers arrived and erected several makeshift buildings where they would stay during planting.

Finally Dearie received letters from her father and Tavish in the same week. After reading her father's letter, she was furious. Tavish had gone to Philadelphia without telling her! Why? Her father mentioned speaking with Tavish, and remarked on her health.

"I know you can't travel at present, but in the future I hope you will accompany your husband," Grayson said.

She realized that Tavish had not mentioned the loss of their child. But then it was not his place to inform her father of such things.

Tavish's letter came a few days later. Cousin Alistair had had an accident and might not live, he wrote. Under the circumstances, he was obliged to stay in Philadelphia a while longer. He did not know when he would return to North Carolina.

Tears streaming down her cheeks, she threw the letter aside. Christmas was not far away. She'd had such wonderful plans for the holidays. Duncan and India McNeill had invited them to their annual Christmas soiree, and Dearie had accepted for them both. Colleen was already at work on a new ball gown for Dearie. She prayed that Alistair would mend quickly so that Tavish could return.

Each successive letter from Tavish described new complications. What sort of accident could Alistair have had? Finally Dearie was forced to accept the fact that her husband would remain absent for a long time. She went out into the fields as the men prepared to sow the wheat. Scooping up a handful of the red earth, she pressed it into a ball in her hand. She reveled in the smell and feel of the clay; it was deep and rich. She would go on without him — she would plant the fields and even harvest the crop by herself. If she had to. What else could she do — except wait until Tavish returned.

Alistair mended quickly — too quickly. He was up and about long before the doctor permitted him.

"Alistair, you should be in bed," Tavish chided him.

"Ah, Cousin, I will surely die if I can't attend the seasonal parties. Truly, I feel much better."

He insisted on being driven about town every night to a different party. On most nights, Tavish accompanied him, albeit reluctantly. Then one night, as he was holding the hand of a beautiful lady, Alistair collapsed in mid-sentence.

The doctor said that an infection had settled in the wound. "By gadding about before the wound was healed, you have made things worse. Now you must stay in bed without moving," he ordered. "If you get up, it will be the last time you do!"

While Alistair was in bed, Tavish tried to sort through his cousin's affairs. This proved to be a difficult task. With his inheritance, Alistair had bought a number of buildings and leased them out. But his records were a shambles. Some months he had not recorded any income, and for others he had recorded the numbers inaccurately. Upon close inspection, Tavish found that many tenants hadn't paid rent for months. It was no wonder that Alistair often found himself in financial straits.

Since Alistair was too ill to respond to questions, Tavish took matters in his own hands.

One of the buildings, a small grocer's store on Walnut Street, was his first stop. The owners lived in a small flat upstairs. When Tavish arrived, the family was having their mid-day meal.

"I'm Master Monroe's cousin," Tavish informed them.

The wife and children were mildly interested, but the man, Mr. Milo, continued to eat.

"I've come about the rent," Tavish continued.

"Can't pay," Milo said, his mouth full of food.

"I see that. You haven't paid in three months."

Milo shrugged. "Business has been slow. Master Munroe said it was okay. We'll pay when we can."

The man's cavalier attitude bothered Tavish. He wasn't the least bit concerned.

"You'll have to pay next month, or you must move," Tavish said.

The man stared back insolently at Tavish. "Tell Master Munroe to come hisself next time."

"Master Munroe cannot come. I'm handling his affairs now. I'll expect the money next month."

Tavish turned and left without looking back. He heard the woman quiet the children. The Milos were obviously poor, but they had no sense of responsibility. Had they made any attempt to negotiate, or to pay at least part of the rent, he might have relented. They deserved to be put out. Strangely, Tavish found that he didn't care what happened to them.

Another tenant was a doctor who had been conveniently out of town each time Alistair came to collect the rent. Alistair had made a note of this fact in the ledger. Tavish called several times and received the same response from the doctor's housekeeper.

"He ain't in," she said, squinting at him.

"When *will* he be in?" Tavish asked.

"Don't know. The doctor keeps strange hours."

"Dr. Jakes owes two months' rent."

She shrugged and closed the door in his face.

On a hunch, Tavish watched the building and observed the doctor entering the building very late one night. He accosted him at the door.

"Dr. Jakes?"

"Yes, I am Dr. Jakes."

"I am Alistair Munroe's cousin, and I've come to collect the rent. It is now two months overdue."

The doctor took out his watch. "It's very late. I've been at a sickbed all night," he said. "If you'll drop by tomorrow, I'll be happy — "

"I have dropped by every day for a week, as did my cousin, Dr. Jakes. I must have the rent now, or I must ask you to vacate the premises."

Obviously irritated, the doctor led Tavish into his office. There he took out a small cash box and huffily counted out the exact amount.

"Thank you, Dr. Jakes," Tavish said, taking the money. "I shall look forward to seeing you every month. Shall I come by about this time, or will your housekeeper have the money ready for me?"

Jakes frowned. "I shall have it ready for you. I'll inform my housekeeper."

"Excellent," Tavish smiled.

By persisting in this manner, Tavish was able to collect enough money to pay for Alistair's medical expenses and still have plenty for them to live on. Soon he was forced to evict several tenants, including the Milos. The new tenants were required to sign an agreement stating that if the rent was one month overdue, they would vacate the premises.

Next, Tavish paid a visit to Alistair's lawyer, Benjamin Simms. Simms had found the properties for Alistair, and was engaged in finding other investments. Tavish asked to see the books. Reluctantly, Simms handed them over.

"There seem to be some discrepancies," Tavish pointed out.

"I've been ill." Simms waved away the comment.

The rest of Alistair's inheritance was sorely depleted, due to the lawyer's bad management. Tavish found that the man had overcharged for services and paid too much in taxes. When Simms was reluctant to hand over the balance of the money, Tavish became angry.

"I think the constable would be interested in these transactions, Mr. Simms," Tavish threatened him.

"I don't like your attitude, Master McLeod," Simms retorted.

"I imagine not," Tavish replied with steely calmness.

Tavish promptly dismissed the lawyer and deposited Alistair's money in a bank. He enjoyed the chastised look on the lawyer's face when he left.

By Christmas, Tavish had completely organized Alistair's affairs. All of the figures had been neatly posted in the ledgers, and there was money in the bank.

Alistair, having followed the doctor's orders, was still in bed. On Christmas Eve, the cousins shared a glass of wine and toasted their recent profits.

"Tavish, you are a natural businessman. Sadly, I am not."

"You asked for my help, and I was only too glad to give it. Now that you have extra funds, you should find other investments."

Alistair nodded and sipped his wine reflectively. "What would you say if I offered you a partnership, Cousin?

You could find new investments. I'm sure I would agree with your judgment. Then we would divide the profits, half and half."

"Alistair, that's absurd. These profits are from your inheritance."

Alistair frowned. "I dislike business, as you know. I shudder to think what would have happened to my inheritance had you not stepped in."

Tavish was intrigued by the idea. The past few weeks had been not only instructive, but stimulating. For the first time, he'd had complete control over the funds at hand. Tavish realized that he liked having money and the power to manipulate it.

"You are saying, Alistair, that I shall have sole judgment as to what is done with the money, and that half the profits will be mine?"

"A tempting offer, is it not?" Alistair raised his eyebrow. "This way you should have things well in hand when you return to North Carolina for harvest."

"But what of Dearie?"

Alistair shrugged. "You can send her money. Has she not servants? Your friend, Calvin, can look in on her. I'm sure she will understand, Tavish. Women always do."

The more Tavish thought about it, the more reasonable the offer sounded. If Grayson would give him no more money, he had to get it elsewhere. He laughed to think that he had once again outwitted the wily old lawyer. And Alistair was right — Dearie would not be lonely. She had Colleen and Calvin to keep her company.

"All right, Alistair. I'll stay. But after the holidays, I must return to Carolina."

"Of course, Cousin," Alistair rubbed his hands together. "Now, how shall we invest the money?"

The holidays came and went. Tavish wrote a brief explanatory note to Dearie, then resolutely put her out of his mind. When he received her pleading letters, he laid them quickly aside. They needed money, and this was the best way to get it . . . or so he told himself.

Tavish decided to sell several of Alistair's buildings. With the profits from the sales, he kept half for future investments. The rest he lent out in mortgages. This provided them with another source of income every month.

He also learned to be flexible with the rent. If a tenant couldn't pay, occasionally Tavish accepted jewels, or even a family heirloom. In this way, too, he often increased their profits.

Once he accepted a brass samovar, which he instinctively knew to be worth twice the amount of the rent due.

"Take it," the tenant said, shaking his head. "I have nothing else to give you, and nowhere else to go."

Tavish took the samovar and promptly sold it. The next month, he was forced to evict the same tenant.

He had hardened himself against feelings of pity or sympathy. If he saw tears, he turned away; if tenants begged and pleaded, he only grew harsher. Even Alistair was shocked at his ruthless behavior.

"Surely you don't mean to turn out Mrs. Delany? She is so old, Tavish. And she was very prompt with her rent until just last month. Shouldn't we allow her one more month?"

Tavish shook his head. "That is how you got yourself into difficulties in the first place, Alistair. We can't make exceptions. Remember, Cousin, you put me in charge of your affairs."

Alistair nodded but he was concerned. Something had happened to Tavish. It was one thing to avenge Murdock's death . . . he had accomplished that. But now, no one was safe from his vengeance. He took all his joy from turning a profit, no matter who was hurt.

Profits continued to grow, however, and Alistair couldn't argue with success. As he mended, he dreamed of the soirees and balls he would have with his new wealth.

But Tavish dreamed only of making more money. It was a game to him, and when he could no longer find investments that would return a quick profit, he turned to gambling.

When Alistair was able to sit up, he invited a few of his friends over for cards. At first, Tavish watched without participating. Being preoccupied with business, he'd never had time for cards.

"Why don't you join us," Alistair suggested. "This time we'll play for money."

"That's good," Tavish remarked. "Anything worth doing is worth getting paid for."

Prowess in cards came easily to Tavish. He looked upon each game as a challenge. The other players were mere opponents, to be outwitted exactly as he had foiled Matthew Grayson. And Tavish never lost.

Soon, Tavish was playing every night. Alistair grew alarmed. "Tavish, one night you are going to lose all we've earned."

Tavish shook his head. "I don't intend to lose — ever again."

Alistair was unconvinced. He watched his cousin manipulate the other players as if they were pawns on a chessboard. It was uncanny how Tavish read his opponents correctly every time.

The story of the duel had spread throughout Philadelphia. Only Jonathan Burns knew Tavish's part, and he wisely kept silent. However, the gentry were scandalized by the affair. Then, Alistair Munroe suddenly had money to spend, and his handsome cousin frequented every gaming table in the city. Again Tavish McLeod's name was on everybody's lips.

At first Matthew Grayson watched his son-in-law with amused fascination. Then, as Tavish began making a name for himself, his interest grew.

When Tavish turned a colleague of Grayson's out of his office for being five days late with the rent, Grayson applauded the action. He would have done the same. But he still did not trust the boy. After all, he had gotten Dearie with child, and he'd obviously squandered her dowry.

When after only four months, it was rumored that Tavish had more than doubled Alistair Munroe's income, Grayson was grudgingly impressed. "Perhaps the boy will make something of himself after all." But success still did not make him worthy of Dearie. As soon as she had the child and was well enough to travel, he would bring her home again.

Although it was not good for appearances, Grayson was not concerned that Tavish might have doubled his money gambling. Making money was the important thing. Matthew Grayson did not believe in the principle of ill-gotten gains. To him there was no such thing.

Unbeknownst to Tavish, Grayson received daily reports on his activities. Often at night, undetected, Grayson observed him at the gaming table. Tavish would have been surprised at the expression of admiration and amusement on the older's man's face. Grayson was reliving days gone by, for he had accumulated his fortune in exactly the same way.

One evening Tavish was to play cards with three men Grayson knew well. Oliver Bidewell, a merchant, owned a number of warehouses on the wharf, and another was a lawyer named Jeremy Gwynne. The third player, James Gunnison, owned a bank. the three players anxiously awaited Tavish's arrival so the game could begin.

Grayson knew that Tavish would be well matched in this game, so he arranged to be present. The proprietor of the house graciously permitted the lawyer to watch the game from an upstairs room. Several other spectators joined him, drinking brandy and smoking cigars.

"You can see better from up here. Anyhow, it makes 'em nervous to have an audience," the owner explained.

Tavish arrived wearing a London brown coat, a high, rolling cape, and dark velvet pantaloons which matched his coat. A silk, swan's down waistcoat and jackboots completed his costume. Grayson thought he looked even more the dandy than his cousin Alistair. Yet Tavish exuded a powerful magnetism when he entered the room. All eyes turned to him, following him to his chair.

The stakes were high, and the game went late into the night. The other spectators in the upstairs room retired, leaving Grayson alone.

Tavish had won consistently, and now only the merchant was bidding against him. Bidwell's forehead was beaded with perspiration, but Tavish remained cool and unruffled.

"Will you bid, Oliver?" Tavish asked.

"Yes. . . . well, I was going to . . . but my money is gone. I have nothing else to play with."

"Nothing?"

"Well, there are the warehouses. But I don't think — "

"The warehouses will do." Tavish's voice was toneless, almost bored.

"Well, I don't think I will lose this time," Bidewell said under his breath."

They played for three more arduous hours. Finally Bidewell lost the warehouses to Tavish. When it was over, the three men sat staring grimly at Tavish. He ignored their stares, continuing to stack his winnings into neat little piles.

"I'll need your signature on paper transferring the warehouses to me, Oliver," he reminded the merchant.

Bidewill flinched. "Tavish, you don't actually intend to take them, do you? I mean, you don't even live here. Why don't I give you an affidavit. I can pay you the money back gradually over time. My wife will perish, I daresay, but . . . "

"No, I'm sorry, Oliver. I shall take your warehouses. I will go down to see them tomorrow." Tavish did not even look up.

Bidewell's face reddened. "You can't do that . . . I . . . please! Without my warehouses I have no business. There would be no place for the goods when the ships put in to port. Allow me to pay out the debt over time! You can charge me what interest you will. I'm willing to swallow my pride."

Tavish's eyes were as hard as flint. "Did you put up the warehouses of your own free will, Oliver?"

"Well . . . I . . ."

"Did you or not?"

"Yes, I did, but — "

"Then you lost them fairly. I shall send my carriage around for you tomorrow. I would like to see them in the morning if you don't mind."

Bidewell pushed back his chair abruptly. He lunged violently at Tavish, but he was instantly restrained by his two companions. "I do mind, sir! I'll send my man with the keys, but I'll not accompany you anywhere, Tavish McLeod. You are no better than a pirate and twice as black." His voice shook with shock and anger.

His expression blank and unreadable, Tavish was left alone to count his money. Grayson watched him a while longer, then, with a bemused smile on his face, he, too, left.

When people commented upon Tavish's scandalous behavior, Grayson assumed a pious attitude and shook his head. "I know, I know. It is shocking. 'Tis a pity that one's true character is often hidden until after the wedding vows."

Grayson was only setting the stage for bringing Dearie back home in the spring. But first he intended to gain the full sympathy of everyone in the city.

"What do you intend to do?" someone asked.

"I don't know," Grayson replied innocently. "What would you do?"

"If she were my daughter and married such a scoundrel, I'd fetch her home."

"Well, now. That's an idea. I shall think on it."

Grayson played his part well. He was scandalized or apologetic depending upon the situation. Everyone gave him advice, which he freely accepted. But his plans had already been formulated — long ago. For Dearie's sake he continued the charade. He was determined that she have another chance, and this time the groom would be of his choosing.

If Tavish had been moody and withdrawn before, he was even more so now. His hazel eyes held a hard, metallic glint. No trace of feeling showed in his face. He had become adept at pushing any troubling thoughts to the back of his mind in order to concentrate on the task at hand. He seldom allowed himself to think of Dearie. He knew that if he did, his carefully constructed facade might crumble.

Although he gave them only a cursory glance, her letters bothered him more than he cared to admit. He knew that she wanted desperately for him to come home, but he could not. It was far better that he stayed away.

"If you are not come home by spring, I shall come to you, my love," she wrote.

Life was strange, he thought wryly. He had intended to send Dearie back to Philadelphia soon after they married, but she hadn't wanted to leave. Now she begged to come. He had hated to leave North Carolina, and now he was loath to return. His thoughts took him no further, for he refused to admit that Dearie only wanted to be with him — wherever he might be.

Tavish was entirely consumed with making money. Everywhere he turned new ventures magically appeared. Soon he would have more money than he'd ever dreamed having. By now he was certain that his fortunes lay here in Phildelphia — not in North Carolina. North Carolina was the backwoods, as everyone had always said. There was no real money to be made there.

When he thought of them, he pitied his friends, Duncan McNeill and Calvin Buie. How hard they toiled for their small reward, scratching out a living from a worn-out land. At long last he understood Dearie. She belonged here in the city, among people like herself. She would be thrilled to return to Philadelphia of that he was sure.

Tavish would have been shocked to know that Dearie had no plans of returning to Philadelphia . . . ever.

Chapter Seventeen

The wheat planting took several weeks. The plantation had but one shovel plow which was pulled by three horses. In this way they covered two acres a day, but the work was slow and tedious. A harrow was used afterwards to level the plowed ground. After leveling, the seeds were cast by hand. The foreman, Ezekiel, supervised the workers along with them.

Once the seeds had been cast, the horses were again harnessed to the harrow. This time the harrow covered the seeds with earth. Dearie watched, fascinated. Until now, she had never realized how much work went into planting.

Dearie helped Tempie and Bess prepare the meals for the men, and she accompanied them to the fields. She helped Tempie ladle the stew onto tin plates, which they handed to the men. Ezekiel looked at her strangely, as if surprised to see her. Then his face broke into a wide grin.

"Looks like we'll get the wheat in afore Christmas. Winter wheat is the best, you know."

Dearie didn't know, but she was learning . . . every day. She tried to tell herself how proud Tavish would be, but she had begun to doubt that he was ever coming back. He'd been gone almost three months. When she voiced her concerns to Calvin, he always reassured her.

"Of course he'll return. He'll be back before you know it."

But even Calvin had begun to have doubts. He couldn't explain Tavish's behavior even to himself. Tavish had written him several letters describing the situation in Philadelphia. At first, Tavish had both reason and obligation to stay, but that time had long since passed. His recent letters had extolled the virtues of Philadelphia, and the money to be made there. The man acted as if he had no intention of ever coming home.

Calvin had half a mind to go and fetch Tavish home. But he was afraid to leave Dearie. Now that Colleen had gone, she was virtually alone except for the servants.

Dearie relied on Calvin more and more. When he offered to escort her to the McNeills' Christmas soiree, she gladly accepted.

Calvin arrived on Christmas Eve dressed in a wine velvet jacket and dark pantaloons tucked into shiny black boots. Dearie clapped her hands. "Calvin, you look like the spirit of Christmas in all your finery."

Calvin beamed. "And may I say, Miss Dearie, that you look lovely enough to win a hundred hearts tonight."

The smile quickly faded from Dearie's face. She might win a hundred hearts, but not the one she wanted. She blinked to stay the tears.

In an effort to lift her spirits, Calvin rambled on. "And your dress surely is a work of art."

"Oh, do you like it?" She twirled in front of him. The gown was violet silk, with flounces woven down from the high waist. More flounces adorned the mancheron sleeves. Lace edged the low-cut bodice and was artfully worked into silk flowers above the hem.

"It is lovely."

"Colleen made it, you know," Dearie was proud of her friend's success.

"Colleen? But I thought she had returned to Philadelphia."

"Why, no. She opened a millinery shop in town. And now she has so much business, she's hired someone to help her."

A smile lighted up Calvin's sharp features and his eyes twinkled. "Ah, well. Perhaps I will pay her visit."

The McNeill plantation, Greenhill, was set back off the road lined with loblolly pines. Lanterns hung from posts lit the carriageway.

"Greenhill is beautiful," Dearie exclaimed when they arrived.

"Old Turquil McNeill, Duncan's father, built the place before the Revolutionary War. Of course Duncan has added more rooms, but I always thought it was the most beautiful plantation in the county, after Rosalie, of course."

Servants helped them out and they ascended white-washed steps which led up to a wide, columned porch running the length of the red brick house. Windows as large as doors were ablaze with festive lights.

Calvin escorted Dearie through the wide oak doors. They stepped into a hallway dominated by an enormous pine tree decorated with candles and strung with fruit. Dearie was suddenly overwhelmed. The smell of the pine tree and evergreen wreaths, the guests, laughter, and the warmth of the flickering candles reminded her of long-ago Christmases when she was a small child. She half expected to be greeted by her own parents. Instead, Duncan and India rushed to welcome her.

"Dearie, we're so glad you could come." India embraced her warmly.

"Welcome to Greenhill," Duncan grinned. "And I see you've brought Mr. Christmas with you." He shook hands with Calvin.

"Come." India drew Dearie's arm through hers. "I want you to meet our children.

The children were quartered in the nursery until later, when they would be allowed to come down and mingle with the guests before bedtime. A servant in a dark blue turban sat rocking a little girl with dark curls, while two boys with russet hair played with wooden soldiers.

When they saw their mother, both boys ran to hug her. "These are my sons, Jamey and Turquil. This is Mrs. McLeod."

James, the older boy, affected a quick bow, but Turquil said shyly, "She's purty," then buried his face in his mother's skirts.

India laughed. "You have already won them over, Dearie."

Dearie looked away, thinking of the child she'd lost. She wondered if it would have been a boy or a girl.

"And this is Lydia," India was saying, moving over to the small child who lay half-asleep in the servant's lap.

At the sound of her mother's voice, Lydia's eyes opened and her chubby arms reached for her mother. India swept her up, cuddling her to her breast. "Look, Lyddie, I've brought a pretty lady to meet you. This is Mrs. McLeod."

Lydia gazed at Dearie with deep blue-violet eyes, then pushed her thumb into her mouth and sighed.

"She's beautiful, India. She looks just like you," Dearie exclaimed. "May I . . . hold her?"

"I'm sure she'd love it. Lyddie adores being held."

Lydia complacently allowed herself to be transferred from one woman to another, then she laid her head on Dearie's chest and continued to suck her thumb.

Emotion welled up in Dearie as she held Lydia. The soft bundle convinced her that she wanted a baby more than anything else in the world. She wanted to have Tavish's baby. Tears sprang to her eyes.

"Dearie?" India had caught the bereft look on her face.

"I'm sorry, India. It's just that . . . well, I lost our baby not long ago. It makes me very sad."

India moved quickly to her side. "Oh, my dear, I am so sorry. I didn't know. Shall I take Lydia?"

"No . . . I . . . could I hold her a while longer?"

"As long as you like. She's almost asleep."

India excused herself to greet the other guests, but Dearie held Lydia for almost an hour before placing the child in her crib. When she rejoined Calvin, her expression was somber.

"Dearie, is everything all right?" he asked, concerned.

"Yes, Calvin. Only I would like to ask another favor. You have done so much already, I hate to impose . . . "

Calvin shook his head. "I will be happy to oblige you if I can."

"I want you to write to Tavish. I have written countless times, pleading with him to return. He says that he must stay to look after Alistair's affairs, but what about his own?" She sighed heavily. "Nothing I say seems to make a difference. Apparently, Alistair is paying Tavish to oversee his investments, and Tavish says he needs the money for the factoring business. Honestly, I don't understand financial matters, as you know. Still, it seems to me that we are forever living hand to mouth. Surely some money has come out of the business thus far."

Calvin rubbed his chin. He had no answers, since he had often wondered the same thing. "I'll be happy to write to him. I feel as you do. He should come home."

Somewhat relieved, Dearie patted his arm. "Calvin, I don't know what I would have done without you these last few months. I owe you a great debt."

He shook his head with a smile, and led her into the sitting room, where all the guests were gathered. Later he

took Duncan aside when Dearie was talking with someone else.

"Duncan, we both grew up with Tavish, but I don't
know what's gotten into him lately. He seems like a different person this past year."

Duncan nodded. "Ever since Murdock died he's been
obsessed with getting revenge. He said he had met
Grayson and gotten the better of him, but he never did
explain how. I guess he took the old man's money in a
card game. Next thing we knew he was married, and had
enough money to put back in the business. I suppose
Dearie had a large dowry."

Calvin shrugged. "I assume so, but she refuses to talk
about her family or Philadelphia. She says that's all in
the past now. But you wouldn't think so the way Tavish
goes on in his letters. He wants us all to pick up and
move there."

Frowning, Duncan ran a hand through his auburn hair.
"Tavish said that?"

"He says that Philadelphia is the place to be these days.
He describes the theaters, balls, and soirees as though he
is having the time of his life. And here sits his wife,
pining away for him." Calvin shook his head. "It's not
right, Duncan."

"No, and it's not like Tavish."

"Maybe you ought to go there and have a look, Calvin.
I'd go with you, but one of us needs to be at home for
Dearie."

"I'm thinking on it, Duncan. If I don't hear something
soon, I will."

January brought cold weather and frequent snow. Dearie
was housebound for weeks at a time. When she ran out of
things to read, she learned how to cook.

Tempie taught her how to bake jelly cakes, ginger
cookies, and pumpkin pie. Dearie had never been in
a kitchen except to visit with Jessamine, their cook in

Philadelphia. Now she became perfectly at home in the kitchen. Tempie was a natural cook; she knew instinctively what spices to use or how much salt and flour were needed. Dearie's first attempts were utter failure, but Tempie only laughed and they did it all again.

They used Clarence as their guinea pig. "Clarence would eat anything," Tempie remarked. "The hard thing is to git him to say he like it."

Dearie fed Clarence a variety of dishes every day, but it was weeks before he said a word. Impatient, Dearie asked him one day how he liked a stew she had made.

Clarence rolled his eyes. "Tastes like something I had once. Called it Brunswick Stew. I b'lieve they used a gray squirrel in it. Is that what you used, Miss Dearie?"

Dearie was horrified. "Certainly not!"

Clarence was puzzled. "Wall, maybe it was a red one. I don't know. I thought they said the gray ones had more flavor to 'em."

Finally Dearie was able to gain the old servant's praise with her apple cobbler. She elaborated slightly on Tempie's recipe by adding rum and brown sugar. Tempie declared that it was better than any she had ever made. But Clarence ate it in silence while the two women watched him expectantly. When he had finished he looked up and smiled. "I b'lieve I might just have another piece of that cobbler, Miss Dearie. One don't seem to be enough."

When Dearie became bored with domestic accomplishments, she persuaded Clarence to teach her to shoot a pistol. At first he was reluctant, thinking that Tavish would disapprove.

"Clarence, I must be able to defend myself. And with Tavish being gone so much . . . "

"I don't know, Miss Dearie. Ain't fittin' for a lady to mess with firearms. 'Tis a good way to get killed."

"I can think of worse ways," Dearie informed him pertly.

Clarence finally gave in, and after several sessions, he allowed that Dearie would be a threat to any varmint that came about.

Dearie beamed proudly. She knew Tavish would be thrilled to see all she had accomplished since he'd been gone.

The bad weather continued until February. For all his good intentions, Calvin was unable to journey to Philadelphia until the weather improved. Finally, toward the end of the month, Ezekiel and his men reappeared to put in the spring crops.

Dearie's spirits rose with arrival of spring. Soon they would have five fields planted. "Oh, Calvin, won't it be wonderful for Tavish to return and find the fields all cleared and planted?" she said, her blue eyes wide with excitement.

Calvin only nodded. "I'm sure he'll be surprised. Let's hope the weather holds. We might ought to wait a few more weeks just to make sure. A late frost could come back and ruin the corn."

"Just look at this glorious weather, Calvin," Dearie insisted. "It will hold. I just know it will."

Ezekiel and his men moved back into the makeshift buildings which Clarence had supplied with a stove and blankets.

The men worked tirelessly, and by the end of the week, one entire field was planted in maize and two others in corn. Dearie personally inspected each mound. Nothing was visible except a small clump of dirt, but in a few weeks the first seedlings would push forth.

Dearie and Tempie cooked an enormous batch of fried chicken and served it to the men along with sweet potatoes and greens. Ezekiel claimed it was the best food he'd ever eaten. The other men stared dumbfounded at the elegant repast, until urged by their foreman to eat.

Now six fields had been planted — three of wheat, two of corn, and one of maize. Almost overnight the wheat sprouted and shot up. Dearie inspected the fields regularly, carefully watching the progress of the crops.

Ezekiel and his men packed their belongings and prepared to return to Rosalie. Dearie hated to see them go.

"We'll be back in a week or two. The maize and corn will need to be hoed and hilled."

Dearie frowned, not understanding. But by now, she had learned that Ezekiel knew what he was doing. He was a good foreman.

Clarence called Dearie to the fields a week later, when the tiny shoots of maize had begun to push through the earth. In the distance, a gentle wind ruffled the tall wheat. Dearie clapped her hands joyously. "Oh, Clarence! We're planters. I can't wait to show Tavish. He didn't think Beauvais would ever become a real plantation again, but it has! And we've done it!"

Ezekiel and his men returned the next week to thin and hoe the sprouting crops. Eventually, they hilled the corn by putting loose dirt around each stalk to provide additional support.

Dearie watched her crops grow eagerly. Her thoughts raced ahead to harvest, when she would proudly bear the corn and wheat to market. She calculated what her crops might bring. Tavish would be so impressed!

One afternoon, the weather changed drastically. Toward sunset, the temperature began to drop and clouds gathered ominously in the sky.

"Ezekiel, tell the men to come in early today. It looks like rain," Dearie ordered.

His black face creased with a frown, Ezekiel gazed up at the huge gray clouds above. "I don't know. It don't look good," he said.

The temperature continued to drop during the night. Dearie awoke the next morning shivering from the cold. She dressed hurriedly and threw a shawl over her shoulders. She ran out onto the porch, where she was stopped dead in her tracks. There was blanket of snow covering the ground. "Oh, no," she cried, oblivious to the freezing temperature. "The corn will be ruined!"

When she reached the field, Ezekiel was already there brushing snow away from the tiny plants. He looked up at her anxious face and shook his head. "I'm sorry, ma'am. But these here plants are about froze. The wheat'll do fine. Snow don't bother it, but we'll have to replant the corn. We always run the risk if we plant too early. We might be able to save a few, but we'll lose most of 'em, I reckon."

"Oh, no! After all that work," Dearie sighed heavily.

"Yes, ma'am. I reckon so." Ezekiel looked up in the sky. "Might have been the wrong time to plant. I b'lieve you and Master Calvin the only ones that put in an early crop. Maybe the moon . . . "

Dearie shook her head. She was tired of superstition. "I read the almanac, Ezekiel."

Ezekiel wagged his head. "Well, something happened to make it snow out of the blue like that. I'll study about it."

Dearie's shoulders sagged. She turned and walked back to the house. Maybe Tavish was right, after all. It *was* too much work for a woman alone. But where was her husband when she needed him most?

Calvin rode over to bolster Dearie's spirits. He had lost some plants, too, although not an entire field.

"You mustn't let it defeat you, Dearie," he said. "This is the plight of the farmer. We are at the mercy of the elements, and there is nothing we can do about it. Someday, when we can predict the weather and make it rain or snow at will, farming will be like other professions. But that is still a dream, I'm afraid."

"Oh, Calvin. I . . . I wish Tavish was here now. I need him more than ever. Did you write him as I asked?"

Calvin looked down at his long fingers. "Yes, I wrote him."

"Well? What did he say?"

"He said he would try to get away as soon as possible. Alistair's affairs have been keeping him quite busy, I understand."

"But what about his wife and home?" Dearie's eyes flashed angrily.

"I expect he plans to be home for harvest," Calvin chuckled nervously. "Tavish would never want to miss that, I'll wager."

"I can't wait until then! That's two more months. I need him now. I'll go to Philadelphia and bring him back myself!"

"No," Calvin said, placing a hand on her arm.

Dearie looked up at him, puzzled. "Why not?"

"No, Dearie. You stay here and see to the planting. I'll go."

"But, Calvin, that's absurd. You have much more to oversee at Rosalie than I do here."

"I have an excellent foreman, and Ezekiel can work with him when he is not here with you. Tavish has been my friend for many years. Let me do this, Dearie."

Sighing, Dearie nodded. A tiny flame of hope rekindled in her heart.

If anyone could bring Tavish back, Calvin could.

Chapter Eighteen

Calvin hated to leave the crops in the field, for anything could happen in his absence. He left specific instructions for his foreman, but he took little comfort in that. Many a crop had been lost due to the oversight of a foreman.

He could only hope that Tavish would be reasonable and they would return soon. Somehow he doubted that would happen. Tavish's last letter continued to praise Philadelphia in reverent tones, and he hadn't even asked about Dearie.

During the long journey, Calvin had time to reflect upon his friend's strange behavior. When Tavish had first spoken of his marriage, he had referred to it as a mistake. He had mentioned annulment, saying that his city-bred wife was unhappy in the country. Everyone thought that Tavish had married the girl for her large dowry. Calvin had imagined Dearie to be a homely woman, and probably unmarriageable, for Tavish had no money or visible means of support.

When he had met Dearie, Calvin had been dumb-founded, and even more perplexed than before. Something must be wrong with her, he reasoned. In vain he looked for defects in what seemed to be a perfect woman.

"She is spoiled and headstrong," Tavish had said.

No doubt Dearie was used to the finer things in life. But she had been without servants and fine clothes for almost a year, and Calvin had never once heard her complain. In fact, she treated her servants with respect, and praised them often.

"She despises life in North Carolina and longs to return to her father in Philadelphia" was another of Tavish's complaints.

Dearie seldom mentioned Philadelphia. She appeared to be quite happy in North Carolina. Even the plantation's deplorable condition upon her arrival had not discouraged her.

Ironically Dearie was exactly the type of woman Tavish had always said he wanted. But now that he had the woman of his dreams, he left her at every opportunity. It was as if he wished to drive her away from him. Calvin recalled the strange reaction Tavish had had to his questions . . .

"Well, Tavish. You wrote that you would explain all this when you returned," Calvin's sharp eyes had scrutinized his friend's face.

"What is there to explain? I married, and that is that."

"But that is not what you set out to do. What about the lawyer who ruined your father?"

"Oh, I have taken care of that," Tavish casually replied. "He has gotten his just desserts."

"What do you mean by that?"

"I'll explain later, Calvin."

But he never did. He had never said another word about it. Now, Calvin promised himself, folding his arms over his chest, he would have a satisfactory explanation for all this. And he would not leave Philadelphia without Tavish.

A carriage was waiting when Calvin's stage arrived in Philadelphia. A servant climbed down and shook Calvin's hand, then loaded his luggage into the vehicle. Minutes later the carriage pulled up to the home of a family friend, Arnold Bromley.

Arnold and his wife greeted Calvin at the door of their home. "Calvin Buie, I never thought to see the day when you would leave Rosalie. I thought you'd taken her to wife, instead of a pretty woman," Arnold said.

Calvin smiled. "A planter is married to his land, I guess. But we do get away occasionally."

After supper when the men were left alone in the parlor, Arnold narrowed his eyes. "What brings you to the city? I know it can't be business. You planters keep our Philadelphia factors alive. Don't tell me you are courting one of our fine ladies?"

Calvin laughed heartily. Then he thought suddenly of Colleen. Of late her pert little face and wide brown eyes had haunted his dreams. He must visit her millinery shop when he returned to Fayetteville. "If you would know the truth, Arnold, I have come to fetch home a friend. He has been gone too long and his wife needs him."

"So you have grown altruistic," Arnold grinned. "The country life must be good for one's soul. Who is this errant husband, if I may ask?"

"He's Alistair Munroe's cousin, Tavish McLeod."

Arnold's good-natured grin faded, and his expression grew somber. "You are a friend of Tavish McLeod? I wouldn't think he had many."

Calvin frowned. "I've known Tavish since boyhood. I gather you know him?"

Arnold nodded. "Although not all know him, everyone has heard of him. Not long ago a friend of mine was ruined by Master McLeod. Perhaps it was unwise to play cards against a man with such reputation, but McLeod was particularly heartless in this case. He took everything my friend had, and seemed to enjoy doing it." He shook his head. "I shall always remember what McLeod said when my friend had to declare bankruptcy."

"What was that?" Calvin asked, alarmed.

"He said, 'You'll live. I lived through it once.'"

Calvin winced. What had happened to Tavish? How could he have changed so much in so short a time? "I am sorry for your friend, Arnold."

"So am I. But he's not the only one."

They talked for hours, and the picture that emerged was not a pleasant one. Calvin began to wonder if his trip had been for nothing. Would Tavish ever want to return to North Carolina now? More importantly, would Dearie want him back now that he had changed so?

It was with some degree of dread that Calvin set out for Alistair's house two days later. Since it was midday, he hoped to find Tavish at home. A servant admitted Calvin to the parlor where Alistair was taking tea.

"Is this really Calvin Buie? You look exactly as Tavish described you. Please sit down and take tea with me." Alistair gestured to a chair opposite him.

"I'm glad to find that you have recovered from your accident."

Alistair sighed. "As well as one can recover from something like that. He shot me in the back, you know. If it hadn't been for Tavish . . . " He caught himself and looked away. "But tell me, Mr. Buie. Will you be staying with us? I'm afraid I have just had my monthly soiree, but I do so love to have visitors."

"No, I am staying with my friend, Arnold Bromley."

Alistair arranged the lace on his sleeve. "I think I know the name. However, you must join us at the tables tonight. Tavish has become quite good with cards."

"So I have heard. Will Tavish be back this afternoon?"

"Only to have a light supper and change for the evening." Alistair raised an eyebrow. "You know that we have formed a partnership, my cousin and I."

Calvin frowned. "I didn't know."

"Oh, yes. We've done quite well in business lately. I daresay I can persuade Tavish to move here permanently. I'm sure his wife would be only too happy to return to Philadelphia."

"I'm afraid not. She has made a home in North Carolina. I believe she intends to stay."

"Surely you can't be serious? I know her father would want her to return, especially now that Tavish is doing so well."

Calvin shrugged. "Tell Tavish to drop round for me and I will accompany him tonight."

"Tonight promises to be an exciting game. Tavish may be well matched in his opponent. He's from New Orleans."

"I shall look forward to it." Calvin smiled weakly.

Tavish arrived in elegant attire, and Calvin was momentarily stunned by his appearance. He wore a brocade jacket and a watered silk vest over white trousers. Although his clothes were the finest, his face was pallid, and there were dark circles under his eyes.

"Calvin," he said, embracing his friend warmly. "I never thought to see you in Philadelphia."

"After all this time, I'm surprised that you remember me, my friend."

Tavish smiled. "It's only been a few months, Calvin. As I wrote, I have been busy."

"I understand that your stay has been quite profitable. Your cousin tells me you have done well in business."

Tavish's eyes narrowed. "Calvin, you have no idea how easy it is to make money here. There are new ventures at every turn. Philadelphia is the center of trade for the entire area. If anything is to happen, it happens here or in New York. It's exciting. If you can stay a while, I promise you'll go back with your pockets full of gold."

"Tavish, have you forgotten that you have a wife in North Carolina?"

Tavish looked down at his hands, studying his nails. "No, I haven't forgotten."

"Do you not plan to return?"

"I do. In fact, I have a short trip planned soon."

"A short trip! Tavish, what has happened to you! You have a business, family, friends, a home."

Tavish laughed. "You call that broken-down plantation a home, but I have a better word for it."

Calvin ground his teeth in silence. The situation was worse than he'd imagined!

"Now, Calvin. We can't be at odds when you've only just arrived. Let me show you the city."

They were shortly on their way to a gambling hall, a dimly lit house set back from the street. A black servant admitted them and took their hats and cloaks.

"Good evening, Master McLeod," he said with a low bow. "A gentleman awaits you in the parlor to your right, sir."

Tavish led the way to an lavishly furnished parlor dominated by a single table. A man lounged in front of the fire, drinking a brandy. He rose when they entered. "Master McLeod?" He was very dark, and he spoke with a slight accent.

Tavish extended his hand. "Monsieur Robard. I am glad to meet you. Allow me to present my friend, Calvin Buie."

Robard bowed. "Will Monsieur Buie be playing with us tonight?"

Calvin raised his hands in protest. "No, no. I know nothing of cards."

"Very well, Master McLeod. Shall we begin? I will have the servant bring the other players."

Calvin sat in a comfortable wing chair by the fire while Tavish and Robard faced each other across the table.

Since meeting Robard, Tavish's expression had altered. His attention was now raptly focused upon his opponent, and nothing else seemed to matter. Presently, two other gentlemen joined them. Tavish acknowledged them briefly with a nod, then returned his gazed to Robard.

Calvin had taken a mild dislike to Robard, and as he sat there he tried to decide why. The man seemed friendly, but his every move was calculated. When he began to shuffle the cards, the flash of a diamond caught Calvin's eye. Then he knew at once that Robard was a professional gambler.

The knowledge bothered Calvin. Did Tavish know? Surely he did. Alistair had referred to the man earlier, but not as a gambler. Calvin wondered if he should try to warn Tavish. However, the game was already underway, and there was no opportunity.

The game continued on into the night. Bored, Calvin walked around to the other rooms. He observed a faro table for a time, then moved back to Tavish's table. Another man stood in the doorway observing the game.

"I understand that McLeod can no longer find an opponent in Philadelphia, so he's taken to importing them," the man said to Calvin in an undertone.

"Really? I should think he would have a good many to choose from, since he is so skilled."

"He's an excellent player. But they're afraid to play him. It's more than a game with him. He plays to ruin his opponent. I've heard that's the way he is in business dealings as well."

"How so?"

"He thinks nothing of putting a man out of his home, or taking away his livelihood. He just doesn't care. You know," the man said confidentially, "his reputation has gotten worse than his father-in-law's."

"His father-in-law?"

The man nodded. "Matthew Grayson."

Calvin was stunned. "Not the lawyer, Matthew Grayson?"

"The same. They're just alike, two peas in a pod. But if you ask me, the younger one's worse. He does everything with a vengeance."

Calvin tried to maintain his composure, but his thoughts were whirling. The idea that Dearie was Grayson's daughter had never occurred to him. Was that what Tavish had meant about Grayson getting his just desserts? Had Tavish married Dearie to get even with her father? Surely, he wouldn't do such a thing! But observing the look of fierce determination on Tavish's features, Calvin had to admit that it might be possible. Torn by emotions of disappointment and anger, he looked away.

A servant tapped him lightly on the shoulder.

'Master Buie? Master Arnold Bromley sent his carriage for you, if you wish to return now."

Calvin nodded. Without a word to Tavish, he rose and abruptly left the room.

Tavish looked up to see Calvin leave. A frown momentarily creased his brow, then he quickly returned his attention to the game. That night, for the first time in a long while, Tavish lost money.

He pondered the situation as he dressed the following morning. Robard was a professional gambler. Tavish had realized that fact halfway through the game. Even so, he thought that he could beat the man. Something had gone wrong. The more he considered the idea, the more likely it seemed that Robard had cheated.

The invitation to a rematch came mid-morning but Tavish declined. By then he was convinced the man was dishonest. Dishonesty would not have stopped Tavish, but his instincts told him to stay away from Robard. Besides, Calvin was in town, and Tavish wanted to talk with his friend.

Tavish sent a note to the Bromley's inviting Calvin to dinner. Alistair set about the arrangements, doing what he could to make the evening a festive affair. When at six o'clock no word had come from Calvin, Tavish rode over to Arnold Bromley's house.

He was coolly greeted by Arnold Bromley. "Yes? How may I help you, Master McLeod?"

"I must speak to my friend, Calvin Buie. We were expecting him at dinner this evening. But since we've had no word — "

"Calvin left early this morning — for North Carolina," Bromley said.

"What! Did he leave word, or some note for me?"

"No. I'm afraid not." Bromley closed the door in Tavish's face.

Tavish stood on the doorstep, perplexed. What had come over Calvin? he wondered.

After returning to the Bromley's, Calvin and Arnold had talked for hours. Calvin had confided his suspicions to Arnold, who had sighed and shaken his head.

"Now I don't know what to do," Calvin said. "I promised Dearie I would bring Tavish back. But now I think . . . "

"I don't know how to advise you, Calvin. It is a very difficult situation. The man seems to be a scoundrel through and through."

On the surface it was true. Apparently, Tavish had completely changed. After much reflection, Calvin had decided to return to North Carolina. He had no idea what he would tell Dearie, but now he realized that it would be better if she did return to her father.

After a few hours of fitful sleep, Calvin had risen the following morning and packed his things. Arnold Bromley had driven him to the stage.

On the way, Bromley had refrained from speaking, but there was heartfelt sympathy in his expression. The early morning fog was lifting as they pulled up in front of the waiting stage.

"Have a safe journey, Calvin. I hope that our next meeting is under more pleasurable circumstances."

Calvin had embraced his friend warmly and climbed aboard the stage. In a way he regretted not saying good-bye to Tavish, but it was better this way. His anger was too great to confront his friend now. Calvin sighed. It would be a long trip back to North Carolina.

Tavish returned to Alistair's house in a temper. Oblivious to his cousin's mood, Alistair fussed around the table arranging plates and wine goblets.

"Well? I hope Calvin isn't ill. The cook has promised us a rare feast for tonight. Venison stew, I believe . . . "

"He won't be here. And neither will I, Alistair." Tavish continued, ignoring Alistair's shocked expression. "Have the servant gather my things. I'm leaving for North Carolina."

Hoping to overtake Calvin on the road, Tavish packed lightly. The groom hastily saddled the best horse in the stable. Alistair trailed after Tavish, trying to convince him to stay.

"Really, Tavish! It's not even harvest time. You said you would stay until then."

Tavish shook his head. "I must go now."

"Just because your friend acted strangely — "

"I'm sorry, Alistair. I must leave now. I will try to return as soon as I can."

"But what will I do? How will I manage our business affairs?"

Tavish sighed impatiently. At the moment, business seemed unimportant. He had to know why Calvin had left so suddenly. "I really don't know, Alistair. I only know that I have to go."

Tavish spurred his horse into a fast clip. Calvin had been on the road for hours, but a coach was much slower. If Tavish rode all night, he could catch up with his friend on the second day.

Thoughts raced crazily through Tavish's head. Certainly, Calvin had been shocked at his newfound wealth. Or perhaps the gambling had disturbed him. But no, Calvin himself had gambled from time to time. They had been friends too long for something so trivial to come between them. What was it then?

Calvin had been a frequent visitor to the plantation, Tavish knew. Dearie spoke of him in every letter.

"Calvin took me to the McNeill's soiree," she had written on one occasion. Another time she wrote that Calvin had escorted her to a ball he had given.

Tavish suddenly wondered if a romantic liaison had developed between the two. He had certainly been gone long enough for such a thing to have happened. He ground his teeth bitterly. Why else would Calvin journey all the way to Philadelphia? To his knowledge, Calvin hadn't left North Carolina in years, except to attend his uncle's funeral.

But if Calvin had come to Philadelphia to declare his love for Dearie, it did not explain his sudden departure. Had he lost his nerve? *Perhaps he was intimidated by my wealth*, he thought suddenly. *Once I was a factor struggling to get out of bankruptcy. Now I am his equal. Dearie would have to choose between us.*

Then Tavish chided himself roundly. Dearie had already chosen. She was his wife. But, he reflected, Calvin knew that he had planned to seek an annulment when he returned. Angered by his thoughts, Tavish spurred his horse onward.

He rode through the night, but he arrived too late at the inn where the stage had stopped for the night. The stage had left two hours earlier, the innkeeper told him. Knowing that his horse was too exhausted to travel farther, Tavish secured a fresh mount, and set out again.

By noon Tavish came upon the stage pulling into a country inn for the midday meal. Wearily, he climbed down from his horse and walked into the inn.

"Tavish!" Calvin exclaimed, leaping to his feet in surprise.

Both men momentarily forgot their angry suspicions in the joy of seeing one another again. Tavish gripped his friend's hand warmly, but then frowned, remembering why he had come.

"You left without a word, Calvin."

Calvin, too, remembered. He sat down opposite Tavish and tried to think of what to say.

"Something is wrong. You've changed, Calvin."

Calvin looked up sharply. Tavish had taken the very words from his mouth. "I? Look at yourself, Tavish. You are the one who has left your home, business, and wife to play cards all night and put people out of their homes by day."

"What! You are the last person to complain about business, Calvin. I've never heard you talk about anything but crops, and the money you plan to make each year. Or has something changed all that?" Tavish's tone was angry and accusing.

Calvin shook his head. "Business is one thing, Tavish. But you've taken your vengeance too far. Innocent people have suffered."

"Innocent people?"

"Your wife, for instance."

"Ah, yes. My long-suffering, hard-working wife. But then you have been keeping her company in my absence, haven't you, Calvin? Helping to ease that suffering, I suppose?"

"What are you saying, Tavish!" Calvin sprang to his feet.

Tavish pushed back roughly from the table, and the bench fell over behind him. "You know very well that what I mean! What kind of friend are you? And what was your purpose in coming to Philadelphia? To ask when I planned to get an annulment!"

Calvin's mouth dropped open in shock. "How dare you accuse me of such a thing! Now I know that what they say about you is true! You have become exactly like your father-in-law. You are no better than Matthew Grayson!"

The color drained from Tavish's face. He drew back his fist and slammed it into Calvin's jaw. Calvin flew backwards, his long form crashing onto an oak bench. Several women screamed and the men circled closer to watch the fight.

"I must ask you to take your quarrel outside, sirs," the innkeeper demanded, held at bay by the savage look in Tavish's eyes.

"I warn you, Calvin. Don't ever say my name in the same sentence as Matthew Grayson!"

Calvin put a handkerchief to this bleeding mouth. His blue eyes narrowed as he stared at Tavish for a long moment. "I was wrong, Tavish. You are not the same as Matthew Grayson. You are worse — far worse. You not only took your revenge upon the man, but you used an innocent girl. You didn't restore your father's good name — you trampled it into the gutter."

With a strangled oath, Tavish leaped upon Calvin. The two men rolled over and over on the ground, only to get up and square off again, splitting benches, upsetting bowls, and overturning tables. The other guests watched, frozen and fascinated. Tavish pounded Calvin with furious blows. Fueled by his anger, Calvin returned every punch, bloodying Tavish's nose, and blackening his eye. The fight raged until the two combatants lay panting across one another, unable to lift their fists anymore.

Several of the men stepped forward to help them up. They swayed unsteadily as they were helped out to the water trough. Taken by the hair, their faces were plunged into the cold water. Satisfied they could do no more damage, the men left them alone.

Tavish looked up, water dripping off his face and smiled weakly. "You always went for my nose, Calvin. How come?"

Calvin chuckled and shook his dark head. "It's the biggest thing on your face, I guess."

"It's been a long time."

Calvin turned toward Tavish. "Yes, it has."

Tavish frowned and looked down at his reflection in the water. His left eye was swollen shut. "Did you mean what you said in there?"

"I meant it."

Tavish shook his head. "Well, Calvin. You never did have a way with words."

He threw his arm around Calvin's shoulder, and they walked slowly back into the inn, in search of a towel and dry clothes.

Chapter Nineteen

Although she had hoped, Dearie heard nothing from Calvin after he left for Philadelphia. However the time flew quickly by, for she found herself busy from dawn to dusk. With the warm weather and frequent showers, the crops flourished. Ezekiel and his men worked all day thinning and hoeing the young plants, then pulling the weeds.

The corn had to be replanted three times. Dearie nearly despaired when cutworms ate the second group of young plants. She tried desperately to rescue the remaining shoots.

"Happens every year," Ezekiel commented wryly.

"But can't something be done about it?" Dearie asked, exasperated. "At this rate, we'll never get a crop!"

"Only thing to do is replant," he said. "And hope those worms got their fill."

So the workers replanted the corn. Dearie breathed a sigh of relief as the stalks again grew tall enough to hill. This time they would survive — she knew it. But then she realized how certain she had been before. Tavish was right. There was so much she didn't know about planting. But she was learning . . . every day.

When she wasn't helping Tempie and Bess prepare meals for the men, Dearie visited the McFarlands. She was glad to see that the color had returned to Louisa's cheeks, and the frightened look had left her eyes. Mrs. McFarland had changed, too. The older woman talked more readily, and even smiled at Louisa. But the happy domestic tableau made Dearie sad somehow. *Will I ever have a family such as theirs?* she wondered.

Tavish joined Calvin on the stage to Fayetteville. The coach was crowded and there was no opportunity to talk. After their fight, an uneasy truce had been established between the two men. Their old closeness had been mostly regained but their present problems remained unsolved. When Calvin occasionally mentioned Dearie, Tavish managed to quickly change the subject. Finally Calvin gave up. The squawling children on board prevented further conversation until they arrived in Fayetteville.

There they secured horses and rode toward the plantation. Again Calvin tried to question Tavish, to no avail. He was unwilling to talk about Grayson, Dearie, or his business dealings. Sighing, Calvin resigned himself to leaving well enough alone. At least he had brought Tavish back as he had promised.

Dearie was just returning from the fields when the men arrived. Her sun-burnished hair had fallen into wispy curls down her neck, and her faded bonnet swung from her hand. Seeing visitors approaching, she tried vainly to brush the dirt from her dress. Then she froze. Her bonnet fell unnoticed to the ground. It was Tavish!

Should she rush to greet him? Or wait to see what he had to say? Not knowing how to react, Dearie stood rooted to the ground.

Tavish slid quickly off his horse and strode over to her. Taking her in his arms, he tenderly kissed the tears from her eyes.

"Oh, Tavish," she choked, burying her head in his shoulder. "It's been so long. So very long!"

The sun played on her hair like a golden halo, and her azure eyes sparkled with tears. Tavish thought that she was the most beautiful thing he had ever seen. Shaking his head, he stared at her in wonder. He had almost forgotten how wonderful it was to be near her.

Calvin cleared his throat. "I kept my promise, Dearie. That ought to be worth a piece of your apple pie."

Both Dearie and Tavish looked up, startled. "Oh, Calvin! Forgive me for being so rude. I have a fresh-baked pie just for you, and Tempie can put the kettle on."

The corner of Tavish's mouth turned up in a quizzical grin. "When did you take up cooking?"

"I've taken up a lot of things since you've been gone. Cooking, quilting, planting. . . . Oh, by the way, Calvin. Ezekiel just finished hilling the corn. He thinks most of it will make it this time."

Tavish looked from Dearie to Calvin and frowned. "Dearie, I thought I told you I didn't have time for planting just yet."

Dearie smiled. "But it's already done. I can't wait to show you the fields."

After they had eaten, Dearie proudly showed Tavish around the plantation. Calvin followed at a respectful distance.

Tavish said nothing, but occasionally he shot a glance at Calvin. Calvin smiled sheepishly. "It does look good, doesn't it, Tavish?"

"Yes indeed. But where did you get all the workers, Dearie? The last I heard, you had only three servants."

"Oh, Calvin had some extra hands and he lent them to me."

Tavish glanced at Calvin. "Extra hands? Since when did Rosalie have extra hands?"

Calvin shrugged. "I was only trying to help, Tavish."

Tavish's mouth tightened into a grim line. "You might have asked first."

Calvin's eyes flashed. "Had you been here, I most surely would have."

Clasping his hands behind his back, Tavish walked back across the fields without another word. Shortly afterwards, Calvin prepared to leave for Rosalie. The tension between the two men was palpable. Tavish disappeared into the house without saying good-bye.

"I'm sorry, Calvin." Dearie grasped his hand affectionately. "Perhaps Tavish is exhausted from the journey."

Calvin smiled stiffly. "Perhaps. Take care, Dearie. I will call on you later." He urged his horse into a gallop.

It tore at Dearie's heart to see the two friends at odds. *Tavish just doesn't understand,* she thought. *It is up to me to make him see.*

Dearie found Tavish in their bedroom, stripped to the waist. He was pouring water into the washbowl. She caught her breath sharply. It had been so long since she'd seen him. She stared, mesmerized, at his strong back and the taut muscles in his arms, as he splashed water on his face. She started to speak, but when he turned toward her the words died in her throat.

She couldn't keep her eyes from his broad chest. His dark mat of hair tapered seductively to a vee at his trousers. She wanted desperately to touch him, to run her fingers along his strong shoulders. A rush of overwhelming desire left her weak, unable to even move.

Tavish took a step toward her. She stood transfixed, afraid that he might move away from her. Now that he was with her again, she was deathly afraid that she might do or say something to make him leave.

She could feel the warmth of his passion as he came closer. His hazel eyes danced with a gold fire, and she knew then that he wanted her too. His fingers brushed her shoulders, and her bones felt as though they would melt beneath his touch. He lowered his hands gently to cup her breasts. Through the fabric of her dress she could feel the heat radiating from him. Now barely breathing, Dearie's eyes fluttered closed.

She felt him loosen the buttons on her dress, and pull it down over her shoulders. In a moment the dress fell to her feet. He undid the ribbons of her pantalettes, bringing them down over her hips. Then, lifting her into his arms, he crushed her to his chest. Dearie's arms wound around his neck and she pressed closer to him.

He carried her to the bed, where he held her in his lap for a long time, as if she was a small child. She opened her eyes to see his mouth lowering over hers. His kiss was deep and urgent, and her lips parted eagerly as he deepened the kiss. How long had it been since they had kissed . . . a lifetime, it seemed! His mouth was soft and tender, becoming bruisingly insistent as he moved from her mouth to her cheeks, nose, and eyelids.

Filled with desire, Dearie tenderly traced his face — the hallows of his cheeks, the curve of his lips, the arch of his dark brow. Her fingers played with his sandy hair, then caught at the thick mat on his chest. He was hers at last!

"I have missed you, my Dearie," he whispered against her hair.

She wanted to ask him why he'd left her for so long, but she was unable to speak. Nothing was important now but Tavish. Her lips traced a line along his jaw from his ear to his mouth. She drank in the feel, the smell, and the warmth of his body. She would never get enough of him!

Gently, he laid her down upon the bed. He bent reverently over her, taking a nipple in his mouth and sucking until it went rigid between his lips. He then moved to the other nipple, outlining it with his tongue until it was taut as a pink rosebud.

Dearie moaned, pulling him to her. He paused briefly to remove his trousers, then he lowered himself over her. She ached to have him in her, but he continued to tantalize her slowly with his fingers until she cried out for him.

When he entered her, she was moist and ready to receive him, and she drew him still further into the velvet recesses of her body. Her hips moved against him as he thrust more and more deeply, rocking them as one. At last, they climaxed together, shudder upon shudder of exquisite sensation cascading over them like waves onto a beach.

Dearie's mind seemed to float freely, suspended in the space above her body. The intense warmth of utter fulfillment permeated her senses, and seemed to touch her very soul. Gradually, her mind became one with her body as Tavish withdrew gently from her. Lying beside her, her reached over to take her hand in his ... something he had never done before.

"Tavish," she whispered, "Why were you away for so long?"

He turned to look at her, and a strange expression flitted across his features. "I honestly don't know" was his puzzled answer. Now his business dealings, the money he had acquired, the games he had won all seemed insignificant. It was as if those things belonged to another time and another person.

"I'm glad you returned," she whispered, nestling against his shoulder.

It seemed that they had just drifted off to sleep when she felt him stir beside her. She opened her eyes to find him gazing at her with a look of infinite tenderness. She held out her arms and he wrapped himself around her. Pressed against him Dearie felt the familiar ache in her loins.

"Oh, Tavish," she whispered. "Tavish."

She loved his name, for it was so much a part of him. Trembling with renewed desire, she traced the line of his strong shoulders, down his back to his firm buttocks. She could not have designed a more perfect body, she thought.

Tavish took his time exploring her body, raining kisses down her graceful neck and over her full breasts. Dearie arched toward him, warmed by the fire of his touch. His fingers moved down to the downy triangle between her legs, and he tentatively caressed the velvet moistness. Then, to her surprise, Dearie felt his tongue probing where his fingers had been. The exquisite sensation heightened her desire until she writhed with pleasure.

Finally Tavish entered her again. This time he thrust inside her more slowly, building to an intensity that was even greater than they'd shared before. When at last their passion came together in a shuddering release, they held tightly to one another, like two sailors adrift in a crashing sea.

"I love you, Tavish," she breathed into his shoulders.

He pulled away from her reluctantly. Then kissed her forehead and smoothed her golden hair against the pillow. "You are so beautiful," he said. "I want to remember you this way . . . always."

What a strange thing to say, Dearie thought as she drifted off to sleep.

The next morning, Dearie awoke to find her husband still in the bed beside her. It was the first time since they had been married that he had remained with her the entire night. She was filled with happiness. Surely now everything will be all right, she thought.

She bathed quickly and busied herself about the kitchen. Hotcakes and bacon were cooking when Tavish finally awoke. Momentarily confused, he sat up in bed, a frown on his face. Then he remembered — he was back in North Carolina with Dearie. A familiar feeling of guilt seized him again.

The problem of Dearie had troubled him often on the long ride back to North Carolina.

"What do you intend to do, Tavish?" Calvin had asked.

"I don't know." Tavish knew that he should send her back to her father. Then why was he finding it so hard to do?

When he saw her he knew why he had hesitated. He didn't want to send her back. Yet she could not stay. He was no planter, he was a factor. He had no interest in building up this wreck of a plantation, and he could pretend no longer. Only lately, he had learned that he preferred life in the city.

He suddenly realized that he had never discussed his wishes with Dearie. He had always assumed that she would decide to return to Philadelphia of her own volition. But she had not. Tenacious as a blackberry bush, she had stubbornly planted herself in the North Carolina soil. He saw that she had changed from the naive girl he had brought here months ago. Now she was a woman — no longer concerned only with what dress to wear, or how many parasols to bring. A glow of admiration welled up inside him, but he immediately pushed it to the back of his mind. It was time to take her home.

"I've decided that we will move to Philadelphia," he announced at breakfast. "I still have pressing business matters to attend to there. I know that you have missed your father and all your friends. I can return to Fayetteville occasionally to attend the factoring business, but I have grown to like Philadelphia as you do."

"Philadelphia!" Dearie stared at him aghast. "But I don't want to move back to Philadelphia!"

The look on her face shocked Tavish. It was as if he had asked her to move to a European country instead of her home.

"I thought you would be pleased. After all you have complained more than once about the rustic life here. And I agree. It is nothing like the sophisticated life of the big city."

Dearie shook her head. "I love it here now. This is my home."

Tavish sighed heavily. "This is no home, Dearie. Surely it is nothing like the fine mansions in Philadelphia. And you are right, there is nothing to do here — no theaters or fine shops or dining halls.

Dearie waved her hand impatiently. "I don't need all those things. For goodness' sake, Tavish. I have rebuilt the house and planted the fields. Ezekiel assures me we will have a good crop to bring to market. One day, Beauvais will be a great plantation, like Greenhill or Rosalie."

Tavish drew a deep breath. He hadn't expected Dearie to react this way at all. "You still have your silly romantic notions. I've told you before, Dearie. I don't have the time to devote to this now. Running a plantation is a full-time job, and one that I cannot now undertake." He hesitated, about to tell her that he was no planter, and never would be.

Dearie smiled sweetly, placing a hand on his shoulder. "You don't have to worry, my love. I've undertaken it for you. And I am doing an excellent job," she told him proudly.

"Whether I agree or not," Tavish said darkly.

Dearie caught her lips in thought. It was true, she hadn't consulted him on the improvements she had made. But he had been away. "Tavish, I'm sorry. Please, can't you see what this means to me?"

"I do see. But I thought you would have taken my wishes into consideration." He looked away, frowning. "I think you'll quickly change your mind when you have to deal with the harvest and milling, then take your crops to market. It is not a woman's job, Dearie."

"I have Ezekiel and . . . Calvin to help me."

Tavish's mouth compressed in a tight line. "I see. Then you surely do not need me." He pushed his chair back from the table and stalked out of the room.

Dearie slumped down in her chair. She had done it again! He had been home less than a day, and she had managed to turn him against her. She had to go after him. No matter what it took, she would accede to his wishes.

She followed him out to the fields, where she found him staring out at the young plants.

"Tavish, I do need you — more than I can say. Please forgive me for being so selfish. I was only trying to help."

He continued to stare into the distance without speaking.

Helplessly she cast about for something else to say. "I. . . . thought you wanted me to adjust to my surroundings. That is what you said. Now you say we must return to Philadelphia. I've tried to do what you wanted me to do. . . . " The tears streamed down her cheeks. "But it is never what you want."

Tavish turned and was stricken by the anguish on her face. He was again flooded with remorse for what he had done to her. Of course she didn't understand. How could she? He shook his head, overwhelmed with confusion. He touched her cheek with his fingertips, then looked away. He couldn't bear the look on her face, and he had no words of comfort to give her.

"Dearie," he finally said, taking her hands in his. "I must return to Fayetteville to see to business there. Please think about what I've said. It is for your own good that I suggest you return to Philadelphia. You will never be happy here, isolated out in the country."

"But I am happy . . . at least, I would be happy if you would stay here with me."

He avoided her pleading gaze. "But I cannot stay here."

He remained for two more days, but they barely spoke. There seemed to be an impassable wall between them that neither one could scale. Wherever he went, Dearie watched him, her blue eyes hurt and bewildered, until he could bear it no longer.

As he prepared to leave she stood near him while Clarence saddled his horse, waiting for him to say something . . . anything.

Tavish shut his eyes, realizing with painful clarity that everything he had done had been to avoid this very moment. He had run away until there was no place to run. He *had* to tell her the truth . . . that the marriage was a sham, that he'd married her to get even with her father.

Tavish took her arm and led her down the lane. *I must tell her now,* he thought, bracing himself. He opened his mouth to speak, but she slid her arms around his neck and pressed her soft lips to his. "Please stay with me," she whispered against his mouth.

Emotion welled up in him, forcing tears to his eyes. "No," he said, holding her apart from him. He looked up into the sky, not half so blue as her eyes. "Damn it all," he said and turned away, feeling unbearably empty.

Her eyes dry and her head held high, Dearie watched him mount his horse. Only the slight tremble of her lips belied her composure.

"I will be back as often as I can, depending on business," he told her.

She nodded, then quickly looked away. "The wheat will be in soon. I will be busy supervising the workers."

Tavish shook his head and nudged his horse with his booted heel. "It's not a woman's job," he said as he cantered away.

"Well, we'll see about that," Dearie said to herself. She lifted her skirts and walked back into the house.

Hearing that Tavish had returned to Fayetteville, Calvin came by to visit Dearie. She had grown so used to confiding in him that she immediately told him what had happened.

"Calvin, what ails Tavish? I don't understand him at all," Dearie cried, tears filling her eyes.

Calvin shook his head, the sharp angle of his face more pronounced. It saddened him to think that he had lost his best friend. "I wish I knew."

"He wants to move to Philadelphia, of all places!"

Although he was shocked that Tavish wanted to move, Calvin smiled at her outrage. "I imagine he thought that you'd be pleased."

"But I'm not, Calvin. This is my home now."

"He's been away. Perhaps he doesn't realize how much you have changed."

Dearie tapped her chin with her index finger. "I hadn't thought of that. Can he not see what I have done? The fields are planted, the house renovated. I thought he would be so pleased."

Calvin sighed, "I wonder if he isn't confused by all the changes?" He was reasoning out loud. "He thought you would be unhappy here, being used to the sophistication of Philadelphia. Now he is offering to return you to the world he took you from. He never dreamed you wouldn't want to leave North Carolina."

The more he thought about it, the more convinced Calvin was that he had hit upon the problem. Tavish had expected Dearie to return to her father long before now. He had intended to beat Grayson at his own game, by taking the dowry and his only daughter away. He had thought that by depositing her at a burned-out plantation by herself she would have quickly run back to her father, and the game would be over. He would have gained his revenge, for Grayson would have been outraged at the hoax.

The game had not ended as planned, however. Dearie had prevailed, turning the ruined plantation into a real home. Then, in an effort to help her husband, she had cleared the fields and planted crops. Women like Dearie weren't supposed to adapt well. In this regard, Tavish had underestimated his bride.

Feeling guilty for what he had done, Tavish had stayed away from her as much as possible. Alistair's accident had provided still another reason to delay facing his problem.

By chance, Tavish stumbled onto a way of gaining more money by investing Alistair's inheritance. One thing had led to another and soon he was making more money than he ever had before. All his energies had been channelled into his new venture, and he had forsaken everything else, even Dearie. Now, trying to make the best of a bad situation, he had offered to return Dearie to her home. He planned to return with her — after all, he had made his mark there.

But Tavish didn't realize that the mark he had left in Philadelphia was a black one, and not easily erased. He was unaware that people considered him a worse scoundrel than his own father-in law.

"Calvin, what can we do?" Dearie asked him.

He was so deep in his thoughts that he hardly heard her.

"It's obvious that I can't return to Philadelphia now. I can't think why Tavish would suddenly want to forsake his home and friends, He's never spoken favorably about the city. And now . . . "

"And now," Calvin said, his dark blue eyes narrow with thought. "We have to convince him that he's wrong."

"Wrong?"

Calvin nodded slowly. "Yes, that's it. We must show him that he needn't go. His life is here."

Her shoulders sagging, Dearie sighed deeply. "Oh, Calvin, I don't think I know how to do that."

Calvin smiled. "We'll find a way. *You'll* find a way."

Chapter Twenty

Calvin invited Dearie to Rosalie to visit the mill before harvest, and Clarence drove her over in the wagon. Wildflowers in pink, yellow, and red were blooming in the woods along the side of the road. Dogwood competed with bright splashes of redbud in the pines and trailing over the fences were lush vines of Carolina jasmine.

Rosalie was situated on a creek that fed into the Cape Fear River. Calvin's father had built the mill, which had provided an extra source of income for the plantation. The elder Buie had had knowledge of mills, since his own father had been a miller in Scotland.

Dearie was full of anticipation as they drove through the tall trees leading up to the plantation. She knew now how Calvin and Duncan McNeill felt about the land. It was as if she were a part of all she saw — the woods, the red clay country roads, and the fields planted in wheat or corn. And Tavish, too, belonged here — not in Philadelphia.

Calvin greeted her at the mill. He lifted her down from the wagon and took her arm.

"Rosalie has one of the best mills in the state," he told her proudly.

He led her into a three-storied frame structure built on a rock formation. It had the same crisp, whitewashed look as the plantation.

"It has three runs of millstones." Calvin pointed to the large, flat stones. "Each stone can grind either wheat or corn."

A short, balding man with a red face was adjusting the ropes attached to a series of pulleys. When he saw Calvin, he wiped his hands on a handkerchief.

"How-do, Master Calvin, ma'am."

"Dearie, this is Amos Diver. Amos runs the mill for me."

Amos smiled proudly. "This is the finest mill anywheres around, I'll warrant."

Amos pointed out the ingenious system of the pulleys and leather belts that transferred the power generated by the water wheel. The kernels and ground flour moved between the floors of the building, and carried through the process of grinding, sifting and bagging by a clever system of chutes and conveyer belts which were also powered by the waterwheel.

"I've never seen anything like it," Dearie exclaimed, fascinated.

Amos beamed. "Yes, ma'am. You just bring the grain and we'll do the rest."

Tavish remained in Fayetteville. Many of the planters had already harvested their wheat crops, and the roads were filled with wagons loaded with grain.

The plantation was abuzz with activity when Ezekiel and his men finally arrived to harvest the crop. Dearie and Tempie had been up since dawn preparing baskets of food for the workers.

"Oh, Tempie," Dearie said, clasping her hands. "It's finally happened. Beauvais is a real plantation. Today we harvest the wheat!"

Tempie shook her turbaned head. "Miss Dearie, I seen plenty of harvests. This is only the first part. We still got the threshing, then comes the milling. Oh, Lordy! We ain't seen nothing yet."

Tempie was right. The harvesting was a much longer process than Dearie had ever imagined. Ezekiel used a cradle, which was a scythe attached to a frame. The cradle had five long fingers that conformed to the blade and extended above it.

Dearie watched in awe as Ezekiel threw the cradle. With a swift toss of his arm, the cut grain fell into the cradle fingers. Then he turned to the side as he completed the cut and deposited the grain. He was like an athlete, expertly brandishing a long pole. Some of the men followed behind Ezekiel, raking the grain into piles, while others bound it into sheaves.

It was a long, arduous process, as Ezekiel could only cut two or three acres of grain a day. Only when Ezekiel signaled could the workers rest or take water. Then Dearie and the other women hurried to open the baskets and distribute the food.

"Where did you learn to throw a cradle, Ezekiel?" Dearie asked.

Ezekiel gave her a sidelong glance. "I've been a field worker all my life, Miss Dearie. I learned by doin'. Throwing a cradle come natural to me. They say I'm good at it." He shrugged. "I don't know. I just do my job."

While the grain was being harvested, Clarence cleared out the barn, and, with the help of some of the workers, erected a threshing floor. When the sheaves of wheat were brought in, horses were harnessed to poles and driven in a circle around the threshing floor. When the heads were separated from the chaff, the straw was thrown to one side with pitchforks. Then the grain was swept up and put into bags to take to the mill.

Dearie was exhausted by the end of the harvest. But as Tempie had predicted, there was much more to be done. Now they had to take the threshed wheat to be milled.

"We'll need more wagons, Miss Dearie," Clarence said. "It'll take us forever if we take one load at a time."

Dearie followed Clarence to the barn, and was astonished by what she saw. The barn was filled to overflowing with bags of wheat.

"Clarence! How many have we got?" she exclaimed, clapping her hands.

"I don't know, ma'am. I don't b'lieve I kin count that far."

Dearie sent Clarence and Ezekiel to Fayetteville to rent wagons. Transporting the grain to the mill took several days even with the additional wagons. After the wheat was milled, Clarence returned with only a fifth of the amount he had taken.

"What happened to all the wheat?" Dearie wanted to know.

Clarence shrugged. "Five bushels of wheat just makes one barrel of flour, Miss Dearie. It don't seem near enough after all we went through, and it took 'most two days."

Taking out pen and paper, Dearie pursed her lips in thought. "Well, we've got thirty-six hundred barrels. That should bring in a goodly sum," she said, thinking out loud. "You go on and get this flour into town. We'll need some money for the corn harvest. I wish I could see Tavish's face when you bring the barrels in. He won't believe it!"

Tavish was more irritated than pleased to see Clarence and his wagonloads of flour. At the time, he was surrounded by several planters who were arguing heatedly over the price of grain.

"What is it, Clarence? Can't you see that I'm busy right now?"

"Yes sir, Master Tavish. Miss Dearie done sent me in with her load of grain. She say can you pay me right away, on account of we got the corn coming in soon, and she gots to have money to pay for the harvest — "

"That's enough, Clarence." Tavish reached in his pocket and handed a purse to Clarence. "Here, take her this. That should take care of things for a while. Now please don't bother me again while I"m trying to conduct business, Clarence."

Clarence nodded. "Yessir, Master Tavish. Uh, beg pardon, Master Tavish . . . "

"Yes?"

"Does you want me to unload them barrels in the warehouse?"

Tavish sighed impatiently. "That will be fine."

"We going to need help, Master Tavish."

"Clarence, there's five men who've been unloading the barrels in the back. They'll help you. I'm sure that's all the help you'll need."

Clarence shrugged. "I don't know."

Tavish shook his head as Clarence left the office. The planters exchanged smiling glances.

Dearie was eagerly awaiting Clarence when he returned to the plantation.

"Well? What did Tavish say, Clarence? Was he surprised that we sent so much?"

Clarence shrugged. "He didn't say much, Miss Dearie. He were a mite busy at the time. But he said to give you this."

He handed her the purse.

Dearie took it and dumped the contents out on the table. "Clarence! There is only five hundred dollars here!"

Clarence jumped at her accusatory tone. "I didn't take none, honest, Miss Dearie. That's all he give me. I'll stake my life on it."

"It's only a fraction of the amount we should have received," Dearie said weakly. "Did he say he would send more later, Clarence?"

"No, ma'am. He didn't say."

Shortly afterwards, Calvin Buie arrived to congratulate Dearie on her wheat crop. He found Dearie sitting in the parlor alone, looking distraught.

"Dearie, what's wrong? Ezekiel tells me you harvested some eighteen thousand bushels of wheat. I came to congratulate you. That's a record hereabouts. Hardly anyone gets as much as thirty bushels an acre."

She looked up at him, her eyes red and swollen. "This is what I got for my efforts. Not even enough to buy seed for next season."

She handed him the purse Tavish had given her. Calvin emptied the contents into his hand. When he saw the pitiful amount, a muscle worked in his jaw. But he forced a cheerful smile to his lips. "I'm sure there must be some mistake. You know how absentminded Clarence can be. You marked the barrels, didn't you?"

She nodded, her lower lip trembling.

Calvin moved toward her and put his hand on her shoulder. "It's all right. I'll look into this when I take my wheat in tommorow. I'm sure there is a simple explanation."

"Thank you, Calvin. You are a true friend." Dearie reached up and kissed him lightly on the cheek. "Please excuse me. I'm so very tired."

On his way into town the following day, Calvin rehearsed what he would say to Tavish. This time he expected an explanation for everything. This last affront was too much, especially after Dearie had worked so hard to produce such an excellent harvest. There was only one thing to do — he had to make things right with the girl.

Calvin arrived at Fayetteville shortly after noon. Most of the planters had gone to lunch, and Tavish was alone in his office. Calvin charged in unannounced. Tavish looked up, a half-smile on his face.

"You could at least knock, Calvin."

Calvin's expression was stony. "You've gone too far this time. Tavish. I will have an explanation for your behavior, and I will have it now!"

Dearie rose early after a troubled sleep. Nothing made sense to her anymore. She seemed unable to please Tavish, no matter what she did. It made no difference that she had produced the best wheat crop in the area — he didn't even care! How could he be so thoughtless? Tears rose in her eyes when she realized that he had been that way all along.

The more she pondered her situation, the more angry she became. How dare he treat her like a child after all she had accomplished!

"I'll speak to him myself." she said aloud. "Let him tell me to my face."

After washing hurriedly, she dressed in a blue velvet riding habit and a matching hat with black feathers. She stepped back from the glass to survey her figure. A dark blue cummerbund hugged her slender waist, emphasizing her full breasts and rounded hips. The blue velvet matched the vivid blue of her eyes. But she was shocked by the coldness of her gaze. Her eyes reminded her of someone else's — her father's. Had she really become so hard and cold? The woman in the glass answered her. *Yes. Yes, you have.*

Dearie turned quickly away. She wouldn't think of that now. Now she must have some explanation from Tavish.

As she was preparing to leave, she saw that Clarence had hitched the horses to the wagon.

"I got to get some supplies, Miss Dearie. I'll drive you in."

Dearie and Clarence arrived in Fayetteville shortly after Calvin. She entered Tavish's office quietly. Seeing the door closed, she sat down in a chair to wait.

Presently she heard shouting from within the office. The voice sounded familiar. It was Calvin's!

"Do you even realize how hard Dearie worked to bring in the wheat?"

"No, Calvin. But I reckon you're going to tell me."

"Oh, why do I bother?" Calvin paced around Tavish's desk, his hands knotted behind his back. "You've changed, Tavish. You're not the same man I used to know."

"Well, as I told you before, you've changed yourself, Calvin. Why don't you tell me the *real* reason you've come?"

"I've come to demand that you do right by that girl. I know you married her to get even with her father for bankrupting Murdock."

Tavish rose from his desk to face his friend. "It was more than bankruptcy, Calvin, and you know it! Grayson killed my father just as sure as I sit here. He took everything my father had — his money, his business, his name — he destroyed Murdock!"

"All right, you've had your revenge. Marrying Grayson's daughter was revenge enough. Then you said you were going to get an annulment. Well, why haven't you? Send her back to her father, for the love of God, and stop punishing her!"

Dearie clapped her hand over her mouth to keep from crying out. She couldn't believe what she was hearing. Tavish had married her to get even with her father. She stood up shakily. "Oh, no. Oh, no, it can't be! Tavish loves me . . . he said . . . "

"You do want me to get an annulment, don't you, Calvin? That would suit your plans perfectly, eh? Then you could step in to play the gallant knight, and carry her off to Castle Rosalie."

"You stupid fool! She'd never marry me. It's you she loves. And why, I don't know — "

The door slammed in the outer office. Tavish brushed past Calvin to see who it was, but only the scent of lavender lingered in the air. From the window, they saw Clarence whipping the horses into a fast trot as he drove Dearie out of town.

Tavish hit the window frame with his fist. "Oh, God! What have I done? What have I done?"

"You've probably broken her heart," Calvin replied, his expression dark.

"Oh, no. I'm so sorry. I never meant for it to be like this." Tavish shook his head, his sandy hair falling across his forehead.

"Then you *do* care."

Tavish rubbed his eyes with his fingers. "I tried not to. Tried tell myself she'd be better off with her father, but. . . . I couldn't let her go, somehow. It was just easier to stay away. Then I didn't have to think about it."

Calvin nodded. He'd figured as much. "You're going to have to win her back, Tavish. Now that she knows everything, it won't be easy. But you owe it to her to try."

Matthew Grayson stared out the stagecoach window at the Carolina woodlands. He passed the time calculating how much lumber the forest would yield, and made a note to inquire into erecting a lumber mill in one of the major cities, such as Fayetteville. The deep verdant green of the pine trees, and the bright dots of jasmine were lost on him.

He had purposely delayed posting the letter which would have informed Dearie of his visit.

She has enough on her mind, what with a child to care for, he had reasoned. Besides, he wanted to be one of the first to greet his grandson. He had no doubt that the baby was a boy — he felt it in his bones.

It had bothered him that Tavish had left the city so abruptly without saying good-bye. The young man must have been called to his wife's bedside for the birth of their child. Grayson frowned. He hoped nothing had gone wrong. But no, he would certainly have been informed.

When he saw Fayetteville, Grayson immediately thought better about investing in a sawmill. He doubted that the town could support such a venture. He shook his silver head disdainfully. Poor Dearie. To think the child had been subjected to this primitive existence for almost a year.

I'll take her back where she belongs, he thought. The deep crevices of his face drew into a smile.

When Dearie returned to Beauvais she immediately ordered Tempie to pack her trunk. While Tempie packed, she paced back and forth in the parlor, trying desperately to collect her thoughts.

Tavish had married her just to get even with her father! Her father had bankrupted Murdock McLeod, causing him to lose everything, and eventually his life! Could her father really have done such a thing? How was it that she had never known?

She remembered when Duncan McNeil asked her if Tavish had spoken to her about Murdock. She hadn't even known who Murdock was! She knew now why Tavish had never spoken of his father.

Dearie was torn between anger at her husband, and fury at her father for causing such pain. The servants tiptoed around as she raged and cried, then fell into a morose silence.

What should I do now? Where should I go? Always she came back to the same questions.

In the midst of her turmoil, Matthew Grayson arrived at the plantation. When Clarence showed him into the parlor, Dearie sat frozen in shock.

"Father!" she exclaimed in amazement.

"My little doll! What has happened! Clarence told me you lost the child. Why in heaven's name didn't you tell me? I would have come immediately."

Grayson took his daughter in his arms. Seeing that she was distraught, he assumed she was still mourning the child.

"Oh, Father. You have no idea what I have been through."

Grayson nodded sympathetically. "I can see how awful it has been for you here. Why, you haven't even any servants to speak of. The conditions here are primitive at best." He clenched his teeth. "I should never have let you come. A short stay in Europe would have been much better, but you were set on marrying that scoundrel."

Dearie pushed him away, her eyes blazing. "Don't you speak to me of scoundrels, Father! You bankrupted Tavish's father. You sent him to an early grave, and you talk as if Tavish were the only one at fault! Then you let me marry him and ruin my life! How could you have done such a thing, Father!" Tears of rage streamed down her flushed cheeks.

Matthew Grayson sputtered in protest, trying to understand what she was saying. "My dear. . . . child, you are distraught. Under the circumstances I fully understand why."

"No, you don't understand! Tavish said you took everything his father had — his home, his business, his reputation in the community — everything!"

"I. . . . I bankrupted Tavish's father? Why Dearie, that is impossible. I don't even know any planters."

"Murdock McLeod was a factor. You bankrupted him in the panic of 1819. And you gave us his business for a wedding present!"

"I did?" Matthew Grayson's mouth dropped open in amazement. His shrewd mind ran back over the details of the transaction, but the names had long since been forgotten. Murdock McLeod sounded vaguely familiar, but he had been one of many. Grayson shook his head. "No, Dearie. I'm sure there has been some mistake."

"No, Father. It is true." She looked down at her work-roughened hands. "Tavish married me to get even with you. To get back some of what he felt you took from him." The words brought fresh tears to her eyes.

Grayson's face reddened. "Now it all becomes clear! All the things I wondered about. Why, the scoundrel! He is worse than I ever suspected. He's a criminal!"

"He's no worse than you, Father," Dearie told him quietly. "I told you before that the two of you are alike. But I never realized in just what way."

Grayson paced furiously back and forth "I will set the law on him as soon as I can get my hands on the rogue."

"Stop, Father!" Dearie silenced him with a hand on his arm. "Are you denying that you did this to Murdock McLeod?"

"Well ... I ... "

"It is true!"

"It is possible. But, Dearie, you know nothing of business. At the time, there were so many bad loans. And Sloan had extended credit far beyond the normal limits. And then, during the panic, I really had no choice but to call in many of my notes."

"There is always a choice, Father."

"But to take a young girl and marry her under false pretenses just to get back at me! I'll have him put in jail for this if it's the last thing I do."

"No. It is I who have suffered, Father. I do not excuse Tavish from his part, but at least I finally understand him." A tear wobbled and fell from her golden lashes.

"Now, now, my child. I'm sure you'll feel much better about everything when we've returned to Philadelphia."

"I'm not going back with you, Father. I don't know where I'm going, but I'm not going there."

Matthew Grayson sank into a chair. "You aren't going back to Philadelphia with me?"

"No."

Dearie left her father in the parlor with a snifter of brandy. A short time later she reappeared, dressed in a traveling gown. When Clarence carried out her trunk her father followed her out to the wagon, a disbelieving look on his face.

"Surely you don't really intend to leave? Can't we talk this over?"

Dearie shook her head. "I'm sorry, Father. I can stay here no longer."

The old man was completely bewildered now. "But where will you go? Have you enough money? Please let me come with you . . . at least until you are settled . . . ."

Dearie brushed his cheek with her lips. "Good-bye, Father."

Watching his daughter ride away, Matthew Grayson wondered if he would ever see her again. A tear trickled down his weathered cheek. He was too old for this.

Chapter Twenty-One

Tavish struggled with his emotions for a time before deciding to face Dearie. It wasn't as simple as just going home. She must hate him now that his deception had been exposed. Still, he was somewhat relieved to have the truth out in the open. After Calvin left, he had gone into the warehouse and counted thirty-six hundred barrels of flour, more than he'd ever dreamed she could harvest. Clarence had never even hinted that there was so much. He'd assumed the servant had brought the entire yield in one or two wagons.

What must she think of me now? I gave her a mere fraction of what her crop was worth. I have cheated her out of everything she deserved.

Now he knew he had to face her regardless of the consequences. The whole thing had gone on far too long.

Riding out to the plantation, Tavish's heart was suddenly lightened. It was all over! They could start anew. They would be man and wife as they were meant to be, without secrets or doubts. Perhaps if he explained everything to her, Dearie would understand. Perhaps if he told her he loved her . . .

Tavish smiled when he thought of saying those words to her. He had been wrong about her along. He remembered the joy in her eyes as she proudly showed him the plantation she had rebuilt. He could still see her jumping in the Cape Fever River to save Louisa Suggs from drowning when she couldn't even swim. Had it not been for Dearie, the girl would surely have died. He smiled when he recalled that the fields, gone to broomsedge and pine trees, were now cleared and planted with grain. He had said that she couldn't do it, that a woman couldn't undertake a responsibility like planting. But she'd proven him wrong, many times.

How could he tell her how he felt? So much had happened to drive them apart. How could he make her believe how sorry he was for everything? And how in heaven could he convince her to stay after all she'd been through?

Tavish was filled with trepidation when he arrived at the door of Beauvais. How he longed to see her again . . . to take her in his arms . . .

The door swung open suddenly, and Tavish found himself face to face with Matthew Grayson.

Grayson was as startled as Tavish. Then, when he saw that it wasn't Dearie come back, the old man turned and walked back into the house, leaving the door ajar.

Tavish followed him inside. "She's gone," Grayson said dully.

"Gone? Gone where?"

"I don't know. She wouldn't say." Grayson sank wearily into a large chair.

He seems like a very old man, Tavish thought. Under his hooded lids his blue eyes were faded and bloodshot, and the wrinkles around his mouth seemed more pronounced.

Tavish took a chair opposite his father-in-law. Here, away from his luxurious house and office, Matthew

Grayson was no longer formidable. In fact, in his present state he looked almost pathetic.

"She hates us both, you know," Grayson said.

Tavish raised a questioning eyebrow.

"Oh, yes. Both of us. I'm as much to blame as you, I guess. Although it all happened years ago." He sighed. "I should tell you, I came to take her back with me. Dearie and the child. I never intended that she stay with you any longer than was necessary. You weren't good enough for her, and I knew that you were not what you pretended to be . . . "

"Then why did you consent to the marriage?"

"Dearie told me she was carrying your child — that she would have her baby in a convent if I withheld my consent."

Tavish never imagined Dearie would do such a thing. A wry smile twisted his mouth.

"I wanted more for Dearie. If I had put my foot down, she'd be in Philadelphia happily married and I would have a grandchild by now."

A muscle worked in Tavish's jaw as he listened to the old man. Grayson was right. If not for him, Dearie would have had a very different life.

"Then I arrive and find that she's lost the child, and never even told me. How could you let that happen?"

Tavish looked away. He hadn't been there when she needed him — ever. "I love her," He said, his voice breaking with emotions. It was the first time he'd ever really meant the words.

Matthew Grayson narrowed his blue eyes. "Well, perhaps you do. But I don't know as that will do either one of us much good now."

"We must go after her," Tavish commanded. "When did she leave?"

"Hours ago." Grayson shook his gray head. "She's too headstrong. It's my own fault. I was always that way too. I wish her mother had lived longer . . . she was so sweet, so womanly . . . "

"I'll get Clarence to saddle horses for us."

" . . . and graceful . . . her little feet and hands were like a doll's. Dearie looks a lot like her mother, you know. that's why I call her my little doll. She was the most beautiful child — everyone said they had never seen such blue eyes and golden curls . . . "

Tavish took Grayson firmly by the arm, ignoring the older man's rambling. This was not time for sentiment; they had to find Dearie.

Grayson continued to talk as if he were in another world. "She had a face like and angel, and for a girl, she was quick. Her tutors all said so . . . " Tavish urged him onto a horse, but Grayson continued to talk until they reached Rosalie.

Dearie might have sought refuge with Calvin, Tavish thought. They found Calvin in the fields supervising the harvest of yet another field of wheat. He waved when he saw Tavish approach, and walked quickly toward his visitors, rolling down the sleeves of his white cambric shirt.

"I'll be glad when this is all over," Calvin said, mopping his forehead with a handkerchief.

"Calvin, this is Dearie's father, Matthew Grayson."

Perplexed, Calvin looked from Grayson to Tavish, then extended his hand. So this was the infamous Grayson, who had ruined Murdock McLeod. He looked like a harmless old man. But what, Calvin wondered, was he doing with Tavish? "How do you do, sir. I've heard . . . a good deal about you."

Grayson looked about him anxiously. "Where is my daughter," he demanded to know.

"Dearie? I haven't seen Dearie since yesterday," Calvin replied. "Why?"

"She has left, Calvin. We . . . I thought she might have come here. She didn't say where she was going."

The look on Tavish's face brought Calvin up short. "Oh, Tavish. I am sorry. Let me get my horse and I'll help you look. She can't have gone far."

They searched all the backroads leading to Rosalie. When toward dusk it began to rain, the men stopped at Greenhill. The McNeills were on the plantation porch having a cool drink before the evening meal.

Hastily, Calvin explained their mission, but neither Duncan nor India had seen Dearie. India insisted they have dinner before returning to Beauvais, and the men were too tired to protest.

At dinner they discussed what they would do the following day. It was agreed that Calvin would ride into Fayetteville, while Tavish and his father-in-law searched the neighboring farms, including the McFarlands'. Duncan volunteered to search the back roads leading to Raleigh.

"Poor Dearie," India shook her dark head. "I hope she's all right."

"We'll find her," Tavish declared, his mouth set in a tight line.

It was midnight before the rain abated and the men were able to return home.

Tavish was up at dawn the following day. He questioned the servants, but none of them knew where Dearie had gone. Clarence was still missing.

"If you find Clarence, you going to find Miss Dearie," Tempie said. "She was shore in a state when she left."

When Grayson arose, the men ate and again mounted their horses. A light rain was falling, just enough to muddy the roads and impede their progress.

They stopped first at Four Corners Tavern, and having no luck there, they proceeded on to the McFarlands' farm. Louisa answered the door. Tavish was shocked at the girl's appearance; she had changed so completely. She wore a blue merino dress and a starched white apron, and her white-blond hair was neatly tucked into a knot at the back of her neck. She was almost pretty.

"Hello," she smiled. "I know you. You are the husband of Dearie,"

Tavish smiled back at her. "Yes. I've come to ask if you have seen her. She . . . we can't find her."

Mrs. McFarland joined her daughter at the door. "They stayed with us last night. It was almost suppertime, and Louisa like to thrown a fit for them to take supper. And it was rainin' . . . "

"Dearie slept in my bed," Louisa supplied brightly.

"She said she come to say good-bye." Mrs. McFarland's voice broke and she looked away, taking a handkerchief from her sleeve.

"Why is Dearie going away!" Louisa demanded. "Are you sending her away!"

"Hush, child," Mrs. McFarland said, putting her arm around the girl.

"Did she . . . did she say where they were going?"

"Musta've been going toward town. They left in a hurry," Mrs. McFarland said.

Tavish nodded. "Thank you." He retraced his steps to his horse.

"I hope you find her and bring her back," Louisa called after him.

Tavish and Grayson turned their horses toward Fayetteville. It was almost noon, and although the sun had come out, the roads were still muddy. Halfway to town, they came upon Clarence driving the wagon. He pulled up when he saw Tavish.

"Clarence, where's Dearie?"

Clarence shook his head. "I expect she gone by now, Master Tavish. I let her off in front of the hotel."

"When, Clarence?"

" 'Bout two hours ago."

"Did she say where she was going?" Grayson asked anxiously.

"No, sir. She said she was going far, far away. As far away as she could get."

Clarence had always been dramatic, but this time Tavish had a feeling the servant was right.

"Well, let's get going. We might be able to stop her yet," Grayson said, applying the crop to his horse.

Clarence stood up in the wagon. "Master Grayson. Don't do that — sir. That horse don't like — "

Grayson came down again with his crop on the horse's withers. The horse reared up, then charged away at a gallop. Tavish ordered Clarence back to the plantation, then spurred his mount after his father-in-law.

By the time Tavish had caught up with Grayson, the older man's horse was running at breakneck speed. Grayson was holding on to the saddle with one hand and gripping the horse's mane with the other.

"Pull him up. Pull him up," Tavish yelled out.

But Grayson couldn't relinquish his grip on the horse for fear he would fall off. Horse and rider plunged ahead blindly. Tavish followed as fast as he could ride, but there was nothing he could do. Soon the horse would tire, he thought. But would Grayson be able to hold on for that long?

Just when it seemed that the horse was beginning to slow, it veered slightly off the road. Grayson was caught by a low-hanging branch, and fell into a deep ditch at the side of the road.

It happened so suddenly, Tavish was stunned. Now free of its rider, Grayson's horse trotted down the road. Tavish jumped from his horse and scrambled down into the ditch.

Grayson was wedged up to his waist in mud. "Help me. Help me." The old man's voice was a pathetic croak. "Please help me."

Tavish waded over to Grayson, but his progress was slow. When he reached the old man, he tried to pull him out, but he kept sliding back down the slimy side of the ditch into the quicksand-like mud. With each pull, the old man slid back further. Tavish struggled, mired in mud to his waist. He couldn't gain a sure footing anywhere.

"Help me, Please help me." Grayson clasped his arms around Tavish's neck, dragging them both down deeper. The mud was now up to Tavish's chest.

Tavish cast about for something, anything, to hold on to. He spied a small tree growing halfway up the bank of the ditch.

He pried Grayson's hands from his shoulder and placed them around the tree trunk. Then, taking a breath, he dove under the mud. Using his back as lever, he positioned himself under Grayson and shoved the older man up, free of the mud.

Tavish emerged covered with mud and slime. Wiping his eyes, he saw Grayson clinging to the tree.

"I'm going to push you, then reach for the top. Grab on to the grass if you can."

"I. . . . can't . . . "

Grayson's grip weakened. He would slide back into the ditch any minute. With supreme effort, Tavish reached the tree and hoisted himself even with Grayson. The old man was breathing heavily, and his eyes were closed. With painstaking slowness, Tavish crawled free of the ditch.

Perhaps he should ride for help. But he knew that Grayson would be dead by the time he returned. His only hope was to somehow pull his father-in-law free. Quickly, Tavish cast about for something to anchor himself with, but he had no rope. He untied the reins from his horse's bridle and knotted them together, but the makeshift cord was not long enough.

In desperation, he retied one end of the rein to the bridle, and the other end he wrapped around his waist. Now, if the horse did not balk, he had sufficient weight to pull Grayson out.

Tavish coaxed the horse forward until he was at the edge of the ditch. Then he lay on his stomach and inched his way back down into the ditch. When he saw that he wouldn't be able to lift Grayson, he switched his position, lowering his legs down.

"Grab hold of my legs," he ordered.

In a moment he felt Grayson's heavy arms clamp around his legs.

Now came the risky part — getting the horse to move without dragging them too far and breaking the reins. Tavish picked up a pine branch and shoved it at the horse's nose. The horse moved a step backwards in response. Tavish shoved the branch again and the horse moved further. Inch by inch they moved, until they were finally pulled free of the ditch.

Matthew Grayson sank into unconsciousness, but he was still breathing. Somehow, Tavish managed to drag him onto the horse, and they rode quickly back to the plantation.

Dr. Prescott arrived from Fayetteville the following morning. Grayson still had not regained consciousness. The doctor shook his head as he left the bedroom.

"It doesn't look good. He's had a nasty head wound, and he lost a lot of blood. With a man his age, it's hard to tell. Sometimes a fever will set in . . . I've left some laudanum for the pain when he wakes."

Tavish ran his fingers through his sandy hair, a worried frown on his face.

The doctor rested his hand on his shoulder, "You did what you could, Tavish. I'm sorry."

The doctor's words rang in Tavish's head. "You did what you could." Tavish's mouth twisted in a wry grimace. He had just saved the life of the man he hated most in the world. And he hadn't even stopped to think about it. He could have left him in the ditch to die, but he hadn't. Why? Then he knew. He'd done it for Dearie. He was her father.

Calvin stopped by on his way from town. His search had been fruitless. "I looked everywhere, and checked with the stage. No woman fitting Dearie's description bought a ticket yesterday."

"Are you sure?"

"The man had been on duty all day long. I could tell he was telling the truth."

"But Clarence left her in town."

Calvin frowned. "Where in town?"

"In front of the hotel. Did you check the guest list of the hotel? Perhaps she intends to wait a day to catch the stage."

"No, I didn't think to check the guests. I'll return tomorrow. But first I'll check with Duncan." He nodded toward the bedroom door where Grayson lay. "I met Dr. Prescott. Will he live?"

Tavish shrugged. "I don't know. I don't know anything anymore."

Calvin smiled sympathetically and left. Perhaps he'd been too hard on Tavish, he thought as he rode to Greenhill. Tavish had been through a lot these past few years. How would he himself have reacted under the same circumstances? Calvin didn't know. But he sensed that the Tavish he had always known was back to stay. If only it wasn't too late!

Tavish took a book and sat beside Matthew Grayson. His father-in-law's face was ashen, and his breathing so shallow it barely lifted the coverlet.

"Please God, don't let him die," Tavish heard himself praying. "Forgive me. I'll make everything right, I promise. Just let him live. . . . for *her* sake."

Chapter Twenty-Two

Tears streamed down Dearie's face as she rode away from Beauvais. She had left her husband and her father, and she had no where to go. She ordered Clarence to stop at the McFarlands' farm. She couldn't leave without saying good-bye to Louisa.

Louisa greeted Dearie with a warm hug, and demanded to know why she had been crying. Mrs. McFarland quickly made a pot of tea and the three women sat down at the table.

"I've just come to say good-bye, Louisa," Dearie said, avoiding Mrs. McFarland's probing gaze.

"But why, Dearie? I don't understand," Louisa asked in her soft voice.

"Child, don't ply her with questions," Mrs. McFarland scolded. "A body has to do what she must."

Dearie nodded, grateful for Mrs. McFarland's intervention.

"But, Mama," Louisa protested.

Dearie smiled at the familiarity. Mrs. McFarland placed a soothing hand on the girl's shoulder. "Let's have us some ginger cakes, Louisa."

"Yes, ma'am."

Louisa obediently got up to fetch the cakes. Mrs. McFarland turned to Dearie and fixed her sympathetic dark eyes upon her. She said nothing, but she nodded her head sagely. Dearie knew the woman understood.

It was strange, Dearie thought. Mrs. McFarland was a woman of few words. She seldom showed any emotion, but when she did her expression was more meaningful than anything she could have said. She had been wrong about the woman, and she was glad. But then, Mrs. McFarland had been wrong about her, too.

Dearie gladly accepted an invitation to dinner with the McFarlands. Then, when the rain continued, they stayed the night. Louisa insisted that Dearie sleep in her bed, and Clarence slept near the fireplace.

Before they departed the following day, Dearie hugged Louisa, and it seemed natural to hug Mrs. McFarland as well. Dearie thought she saw the woman's eyes fill with tears before she looked quickly away.

Louisa ran after the wagon waving, picking up her skirts so as not to muddy the hems. It tore at Dearie's heart to leave her, for she loved Louisa and the McFarlands. Now she would never see them again. Her lip trembled and the tears gathered again in her eyes.

Clarence said nothing on the long ride to Fayetteville, but he looked over at Dearie often, shaking his head. As they were pulling into town, he finally spoke.

"Master Tavish is a good man, Miss Dearie. I knowed him since afore his daddy died."

Dearie remained silent.

"Well, I know he don't act right all the time. But he cares about you, he surely do."

"Clarence, please let me off in front of the hotel."

"What you going to do, Miss Dearie? Where you going to go?"

"Somewhere far away, Clarence."

The old servant grumbled under his breath until they reached the hotel, then he removed Dearie's luggage from the wagon and deposited it at the door of the hotel. He moved slowly, as if he hoped that someone would arrive to prevent her departure.

"Well, it ain't safe for a lady to go traveling around by herself," he remarked when it was clear that she really meant to go. "Why, anything could happen . . ."

Dearie silenced him with a hug and a kiss on his old cheek. "Take care of yourself, Clarence." She pressed a one-dollar gold piece into his hand.

"Oh, Lordy, it gold! I'm going to keep this for my lucky piece, Miss Dearie. Thank you, ma'am."

Clarence left Dearie standing in front of the Fayetteville Hotel. She had only to buy a ticket to be on the next stage, but she didn't know where to go. As she pondered her options, Georganna Arms flounced down the sidewalk.

"Why, good day, Mrs. McLeod. Are you leaving us after all?"

Dearie looked up sharply. "Yes, as a matter of fact I am planning a short visit."

Georganna touched the trunk with the tip of her parasol. "You must be planning to stay quite a while with such a large trunk. But we ladies always overpack, don't we?"

Dearie's face flushed and she was too angry to speak. Fortunately, Colleen saw her from across the street and hurried to her side.

"Well, have a *lovely* visit, Mrs. McLeod," Georganna said, moving away. Dearie watched as she walked away, her hips swaying seductively while all the passing men doffed their hats and smiled at her. Dearie was seething with anger.

"Miss Dearie, where are you going?" Colleen asked when Georganna was out of earshot.

"I'm leaving, Colleen. I planned to come over and say good-bye after I bought my ticket."

Colleen took Dearie firmly by the arm and led her over to the shop. "The stage isn't due for at least an hour. We must have a talk."

Dearie allowed herself to be led into Colleen's neat little shop. Once inside the shop, Colleen went into the back room to make a pot of tea. The back room held bolts of materials, a small bed, a washstand with pitcher and bowl, and a stove. Dearie smiled. Colleen had made a cozy little haven out of the storeroom. How like her.

"Well, miss? What do you think?"

"I love it, Colleen. I didn't realize that you were living here, too."

"Well, I thought it'd be best to cut my expenses. Now that the shop's caught on, I've no mind to leave. I've planted my roots, if you follow my meaning."

Dearie's smiled faded. "I do know, Colleen."

Colleen poured them each a steaming cup of tea, and they went back into the shop. "Miss Dearie, what's happened?"

Dearie shook her head wearily. "Everything, Colleen. Everything."

Dearie launched into a detailed description of the events that had transpired over the last several months. Having been so busy with the harvest, Dearie had not visited her friend for some time.

Colleen slowly sipped her tea and listened attentively. Finally she set her cup aside. "Oh, Miss Dearie. That's the worst I ever heard! What are you going to do?" She shook her dark curls. "If it was me, I don't know what I'd do."

Dearie wrung her hands. "Colleen, I don't know what to do or where to go. I just know that I have to get away."

Colleen nodded. "Why don't you stay here with me for a while until you've decided? You could write to some schools, perhaps. With all your schoolin', Miss Dearie, you would be a fine governess."

Dearie caught her lip in thought. She hadn't thought of being a governess. At least with such a position she would receive lodging and wages. "That's a good idea, Colleen. But are you sure that you have room?"

"Of course I'm sure, Miss Dearie. We'll move the couch out of the main room. It's as comfy as you please."

Dearie breathed a sigh of relief. How good it was to be with Colleen again. Colleen always knew the best thing to do.

As Colleen had recommended, Dearie obtained the names of several institutions in Raleigh and Wilmington, and wrote inquiring about a teaching position. She also posted an ad to be placed in the local papers, advertising her services as a governess.

"My goodness, Colleen," she said when she'd finished. "I don't know what I'd do if I got one of these positions. I've never even been around children."

Colleen waved aside her comment. "There's nothing to it, Miss Dearie. Me mum taught school after me father passed away, and she could hardly read. She learned along with 'em, she said. After that she learned to read very well."

Dearie frowned. "I thought your mother was a seamstress."

The little maid laughed gaily. "Well, of course she was. But our village was so poor, there was no money in it. And she had all of us to feed."

Dearie laughed with her. "Colleen, I've never known you to be without a family anecdote for every situation that arises."

Colleen blew a dark curl off her forehead. "That's right, miss. I've got a big family."

Dearie shook her head. Life would certainly be dull without Colleen. While she was waiting for a reply to her letters, Dearie busied herself about Colleen's shop, doing odd jobs to keep busy. However, when customers came in, she quickly retreated to the back room. As far as her father and husband were concerned, she had left Fayetteville.

Living with Colleen was a tonic for Dearie. Whenever she begin to think of her plight and how poorly she had been treated, Colleen was there to cheer her.

"There's no denyin' that men are a great deal of trouble, Miss Dearie. A woman in our village had six husbands, each one worse than the one before. One followed the ladies, the next drank himself to death, and the last one used to beat her something terrible."

Dearie sighed. "I suppose she decided never to marry again?"

"No. She finally found a good one, but he died right off of the fever."

"Oh, Colleen. What a morbid story."

Colleen's mouth curved up in a mischievous smile. "Well, everyone said she had no luck at all. But you know, the uncle of her last husband up and left her a big house full of servants and enough money to last her the rest of her days." Colleen shrugged. "We never saw her after that, of course."

Dearie rolled her eyes.

The shop bell rang and Colleen hurried out to greet her customer. Dearie stayed in the back room, leafing through a book of fashion plates.

Colleen saw only a broad back as her customer bent over a display of hats. She was surprised, as men rarely visited her store. She smoothed her white cambric gown and brushed the curls off her face.

"Good day, sir. May I be of service?"

When Calvin turned around Colleen's smile froze on her face.

"Colleen, how good it is to see you. I had heard that you opened a shop . . . "

His eyes drank in every detail of her face and figure. Her white dress showed off her dark curls and emphasized the pearly luster of her skin. He watched a pink flush spread from her face to her pretty breasts, outlined by her tastefully low-cut dress. Before, he'd thought her pretty in a quaint, old-fashioned way. Now he saw that she was beautiful — more beautiful than any woman he'd ever seen.

Colleen watched the course of his gaze as it traveled over her body and back to her face. She saw in the dark blue depths of his eyes a longing, a hunger she'd never noticed before. Calvin wanted her! That realization gave her enough confidence to speak.

"Yes, it's glad I am to see you again, Master Buie. Is there aught I can help you with?"

The formality of her tone embarrassed him. Shyness overcame him. "Well, no. I really didn't come in to shop for myself . . . " He paused, realizing that his answer sounded awkward.

Colleen lowered her lashes. "Perhaps it's a lady friend you're shopping for, Master Buie. I have many customers who venture in to buy a parasol or shawl. Allow me to show you some of my newest arrivals."

She led the way to a low table. Calvin followed like an obedient puppy, savoring the scent that trailed behind her — a mixture of lemon, lavender, and rose. It was heavenly. So intent was he on the woman in front of him that he caught his long leg on a table and tripped, falling over the display and onto the floor.

Colleen hurried to his side. Helpless, Calvin held up his hands, draped in feathers and fringed shawls. The sight was so comical that Colleen giggled out loud, and soon the both of them were laughing uncontrollably.

When they had recovered, Colleen noticed that Calvin was studying the attractive rise and fall of her breasts.

She quickly retrieved a sandalwood fan from Calvin's knee and began fanning her flushed face. "Oh, Master Buie. What a sight we are. Here, let me help you up."

"Please call me Calvin."

Colleen offered her hand with a shy smile. "All right, Calvin."

With some difficulty, Calvin rose from the floor. However, he could only hobble to a chair, as he had injured his knee in the fall.

"Oh, dear. Let me get a cool compress." She hurried to the back to get a moistened cloth.

Dearie had been reading a book of fashion plates, and she looked up in question when Colleen appeared.

"It's Master Calvin, Miss Dearie," Colleen whispered. "He's hurt his knee."

Colleen hurried back out into the shop. She knelt next to his leg and quickly pushed up the trouser leg.

He looked at her questioningly, but she tossed a curl off her forehead. "Oh, don't worry. I've several brothers," she said, then was immediately embarrassed by her remark. Again she felt the blood rise in her face as she wrapped the material around his well-shaped leg.

She raised her eyes to lock with his and caught her breath. His fingers touched the soft skin of her chin.

"Colleen . . ."

His touch sent a fiery current coursing through her body, and she was galvanized into action. She hurriedly wrapped the bandage around his leg and pulled his trouser leg back down. "There, that should hold," she said, ignoring his tender look and the pounding of her own heart. She rose and turned, thinking to flee into the back room. What else could she do? The man had virtually undressed her with his eyes! But what was worse was that she couldn't seem to control the response of her own body.

"Colleen," Calvin said. "Don't run away again."

Her eyes searched his helplessly as he stood to face her. He was so tall, so marvelously tall. Before she knew what was happening, he stooped to gather her in his arms, He lifted her up as if she was feather-light, and pressed her closely to him. His lips swiftly claimed hers, in a kiss more wonderful than she had ever dreamed.

How could a man's lips be so soft? She wondered. Breathlessly she clung to him, investing every ounce of her strength in the embrace. He tasted and savored her lips, reverently caressing them over and over. Her mouth parted to receive his tongue as he thrust it between her small white teeth.

"Oh," she protested feebly against his warm lips. But she had no more will to resist. He deepened the kiss and she responded instinctively. She felt her breasts straining against his strong chest.

From the corner of her eye, Colleen saw movement outside the shop. Two ladies were ogling the hats in the window. Colleen broke away from Calvin's embrace and would have stepped away, but she was two feet off the floor.

"Calvin, you must put me down," she whispered in desperation.

"And if I say no?" He nuzzled a dark curl at her ear. "I can hold you for ransom."

The bell jingled, announcing the ladies' entrance, and he immediately set her down. Fortunately a dress rack shielded them from the ladies' view.

Shaking, Colleen waited on the ladies, casting an occasional covert glance at Calvin, who appeared to be inspecting the shawls as he replaced them on the table. When the ladies left, he immediately returned to her side, grasping her hand.

"I should have kissed you long ago, Colleen. But I have always been bumbling oaf as you can see. Talking to women never came easy to me."

"Well, you never seem to have much trouble talking to Miss Dearie," Colleen pointed out.

"Ah, but there was safety there. She was married to my best friend." Then, remembering his purpose, Calvin hit his head with his hand. "Your lovely face has made me completely forget my purpose here. I came to ask you if you've seen Dearie. She has disappeared from the plantation. Tavish, her father, and I have been looking for her."

Colleen looked away, pursing her lips. She had no idea whether Dearie wanted to talk to Calvin or not. Her eyes strayed to the back room. That moment, Dearie walked through the door.

"Calvin, it is so good to see you," Dearie said, clasping his hand.

"Well, I'll leave you two alone," Colleen said. Old feelings of inadequacy wafted over her again. But Calvin caught her hand and pulled her to his side.

"Colleen, I won't let you out of my sight, now that I've found you again."

Colleen breathed a sigh of relief. It was really true, Calvin cared for her!

Calvin and Colleen sat down next to one another on the settee while Dearie took a chair opposite. Dearie's eyes went from one friend to another, and she smiled. She couldn't think of a better match. But why had it taken so long, she wondered.

"Calvin, I am so glad you came by. I wanted to say good-bye before I left."

"We were all sure that you already had left. Clarence said you'd taken the stage."

Dearie looked down at her hands. " 'Tis just as well, Calvin. I'll be leaving just as soon as I receive confirmation of a post."

"Dearie, I think you should return to the plantation with me. There's been an accident. Your father has been injured in a fall, and Dr. Prescott does not know if he will recover."

Dearie's hand flew to her mouth. "My father! Oh, no!"

"I'm sorry to bring you such bad news. Tavish rescued him after the fall, and brought him back to the plantation. He has been at your father's side around the clock."

"Tavish! Rescued my father!" She shook her head in wonder, then rose quickly. "I'll get my things. Of course I'll return with you, Calvin." Dearie rushed into the back room to get her things, and Calvin turned to Colleen.

"Colleen," he said, fingers touching her cheek. "Will you be here when I return?"

Colleen lowered her lashes. Calvin lifted her chin, and her eyes were captured by his loving gaze. "Yes," she said, breathless.

"That's good," he said, "because I've waited a long time for you."

Colleen smiled. She knew exactly what he meant.

Dearie returned with her traveling case and shawl. Taking her arm, Calvin ushered her to the door of the shop.

"Oh, Calvin," Dearie said. "I hope I'm not too late!"

Calvin patted her shoulder. "Don't worry. You won't be too late." He caught Colleen's hand and squeezed it. "It's never too late," he whispered, a twinkle in his eyes.

Chapter Twenty-Three

Calvin rented a carriage at the stable and drove Dearie to Beauvais. Dearie was silent, absorbed in thought. So much had happened during the last few days. Her life had fallen apart — her father was dying, and she dreaded seeing Tavish again. She hadn't wanted to see him again — ever.

Calvin looked over at Dearie from time to time, ready to lend a sympathetic ear if she should want to talk. But she said nothing as she stared wistfully at the passing landscape.

Calvin was content to remain silent. His thoughts dwelled on Colleen as he remembered her, framed in the doorway of her shop like a tiny Dresden figurine. His heart was so light he felt like singing. But he stifled the urge for Dearie's sake. Instead, he tapped his boot against the footboard as if keeping time to a lively tune.

Rosalie would soon host another ball, he thought with a smile. And on his arm would be Colleen! They would walk in the gardens and he would ask her to become his bride. Or perhaps he would ask her sooner, then they could announce the engagement at the ball. His skin tingled with the thought, and his heart kept time with his foot. He was in love.

For a while, Dearie was so lost in thought that she noticed nothing. However, she turned at the sound of tapping to see Calvin swaying back and forth, his foot keeping time with an inaudible tune. Completely absorbed, his wide smile betrayed his sheer happiness.

Dearie couldn't help but giggle. "Calvin, if I didn't know better I'd say there was a jig going on in your head."

Calvin stopped abruptly and nodded, still smiling. "Well, I was thinking of a ball I aim to throw real soon."

"Did you have a certain somebody in mind to invite?"

His face flushed. "I reckon I do."

"It wouldn't be Colleen, would it?"

His face was bright red now, and he looked away in embarrassment. "I reckon it is."

Dearie grabbed his arm and hugged it. "Well, it's about time, Calvin!"

Tempie greeted them at the door of the plantation, her broad face solemn.

"Oh, Miss Dearie," she cried out. "I never thought they'd find you in time. Master Grayson is awful bad. He taken a fever and we can't get it down."

"It's all right, Tempie. I'm here now."

Tempie led the way to Master Grayson's bedroom. Tavish was sitting next to the bed, half asleep, his chin on his chest. The opening door startled him, and he sat up looking around him, bewildered.

"Dearie," he called out, moving quickly toward her, but she held him off with a chilling look.

She rushed to the bed, and sitting on the side, took her father's hand in hers. "Father," she whispered. "Can you hear me?"

"He don't act like he hear nothing, Miss Dearie. He don't eat, he don't sleep. He just toss and turn," Tempie reported twisting her white apron.

Tavish waited on the opposite side of the bed. It was as if there was an impassable obstacle between Dearie and himself. He noted with a wry grimace that once again the obstacle was Matthew Grayson.

"I will take over now, Tempie. Set the pots to boiling. I'll need fresh rags to change his bandage. . . . Oh, and some cool compresses to help lower the fever."

"Oh, yes, ma'am. We got that already. Master Tavish, he been changing the bandage regular. 'An he told us to boil the ones that been used. The fresh bandages is on the table and the compress is on the tray. Master Tavish said to bring in a cool one every ten minutes. Been keeping Bess a'runnin' to the well."

Tavish had done that? How strange. Dearie looked up, surprised. Tavish held her gaze for a moment, before she looked away again. "Well, anyway, Tempie, set a pot of chicken soup to boil in case he wakes."

"We got that, too," Tempie said.

Tavish managed a slight grin.

"Who would have thought you could be so handy?" Dearie snapped, leveling a long, cool gaze at her husband. "As long as you've been away from home, I wouldn't dream that you'd know anything about tending a sick person."

"I don't know a lot," Tavish replied honestly. "But I'm willing to learn."

His humble tone unnerved Dearie. He had always held himself so tightly in control. Now his hazel eyes were softly imploring. She looked away. She had suffered too much pain already.

Witnessing the entire scene, Calvin cleared his throat self-consciously. "I must be on my way. If you need me . . ." He looked from Tavish to Dearie. They were like two opponents facing each other across a playing field. "Send Clarence."

"Thank you, Calvin," Dearie told him, with a smile of deep gratitude.

Tavish walked his friend to the carriage. Calvin draped an arm around his friend's shoulder. "She'll come around, Tavish. She needs time."

Tavish sighed heavily. "I don't want him to die, Calvin. I never wanted him to die."

Calvin saw the anguish in Tavish's eyes. He understood now why the Lord claimed revenge and withheld it from man. The price was too high. Tavish had gained very little, and he stood to lose a great deal more if he lost Dearie.

"I wish I could help you, my friend."

"You've already helped by bringing Dearie back. Perhaps her father will mend now that she has returned." But will she? Tavish wondered sadly to himself.

After Calvin left, Tavish returned to Matthew Grayson's bedroom. Dearie sat in a chair at his bedside. She had fallen asleep, her head resting on the old man's hand. She was a beautiful sight, her golden curls feathered out across the coverlet, her soft lips parted in repose. Tavish softly closed the door leaving them alone.

He returned to the bedroom he had shared with Dearie and collapsed on the bed. It was best to sleep while he could. Having only rested a few hours during the last few days, he fell immediately into a deep sleep.

He awoke hours later to the smell of chicken broth, and remembered that he hadn't eaten since breakfast. Dearie was sitting at the kitchen table when he arrived, but she quickly pushed her chair away as if she had no wish to sit near him.

Tavish ate his meal alone, and then returned to Grayson's room. Dearie was removing the soiled bandage and replacing it with a new one.

"What have you been using on the wound?" she demanded.

"Just some herbs my mother used for wounds. I don't know the names. She kept a little pouch full of them for emergencies." Tavish pointed to a black leather pouch on the dresser.

"They seem to be easing the swelling some, whatever they are." Again she was struck by his attention. Why would he even care?

Tavish watched her wrap the bandage around Grayson's head, taking care that it was not too tight. Then she bent to kiss the spot where the wound was. Suddenly, he felt a quickening sensation in his loins. He wished that she would kiss him — in fact, he could almost feel the petal softness of her lips on his. Forcing his eyes away from her, he studied the room. He looked at it as if he were seeing it for the first time. The pine furniture was old but polished and the walls had been whitewashed a gleaming white. At the open window, gingham curtains fluttered. It was a pretty room. He could see his wife's touch in every detail of the simple decor. He'd been in the room many times before and never noticed — he wondered why.

"If you would like to rest — "

"No. I'm not tired," she cut him off sharply.

He busied himself by chopping wood and inspecting the corn crop. After each chore, he stopped to look in on Dearie. She sat frozen by her father's side.

She must love her father a great deal, Tavish thought. He wondered if she could ever love him that much.

Dinner was a solemn affair. The servants quietly set down the food, then quickly disappeared. Dearie condescended to eat with Tavish, but she neither looked up nor spoke. When she had finished, she immediately returned to her father.

Later, the servants were all abed, and Dearie was still in with her father. Exhausted, she had fallen asleep in her chair. Tavish gently picked her up and carried her to their bed. He loosened her dress and observed the soft rise and fall of her breasts in her open bodice. He longed to undress her and lie beside her, but instead he drew a coverlet over her and returned to Grayson's bedside.

Golden shafts of sunlight slanted in through the window, waking Dearie. She sat up confused, not remembering where she was. She washed hurriedly, changing into the extra dress she had brought, and returned to her father's room.

Tavish was asleep in the chair next to the bed. In spite of herself, she smiled. A lock of sandy hair had fallen across his forehead. He looked like a young boy who had become exhausted and fallen asleep right where he was.

"Water . . . water . . . give me water." Grayson's voice was so soft it could barely be heard above Tavish's heavy breathing.

"Father!" Dearie flew to his bedside. She quickly poured cool water from the pitcher into a goblet and pressed it to his lips.

The old man's lips were so parched they stuck together. By the time he opened them to receive the water, he was drained from the exertion and fell back against the pillow.

Tavish awoke. "Oh," he blinked in surprise. "The fever's broken. Thank God!"

Dearie looked at him in astonishment. Tavish was thanking God for her father's recovery! She shook her head in disbelief, and turned her attention back to Grayson.

"Father, I'm here. It's Dearie."

"Dearie," Grayson repeated. "Ran off, can't find her . . . "

Frowning, Dearie exchanged a glance with Tavish. Was his mind affected, or did the fever still linger?

"I'll send Clarence back to town for Dr. Prescott," Tavish volunteered.

Dearie nodded. He had read her mind.

Dr. Prescott returned with Clarence in the late afternoon. Dearie and Tavish were both there when he entered Grayson's room. After checking him over, the doctor pronounced his patient much improved.

"I must tell you, I didn't hold much hope he would recover. It was a nasty wound. But it has healed mighty quick, probably due to the herbs you used in the bandage. Dearie, I didn't know you were a herbalist."

Dearie colored and looked at Tavish. "They were Tavish's. His mother left them."

"Of course . . . Mary. Well, they've done wonders. I wouldn't doubt that they helped break the fever.

"Maybe it was the tea," Tavish suggested.

"Tea? What tea?" Dearie frowned at Tavish.

Tavish nodded toward the pouch again. "There was some tea in there. Mother always swore by it . . . said it'd cure anything but poison ivy."

"But," Dearie protested, "he hasn't even been able to drink anything."

Tavish nodded. "I spooned it into his mouth. It didn't come back out so I figured he swallowed it."

"You know, I've heard of Mary's famous tea. I'll have to take a look at what's in that pouch one of these days, Tavish."

Dearie's mouth clamped shut and she stared at Tavish.

Matthew Grayson gestured at Tavish with a shaky hand. "Pulled me out of the ditch . . . Mud everywhere. Ruined my coat . . . "

"I know, I know, Father."

"Saved my life . . . "

Dearie nodded, a tight smile on her lips.

Dearie and Tavish took turns sitting with Grayson as he slowly recovered. Each day he was more alert, and gradually his face lost its ashen pallor.

In a week, he was able to sit up, and his appetite immediately returned. Occasionally he complained of a headache, but the doctor said that was to be expected.

Tavish spent hours in the old man's room. Dearie was surprised to walk by and find them deep in conversation one day. On another occasion, she was startled by a loud whoop. Her face white with dread, she hurried to the door, thinking that her father had taken a turn for the worse. She was taken aback to find that he was only laughing. Tavish had set up a makeshift table on the bed and the two of them were playing cards!

"You think you can outwit me, you young pup," Grayson roared, with more energy than she would have thought he had.

"Well, no," Tavish replied, laughing. "You've probably forgotten more than I'll ever know about the game."

"I don't know," Grayson said with a sly grin. "I've seen you play. You could give me a run for my money even in my heyday."

"All right, then. Let's see the color of your money."

"Dearie, bring me my purse, child."

"What! Father, are you daft! You are in no condition to be gambling. I'll not have you — "

"Oh, hush! If I weren't in any condition, I wouldn't be doing it. Now do as I say."

Dearie did as she was bidden, but her expression showed her disapproval. Later she had to chuckle. Her father was certainly getting back to his old self.

After dinner, Tavish joined Dearie in the kitchen, where she was baking an apple cobbler. He stood very close to her as she stirred the pie filling. When she set the ladle aside he sampled a taste.

"Apple cobbler is my favorite. When did you learn to make it?"

Her mouth tightened into a straight line. "When you were gone. There wasn't much else to do."

She turned abruptly and left Tavish holding the dripping ladle.

As Grayson was sleeping well now, there was no need to keep a vigil at his bedside. For several nights, Dearie had slept alone in their bedroom while Tavish took a blanket to the porch. Finally, his muscles aching from the hard planks, Tavish waited until he was sure she was asleep and quietly slipped into their bedroom.

He quickly took off his clothes and eased onto the bed beside her. She stirred slightly, but she didn't awaken. Too late, he realized that it was a mistake to lie next to her when he wanted her so much. Before, he had been able to put her from his mind, but now that was impossible.

The warm weather had caused her to wear only a thin nightdress. In the semidarkness, he could clearly see her body beneath the gauzy material. Her full, round breasts strained against the material as she breathed. Her firm, lithe figure curved at her small waist, rounding softly at her hips. It was agony to see her thus and not be able to touch her. He reached out to cup one full breast in his hand, but she turned away, rejecting him even in sleep.

Frustrated, he pummeled his pillow and turned on his side, putting his back to hers. He could take what was rightfully his if he chose. But he wanted her to want him, otherwise it would be meaningless. And their marriage had been a sham for too long as it was.

As Matthew Grayson mended, Tavish helped Dearie with the chores. He seemed to know what she wanted done intuitively, and was on hand before she called. Despite her coldness, he went about his tasks as if everything were perfect between them. Dearie shook her head in amazement. Tavish had never been like this. But she told herself that he was only trying to make up for all the times his behavior had been abominable.

One evening after dinner, he caught up with her as she was taking a walk.

"Mind if I join you?" he asked.

She shrugged carelessly.

"Dearie, are you ever going to speak to me again?"

She looked up at him, weighing her answer. " 'Twould be foolish not to. But the truth is, I have nothing to say."

He gazed at her, trying to force her attention. He wanted desperately to tell her how sorry he was, but she acted as if she was walking alone. He caught her hand but she pulled it quickly away.

"It is getting late," she said, turning.

"Dearie," he said, pulling her to him.

"No," she cried, pushing him away. The pounding of her heart signaled her response to him. She knew that if she yielded, she would lose herself to him again, and the risk was far too great. Picking up her skirts, she turned and ran back into the house.

Chapter Twenty-Four

Several days passed, and Colleen vacillated wildly between joy and despair. She had been overjoyed to learn that she had been wrong about Calvin. He hadn't been in love with Dearie at all! At least that is what he'd said, and the look in his eyes had told her more than words could ever say. Yet Colleen was afraid. She shook her dark curls. Surely, she wasn't mistaken.

She knew that she was in danger of falling head over heels in love with the man — in fact, she already had. This knowledge plunged her into an agony of despair, for she had no idea how to act. "Never give yourself away," she counseled herself. "Never let a gentleman know what ye're thinking. It never works when the woman falls in love first."

All the wise advice she had given Dearie now seemed trite and inappropriate, for she could think of nothing but Calvin. His dark hair and sparkling blue eyes haunted her dreams every night. She awoke, drenched with perspiration in the middle of the night, yearning for his touch.

She chided herself for thinking about him so much, but it was no use. Each time the bell on her little shop rang, she flew to the door in happy expectation. It was usually a woman seeking a new parasol or hat, and her face showed her disappointment.

"Are you ill, my dear?" Hannah Prescott asked her one afternoon. "Your face has gone so white all of a sudden."

"No, ma'am. I'm fine, thank you. It must be the heat."

"Well, in any case, I'd be happy to send Dr. Prescott over to see you if it turns into a fever. We can't have the town's favorite milliner coming down with sickness."

Colleen managed a weak smile. "Yes, ma'am. Thank you, Mrs. Prescott."

The days dragged slowly by, and Calvin did not return. Colleen was overcome with doubt. Had she misinterpreted his intentions? Had her senses been overwhelmed by the moment? Soon she had convinced herself that Calvin had meant nothing of what he'd said.

She became so distraught that she thought about leaving Fayetteville again. Then, almost a week later, Colleen was arranging the window displays when she heard the bell ring behind her.

"I'll be right with you," she called out from her position on a three-legged stool.

"And what if I don't choose to wait?"

Colleen turned quickly, and found herself nose to nose with Calvin. Her dark eyes opened wide with surprise, and when he put his strong arms around her, she melted into his embrace. Then she quickly drew back.

"Well, Master Buie, you certainly took your time about — " she started to say, but his lips came over hers, stifling her reprimand.

Over and over again, he kissed her small red mouth, hungrily taking her bottom lip in his teeth, then thrusting his tongue to meet hers. Against her own will, her mouth parted in response, savoring the taste of him again.

His mouth moved from her lips to her eyelids, tracing the line of her brows, down her cheek to her pert little nose.

"I believe you have the smallest nose I've ever seen," he breathed as his lips moved toward her ears.

"It's served me well enough all . . . these . . . years." What started out as a saucy retort became a breathless whisper as Calvin's tongue explored her small ear, sending shivers of delight throughout her body.

Colleen desperately searched her mind for some family maxim regarding such behavior, but her mind had gone blank. Her senses had taken complete control of her — everywhere Calvin touched started new feelings of pleasure, until she was breathless with longing.

The long hands which had held her so firmly now ranged above and below her waist. One hand came around to cup a soft, rounded breast, and Colleen took in her breath sharply.

"Master. . . . Buie . . . "

"Calvin," he corrected.

"Calvin! We're right in front of the window for all the world to see!"

"I don't care," he said, sliding his other hand along her shapely hips.

Abruptly, Colleen pushed him away. "Master . . . Calvin. 'Tisn't seemly. I don't know ye're intent . . . but . . . "

"I intend to marry you. Will you marry me, Colleen?"

Colleen was so astonished that she lost her balance on the stool, falling forward into his open arms.

"Does that mean 'yes'?" Calvin said, laughing and hugging her to him. Colleen was speechless.

"Well . . . I . . . "

"Say 'yes'."

"Yes."

Calvin insisted that Colleen close the shop and take a drive with him out to Rosalie.

"After all," he told her, "you've never seen the house you'll be mistress of."

Colleen only nodded, completely overwhelmed.

On the way, they stopped briefly at Center Church to post the banns with Reverend Ferguson. Within a short time, they were back in the carriage again, having received the reverend's blessing and hearty congratulations.

"Oh, 'tis all so fast," Colleen said. "Me head is spinning."

Calvin caught her hand and squeezed it. "Do you think I aim to give you time to think? You might run away again!"

"Oh, tush. I'd never run away."

Calvin raised his eyebrow. "Every other time I came around you always left the room. Sometimes I looked for you, but I could never find you. Remember when I asked you to come over to Rosalie?"

She nodded.

"You never came. I was sure then that you had another beau."

"But I thought . . ." she said, shaking her dark curls. "Oh, never mind. 'Tis all past now." When she smiled at him, her dimples indented her cheeks. Calvin immediately stopped the carriage and kissed each one, which set her to giggling.

They arrived at Rosalie in the early afternoon. Bright sunlight glanced off the whitewashed brick of the plantation house. Colleen took in her breath sharply, for she had never seen anything so grand. Immediately, she felt self-conscious, unequal to the task she had undertaken.

Calvin drew the carriage to a stop in front of the house and a servant hurried to greet them.

"How do, Master Calvin, ma'am."

"Hello, Jeffrey. This is Miss Colleen McCurdie, soon to be the new mistress of Rosalie."

Jeffrey broke out in a wide smile. "Well, I declare, Master Calvin. It's about time. Welcome, miss. Welcome."

With Calvin's strong hand holding hers, Colleen's courage returned. He led her up the steps and into the foyer of the house. It was beautiful, as beautiful as any house she had ever dreamed of. For a fleeting moment, she thought of her mother. How she would have loved this house.

The staircase and walls were paneled in a dark walnut, and a crystal chandelier hung in the entryway. He took her through the elegant parlor off the main foyer to the sitting room and dining room. Everywhere were beautiful paintings and carved wooden furniture, and plush Oriental carpets lay underfoot.

Then Calvin led her upstairs to the bedrooms, saving the master bedroom for last.

"And here is our bedroom, Colleen," he said, showing her into a huge room overlooking the gardens and orchard. A long four-poster bed dominated the room, but aside from an armoire and low lamp table, the room was sparsely furnished.

Light from many windows flooded the room, and it adjoined a small sitting room with a fireplace. Colleen couldn't help envisioning how gaily she would decorate such a room with the fabrics she already had.

As if he read her thoughts, Calvin chuckled. "You may want to spruce up the place a bit. I'm afraid it reflects my bachelor taste. I never did have a sense for color — they all run together for me. So that will be your task, if you'll have it."

Colleen went into his arms, nestling her head against his flat stomach. "Of course, I'd love to redecorate if you'd like." Then she frowned suddenly and looked up at him. "But, Calvin, you don't think I'm too . . . short for you?"

He lifted her up to his height. "No, ma'am. I'd say you were just right."

After a walk around the gardens and a ride through the fields, Calvin and Colleen sat down to a sumptuous meal of fried chicken, new potatoes, and hominy. Afterwards, they sat on the porch and talked until the moon rose. So lost were they in one another, they had no idea of the time.

"Was Rosalie your mother's name?" Colleen asked.

"My grandmother's. She was a fine lady, the daughter of a wealthy landowner who died and left his family penniless. She married my grandfather, who was a miller by trade. He worshipped her, of course, and with good reason. She was sweet and generous, never putting on airs. The only thing she insisted upon was an education for her children. This she accomplished by teaching them herself."

"I would like to have known her."

"So would I, but she died before I was born." With his fingers, he lifted up Colleen's chin. "I imagine she was much like you."

Finally, when the night birds began to call, Colleen was reminded of the hour, "Calvin, I must get back to town. 'Tis growing late."

"No, Colleen. It's too late to return to town. You'll stay here tonight. With me."

"But . . ."

He silenced her with a kiss. "Come, my Colleen. Let's go to bed. Our bed."

Colleen swallowed hard. She hadn't thought that this would happen until later . . . after they were married. But he was so forceful, so commanding, as if he knew exactly what he was about. It would be difficult and pointless, she realized, to argue with him. And she wasn't sure she wanted to.

Calvin pulled her arm through his and led her up the wide steps. Colleen's heart pounded so loudly she was sure he could hear. "This is nothing like Jimmy McGregor's barn," she said aloud.

"What, dearest?"

She smiled up at him crookedly. "I . . . said this is nothing like anything I've ever seen before."

At the top of the steps, he swept her into his arms. "Oh, my love. My dearest love." With long, eager strides, he carried her into the bedroom and put her gently down on the bed.

"Calvin, shouldn't we wait . . . ?"

"We've waited too long as it is . . . " he said, his eyes warm with tenderness.

She watched him quickly doff his coat and pull the white cambric shirt from his trousers. As he moved toward her, she looked in awe at the dark hair matting his broad chest. He had a magnificent torso with finely toned muscles. He was slender, but not too much so for a man so tall.

He knelt on the bed beside her, and with patient deliberation loosened the fastenings of her dress. He undressed her as he would a child, carefully tugging her bodice down over her shoulders. Strangely, she was not embarrassed by his open admiration of her full breasts straining against the gauze of her chemise. She felt the chemise and dress fall from her body, and then her pantalettes came off. Unembarrassed, she invited his admiring gaze. She realized then that Calvin was right. They had waited far too long already.

He caressed each breast lovingly, fondling the nipple between his thumb and forefinger, then covering each one with his mouth until Colleen writhed beneath him. She ran her hand through his soft dark hair, the hair she had admired so from afar. Then she pulled him close to her, wanting to feel the mat of dark hair against her swollen nipples. He was not too tall at all. In fact, they fit together perfectly, as if they were made for each other.

Gently Calvin eased away from her, tracing a line from her nipples down to her stomach and legs. She was so beautifully formed, so small and petite. He wanted her more than he had ever wanted any woman, but he was half afraid that he might crush her with his weight. Then she pulled him to her again and his misgivings fled. It had to be.

He moved away for a moment to divest himself of his trousers and Colleen stared in awe at his tumescent shaft. He smiled at her expression. "I promise I will be gentle, my little darling."

By now, Colleen had begun to believe him. His fingers moved to the mound of her womanhood, tenderly caressing the soft velvet recesses until she was moist with anticipation. Slowly, he lowered himself over her, balancing his weight on his elbows, but she pulled him to her forcefully.

"I love you, Calvin," she said.

"Oh, Colleen, how long I have wanted you to say those words. I never thought to hear them."

He thrust deeply into her. She winced, but urged him further, past the obstruction of her maidenhood. They moved as one, rhythmically, their lips hot upon each other as the cresting wave of their passion took them up beyond their bodies, to a realm of pure happiness.

Colleen had no idea what was happening to her. She had been somehow swept away from herself and . . . she didn't care. She clung to Calvin until the wave of ecstasy subsided, and he lay against her, spent and sated.

He lifted his head, and Colleen touched the little beads of perspiration that dotted his forehead. "I don't believe we can wait a month, Colleen. I must have you with me every night, every day . . . every waking minute."

Colleen giggled softly. "You'll tire of me, Calvin."

"Never," he said, firmly. "Never, my dearest."

It was mid-morning before Calvin drove Colleen back to town. On the way, they eagerly made wedding plans. The ball Calvin had planned would now be a wedding reception.

"We'll invite everyone in the whole county," he said. "They've all been after me to marry. So now we'll give them something to celebrate!"

"Oh, I must tell Miss Dearie. I hope she will stand up for me at our wedding."

Calvin's expression darkened. "I think it best to leave them alone for a time. Dearie and Tavish have much to work out between them."

Their parting was lengthy and tender as neither Colleen nor Calvin could bear to say good-bye. They lingered at the back door of the little shop for almost an hour before Colleen finally reached up to kiss him lightly on the lips.

"Good-bye, my love."

"No. One more kiss, Colleen. After all, it must last me for days, since I'll not be back until the end of the week."

Colleen nodded and kissed him full on the lips. He deepened the kiss and crushed her to him. They pulled apart, breathless, when they heard the rush of carriage wheels behind them.

It was Clarence. He pulled off his hat immediately, realizing that he had disturbed their tryst. "Beg pardon, Master Calvin, Miss Colleen. Miss Dearie sent me for the rest of her things."

"How is Master Grayson?" Calvin asked.

"Oh, he 'most well. He got out of bed yesterday. Won't be long 'til he head on back to Philadelphia."

"What about Miss Dearie? Will she go with him?" Colleen wanted to know.

Clarence wagged his head. "Oh, I 'spect Miss Dearie going to go back with her pa. She don't talk to Master Tavish a' tall. Looks like he's been trying to mend his ways, but she won't have none of it."

"Perhaps I can be of some help," Calvin suggested.

Clarence shrugged. "Won't hurt to try, I reckon. But it look to me like the two of them is as far apart as two bodies kin be."

Chapter Twenty-Five

Tavish watched Dearie sitting in the parlor with her father. They talked animatedly, Dearie's laughter ringing throughout the room like a bell. It was good to see her so happy — it lightened his spirits. But when she saw Tavish, her smile faded and her blue eyes grew cold.

Icy fingers clamped over his heart, and he withdrew hastily. He no longer wished to be the cause of her unhappiness.

Weeks of reaching out to her had yielded nothing, not even a warm glance. At night they slept next to one another like wooden statues. When he tried to touch her, she recoiled from him as if he were a hateful thing. Eventually, he stayed away from her entirely.

The summer harvest was beginning, and Tavish made frequent trips to town to maintain the business, but he returned as quickly as possible. Dearie did not notice his comings and goings, as she was too preoccupied with her father.

Ezekiel and his men came over from Rosalie to begin harvesting the corn, but Dearie paid no attention to them. Tempie and Bess busily supervised the preparation of the worker's meals without Dearie's help. She didn't seem to care anymore.

"The men say they're going to bring in a lot of corn," Clarence reported.

Dearie nodded with a thin smile. "That's good," she said, returning to her father's room.

Matthew Grayson recuperated quickly under Dearie's management. Who would not? Tavish thought. Who would not welcome the patient ministrations of her soft hands, the frequent kisses from her petal-pink lips?

As the weeks wore on, Tavish knew the time would soon come when Grayson would be well enough to return to Philadelphia. What then? Would Dearie go with him? The answer was obvious. She would be going back with her father. What an ironic twist of fate that she would be returning now — when he would do anything to make her stay.

One day Tavish went into town and stayed longer than usual, returning too late for the evening meal. Dearie pretended not to notice, filling the awkward silence with idle chatter. Finally her father grew irritable.

"I was looking forward to our card game this evening. Where's Tavish? Since my health has returned, I'm bound I'll beat him before I leave."

Dearie said nothing, pushing her food around on her plate. Grayson shoved his chair back from the table. "Well, when he comes in, tell him to stop by my room."

But Tavish did not come in that evening at all. Dearie found herself pacing back and forth in front of the parlor window, searching the dark, moonless horizon for any sign of a rider. But toward midnight, she retired, finally drifting into a fitful sleep.

When Tavish arrived at noon the next day, he gave no explanation of his absence. However, he did favor

Grayson with a short game of cards before the evening meal.

Dearie cast disparaging looks at him, as if to say, "You've gone back to your old ways." What could he say? How could he hope to convince her that he had changed? He tried several times to speak with her alone, but she always found some excuse to leave.

Finally he caught her arm as she came from her father's room.

"Dearie, I must speak to you . . . please."

She looked up at him as if she couldn't be less interested. "All right."

Tavish had no idea what he would say, but he had to say something — they had been at odds for far too long. He led her to the porch.

A cool evening breeze ruffled the golden curls around her face. She looked so innocent, so angelic. "Dearie, it's not easy for a man to admit he's been wrong . . . but I have been. I was wrong about you . . . wrong to marry you . . . wrong to bring you here."

Dearie looked away, chewing her lip. She knew he was going to suggest she return to Philadelphia with her father. It was what he had always wanted anyway. "It's all right. You don't have to say it."

"I don't?" He looked relieved. "It's been on my mind for a long time. So many times I wanted to speak to you about it, but the time has never been right. It makes it easier to know that you understand."

"Oh, I do," she said with vehemence. Her eyes sparked with blue fire. "It's what you've always wanted — for me to return to Philadelphia."

"Well . . . I . . . " He suddenly realized that she didn't understand at all. "No . . . that's not what I meant."

"Of course you did. What else could happen now? Our marriage was based on a lie. Now the lie has been exposed, and there is nothing left. What recourse do I have?"

He seized her words. "Nothing left . . . "

"We must simply pick up the pieces and get on with our lives," Dearie said, looking past him.

He nodded silently. "Then you have made your decision."

"Yes," she replied, leaving him alone on the porch.

Later, when they retired to their bedroom, they were like two strangers. They politely apologized as they brushed past one another, turned away to dress, then approached the bed from opposite sides. The bed was small, but the distance between them was greater than any ocean.

This could be the last night I will ever sleep next to her, Tavish thought. As he looked at his wife, bathed in the dim light of the candle, he thought that she had never looked more beautiful. He memorized every detail of her body, especially her face. It would have to last a long time, perhaps forever. As he looked over at her, he had the overwhelming desire to kiss her . . . just one last time. She seemed to be already asleep, for her breathing was deep and regular.

Bending over, he kissed her soft lips, then he couldn't resist touching the skin of her arms with his fingers. Her eyes flew open in alarm, but her surprised expression did not deter him. Now he couldn't stop. He wanted her more than he had ever wanted anything in his life.

"No, Tavish," she murmured against his heated kisses.

"Please let me, I want to . . . "

Despite her protests, he covered her face with white-hot kisses. Her chemise was torn off and fell limply to the ground. But all the while, Tavish never moved away from her, raining more kisses along her shoulders and breasts.

Dearie began to respond to his heated embrace although she fought against the feeling. He tugged and pulled at her nipples with a passion greater than they had yet experienced together. She moaned with pleasure, offering first one, then the other nipple to his waiting mouth. She was caught in the same hunger, for she had longed for him equally as much. The warmth of his kisses burned a fiery trail down her abdomen to the dark triangle of curls between her legs. With more kisses and flicks of his tongue, he parted her legs. Then he plunged his tongue into the velvet passage, already moist and ready for him.

Dearie moaned, unable to withhold herself from him, and dragged her fingernails across his broad shoulders. When he could wait no longer, he lowered himself over her and plunged deep within her, driving hard, as if he wished to possess all of her. Dearie's breath came in little gasps as she moved with his frenzied thrusting. Her mind had long since ceased protesting, allowing her body full reign.

At last, when he began to reach his peak, he took her with him . . . spiraling high above the earth, far beyond thoughts, feelings, and emotions. Then, he gently withdrew from her, and she felt as if she were being let down on a soft, fleecy cloud. She opened her eyes in wonder to see Tavish frowning down at her.

"I'm sorry," he said, rolling abruptly away from her.

Dearie awoke late the following morning. She stretched lazily, relishing the memory of the night before. She reached out to touch her husband, but he wasn't there. She was not concerned, for Tavish always rose early these days.

Dearie washed and dressed with care, selecting a blue calico day dress and ivory combs to pull back her blond curls. She and Tavish would have much to talk about, she thought, as she hurried to the dining room.

Her father was seated at the table drinking a cup of coffee. When he looked up, she could tell by his expression that something was wrong.

"Where's Tavish?"

"He's gone, my dear. He left early this morning before I got up. He . . . he's left you a note, and there's a purse next to it."

With shaking hands, Dearie picked up the note.

My Dearie,

How many times I have wished we had met in a different time and place. I loved you the minute I laid eyes on you, but then I set my love aside when I learned that you were Matthew Grayson's daughter.

I had vowed to avenge my father in whatever way I could, and you became a part of that plan.

In this way I used you as no man had a right to, for you had no part in my quarrel. And I wanted to send you home, but I couldn't bring myself to part with you. So I stayed away, trying to forget the feelings I had for you. The longer I stayed away, the easier it was to put off what was surely inevitable.

Now that you know everything, I suppose it will do no harm to tell you I still feel the same. I love you as I have loved no other woman, and will love no one again. But I can understand why you would want to return with your father.

I have left a purse with the proceeds from the business, which I had withheld from your father to replenish what Murdock lost. It no longer seems to matter now.

Tavish.

Dearie laid the letter aside with a heavy sigh. She took up the purse and was astonished to see that it held almost six thousand dollars! As he emptied the money onto the table, a set of keys dropped out of the purse.

"These are the keys to his office! He's giving you the business back!"

Matthew Grayson sighed deeply. "Well, I don't want it. I can't run it anyway."

"What should I do?"

Grayson shook his head. "Well, Dearie, I declare I don't know. But I believe I feel well enough to travel. Please have Tempie pack my things. Clarence can drive me into town."

"Yes, Father. And she can pack my things, too. I suppose I shall be traveling with you."

"Are you sure that is what you want to do, Dearie?"

"I . . . yes . . . I mean . . . well . . ." Tears welled up in her eyes. "My . . . my first loyalty is to you, Father, after all."

Matthew Grayson studied his daughter. "No, I don't think so. You are married, and your first loyalty should be to your husband."

"But he betrayed my trust. He's a scoundrel. You said so yourself."

Grayson chuckled. "But he's no worse than I. You yourself pointed that out not too long ago."

He took her hand in his. "Dearie, I never thought I'd say this, but I've gotten to know Tavish in the past month. He *is* a lot like me and I don't mind it. What's more, he loves you. Probably said as much in that letter, I'll warrant."

"But — "

"I've done a lot that I'm not proud of, Dearie. But perhaps I'm not too old to learn. I do know what it is to lose someone you love. If you love him, you'd best go after him, child. Love doesn't come that often . . ."

Dearie quickly got up from the table. From the peg near the door, she retrieved her bonnet and parasol "Tell Clarence to hitch up the wagon, Tempie. I'm going into town."

"Father, thank you," she said, rushing back to kiss Grayson's wrinkled cheek.

"Dearie," he called out when she had reached the door. "Don't forget. You owe me a grandson."

She smiled and hurried out the door.

Dearie thought about her father's words on the way to Fayetteville. Tavish was exactly like her father in many ways. She remembered the cook, Jessamine, predicting as much. Looking back over the past year and a half, she marveled at her naive expectations. She had imagined that she would be mistress of a grand plantation, that she would oversee hundreds of servants and do nothing more strenuous than throw an occasional ball or soiree. She had learned . . . the hard way. Being mistress of a plantation was hard work, and she had never known work before.

Always before, she had relied upon men to take care of her every need. Her father had spoiled her, but Tavish had not. Tavish had forced her to look after herself for the first time in her life.

Both her father and Tavish had made mistakes. Well, so had she. She had made the disastrous mistake of expecting them to be perfect. And they were not — they were human.

They had forgiven her for her shortcomings — for her willfulness and her naiveté. But she had not forgiven them.

Only when she had thought that her father was dying did she forgive him for everything he had done. But she hadn't extended that same courtesy to her husband. Dearie was suddenly ashamed.

Tavish said that he had been wrong. He had asked for her forgiveness, but she had withheld it. Now she stood to lose the only man she would ever love, by holding on to false pride.

As they neared Fayetteville, Dearie desperately hoped that Tavish had not left immediately on the stage. The wagon lumbered into the town and Dearie craned her neck to see any sign of her husband. As they came in sight of the Fayetteville Hotel, her heart leaped to her throat as she saw Tavish step out onto the front porch. Immediately behind him came Georganna Arms.

· Dearie caught her breath in surprise.

"Why, that high-toned floozie," Clarence muttered under his breath.

The wagon pulled up in front of the hotel and Dearie jumped down without waiting for Clarence to help her. Tavish looked down at her, a smile lighting up his face.

"Tavish!" she cried, running into his open arms.

He kissed her hair and face, and held her to him as if he would crush her.

"Oh, Tavish! I thought I could never love you again, but I've always loved you! When I finally realized how foolish I had been . . . "

"Hush, hush," he soothed. "It doesn't matter now. All that matters is that we're together now, Dearie. That is what you want, isn't it?"

"Oh, yes, Tavish. That is all I want."

Georganna Arms was watching them with an obvious look of distaste on her face.

"Tavish," she said.

"Georganna, I have told — "

"Wait, Tavish," Dearie put her finger on his lips.

"Georganna, do you know what this is?" She held up her ring finger, and her golden wedding ring caught the light of the noonday sun.

"Well, of course I do," Georganna sputtered, affronted.

"Good, I'm glad. Because this ring is never coming off, and if I catch you or anyone else around my husband, I'll blow you from here to kingdom come." Dearie's fierce look took Tavish aback.

The impact on Georganna was even more amazing. Her face turned varying shades of red. "Well, I never," she huffed, picking up her skirts and scurrying off down the street.

"Dearie, what possessed you to say a thing like that? I believe you scared the daylights out of her."

"Oh, I meant it. Clarence taught me how to shoot a pistol and I'm good at it."

Clarence grinned sheepishly at Tavish and shrugged his shoulders. "Ain't no help for it, Master Tavish. When Miss Dearie decide she going to do a thing, she going to do it. And that's that."

They were still laughing when Calvin rode up in a cloud of red dust.

He eased his long body down from his horse. "Looks like I'm too late to help you work out your problems," he said with a grin. "That's good, because we want both of you at our wedding."

"What's this, Calvin? Who's the lucky lady?" Tavish asked, grinning.

Colleen waved to them from across the street, and hurried to join them. Calvin swept her up into his arms and planted a kiss on her rosy cheek.

"Why Calvin, I declare. What will people say?"

Calvin chuckled. "They'll say, 'It's about time, Calvin.'"

Everyone laughed, and Tavish hugged Dearie to him.

"Oh, you . . . " Colleen said, her face flushed. She smoothed down her dress and bent to retrieve the letter which had fallen from her hand. "You got a reply back, Miss Dearie. I expect it's for that position as governess."

Dearie took the letter from Colleen and tore it in half, her eyes locked with Tavish's. "I won't be needing that now, Colleen. I'm not going anywhere . . . but home."

*　　*　　*　　*

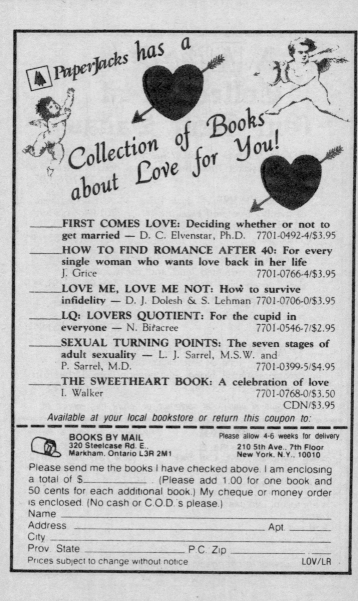

FREE!!
BOOKS BY MAIL
CATALOGUE

BOOKS BY MAIL will share with you our current bestselling books as well as hard to find specialty titles in areas that will match your interests. You will be updated on what's new in books at no cost to you. Just fill in the coupon below and discover the convenience of having books delivered to your home.

PLEASE ADD $1.00 TO COVER THE COST OF POSTAGE & HANDLING.

- -

BOOKS BY MAIL
320 Steelcase Road E.,
Markham, Ontario L3R 2M1

IN THE U.S. -
210 5th Ave., 7th Floor
New York, N.Y., 10010

Please send Books By Mail catalogue to:

Name _____
(please print)

Address _____

City _____

Prov./State _____ P.C./Zip _____

(BBM1)